MIRROR WORLD

MIRROR WORLD

John Calicchia

Copyright © 2015 John Calicchia
All rights reserved.
ISBN-13: 9780986102004 (Psychangel Books)
ISBN-10: 0986102008
Library of Congress Control Number: 2015912733
Johncalicchia, Wrentham, MA

All rights reserved. No part of this publication may be reproduced, distributed, or transmitted in any form or by any means, including photocopying, recording, or other electronic or mechanical methods, without the prior written permission of the publisher, except in the case of brief quotations embodied in critical reviews and certain other noncommercial uses permitted by copyright law. This is a work of fiction. Names, characters, businesses, places, events and incidents are either the products of the author's imagination or used in a fictitious manner. Any resemblance to actual persons, living or dead, or actual events is purely coincidental.

FOREWORD

I have always loved reading fiction. A book for me has always been a magical place where I could experience the lives of the characters in the story, so much so that at times I felt as if I actually knew them and lived in their worlds. Did I? Can psychology explain this? It can. When people experience in their imaginations the thoughts, feelings, or events of another person, psychologists call it vicarious learning. We learn through the lives of characters we read about. We see ourselves in their shoes struggling with pain, difficult choices, redemption, hope, and love. This is a good thing, for psychological research has shown us that reading narrative fiction can foster human capacities such as empathy, interpersonal sensitivity, kindness, tolerance, and heroism. I hope this book helps this in some small way.

There is another purpose behind this book, one that you must discover for yourself. This book is filled with powerful hidden secrets. But I have to be honest; these powerful hidden secrets were taken from others, with their blessing. You see...the science of psychology has produced research that is so helpful in understanding and helping the human condition. Psychological research helps us understand and deal with many issues: stress, bullying, racism, body image, self-perception, and peer pressure. It also shows us how to lead more fulfilled lives, to be happy, and how to love others and ourselves. The problem is that all of these hidden secrets are in scientific journals—which nobody reads. I decided to take some of the most notable and famous psychological studies or concepts and share them with you. But I didn't want to bore you with scientific journals and statistics. So...I used the characters and storylines within *Mirror World* to reveal the findings of these famous psychological studies. For a quick example, do you think you would deliver painful electric shocks to another person until that person cried out in pain, or was perhaps dead? *Not me* you're saying. I wish that were true. But research has clearly shown that, in the right situation, 95 percent of people will deliver painful electric shocks to another, especially when they can blame their actions on an authority figure that told them to do it. Sound familiar? If you want to learn more about this study, you can read a psychology journal. Or maybe you want to skip the psychology journal and experience the revelation through a novel. Check out what Longtooth the dragon does when she's told to eat the head of a kind old dwarf!

This book has been a journey and a quest to share important psychological knowledge—through fiction—with people for the betterment of their lives. But more than that, it has been fun to write. I hope you enjoy the story.

All the best,
John

Coming in 2016!
Mirror World: A User's Guide for understanding famous psychological studies in the book

Be sure to check out my website
www.johncalicchia.com
for more information about *Mirror World* and
the psychology behind it.

DEDICATION

**To Cathy, Alyssa, and Caitlyn,
The Angels
Who Surround Me.**

Many thanks to my family and the people who read the first drafts of this book. Special thanks to Dave, brilliant beta reader and editorial consultant and Justin for polishing the book cover.

TABLE OF CONTENTS

   Foreword v
1 Trouble in the Morning........................... 1
2 A Day at the Zoo 9
3 Friends and Malls................................. 16
4 The Choice.. 25
5 Alone 35
6 Good Company 39
7 The Obedient Servant 56
8 Specular Knowledge 70
9 The Wound 77
10 Dark Reflections 88
11 Journey from Castle Larkin..................... 94
12 Road to Ruin 107
13 Legends for Friends 117
14 Perceptions of Beauty........................... 130
15 A Fallen Angel 138

16	Inner Conflict	142
17	Spirals in the Sky	151
18	My Fault	158
19	Helpless Friends	164
20	Still Best Friends	177
21	Freedom and Fear	190
22	A Lesson from Death	199
23	Abode of the Dead	207
24	Crazy Angel	218
25	Trust in Kindness	233
26	Constantine	255
27	The City of Angels	269
28	The House of Gabriel	277
29	Angels and Demons	287
30	The Castle of Dark Mirrors	306
31	Gambit	321
32	Amazing Grace	329
33	Payback	335
34	Renunciation	344
35	A Proposal	348
36	Constantine Renewed	361
37	The Real Me	369

> SEE ME NOT, YET I SEE YOU.
> SEARCH IN ME TO FIND WHAT'S TRUE.
> CLOSER NOW, IT'S YOU I SEE.
> CAN'T YOU FIND THE REAL ME?
>
> —FROM THE *LARKIN REDBOOK*

CHAPTER 1

TROUBLE IN THE MORNING

OK, calm down. You can't smash it into a million pieces without cutting yourself, and then you'll really be in trouble.

"I hate you, I hate you, and I hate you!" I hissed at my reflection in the mirror. "Why do you always have to give me a hard time?"

I stood in front of my bedroom mirror, unable to move, transfixed by the image that stared back at me. It really freaked me out. It looked like me—but it wasn't me. There was just something wrong with it. Was I going crazy? I found it difficult to move. A tap on my shoulder made me jump, and I shivered as I looked away from the mirror.

"Caught ya lookin' in the mirror!" My little sister said as she danced happily behind me smiling broadly. "Hey, big sister, no uniforms today at school, remember? Can I borrow your green headband? It will make a perfect match to my awesome shirt." Terry paused and tilted her head to the side. "Lyssa, you all right? You look like crap."

"Terry, thanks a lot, not everybody can look like you in the morning."

Terry was a freak of nature and an amazing athlete. She had piercing blue eyes, the most gorgeous, silky red hair, and perfect skin that never needed a drop of makeup. Every morning she ran a brush through her hair, quickly washed her face, and she was ready to go.

"Lyssa, you know I think you're gorgeous. The only reason I said you look like crap is because of your eyes. Were you crying?" Terry said softly as she warmly placed both her hands on my shoulders. "C'mon, you can tell me. I heard you yelling at the mirror when I walked in. When you do that I always know it's 'cause you're scared or worried. What's going on?"

"I don't know," I said, glumly shaking my head back and forth. "Remember I told you the strange feelings I get sometimes when I look in the mirror: like it's not me or that maybe someone is—I know this sounds crazy—looking at *me*?"

"Yeah, Lyssa, I remember. Just the other day I had the feeling that somebody was staring at me, and sure enough, when I turned around, it was creepy Randle from the back of math class. Isn't it weird how you *so know* somebody is staring at you? But really, Lyssa, the mirror?"

"Yes, Terry. But here's the thing—and promise not to tell anybody; you're the only person I've ever told about this. It's getting worse. A lot worse! Before you came in the room, I couldn't move away from looking at the mirror. Am I going crazy?" I covered my face with my hands, determined not to let Terry see me on the verge of tears.

"Listen, big sister, you are definitely *not* going crazy! You must just be stressed out. You need to take some time for yourself. All you ever do is look out for your friends and try to help everybody. You have the biggest heart of *anyone* I've *ever* met, and I think at times you need to be a bit more selfish. Take care of yourself too!" Terry said as I stood up and gave her a hug.

The problem with hugging my little sister was that she started out soft, and then she always tried to squeeze the stuffing out of you, to make it funny at the end. She let go of me before I exploded and spun around so fast that her ponytail lightly brushed across my chin. It made me laugh. Before she left my room, she paused at the door, spun around, and smiled. Her fingers pointed toward me, thumbs up, in what she called her six-gun position.

"Hey, Cailyssa, I forgot to show you the cool slogans I added to the front of my volleyball shirt!" Terry slid across the room and quickly opened her jacket to display her shirt. "Block This" was written in all caps across the front of her shirt with a fat marker, and "You Wish You Could Hit Like a Girl" was on the back. I laughed harder this time.

"Hey, Lyssa, we need to talk more about this mirror thing. You and I! After school! Froyo at our favorite place… *yogurt beach!*" Terry said as she ran down the stairs to catch breakfast before school.

Terry was just what I needed this morning. She came into my room, listened to me complain, and wrapped an enormous bubble of happiness around me—just like she does to everyone. I wish some days I could be more like that. Why do I often feel like I have the weight of the world on top of me?

"Honey, stop talking to yourself. You're going to be late for school. Come down and eat breakfast. I made pancakes and don't have time to drive you if you miss the bus." That was my father talking. The sound of his voice and the thought of a hot breakfast relaxed me, but I still wanted to take my hairbrush and give the mirror in front of me one good smack! Caught up in a whirlpool of thoughts, I headed downstairs for breakfast.

"Good morning, honey," my mother said. "You look great today! Is that a new outfit?"

Silence.

"Lyssa, I said you look great today. Didn't you hear me?"

I was about to make a sarcastic reply, but I bit my tongue just in time. It wasn't my mom's fault that I was in a conflicted mood today. She was just trying to be positive and lift my spirits when it must have been obvious to everyone that I wasn't too cheerful.

"Uh, yeah, mom. It's a new outfit." There was no use commenting on the part about looking great; we both knew that wasn't true today! "Mom, I just want to eat breakfast and go to school, please."

I was still worried about the mirror thing, and I really didn't want to talk or listen to my parents this morning.

My father looked at me with a raised eyebrow, recognized it was best not to disturb the peace, and quietly said, "Your mom's right; you look great today."

"Thanks, but I really don't want to talk this morning," I grumbled. I gave them both a hug and then decided to bury my face in pancakes and bacon. Isn't it amazing what food can do? I ate, felt a little better, did a quick mental checklist that everything I needed was in my backpack, and headed for the front door.

Then I saw it in front of me. It was like a vision from heaven. It was golden, it was sweet, and it had the most incredible smell. I couldn't resist. I ran toward it, wrapping my arms around it, and buried my nose in the softest, most perfect spot imaginable.

"You are the best dog in the whole world, Cali," I said, nuzzling the fur of my golden-retriever puppy.

She looked at me with adorable chocolate-brown eyes that shone like pools of endless love. Her happiness to see me spread into my body, and all of a sudden, I felt how much I loved this furry critter. The only thing better than getting love and attention from one dog is getting it from two dogs.

"I love you, too, Bentley," I said as my Bernese mountain dog plowed into me, knocking me over in his excitement to see me. *Dogs are proof that God loves us*, I said to myself.

Both dogs attacked me with a love fest of licking, sniffing, and snuggling. It was simply the best feeling in the whole world. With dog-infused love, I quickly hugged my mom and dad good-bye and went out to wait for the bus with my kid sister, Terry. Usually I drove to school, but my car was in for repairs, so that meant we had to catch the bus. "Please," I thought to myself, "please don't let Billy be on the bus."

The feelings of elation I had felt a few moments ago with Cali and Bentley evaporated immediately as the bus pulled to a stop.

A sick feeling crept into my stomach as I saw the side of Billy's face in the window. Reluctantly, and with an odd feeling of premonition, I walked onto the bus and made my way to an empty seat. No sooner had I sat down than I heard the most disgusting sound in the universe.

"Here's *Kissa* Larkin, stuck on the bus. Where is your boyfriend, Daemon?" Billy Bloomfield yelled as he stood up.

"Billy, just leave me alone today. I don't feel like dealing with you! BTW my name's Cailyssa, pronounced K-lyssa, not *Kissa*." I said it as politely as I could, but underneath I was seething, and I deliberately avoided any eye contact.

"What's the matter, *Kissa*, you too good to talk to the rest of us, or do you miss your boyfriend?" Billy taunted as he made a kissing face to the rest of the bus and finished with an obnoxious burp that seemed to last for minutes and vibrate every window on the bus.

Billy was one of the worst bullies in the entire school, and most people were afraid of him. Not me. First of all, we used to be friends before he became a bully. And I *especially* dislike boys who like to bully people in front of a crowd to make themselves feel good. Oh yeah, I hate when he calls me stupid names like Kissa. As Billy was still laughing about his own stupid joke, I saw him actually pick his nose and wipe it on the seat in front of me. He continued to laugh, and his chins were shaking up and down as the spittle flew out of his mouth.

I looked across the aisle and saw my little sister's hands ball up into fists. That could mean only one thing.

"Billy, why don't you shut up and eat some of the jelly doughnut that you dropped on the front of your shirt," my little sister howled.

Now let me tell you, my sister has a pair of lungs and can out scream a crowd at a Patriots game. So the entire bus turned around and looked at Billy's shirt. Sure enough, right in the middle was a huge splat of jelly and a trail of crumbs from the doughnut that had fallen from his mouth.

"Shut up, you little pimple, before I squash you," Billy yelled back.

Of course he didn't do anything. Although my sister was a couple of years younger, she had that if-looks-could-kill face on, and Billy sure didn't want to risk getting his butt kicked by a girl. My sister, Terry, was pretty much not scared of anything, especially Billy Bloomfield. Terry's nickname was Tink because her favorite hat had a picture of Tinker Bell on it. The hat said "Don't even Tink about it!" Not many kids could get away with wearing that hat at her age, but the hat was a perfect description of my sister's personality. You don't mess with Terry or Tink! Nobody ever gave her a hard time about the hat—or about anything else for that matter. Everyone loved my sister. She was totally out there—smart, athletic, bold, loyal—and had so many friends. *She's so different from me*, I thought as I looked at her.

When Billy turned to yell at my sister, the squashed blob of doughnut on his shirt became visible for the whole bus to see. Half the bus started yelling and pointing to the doughnut on Billy's semiwhite T-shirt. When Billy realized he had become the brunt of everybody's humor, his face turned bright red, and his whole huge body trembled with embarrassment and anger.

"Thanks for doing that, Tink, but I don't need your help," I said to Terry.

"I couldn't help it! When I saw him making fun of you, I wanted to punch him so bad." My sister tried her best to whisper this; of course Terry's voice is completely incapable of whispering, and everyone around us heard and began to giggle. Billy was too busy trying to clean the doughnut off his shirt to hear what we were saying.

I whispered, "Let's just leave Billy alone. If he gets too upset, he might just explode here on the bus and splatter us with the food and the disgusting things that are in his stomach."

We both laughed, and I looked down at my little sister, thinking how much I loved that she stood up for me. The bus finally arrived at school, and I made sure to get out of my seat quickly before Billy could block the aisle. Believe me, you don't stand close behind Billy Bloomfield's butt—unless you are able to hold your breath for a very long time.

CHAPTER 2

A DAY AT THE ZOO

I must have inherited my father's warped sense of humor. We both refer to school as "the zoo," since it's filled with a bunch of different species. If you were an alien and I were giving you a tour of my school, I would introduce you to all of the species. There are emos, geeks, jocks, populars, nerds, punks, brainiacs, goths, stoners, boarders, losers, cheerleaders, chubs, criminals, beauty queens, regulars, and assorted other types. Each species has both male and female, although sometimes it's hard to tell them apart.

The worst part about the zoo was that, other than being female, I was the *only* kid who didn't fit into at least one group. I wasn't sure what all the people really thought of me, although the words "strange" and "unusual" were often used to describe me. It's not like I was ugly or anything. In fact, Mrs. Hennery, the art teacher, asked to photograph me as a fitness model for one of her projects. I thought that was weird, so I thanked her and ran away. I wasn't ugly, but I certainly wasn't beautiful either. Most people tend to stay away from me except my few close friends. I didn't have any hideous open sores oozing from my face or anything; it was just that I was different…in a strange and unusual way. I've always felt that way. It used to bother me when I was little, but by now I've just learned to accept it.

I entered the zoo—excuse me, school—and walked to my homeroom to begin the day.

"Hey, Lyssa, come over here. I have to show you something." It was my friend Phoebe, and she was extremely wound up to share something. "You won't believe who texted me last night!" Phoebe said excitedly in her pitchy, singsong voice.

"Can you give me three guesses?" I smirked.

"Sure I can, but you'll never guess who…"

I straightened my sweater, crossed my arms, and slid my hand under my chin while looking at the ceiling.

Slowly and dramatically I said, "Let's see. I see a boy… with dark, curly hair, brown eyes, and a gorgeous smile that makes you crazy. He's texting you a message and sending you a pic of him on the football field."

Poor Phoebe, I shouldn't have done this to her, but sometimes it's too much fun to resist.

"Someone told you! Either that or you took my phone and looked at the picture. Give it back right now!" Phoebe was becoming upset and started looking through my pockets for her phone.

"Phoebe, your phone is in the right pocket of your backpack, where you left it last night. Remember? You're just about to find it. Relax."

Phoebe launched herself on her backpack, frantically searching. "Oh, thank God! Here it is." Phoebe grabbed her phone and turned her back on the teacher so he couldn't see. "This is weird, Lyssa. How did you know Scott sent me a picture of him like that? Did I tell you about that or something? And it's weird that you always know where my cell phone is when I lose it. You're so annoying, but you are my best friend."

Phoebe went on to show me the pic Scott had sent her, being careful to point out his muscular thighs. I listened to Phoebe to be polite, because I knew it was important to her, but I just couldn't understand how any girl could be so boy crazy. I also thought that Scott was a jerk, but I didn't want to remind Phoebe about that right now and ruin her moment. Phoebe dated him last year, and Scott broke up with her for a cheerleader. I always suspected that maybe Scott was abusing her.

The bell rang, and we all took our seats in our first class. I stared at the clock as the teacher called out our names, and I began having one of my famous spaced-out, dreamy moments.

The sound of Mr. Larkin's booming voice brought me back to reality. "Cailyssa, are your body and mind among the living, or shall I record you absent for the day?"

"Sorry, Mr. Larkin, I'm here," I mumbled.

As I said that, the class all turned and gave me the look that all the people in school seem to use when they glance at me: there goes Cailyssa again, lost in her strange and unusual mind. I went back to my private world and closely examined the thought that I knew would bother me all day. *How did I know that Scott had sent that picture to Phoebe?*

"You'll have thirty minutes to complete the exam. Good luck," Mr. Larkin's voice echoed across the classroom.

I loved his science and psychology classes, but his tests were always a challenge. He usually gave students a bonus question or two that were very difficult to answer. I usually got one right every week. It was strange. I almost thought that Mr. Larkin wrote some of the questions just for me, and for some weird reason, I almost always knew what the question was going to be.

Truth be told, Mr. Larkin might know me better than I know myself—after all, he is my uncle. But I didn't know he was my uncle when I was young. I always thought he was just a friend of the family. It's weird that my parents always told me that. I spent much of my childhood with him. I loved him, and he was a second father to me. One of my most vivid memories of Uncle Spencer occurred when I was twelve years old; it was the night of the big family fight. After that he didn't come over to the house anymore, and Tink and I only saw him at school.

The night of the fight, I heard him and my father whispering in the living room. Their voices grew more intense, and they began yelling. I remember sneaking to the edge of the stairs to hear them.

"Jack, don't you think it's about time you told her?" Uncle Spencer said to my father.

"Not yet. She's too young, Spencer, and I'll tell Cailyssa when I'm ready, not you! Don't dare tell her any of the crazy thoughts in your mind or that we talked to our father tonight. You only talk to her during class, and treat her like any other student. And if I find out that you've told her anything, I will personally whip your butt—and don't think I won't do it!" my father yelled.

"Some things don't change, Jack. You're still the imbecilic young brother that I needed to watch out for all these years."

"Spencer! I don't need *you* to watch out for me or my family. And don't go on about that nonsense, needing to watch out for Cailyssa. I can look after my daughter just fine without your help."

"Jack, Cailyssa...knows," Spencer said very slowly and with great sadness in his voice.

"Cailyssa knows *what*? That you're her uncle? Big deal, your name is Larkin." My father's voice sounded tense.

"No, Jack, that's *not* what I'm talking about; she knows—"

"Stop it!" my father yelled. "I don't want to hear any of your crazy theories, and if you ever say anything to Cailyssa, I'll—"

"Please, Jack, calm down, and stop puffing out your chest like a bantam rooster. You're no longer a young boy threatening me with your fists."

"You pompous, old snob, I hate when you lecture me with that Oxford professor's voice," my dad replied.

"That's enough, boys! And I do mean 'boys!'" My mother interrupted both of them with her I-mean-business voice. "If you don't stop it right now, I'll grab both of you by the ear like your mother used to and lead you outside for a time out."

I heard this conversation on a steamy August night, right before the school year started. What *did* I know? Was there some great family secret?

My daydream was suddenly interrupted. "Cailyssa? Don't you think you should begin the exam? You have been staring at your paper for ten minutes," Mr. Larkin said in his kind but firm voice.

"Ugh…sure, yeah, I'm just thinking about the bonus question," I replied lamely.

"I think you'll find the bonus question especially compelling today. It's about mirrors and seeing the future," Mr. Larkin whispered.

The look in his piercing blue eyes reached deep into my heart, and I had the unshakable sense that he knew how my morning had begun. I decided to close down the inner theater of my mind and work on the exam, while wondering how I could possibly finish in time.

I finished the test, and Mr. Larkin smiled calmly at me as I placed it on his desk. I paused for a moment and looked at his blue eyes. I really missed him some days, and I wanted to ask him what he and my father had fought about. But now wasn't the right time.

The school day went by fairly quickly. I kind of like school. It's always been really easy for me. The only problem was that sometimes I got lost inside my own head. The picture thing with Phoebe was still in the back of my mind as I left math class. Maybe it was just luck? I mean, don't most people have hunches about such things? Part of my mind screamed at me to stop. *No, Cailyssa, make a mental note here. Most people do not see the future!*

School was out for early dismissal, and I was looking forward to meeting up with my three best friends at the food court in the mall. As I left, little did I know that I wouldn't set foot in that school for what would feel like a very long time.

CHAPTER 3

FRIENDS AND MALLS

"Let's take my car to the mall," Phoebe suggested.

"Sounds good to me. I had to take the bus," I said. "We'll pick up Madison and Jessica on the way. I'm sure they're both begging their moms for more cash for the mall."

"I have twenty-five bucks, and I really need a new top—especially if Scott takes me out this weekend," Phoebe said excitedly.

We picked up Madison and Jessica and made our way to the mall. I was with my three best friends, and I always thought we were kind of a gang, since we had known each other since first grade. We didn't constantly hang around together, but we always had this kind of connection, and we just felt really relaxed around each other: we felt like we could be ourselves—even though we were all radically different. Madison was the leader of our gang or at least she thought she was. Mads was tall and blond, with Barbie-doll looks. She was the head cheerleader and had been asked out by most of the boys at school. Despite her supermodel looks, Madison lacked self-confidence. She didn't think she was that smart—although she was—and she felt a lot more nervous than she looked. I was one of the few people who knew this about her, and she trusted me to tell no one.

Jessica was the athlete. She grew up as a tomboy with three older brothers, and she could go toe-to-toe with any of them. She played lacrosse and soccer and was the captain of both teams. She had short brown hair, brown eyes, and an impish grin that often said, "I'm up to no good, so watch out." She was clearly the most confident of us four girls. We all decided that whatever she did in life, she would be really good at it.

Phoebe was my best friend. She wore all her emotions on her sleeve—and there were many of them—with a dramatic flair that always made you feel like *High School Musical* was about to pop up around you. Phoebe had multicolored hair (since she loved to be different), brown eyes, and a body that was shapely and huggable—not fat, although she thought she was. I noticed today that she had more than her usual package of excessive jewelry and makeup.

"Is that a bruise on your wrist, Phoebe?" I said with concern.

Phoebe became anxious and started adjusting her jewelry, trying to hide the marks on her wrist.

"No, it—it's fine; I must've bumped into something. You know how goofy I can be," Phoebe nervously replied as she covered her wrist with her jewelry.

"Are you kidding me?" I said worriedly. "It looks like somebody was trying to pull your arm out of its socket by grabbing your wrist. Phoebe! Tell me honestly, did Scott do that to you?"

"No—I, I mean…he didn't mean to. It's just that we were arguing, and I tried to run away. I knew I shouldn't have, but when I did…he was just trying to pull me back to him. He said he was sorry. Please don't tell anyone, Lyssa. He won't do it again." Phoebe looked straight ahead, trying to drive as she wiped the sweat from her shaky hands.

"Phoebe, you promised me if he ever hurt you, you would leave him. You don't need *him*. You're too good for him, and what he's doing to you is abusive!" As I said this, I could feel my blood begin to boil. I usually don't get mad, but when I do, watch out! I was envisioning taking Scott's arm, pulling it out of its socket, and smacking him in the head with it.

We arrived at the mall, and the three of us spent a wonderful afternoon of laughing, shopping, and gossiping. My friends played their favorite game, which was called "Makeover Cailyssa." They took me into a designer store and convinced me to try on just one outfit.

"Lyssa, you could really look stunning with some new clothes and a bit of makeup," Madison stated firmly.

"Yeah, Lyssa, why don't you let Madison pretend you're a Barbie doll, and she can style you," Jessica said sarcastically.

"Jessica, don't hate me because I'm beautiful," Madison said as she flipped her blond hair around like a runway model.

"Puhlease, Mads, how could I be jealous of a Barbie doll who doesn't even sweat?" Jessica said in her half-serious voice.

Anyway, after I tried on a new outfit, my friends all told me how beautiful I was. Of course I didn't believe them, so I went back to the dressing room and avoided looking in the mirror. I put on my favorite old black jeans, a soft, faded T-shirt, and my favorite purple Converse sneakers.

"Thank God," said Jessica. "Cailyssa is back to normal. I thought you might get stuck in Barbie World."

"Let's go eat; I'm starving," Phoebe said anxiously.

Phoebe was always hungry, and today she was more nervous and hungry than usual. I didn't say anything more about the bruise on her wrist, but I could tell by the way she adjusted her jewelry that she was trying to hide it. Every time she touched it, she made a nervous kind of twitch, and I occasionally saw her wipe a tear from her eye. I hated Scott! As she took out a small makeup mirror I glanced over her shoulder, and the mirror sent a flash to my mind. *Oh God, no!*

"Phoebe, do me a favor and stay close to me. I think something bad might happen, and you might need my help," I said nervously.

"Oh, Lyssa, what could happen at the mall?" Phoebe mumbled as she continued doing her lipstick.

As I entered the food court, a nervous, sick feeling entered my stomach. Daemon was sitting there, alone as usual, drinking a Coke. Daemon was the only boy at school who made me nervous. It was a good kind of nervous. Daemon had silky, longish black hair, gray-green eyes, and a very tall, solid athletic body. He could have been a star athlete, but he preferred reading and music. All the girls at school thought he was extremely hot—but he dated no one, hardly talked to anyone, and no one really knew him but me.

He lived in an old house at the edge of town with his father. His mother died when he was young, and his father was a coroner. Kids would joke that Daemon was weird because his father made him watch as he examined dead bodies, which of course was a lie. I liked Daemon—not only because he was different like me but also because he was the only other kid at school who, like me, did not belong to any of the groups at the zoo. I kind of saw us as the only two outcasts.

As we walked by Daemon, he stood up and walked toward us, his six-foot-five-inch muscular frame towering over us. This was most unusual. Daemon was extremely shy and was not interested in most social opportunities, unless I was alone. As he approached, his eyes bore in on me. I stood there, unable to move.

"Hello, Cailyssa," Daemon said in his husky voice. He had a commanding tone about him and steady confidence that made him appear ultra cool.

"Cailyssa says hi," Madison interjected, using the best of her social-butterfly skills.

Daemon continued to look at me as if Madison didn't exist. "I believe I was talking to Cailyssa," Daemon said as he stared at me with his intense gaze. Mads looked like a flower that was wilting in the hot sun.

"Cailyssa, can I talk to you for a moment in private?" I walked away slowly with him, not sure what to expect. He had never seemed this intensely serious before.

"Hey, Daemon, what's so important that you need to be rude to my friends and drag me over here?" I said this firmly as I regained my confidence and broke out of my frozen state.

"My apologies. I was talking to Mr. Larkin, and he was wondering if you and I would stop by his house later this evening and help him with something. Perhaps you could meet me there after you're through at the mall."

Daemon had a way of talking that made him seem two hundred years old. I thought this request was a bit odd, but I was hypnotized by the way he said it. He just seemed so sincere that I couldn't say no. You see, before high school, Daemon and I were inseparable. We'd gone to the same schools since we were babies in day care. We were always together, and we were best friends. I felt regret that we had drifted apart a bit lately. We used to see each other every day. Now, although we found time to take walks together in the woods, Daemon did not want anyone to think he was dating me, so he rarely talked to me at school. My friends thought he was stalking me, 'cause he always seemed to be around—like today. I just figured that puberty forced two good friends to push each other away. Seeing him close again made me want to go back to third grade and play on the swings with him.

"Sure, Daemon, I'll text you when I'm leaving the mall. We can meet up with Mr. Larkin after that," I said as I tried to hide the excitement in my voice. *Was this a date?*

"Sounds great. Thanks, Cailyssa. It seems like a decade since I've talked to you alone," he said with a sparkle in his eye as he turned to walk away.

I said good-bye and walked back to my friends, who were all staring at Daemon leaving and talking about how absolutely gorgeous he was. They all wanted to know the details of the conversation. However, I'm a very private person and told them nothing, which drove them absolutely out of their minds—especially Madison, the gossip queen.

As we left the food court, I was daydreaming about Daemon when Scott and his two hulking companions appeared out of nowhere.

"Yo, Phoebe, where's my girl going with all her friends when she could be standing here next to me?" he said with his cocky voice and gangster stance.

Phoebe began to walk over, and I held her elbow and told her to stay with us.

Scott looked irritated and came stamping over with fire in his eyes. "Excuse me, girls, Phoebe's coming with me!"

As he pushed his way past me and grabbed Phoebe's hurt wrist, my brain exploded with anger. Scott yanked her wrist, and she cried out in pain. Phoebe tried to pull away, and Scott suddenly let go of her wrist. She fell on the ground.

"Don't worry; she won't get hurt falling on that fat butt!" he said as he laughed with his two thug friends.

When I went to pick Phoebe up, I felt Scott's hands grab my elbows from the back and pin them to my sides. "No helping her up, Cailyssa. Let's see if the beached whale can get up on her own." His arrogant voice and foul breath screamed in my ear.

I stepped hard on his instep, and when he gasped I elbowed him in the stomach and spun around, just as I had practiced many times. Scott swore at me and approached angrily as his friends laughed at his predicament.

"Scott, leave us alone. I don't want any trouble. We're sick of your abuse, and so is Phoebe!"

"No girl's gonna tell *me* what to do." Scott stormed up to me and pushed my shoulder hard.

"Scott, do you see the star on my purple Converse sneaker? I'm going to take that sneaker and wipe it across your face so fast, you'll never know what hit you!" I said without fear, knowing full well I could do it.

Scott went to push me again. I saw red. Anger consumed me, and the next few seconds were like slow motion. Scott's hand came forward to push my right shoulder, and I slid my weight to my left foot. As his hand missed my shoulder, I jumped up, spun around, and gave him a roundhouse kick with my right leg to the side of his face—just as I had promised. He went down like a ton of bricks, blood dripping from his mouth, and I knew from the crunching sound that at least a few of his teeth were broken or loose. Everyone stood there in shock. I grabbed my girls and hustled out of there as Scott's friends tried to revive him.

"Whoa!" said Jessica as we ran back to Phoebe's car. "That was amazing! You told us you took that kung-fu stuff, but we never imagined you really could do it."

Phoebe was sobbing, and Madison and I were holding her arms, putting her in the backseat of her car, and getting ready to leave the mall. I saw Daemon in the distance. Had he been watching? I drove and dropped Madison and Jessica off at their houses. I calmed Phoebe down and gave her the biggest hug when she dropped me off at home. She drove away sniffling, promising not to talk to Scott again. I told her to call the police if he showed up at her house.

I went to my bedroom, avoided looking at the mirror, and got changed to meet Daemon. What a *day* this had been, and it was not even over. I was going to meet with Daemon! Dreamily I thought to myself, *was it a date?* Even more bizarre, I was meeting Daemon at Uncle Spencer's house—which my father had banned me from ever entering again. And I had just knocked out a few of Scott's teeth with a *kick to the face! What was I doing? How would this day end?*

CHAPTER 4

THE CHOICE

I came down from my bedroom. My whole family was about to eat dinner. I usually have a big appetite, but tonight I had other things on my mind. I needed to avoid any hint of suspicion, so I sat down with my family and reluctantly enjoyed some of my father's amazing Italian cooking.

"Did you have a good day, Lys?" my mother said.

"Uh…yeah, sure, Mom, it was great. Just another boring day at school, and then I stopped by the mall." I tried to sound like it was just another day, but I could feel the nervousness creeping into my voice.

"Lyssa, you look like something's bothering you. You haven't eaten much of your dinner, and you keep staring down at your plate." The suspicion in my father's voice was scaring me, but I tried to remain cool. If he knew what was about to happen today—especially the part about Uncle Spencer—he would freak out and probably ground me for the rest of my life.

"I'm *fine*, Dad. I was just thinking about what to get Phoebe for her birthday. I need to go back to the mall tonight and make sure I pick out something perfect."

When Terry heard what I said, she immediately said, "Can I go to the mall with you? I need to get new knee pads before our game on Saturday."

Before I could say no, my mom and dad gave me the look. It was clear that the only way I was going to get the car to go to the mall tonight was if I took my sister. *Oh great*, I thought. *I can just see Dad blowing a gasket if he finds out that I took Terry to Uncle Spencer's house.* I skipped dessert, grabbed Terry's arm, and ran out to the car to text Daemon.

"Listen, Terry, BTW we're not going to the mall. I promised Daemon I would meet him at Uncle Spencer's house!"

"Whoa, you're like breaking every rule possible. You're going out on a date without telling Mom and Dad to the forbidden house of Uncle Spencer. Are you nuts? You'll be grounded for the rest of your life, and so will I since I went with you!" Terry said excitedly. "Lyssa, this is *so* cool. I can't wait!"

"Listen, Tink, I didn't want you to come. Mom and Dad forced me, and it's really important that I go. And if you say this is a *date* again, I'll drop you off on the side of the road."

"Just one question. Is Daemon *the* Daemon I'm thinking of—gorgeous, rich, large, dark, and scary—who lives in a creepy house down by Uncle Spencer?" Terry said as she bounced up and down in the seat.

I just shook my head, and my silence answered Terry's question. I focused on driving and getting to Uncle Spencer's house as quickly as possible. For some reason my hands were sweaty, and I was gripping the steering wheel like I was holding the ledge of a cliff. *Was I nervous about seeing Daemon?* Nah, I was actually looking forward to seeing him and being at Uncle Spencer's house again. I spent so much time at his house when I was young.

"Cailyssa?"—Terry used my full name, which she never did unless—"I'm really scared and excited, too. I miss Uncle Spencer and his awesome mirror house."

"Don't worry, Tink. This is no big deal. We'll be back home before you know it." I tried to speak calmly to reassure Terry.

"If this is no big deal, why do you look so tense—like you're trying to pull the steering wheel off the car?" Terry said as we pulled up to Uncle Spencer's house.

Uncle Spencer's house was at the end of a cul-de-sac and had a long curving driveway graced by beautiful pine trees. I saw Daemon's car in front, a black Porsche with tinted windows. I got out and grabbed Terry's hand as it started to rain. We felt like two little girls again, holding hands, walking up the brick pathway to Uncle Spencer's enormous black front door. On the middle of the door was one of those old-fashioned knockers with a tiny mirror in the middle. It was shaped like a heart but had this scary medieval stuff carved around it. I was just about to use the knocker when I glanced in the mirror. My heart froze, and a chill swept through my bones; I felt like something bad was gonna happen, and I was more scared than I thought possible.

The mirror flashed, and I briefly saw a face. But it wasn't mine. It was a dark face with piercing red eyes glaring at me.

Before I could use the knocker again, the door swung open quickly, and Terry and I ran to Uncle Spencer. We both wrapped our arms around him, and I felt like I was a little girl again playing on the swings in his yard. I spent so many of my early years on this planet with Uncle Spencer. He was my second father, and I still loved him dearly. I didn't realize I was still shaking until Uncle Spencer's warm voice brought me back to reality.

"It's all right, Cailyssa, nothing can harm you here. You've always been safe when you're with me here." As I wrapped my arms around Uncle Spencer again, I felt the warmth and safety of his large body. *Did he know about the doorknocker?*

As I was hugging Uncle Spencer, I looked over his shoulder and saw a pair of boots standing in the living room. The boots were large and black and were laced up the side rising to just under the knee. The black leather pants tucked inside of them clung tightly to strong legs. The figure was complete with a dark maroon tunic and some kind of medieval vest. I almost thought I saw the hilt of a large sword above the figure's shoulder-length black hair. It's a good thing then that I saw the eyes and knew who it was.

"Daemon? *Is that you?*" I said with a stunned look on my face.

For some unknown reason, my body took over, and I ran to him. We both hugged tightly—just like we did when we were little kids. Before I could say anything about Daemon's unique attire, Terry was tapping my shoulder.

"Soooo—let me see. This is some kind of weird medieval date, and you brought me along to take pictures," Terry said in her most sarcastic voice.

"This is not a date, Terry. But perhaps your thoughts of medieval culture are appropriate at this auspicious occasion. I have missed you both very much, and there is much catching up to do but little time to do it. We must talk very seriously about the future," Uncle Spencer said, and I knew it was important.

We all followed him into the living room, and I noticed Uncle Spencer's house had not changed much since I was a child. He had mirrors all over the house from cultures he had traveled to throughout the world. Some of them were more polished stones than mirrors. Uncle Spencer always said that one does not need a mirror to make a reflection, and many cultures used stones and water as we do mirrors. We walked into the living room, by far the largest room of the house, and Uncle Spencer asked us all to sit on the couch. It was good to have Daemon and Terry beside me as I looked into Uncle Spencer's vast wall mirror. It was probably eight feet high and stretched across the entire room. It was outlined by a golden frame with faces of angels and devils carved in an intricate design. I had spent many hours as a young child staring at my reflection in this mirror. Then in high school

I started hating mirrors and rarely looked at one. Today, as I sat across from it staring at the three of us sitting on the couch, I had this dreadful feeling come over me.

"I wish we had time for a party—and I promise you one when we return—but as for now, time is of the essence. The moon is full, and our journey is soon to begin." Uncle Spencer said this as if we knew what he was talking about.

"Uncle Spencer, I don't know what you mean. Daemon asked me to meet you here to help with something, and I need to get home to finish my homework. Terry does too," I said.

"Of course, of course, I didn't mean to presume. You may well go home to finish your homework—or you may decide to journey down another path. Rather than me telling you, let me show you with great urgency what the mirror has uncovered," Uncle Spencer said gravely.

"Are you going to tell us the Larkin family secret that you and our dad were arguing about?" Terry said excitedly.

Without answering Terry's question, Uncle Spencer became very quiet. He began to breathe deeply, and I felt the temperature in the room drop till the end of my nose felt like an icicle. I remembered stories from my childhood that Uncle Spencer told me in front of this mirror. He said that mirrors throughout the world recorded all of the world's history. He said mirrors could show the present, yet if one looked hard enough and closely enough, this mirror would show the past and the future. I don't think I ever believed him—until now.

"Terry, *I* will not tell you the family secret, but Cailyssa will someday. She's known about it for a very long time!"

"Cailyssa, please begin the story," Uncle Spencer said with great expectation.

"I'm not sure I know the story. What is it that I am supposed to know? I only heard you and my dad arguing. I don't know any Larkin family secret!" I said angrily.

Uncle Spencer never said a word. His large hand swept across the room and focused our attention on the large mirror as if he expected me to use the mirror to tell the story. My mind flashed, and I felt the liquid reflection of the mirror pool in my mind. Before us, on the mirror, was the town we lived in—although not as we knew it. It was dark and gloomy, and people seemed scared, running from shadow to shadow, avoiding each other. The next image was of us flying over the town. I heard crying and anger, and I knew it was the result of evil. People were afraid of each other—and of death. There were horrible things going on in my town, and it seemed so real. Darkness was covering the world!

The next vision was of my parent's house. It was dark, and most of the lights were out. My parents looked cold and scared, and they were huddled in the kitchen, whispering angrily at each other. My two dogs were on the floor looking skinny, dirty, and hungry. They yelped when my father threw a glass at them. As it shattered, my mother picked up a knife and pointed to the back door, yelling at the dogs to get out. My father and mother followed them out the door. My father grabbed an ax from the side of the garage. There were two shallow graves in the backyard. There were no headstones on the graves, but I knew they were for my dogs.

At that point the reflection of the mirror stopped. I had stopped it! I fell back into the couch, sobbing. Could this possibly be the future?

"Cailyssa, I'm sorry you had to see that. Daemon and I were hoping it would be otherwise. But you showed us only *one* possible future," Uncle Spencer said, slowly pronouncing each word.

"Please, please, please, Uncle Spencer. I know what we saw, and every fiber of me knows it could be true one day. What can we do to stop it?" I asked firmly.

"Long ago, your grandfather—who was much like you—sat on this couch and was faced with a similar vision. He had to make a choice. The choice he made was the right one. Your life would not be what it is had your grandfather not died to save you and everyone else," Uncle Spencer said with sadness, remembering the death of his father.

"Our dad told us he died of a heart attack," Terry interjected.

I knew what our dad had told us was not true, just as I knew that I needed to face the same choice my grandfather had all those years ago. This was why my father had protected me from Uncle Spencer. He knew in the deepest part of his heart that I could be charged with carrying on the Larkin family traditions, and he loved me too much to let me die as my grandfather had. But I was not ready to die. "Uncle Spencer, I will not let whatever we just saw in the mirror happen. What is the proper choice?" I stood up as I said this. I was feeling brave at the moment.

"Dear Cailyssa, you may go home, finish your homework, and hope all is well. Or you may make another choice, and I'm not sure what will happen if you choose this path."

"If I choose this path, will my parents and dogs be saved? Will the happiness and lives of everyone in town be safe?" I said a bit nervously.

"They may. Or they may not. And you and all of us here may die in vain trying to make it so!" Uncle Spencer's voice was solemn.

I knew what I had to do. I had to try to save my parents, my dogs, my friends, and everyone else. But I couldn't risk the lives of the three people with me trying to do it. So I decided to do it alone.

"You only have a few moments, Cailyssa. The moon is full, and the choice will not be open to you for long. You must decide. Go home and carry on with your life, or step up to the mirror and touch it," Uncle Spencer said as he placed his hand on my shoulder.

Knowing what I had to do, I walked slowly up to the mirror, ready to kick it as fast and hard as possible. I always hated mirrors anyway. Why not break the biggest one I could find? I walked up to the mirror, and with my best kung-fu stance, I kicked hard. The mirror didn't break, but my foot went through. I looked down, and the liquid pool of mirror reflection swallowed my leg and began to travel up, sucking me in, covering my entire body. I thought I would die when my body was totally covered. I tried to pull back, but it was too late. I tried to scream, but the liquid reflection of the mirror ran into my mouth. I lost control. I looked back at Uncle Spencer, Daemon, and Terry…as the mirror swallowed me whole.

CHAPTER 5

ALONE

I stood at the edge of a cliff and peeked through the mist that seemed to swirl around me as if it wanted to grab hold of me and throw me off. I did not move. Maybe this was a bad dream and, like in the movies, I'd wake up soon when one of my dogs licked my face. A black shape approached me, parting the mist as it flew by. Its small black form was heading straight toward me. As it approached I could see that it was a large crow. It flew to the right, directly in front of me, and perched itself on a dead branch of a tree. Its red beady eyes bore into me, and it raised its head and shrieked. This was real; there was no hope of me waking up from this nightmare.

"*Cailyssa Larkin,*" a voice whispered. It sounded like it had come from the swirling mists or the crow; I wasn't sure which. "I have long awaited your arrival. I have been watching you for many years."

The crow flew off the dead tree and through the mist, which seemed to disappear as the bird flew through it. I looked out across this place. It was dark and forbidding—as if all the good feelings had been sucked out of there. In the distance was a monstrous volcano, hot lava dripping out the top and down the sides. To the right of me was a gloomy forest. Rocks that appeared to be black coal or ash covered the ground. There were no living creatures other than this ugly, wretched crow. I finally found the courage to look down at my feet. At the bottom of the cliff were seven luminous pools, each one of them holding a reflection of me peering down from the top. I looked off to the side and saw a small path. I figured it was best to get away from this edge.

I followed the path down, and it led to the seven pools. In the middle of the seven pools was a stone pedestal with a circular stairway leading to the top. I walked up each stair slowly and reached the top of the pedestal to find that "Larkin" was chiseled in all caps into a stone throne.

The black crow landed on the top of the throne and now spoke openly to me. "Take your seat, Cailyssa. A Larkin is back in Mirror World, and I have a present for you."

My body moved as if some unknown force guided it. I stepped up to the throne and sat down.

"Behold thy present," the crow said. His head turned to look down at the pools.

As I looked at the seven images before me, I couldn't believe my eyes. I always hated mirrors because when I looked at one, I always felt fear and saw something about myself I didn't like. *But now I liked what I saw. How could that have changed?* I looked from one image to the other, and I became more beautiful and magnificent in each. By the time

I reached the seventh image, I was the most glorious, beautiful, intelligent, and graceful person I could ever hope to become. I was pure angelic perfection!

The crow looked back at me with its red eyes sparkling with fiery intensity. "I knew you would like your present," it gloated with satisfaction.

I was stunned. *Is this the real me? Have I been looking at myself wrong all these years?* I remembered a time as a little girl when my Uncle Spencer found me crying in front of the mirror. He told me that mirrors were magical; they could show you anything, depending on what you looked for. He said some people would look into a mirror and see only what they hated about themselves, wishing to change something. These people were never happy. Others could look into mirrors and see their true selves and be proud and happy. I remember hugging my Uncle Spencer and hoping one day I would see my true self.

A sudden fury erupted in me. I jumped off the chair and grabbed a stone and hurled it at the head of that stupid black crow. "I don't want your stupid present! None of those reflections in the pools is the real me!"

I suddenly realized where I was, and fear crept into my bones. The crow flew into the air as it narrowly escaped my well-placed rock. It hovered in front of me and exploded into a swarm of black wasps that I thought would sting me to death in a thousand places. The swarm of wasps became a horrible evil skull with dreadful red eyes and sharp black teeth: the face I had seen in the doorknocker.

"To deny my gift is to seek death. So be it for the next Larkin," the hideous voice screeched at me.

In the next second, the face disappeared, and the world turned cold and deadly silent. I was afraid to look down at the pools, sensing movement within them. When I finally looked down into my unreal images of perfection—they turned into the evil skull, which was now laughing at me. Before I could pick up another rock and throw it at one of the pools, a terrific explosion sent water from the pools towering above my head. The earth shook and the ground trembled and I felt sure I was about to die. When it stopped I found myself cold, wet, and alone. I fell to my knees and slid to the ground. I noticed the cuts on my knees, where the sharp rocks had dug into my skin. I was so brave at Uncle Spencer's house, but now I just wanted to go home. I heard noises in the dark forest on the side of me. I heard the clanging of metal and the gnashing of teeth. This day was about to get a lot worse.

CHAPTER 6

GOOD COMPANY

I was still on the ground, covering my face with my hands. I managed to peek through my fingers at the forest where the sounds were coming from. I saw them. Out of the forest marched a dozen of the most horrific-looking evil shapes I had ever imagined. They were slowly approaching me, moving up and down as they walked. I could hear them talking in some unfamiliar language and pointing in my direction.

When you're really scared, your body takes over, and right now mine was telling me to run for my life. As the group of creatures approached me, I could see them a bit more clearly. They were each about seven feet tall and hunched over, and they walked on skinny legs with backward-jointed knees—like birds. Their faces appeared to be covered with green-and-black skin, their heads were entirely bald, and their ears tall and pointy. They were dressed in medieval armor and had various weapons with them: swords, maces, and evil-looking daggers, twisted and black. I saw the crow approaching them. They cowered at the sight of it and fell on the ground. The bird appeared to be hissing orders to them, and they immediately regained their feet.

They pointed at me again and began closing in on me. As they came closer, I could see the face of the one who appeared to be in charge. His blood-red eyes bore into me, and his black pointy teeth were held open with a vicious grin. As he saw me, he pointed to his associates and unsheathed an ugly dagger from his belt. He pointed the dagger directly at me, and I heard his voice. It sounded as if he was saying my name. Next, he put the dagger up to his mouth and slowly licked the blade, enough to draw thick, black blood from his own tongue. This seemed to drive the creatures wild, and I knew they were going to charge me at any minute. I was frozen with fear until I saw the evil creature lick the blade of his dagger. At that point only one thought pervaded my mind: run like hell!

I ran down the stairs as fast as my legs could carry me, my purple sneakers barely touching each stair. At the bottom I didn't know where to run, so I decided to run in the opposite direction from my knife-licking new friend. I could hear them pursuing me. They were screaming and hissing, and their armor and weapons were clanking about them. I stooped as one of them swung at me. I was surrounded, so I ran back up the stairs to hide behind the throne. *Bad idea!* Three of them came up the stairs and surrounded the throne. They began waving their weapons at me. It looked as if they were drooling and bleeding from the mouth—as if they had cut their own tongues. Now I saw them each making small cuts in their tongues, arms, and legs. As the blue-black blood dripped down their bodies, it sent them into a frenzy.

The leader reached his hand out for my arm. It looked to be dinnertime, and I was the meal, with no place to run and no one to help me. I decided I wasn't going to go without a fight. Maybe these creeps had knives, but I bet they'd never met a girl with my kung-fu moves. I was planning to kick the first one in the head and grab his dagger and then run through the others. However, when he reached for my arm, his foul smell hit me in the face. I stood there frozen with fear—the sacrificial lamb at the slaughterhouse.

Just then, a whooshing noise came from nowhere, and the head of the creature in front of me slowly fell off its body, severed in one clean shot. I barely caught a glimpse of the figure clad in black that flew past with two beautiful white wings and apparently some razor-sharp claws. As the creatures saw the head of their leader fall to the ground, they began looking nervously around. From behind me a cloaked figure was approaching, his hands raised above his head. Blue bolts of electrical fire came from his fingers and scared the creatures in front of me. They seemed scattered and confused without their leader. Out of nowhere another figure dashed in from my right. I heard the *ting* as he unleashed his sword from behind his back. The sword must've been six feet long and gleamed with a bright silver-white light. A figure wielded it with such awesome precision and grace that it seemed almost cruel as he cut a path through the horrible creatures, leaving most of them dead or retreating. The threat seemed to be over, but I was unsure who was helping me; maybe they would eat me, too!

Before I could walk down the stairs, the white-winged figure flew down quickly and landed on the top of the throne with ease. I blinked three times in shock when I saw the figure's face, and then I caught hold of myself.

"Terry, what the hell are you doing *here*?" I blurted out. "You could've been killed! There are crazy creatures here and dark, evil birds and who knows what else. Get your butt home before I kick it there." I had to protect her! But I was losing my steam now as I looked into Terry's beautiful face.

"OK, Lyssa, take a chill pill and look at this," Terry said as she slowly unfurled her beautiful white wings. She then crossed her arms, closed her fists, and popped three long, razor-sharp blades out of each hand. Then she struck the most awesome movie star pose, winked at me, and *very* slowly adjusted her Tinker Bell hat.

"Say what you want about this girl, but she's got *style*," Terry said as if we were back home standing on the porch. She then back flipped off the stone throne and landed with perfect balance on the ground.

The stress of what I had been through and the surprise of seeing Terry as some superhero overwhelmed me. My knees got weak, my head started to spin, and the world became black around me. With a tremendous force of will, I managed to sit down on the throne only a split second before passing out.

As I awoke I heard Uncle Spencer's warm, reassuring voice. "Dear Cailyssa, sit up and drink a little of this, and you'll feel better in a few moments."

I opened my eyes and expected to be back at Uncle Spencer's home on his couch. But when I saw Uncle Spencer, I almost fainted again. He was draped in the cloak, but at least the firebolts were not still coming from his hands. I had a million questions jumbled in my mind to ask Uncle Spencer. So I stood up and brushed the dirt from my clothes, only to notice that the warrior who had killed the evil creatures was now on one knee in front of me with his head down.

"Thank you, sir," I said. "Please don't kneel in front of me. You're embarrassing me. My name is Cailyssa, and I'm not some royal princess."

"By your leave, I shall stand. I am in your service and offer protection," the proud warrior said. He rose to his full height, and I looked into Daemon's gray-green eyes.

I lost it! The five-year-old in me who missed her best friend ran to him and threw her arms around him, clutching him tightly. I noticed after a minute of my slobbering embrace that Daemon was standing there like a stone statue. Now, there's nothing that a girl hates more than laying an emotional hug on a guy and having him stand there like a rock as if she didn't exist. I stepped back.

"Most people at least have the courtesy to return a hug, *Daemon!*" I said with an angry look.

"If you so wish it, I will embrace you. But I must warn you that I do so with great reluctance." Daemon looked directly over my head, making no eye contact whatsoever.

"Uncle Spencer, what's going on here? Terry's got wings, you're dressed in a Halloween cloak, and Daemon is playing the knight who doesn't know me! Please tell me this is a nightmare and I'll wake up soon."

"Cailyssa, this is no nightmare, I can assure you. It is far too dangerous to discuss these matters here. We need to be on the move quickly and without delay."

"Where do you want to go? Any ice-cream shops in the neighborhood? Perhaps you could grab me a sundae," I said in my most sarcastic voice.

"I am sorry, Cailyssa, ice cream is not to be had today. Terry, you fly ahead and report back if those raxs are in front of us. Daemon, go behind to protect us from the rear. Let none pass. Cailyssa, take my hand and come with me. I'll show you the way," Uncle Spencer said with great authority, and everybody responded immediately.

I felt bad for my earlier sarcastic remark about ice cream, and I grabbed Uncle Spencer's big, warm hand.

"Sorry about my wisecrack, Uncle Spencer. I'm just feeling a bit more strange and unusual than on most days," I said sheepishly.

"As you should, Cailyssa. Few people have ever seen this realm, and it can be quite—how should we say—overwhelming, even for the bravest of us," Uncle Spencer said as he began to quicken our pace.

"Could I at least ask where we're going?" I said in my steadiest voice. My nervous, weak feeling was returning.

Uncle Spencer looked at me, drew back his hood, and gave me that warm, hearty smile that I love. "Of course, so rude of me. I presumed you knew."

"Knew what?" I said. "Why does everybody presume I know things?"

"I thought you knew where we were going," Uncle Spencer said matter-of-factly. "We are going to your house, Cailyssa. Better known in this world as Castle Larkin."

I kept walking with Uncle Spencer as the words "*my house?*" and "*Castle Larkin?*" kept falling from my mouth.

As we walked, the blackness of the forest vanished a bit, and the land became greener but still a bit shabby. The road narrowed to a path, and we began walking through a forest. The trees were immensely tall, with pine needles only at the top and thick dark-red trunks to support them. For some reason, I felt much more calm here. I had let go of Uncle Spencer's arm a long time ago, and I was trying to sort out the details of this remarkable day in my head. Just then Terry swooped down from the tops of the trees and landed in front of Uncle Spencer. At the same moment, Daemon appeared out of nowhere behind me.

"Not to worry, Cailyssa, there is no danger. We are protected here by the charms that guard your castle lands. Terry and Daemon sensed this and have joined us to provide good company!" Uncle Spencer said this as if he was in a buoyant mood and this was a fun adventure. "And of course I have sent word for Halodire to pick us up at the water's edge."

We walked in silence for the next several miles until we came to the edge of the most beautiful Crystal Lake. The water was a deep blue and glistened with a sheen that made every reflection sharp and clear. As I looked down at the lake's reflection, I could see the forest, the clouds, and a structure that must be Castle Larkin in the distance. A long gondola approached with a single oarsman standing on its back edge, pushing the boat through the water with a long pole.

"Hey, Uncle Spencer, who is this Halodire dude, anyway? He looks really tall from here. I sure hope he is friendly and cute," Terry said with unnecessary enthusiasm.

"Terry, don't even *tink* about going on boyfriend patrol in this crazy world. We're not even supposed to be here. Think how Dad would react if you brought home a nonhuman boyfriend," I said to hide my nervousness as the figure approached us in the boat.

I moved closer to Uncle Spencer's side. "I hope this guy is friendly. Like Terry said, he sure looks big."

"Of course he's big, Cailyssa. He is one of the high elves of Charlock. All of his kind are known for their tall statuesque forms, and, as Terry rightly said, their tremendous beauty. Although his size and stature may intimidate you, don't be scared. He is from a gentle race. Aside from that, he is your bound servant. He has served the house of Larkin as gatekeeper of the great castle for over a thousand years."

As the long boat touched the shore, Halodire gracefully exited the boat, drew back his hood, and bowed slightly in front of me. "Welcome home, Cailyssa. I have watched you for many years, but I must say that your beauty is far more spectacular in person." He took my hand and kissed it and then stood up in front of me.

I must say, I'm not often taken by guys with good looks, but Halodire was simply the most gorgeous man that I have ever seen. He was tall and broad shouldered, with blond hair that fell to his shoulders. His chiseled face was strong and handsome, and his blue eyes seemed to look through you and capture your heart as though he were holding it in his hand. He flashed a dazzling smile after he kissed my hand, and I simply melted with adoration.

Terry jumped in front of me. "Hey, Hal, my name's Terry, and I have the coolest white wings. So if you want to go flying sometime, let me know. I mean we could always—"

I pushed Terry out of the way, seeking to regain my connection and place in front of Halodire. The two of us actually began fighting and pushing each other out of the way to stand in front of this man and beg for his attention. This was totally unusual. Terry and I were never boy-crazy teens, and we usually treated boys as semi unimportant. Now, however, Halodire had us fighting like two insane Barbie dolls over the last Ken doll on earth. As Halodire continued his perfect smile, Daemon stepped between us. His sword was drawn, and he was glaring at Halodire. Halodire quickly stopped smiling and took three paces back, obviously scared of Daemon.

"You will stop your sorcery! Never use your halo charm again on these young ladies, lest I separate your limbs from your body at a leisurely pace." Daemon said this with great authority and presence, and even Uncle Spencer seemed to take a step back from the intense power he projected.

Uncle Spencer intervened. "Now, everyone, let's calm down. We have more to do than quibble between ourselves. Everyone onto the boat; Halodire will take us to the castle."

We boarded the vessel, and Terry and I sat next to each other, not saying a word. We were both embarrassed about our actions and couldn't believe that any guy could make us act that way. As I glanced at the water, I was amazed that the beautiful blue-black lake showed no wake of the boat as we traveled. There were simply no ripples in the water at all, and my reflection and those of my friends were perfectly clear. As we approached the castle, I saw its reflection in the water. I gazed along the water to the shore, and I saw the bottom of the real castle. It was an inviting castle made of a beautiful red-gray brick with a green roof. At the front of the castle was a gatehouse of the same color and structure. When we arrived at the gatehouse, Halodire disappeared inside, and the two large wooden doors at the front of the castle opened.

"Come inside; come inside!" said Uncle Spencer with great glee. "It has been many years since a Larkin has visited the castle, and I have missed it so. The last person to live here, Cailyssa, was your grandfather Artemus Larkin. He brought your father and me here several times when we were young, although your father denies any memory of the experience."

Uncle Spencer gave us a quick tour of the castle, at least from what he could remember. The castle was more like a home with grand bedrooms and living rooms draped in comfortable royal colors, such as purple and maroon. There was also a female touch of style in the flowering tapestries and rugs, said to be the work of my grandmother, Elissa Larkin. The castle's keep was to the back, and Uncle Spencer promised to show it to us after dinner. Halodire busied himself in the kitchen with six small elves that were scurrying about, preparing food. These were the types of elves I was used to from childhood Christmas stories and cookie boxes. They were short, chubby, and jovial, often teasing and laughing with each other as they worked. Halodire explained that he was a high elf and that these other elves were only distant relations. He seemed to look down upon his distant cousins and treated them somewhat harshly when they dropped a plate or made too much noise with the silverware.

We sat at a grand round ballroom table, and the meal was served. Terry and I ate like we had been starved for three days, and Uncle Spencer enjoyed the wonderful food, too. However, although Daemon sat there happily enough, he did not partake of any of the food; he sipped slowly from a large goblet that contained a wonderful broth that tasted like lemon and honey. When the meal ended, I was determined to blurt out all my questions to Uncle Spencer. But before I could, Uncle Spencer led us to a patio overlooking the lake.

The reflection from the lake was as clear as a bell. Before I could say a word or ask a question, the reflection changed to a face.

"Dear Cailyssa, seeing you here makes me sad that I can no longer take human form and wrap my arms around you. The last time I did, you were a tiny child, and I can honestly say that holding you was one of the most joyous memories of my life." This was my grandfather, Artemus Larkin, speaking, and no one needed to tell me that; I knew it in my very soul.

The tears began to well in my eyes, and I could see Terry was trying to cover her eyes with the tips of her wings.

"Papa, is that really you?" I said in a choked-up, tearful voice.

"You know it's me, and so does Terry. Now if she would just move her wings, I could look at her beautiful face," our grandfather said.

Terry folded her wings behind her back and couldn't help letting the tears drip off her cheeks onto her trembling hands.

"Let's not make this a sad event. Few humans and spirits, such as myself, ever get to talk to each other like this. I have been waiting for this moment for a long time. As I watched you two grow up, I knew that one day we would be here together. Let me welcome you to Castle Larkin. I see my dear son Spencer is here, too. But where is my best friend Daemon?"

"Unfortunately, I could not convince him to visit with your image. He says he is too ashamed to see you again, and he is still begging for your forgiveness," Uncle Spencer said sadly.

"It is unfortunate. Daemon should know that there is nothing to forgive. I will forever hold him close to my heart. I will always love him as a son," my grandfather said with great distress. "Cailyssa, there is much you know about this world, but let me refresh your memory in case your specular skills are not fully developed. When you touched—or, should I say, tried to break—the mirror at my son's home, you entered into the world of Speculus Locus, often called just Speculus or, in the common tongue, Mirror World. Long ago when the earth was created, this place was made. It is a confusing place, and much is not known about it, but it is somewhere between heaven and hell. Most of those who live here are trying to make it to heaven and have not yet proved themselves. This place also houses the forgotten species that left the earth, such as the elves.

"The dark lord also resides here, and he uses his powers to corrupt the inhabitants of this place. The dark lord has the power to influence the reflections we each see—be it in water or a mirror. Since the dawn of time, he sits in his dark tower trying to bend all reflections to his will. His wish is that all will look upon themselves—and each other—with spite, hatred, and misery so that all life destroys itself. The laws established by the Creator bind him, however. He cannot directly control or change a person. He can, however, corrupt a person through reflections and temptation so that each person sees himself or herself in an evil way. Such people do not see their true selves in the mirror. They see themselves filled with hate and misery until they are destroyed. Their souls, originally reflected as good in the mirror, are ruined.

"Alas, I wish I could stay longer and be with you all, but I must return. I love you all. Be comforted that the Creator, the angels, and those of his realm have faith in you. Your duty is to help so that, one day, people will see their true selves in every reflection and find love, happiness, and joy to feed their souls. Don't forget: look to those you meet for help and guidance. Only through friendships and trust can an army be mustered that can defeat the plans of the dark lord. All my love to you. Good-bye."

I stood there stunned, trying to take in all this information. The strange thing was, I knew much of it before my grandfather had said it. It was almost like he was reminding me of something I already knew. I also knew, on another level, that much was expected of me. That's what really scared me, because I wasn't sure I could expect much from myself.

Uncle Spencer led us back to the round table, where Halodire had prepared a tremendous round of desserts and sweets with his little elf friends. Terry and I were hardly in the mood to eat, and we sat there and only nibbled on chocolates that we would have shoveled down any other time. Uncle Spencer came out, and so did Daemon. Uncle Spencer was carrying a large box with several items that he placed on the table. When Daemon walked by me, I looked at his back and saw two huge gashes and long trails of blood.

I jumped up and ran to him. "Daemon! Oh my God, you're hurt! Let me get something to stop the bleeding," I said as I was looking around for a clean cloth.

"Please, Cailyssa, don't worry. I'll be fine," he said as he strode past me.

"What do you mean you'll be fine? You have two long cuts on your back that are bleeding. You need a doctor." I scrambled over and put the clean cloths on his wounds.

Daemon looked up at me with deep gullies under his eyes. It appeared that he had been crying. "Cailyssa, there is nothing that can stop the tears of blood from an unforgiven being such as myself. Today, however, I stop shedding tears, for it may hinder my duty to you." As Daemon said this, the blood miraculously began disappearing from his back, and he rose and left the room.

"He will be fine, Cailyssa. This has been quite difficult for him. But I'm glad you're here. If you were not, I am quite sure that Daemon would already have killed himself. Please sit down. I have several presents for you," my uncle said. He walked around the table and placed a long bundle in front of me.

I opened it and revealed two beautiful swords with slim samurai blades and polished metal handles that gleamed reflections in all directions. The words "Sacrifice" and "Justice" were etched into each blade with fancy lettering. I picked them up and hefted them in the same way as I did the bamboo sticks in my kung-fu class. They felt light and balanced, and it felt wonderful to move my body in a sequence of fighting moves that helped relieve some of the stress I had been experiencing.

"Whoa..." said Terry as she jumped up from the table. "That's the coolest two-handed fighting style I've ever seen. Maybe when we get back home you can teach me, and we'll make one of those cool martial-arts movies."

I wiped the sweat from my brow, trying to relax. I knew what the next two surprise presents would be. I opened the case that contained a round moonstone, its reflection shimmering like a mirror. I knew that, like a compass, it would guide me on this journey. Last, I slowly opened the book Uncle Spencer had slid in front of me. It was bound in red leather with "Larkin" inscribed on top in dark-gold letters. It was thick, but it opened to only two pages. The first page was a mirrored pool of reflection that instantly transmitted to my brain a slideshow of the happiest memories of my life. I could see my mother, my father, my dogs, and every happy memory that had ever been in my mind. On the second page, written in an ancient script tilted backward upon the page, was a poem that somehow I knew I had read many times before. Most people would need a mirror to read it, but not me.

I closed the book, put the moonstone in my right pocket, and resheathed the swords in the leather scabbards. I picked them all up without saying a word and carried them up to my bedroom. I lay down upon the bed, hoping that sleep would consume me. Yet the poem was etched into my brain. I could clearly see what I had to do, but I was too afraid to do it. That night I prayed myself to sleep, knowing that the last four conscious words from my mouth were, "God, please help me!"

CHAPTER 7

THE OBEDIENT SERVANT

A large dwarf sat on a ledge outside of his cave and peered into a black lake below. As he looked down, he gazed at the reflection of himself. He hated looking at himself, but he could not divert his eyes from his own grotesque image. He looked at his rotund face with several layers of chins that supported his large, blubbery mouth. Encroaching folds covered his beady eyes, and his long braided beard was dirty with coal and food. He was dressed in his mining outfit. Bulging stomach pressed against every square inch and threatened to bust the heavy leather shirt apart. His belt was of no use to hold up his stained green pants; it was hidden under layers of belly, and it made a big, red, painful crease in his lower gut. Yllib the dwarf sat looking down into the black lake, hating the image of himself floating in the water.

The dwarfs here lived in small caves carved in the side of the mountain. Each cave had a ledge, and each morning the dwarfs would come out from their shabby, smelly caves and sit at the edge and gaze down at the black lake. This morning, Yllib looked down from his ledge and saw the thousands of dwarfs that he commanded looking down at the reflection with him. It was early. The light of day had not arrived, and they stared into the black water—disgusted with themselves—awaiting the directions from the master. Suddenly the reflection in the lake changed, and the dwarfs stared at their dreaded master.

"I hope you have been working hard lately. I shall be visiting your putrid coal mine today, and if I don't find the monthly total acceptable, the punishments will be unbearable, and your food will be rationed for a week." Ttocs's cruel grin widened and disappeared before the dwarfs.

Ttocs served the dark lord of this world as his first lieutenant. He loved visiting the dwarfs, since he could unleash his cruelty and barbaric sense of humor. Dwarfs were very sturdy and could be beaten relentlessly without fear of killing one of them. Ttocs readied his black tunic and pants and made sure that the vicious spikes that protruded from them did not cut him as he put them on. He whistled loudly, and his red dragon, Longtooth, appeared from her filthy hole as she spit out the bones of the creatures she had just devoured for breakfast.

"Come to me, Longtooth," Ttocs said. "We journey to the dwarf lands today, and I look forward very much to beating my fat-bellied friends."

Yllib watched the glum messenger disappear as he readied himself for another day managing the coalmines. He put on his miner's helmet and his old crusty boots and emerged at the edge of his cave. He paused for a moment and thought of his life long ago when he was young. He remembered his family picnics when they owned their own mine. They were a happy family, bound by love and honor, descended from a noble race of great dwarfs. How did he end up here, doing the horrible things he did? He erased any happy thoughts from his mind, and he picked up his whip, which he fondly called Sting. Yllib made sure the handle was secure and that the tips of the five metal balls were clean of the flesh that he'd sliced the previous day. He rolled the whip, attached it to his belt, and walked down the long path to the dining hall below.

Yllib entered the dining room, and a hush overtook the room. The dwarfs hated Yllib and feared his whip, but many of the dwarfs pretended to be friendly toward him, hoping to gain his favor. The dining room was nothing but a flat stretch of rock with long wooden tables and benches. The morning gruel was served, and each dwarf stared glumly down at his wooden bowl, hoping to find a small bone or a hint of meat in the thick sloppy mess. They ate quietly, preparing themselves for another day at the mine and dreading the arrival of Ttocs.

"Make room, you stupid piece of dragon dung!" Yllib yelled at Dolhar, the closest dwarf to him.

The dwarfs all slid down the bench and began to eat hastily, knowing that Yllib would soon grab each bowl and steal as much food as he could. Yllib sat here every morning across from Dolhar, the oldest dwarf in the mine, who for some odd reason put up with Yllib's abuse and actually seemed to show some interest in him.

"You better save the last of your bowl for me, you worthless old slug," Yllib said to Dolhar as he slobbered up the gruel from his own bowl.

"I always save a little for you, Yllib. I seem to have lost my appetite, knowing that Ttocs and Longtooth will be visiting today. It's a shame what happened to poor Gothir last time they came," Dolhar said with obvious sadness. "I always considered Gothir my friend, and I consider you, Yllib, my friend, too."

Yllib wiped his arm across the table, knocking all the bowls to the floor, and he jumped up from the bench. He grabbed Sting from his belt, getting ready to whip Dolhar.

"No one is *my* friend; there is no such thing as friends in this place. If I hear you use that word again, you'll taste my whip, you stupid old fool," Yllib said as he stormed out of the room.

The other dwarfs looked over at Dolhar, who was staring straight ahead. But if you looked closely, you could see the tear that rolled down his right cheek.

Dolhar stood up and said loud enough for all to hear, "Yllib, your father was my friend and always will be!"

Yllib froze at the front door. The dwarfs gasped, fearing that a wild beating was about to happen. But Yllib did nothing. He continued walking out the door to await the train that took them all to the mine.

The dwarfs quickly finished their breakfasts and sluggishly walked to the train, dreading another day of digging for coal. Dolhar was the last one on the train, and that meant he would be the first one off. He took this place, knowing full well what would happen to him. The other dwarfs on the train tried to help Dolhar into another seat. Dolhar was very old, and some days he had difficulty walking or even standing up. Without the help of the other dwarfs, he would already have been dead. But Dolhar was very well liked among the dwarfs; he was the kindest and funniest among them. He seemed to remind everyone of his favorite uncle or grandfather. Today, Dolhar refused to budge from the last seat on the train.

The train stopped at the mine, and the hideous, fat form of Yllib waited at the door of the train. He had his whip, Sting, in his hand, and he looked to be in a most foul mood, after what Dolhar had said in the dining room. Without help, Dolhar took his old self down from the train and stood to face Yllib. Without mercy, Yllib pulled back his whip, and the five shiny metal balls bit into the flesh of Dolhar's shoulder, bringing him to one knee. Without stopping, Yllib readied the whip again and slashed it across Dolhar's back. Dolhar did not scream out in pain; he simply trembled and fell on his hands and knees. He felt in his heart that Yllib really didn't want to do this. Before Yllib could lash out again at Dolhar, a huge red dragon appeared in the sky and overflew the dwarf's train. Upon seeing Longtooth and Ttocs, the dwarfs ran to the mine as fast as they could, often stepping upon poor

Dolhar. With help from his friends, Dolhar was able to make it into the mine and begin to work.

"Ttocs will be here soon to count our coal. You'd better be working extra hard today to ensure we have enough for the dark lord's ovens," Yllib said as he walked frantically through the mine.

The dwarfs worked as hard as they could, knowing that by lunchtime Ttocs would have counted all their coal. He was never happy with the amount.

"Land there near the coal pit, Longtooth!" Ttocs screamed.

As she landed, Longtooth looked at Ttocs with her large golden eyes and wondered how she could serve such a horrible master. Longtooth came from the island Dragonlance. Long ago, she was a proud and beautiful dragon, and she served her old master, Zane, faithfully for many years. One day Ttocs and a group of demons attacked her and Zane as they slept. Ttocs murdered her master, and she was then forced to serve him. According to dragon lore, a dragon must serve a new master if her master is defeated in battle. However, Ttocs did not defeat her master in battle, he simply murdered him as he slept. Nonetheless, Longtooth was bound to this new master—although some days she wished she would die rather than serve him. She looked into the black pool and saw her long red body. It was filled with scars and missing scales. Longtooth had once been a magnificent and noble red dragon. But she had long since forgotten who she was and the love she held in her heart. Legend has it that dragons were placed upon the earth to give men wisdom and to help them to see the power of love in one's heart. It was said that a dragon could remove its heart and show it freely to men so that the love of the Creator would be within them. However, Ttocs's beatings and savagery had long removed her beauty and any traces of nobility within her.

"Yllib! You useless, disgusting excuse for a dwarf. Where are you?" Ttocs bellowed at the door of the mine, expecting that Yllib would be waiting there for him.

When Yllib heard the sound of his master's voice, he ran through the mine as fast as his stout legs could carry him. He appeared in front of Ttocs, out of breath, with drool dripping down the sides of his mouth.

"It's a good thing you have a beard. It's quite useful to catch your drool and food," said Ttocs sarcastically.

"I...I...I...was making sure the dwarfs were working hard, master," Yllib said as he tried to catch his breath.

Ttocs slowly walked around Yllib. In his right hand was his mace. It was a carved black stick with three chains stemming from the top. At the tip of each chain was a black skull with sharp spikes sticking out in all directions. Yllib could hear the sound of the mace as it was swinging behind his back. He stood there, terrified of what might happen to him next. Ttocs walked up to one of the mining carts and picked up a handful of clips that looked like large metal clothespins. He walked in front of Yllib and looked upon him with great disgust.

"Obviously, you take no pride in your appearance. You disgust me. Have you been stealing the dwarf's food?" Ttocs said with great disdain.

"I only work to serve the great Ttocs and his master—"

"Quiet!" Ttocs bellowed. He swung the mace on top of Yllib's mining helmet. Yllib fell to the earth with a thud and actually found himself crying as if he was a little boy again.

"Get up, or I'll beat you again!" Ttocs howled.

"Yes, Master, I was only trying to help," Yllib said as he wiped the tears from his eyes.

"I plan to tour the mine with you in a moment. But I wanted the dwarfs to know that I am aware of your food stealing, and I have determined the appropriate punishment," Ttocs said this with a great evil smile. "Take off your shirt, you miserable slug!"

Yllib slowly took off his shirt, dreading the punishment that Ttocs was about to unleash. Ttocs slowly walked up to Yllib and took one of the large metal clips in his hand. He opened the metal clip and clenched it over Yllib's expansive flesh. The sharp clip bit in, and it pinched Yllib's flesh painfully.

"Now that's an improvement," said Ttocs. "I think I'll clip a few more on you just to remind you not to steal food from the dwarfs." Ttocs laughed as he said this, and he proceeded to slowly walk around Yllib placing pinching clips as he laughed loudly at the dwarf's displeasure. Yllib now had clips all across his stomach and back, and he did his best to hold in his tears. He couldn't help himself; he whimpered, hoping that somehow this would all end. Last, Ttocs picked up a piece of coal and walked behind Yllib. Across Yllib's back he wrote, "I steal food."

"Now that you're ready, let's take a tour of the mine. And stop your sniveling and whimpering. I hate to see a sniveling dwarf cry," Ttocs said this with great pleasure, and his laughter could be heard all the way inside the mine. Longtooth had been watching this from afar. She turned her golden eyes away and looked into the lake below; she was disgusted by such cruelty.

As Ttocs and Yllib walked through the mine, the dwarfs worked harder, in fear of the dreaded mace that Ttocs held in his hand. Ttocs paraded Yllib openly around the mine, making sure that each dwarf got to look at his back and see the painful clips all around his body. As they approached the back of the mine, several dwarfs worked close together, attempting to hide old Dolhar from Ttocs's view.

"What have we here? Are you dwarfs hiding something?" Ttocs said as he pushed the dwarfs away, only to see old Dolhar sitting down on a rock. "Hiding a dwarf who is supposed to be working? Get him up, Yllib, we will make an example of him. The beatings will continue until morale improves," Ttocs said as he laughed wildly.

Yllib walked over to Dolhar and picked him up by the arm. They followed Ttocs out of the mine. As they were walking, Dolhar proceeded to gently remove the clips that pinched Yllib. When they came out of the mine, all the dwarfs followed.

"Yllib! Who said you could remove my clips?" Ttocs glared.

"He didn't remove them; I did." Dolhar walked up fearlessly to face Ttocs.

"You were already in trouble for not working, old dwarf. How dare you defy me?" Ttocs pulled up his mace, ready to pummel the old dwarf to death. He stopped in midair and slowly lowered the mace, as Dolhar stood proudly to face his punishment.

"I have a better idea for you, dwarf. Killing you swiftly would provide me no great enjoyment. I would rather see you die slowly. And of course, I hate to waste a good old dwarf, since Longtooth has not had her lunch. Longtooth, come here. I have a snack for you," Ttocs said with great anticipation.

Longtooth landed next to Ttocs, her wings folded into her sides and her large golden eyes staring at the ground.

"Longtooth, be happy. I have a lovely old dwarf for you to eat. Start with his feet and slowly nibble your way up so that he dies slowly. *Eat his head last!*"

The dwarfs gasped in horror as Ttocs said this.

Longtooth stood for a moment unmoving.

"Feast upon him, Longtooth! I command it!" Ttocs said.

Again Longtooth did not move a muscle.

"I said, feast upon him, Longtooth! I command it!" Ttocs roared louder.

Still Longtooth did not move.

"Do what I command, Longtooth! Obey me, you scarred, hideous beast!" Ttocs screamed in fury.

Longtooth looked at her master and then slowly over at the old dwarf. She felt sick. How could she do such a thing? But she knew that if she did not, Ttocs would brutally beat her with his mace and notify the dark lord of her disobedience, and she would be killed. Longtooth glanced back at her reflection in the lake. She knew she could not do this thing, for she would forever lose her soul and never join her deceased family in the stars.

"Enough of your disobedience, Longtooth. I should've known better than to trust a female dragon, especially one as stupid, old, and ugly as you! You'll now feel the wrath of my mace!" Ttocs whirled his mace above his head, ready to strike Longtooth and remove more of her beautiful scales.

Longtooth heard voices within her mind: *Do what you know is right*. It was her parents, and what they said rekindled the love in her heart. It made her noble and proud once again to know that she could still do the right thing. She stood up straight and tall and unfurled her fifty-foot wings. She raised her head, and her great golden eyes, ringed with fire, bore down upon Ttocs as he approached. She bellowed a hideous roar that echoed off every mountain in the dwarf lands. Then she reared her head back and spit out a vicious ball of flame at Ttocs's feet. The first lieutenant of the dark lord, Ttocs, stopped in his tracks, shaking in fear at the sight of Longtooth's rage, his pants stained in front where he had wet himself.

"You should change your pants, master. You seemed to have soiled yourself." As Longtooth said this, she gently walked over, picked up the old dwarf, Dolhar, and simply flew away.

Ttocs's fury was unimaginable. The dwarfs were now pointing to him and the stain on his pants, laughing. He charged and mercilessly tried to beat the dwarfs as they ran from him.

Suddenly, the atmosphere changed. Ttocs froze in place as a black shadow swept over the land. A swarm of wasps appeared in the shape of an evil black skull. The dark lord had arrived. The mouth of the skull opened, and an evil hiss spread a swarm of wasps around Ttocs. The wasps lifted him up and carried him back to the dark lord's castle, stinging him relentlessly as they flew. Even though the dwarfs were glad to have a reprieve from the beatings, they couldn't help but be terrified at Ttocs's awful screams of pain.

Meanwhile, Longtooth landed far away and put Dolhar down gently.

"Thank you, my friend. The dark lord's wrath will be awful when he finds what you have done. But I appreciate you saving my life. I have known several dragons throughout my long lifetime, and each has been a noble and proud creature. But what you have done today is perhaps the bravest thing I have ever witnessed." Dolhar affectionately stroked the dragon's nose.

"Thank you, master dwarf, for your kind words. But perhaps you should leave before the dark lord finds me and sends me to my final resting place." Longtooth spoke with great sadness as she lay down upon the ground, waiting to die.

"I have no intention of leaving you or watching you die, great dragon, for now our lives are bound together, and I'll fight to the death to protect you from the dark lord and Ttocs." Dolhar proudly stood up and looked into Longtooth's beautiful golden eyes. Longtooth rose, and Dolhar climbed upon her back. She flew into the sky, feeling she had regained her honor. Her dragon heart began to swell. The love she held had been rekindled, for now she was again bound to an honorable and caring master. She would die to protect him. If Ttocs tried to kill her master, this time she would have his head.

"Where are we off to, master dwarf? The dark lord and Ttocs will soon be on our trail," Longtooth said, as she spiraled gracefully in the air.

"Fly north. Today is a good day, great dragon! Look at our reflection in the lake below—I feel it is changed. The color is bright. The air is clean, the water looks beautiful, and the sky is clear," Dolhar said as he proudly sat upon Longtooth's back, his long hair and beard blowing in the wind.

"Yes, I can see what you mean. I can feel the change, too. It's been a long time overdue," Longtooth said as she flew toward the north.

"*Long* overdue, my noble red friend—fly us with haste to the north! The change in the world is unmistakable, and it can mean only *one* thing. A Larkin has returned to Mirror World!"

The dragon and the dwarf, now one, flew on toward Castle Larkin. For the first time in a long while, they both felt something that they had not felt in a very long time: love and hope.

CHAPTER 8

SPECULAR KNOWLEDGE

I awoke the next morning and stared at the ceiling, expecting to see the old familiar light in the middle of my bedroom at home. Instead, I found myself in the master bedroom of Castle Larkin. The ceiling above me was adorned with a painting that replicated art found in the most beautiful churches in the world. The painting depicted various types of angels, from tiny cherubs to large warriors. They all seemed to be looking at something in the distance, their faces beaming with happiness and bright sunshine. As I examined the intricate painting—which appeared to be inlaid with precious gems and gold—I heard a soft knock on my door, and a familiar voice brought me back to reality.

"Lyssa, come on down and eat breakfast. Those little elves have gone crazy and put up a huge brunch," Terry's familiar voice said from behind the huge ornate wooden door.

I hopped out of the enormous bed, grabbing one of the huge posts that anchored each of the four corners. I placed my foot upon the thick carpet, which felt great between my toes, and I looked across the room at a floor-to-ceiling mirror. For some reason mirrors didn't bother me as much today. Next to the mirror was a changing table with what appeared to be new clothes laid out for me. I'm usually not into leather, but I guessed that's what they wear in this strange place. I put on my dark-blue leather pants and a loose-fitting shirt that was made out of the softest white material imaginable. Across the top of the shirt and down the arms it was adorned with an intricate pattern of beautiful purple and maroon stitching that seemed to sparkle in the sunlight coming through the vast window to my right. I laced up my black boots and buckled the clasps at the top. I tapped on the heels of my boots for fun, and I was stunned to see that a sharp blade sprang from the toe of the boot. I carefully replaced the blade in its spring-mounted launcher and stood up. Across from me on the changing table were the moonstone, my red wordless book, and my swords and scabbards. Memories flooded back to me from the day before, and uneasiness crept into my stomach. I placed the moonstone and book in a leather pouch, and I grabbed a beautiful green tunic that hung from the wall and wrapped my swords within it. I opened the wooden doors of my room and headed down the castle stairs.

When I reached the dining hall, I could see the elves scurrying around, placing platters of food and freshly cut flowers on the long wooden table. Uncle Spencer and Daemon were sitting on one side of the table, and Terry and Halodire sat on the other. They all looked up at me as I approached the table. The largest chair at the head of the table was open, and Uncle Spencer gestured for me to sit there.

"Cailyssa, I must say you look absolutely radiant in your grandmother's travel outfit," Uncle Spencer said with great sincerity. "Please sit down and join us for breakfast."

I grabbed an apple and a cake, and I sat down and watched Terry and Halodire greedily consume their food. Of course, Uncle Spencer ate slowly, like a perfect gentleman. Daemon, however, sat there without a morsel of food on his plate and only a large goblet of some gold liquid. He refused to make eye contact with me and simply stared straight ahead. When he did dare to speak, he only spoke in whispers to Uncle Spencer that I could not hear.

"Good morning, Daemon," I said in my most encouraging voice, trying not to show the irritation I felt.

"Good morning, Cailyssa," Daemon seemed to say this rather reluctantly and only gave me the briefest glance as he continued to talk to Uncle Spencer.

I guess this meant he was still going to play the cold soldier boy again, but I wasn't going to let him do that for long. There was no way I was going to let my best friend from childhood treat me that way. We had spent too many hours together enjoying each other's company for him to act like this. In fact, I remember when I was younger, *he* was always following *me* around, trying to hang out with me. The other kids used to tease us and chant rhymes that suggested we would be married someday. I think, when I was in preschool, I actually asked him to marry me, and he said *yes*. However, it's kind of hard to make marriage work when you're four years old. But even as we grew older together, Daemon and I were inseparable. You know how you just feel entirely comfortable with your best friend; you can totally relax and be your real self. That's how I always felt around Daemon, and I knew that's how he felt too, except for now. So there was no way I was going let him continue the distant soldier-boy routine without giving him a good talking to.

"Lyssa, you're doing that spaced-out look, and you're not even touching your food. The elves are going to be quite upset if you don't eat some of the delicious crepes. This is the most amazing breakfast I have ever had!" Terry said as she scooped the food into her mouth with no shame.

"Cailyssa, I was wondering if I might have a word with you after breakfast," Uncle Spencer said.

"That sounds great. I'm hoping you can help me out with what my grandfather called my specular skills."

I finished eating, grabbed my stuff, and walked with Uncle Spencer toward the keep of the castle. From the corner of my eye, I saw Terry walk over to the balcony, step up on the rail, and gracefully fall over the edge. My heart stopped until I saw her beautiful white wings unfurl as she gracefully spiraled toward the large field below. Uncle Spencer opened the doors of the castle keep and escorted me inside. It looked like a mausoleum, and before me I saw the tombs of my grandfather and grandmother at the front, followed by hundreds of stone caskets. The room was lined with mirrors and candles in a hallway that seemed to stretch on forever. The ceiling was one hundred feet high, and sunlight peered in through skylights that gave the room a shimmering radiance.

"As you probably know, Cailyssa, here in this burial chamber lie your relatives for many generations. They have moved on, like your grandfather, into the spiritual realm," Uncle Spencer said with great pride.

"Uncle Spencer, this room is enormous! I bet we could find relatives here from a thousand years ago," I said in awe. "How far back can you trace my family genealogy?"

"Now, if I were to answer your question, I would not be helping you with what you called your specular skills. You did ask for my help in that regard, did you not?"

"Yeah, I did, so what exactly are specular skills? I'm kind of tired of everyone expecting that I know things before they happen. I mean, just because I have an occasional premonition about the future doesn't mean I'm special. Doesn't everybody occasionally see a bit of the future?"

"Cailyssa, put simply, *no*—people do not often have prophetic visions of the future. Don't you remember, when you were in my class, the shock on Phoebe's face when you foresaw Scott's picture before she showed you?"

"Yes, but that was, I mean, doesn't everyone—" I helplessly mumbled.

"Cailyssa!" Uncle Spencer's voice boomed. "I must be stern with you since I love you so dearly. Stop denying the gifts that have been given to you. Your specular training must come from within you; it is not something I can teach you. Now, turn and face me, and be prepared to answer a question.

From examining this room and using your specular skills, tell me how far back your family's lineage can be traced." Uncle Spencer's demanding professor's voice shocked me into formulating an answer.

I gazed at the stone coffins of my relatives lined up in endless rows, and then I turned my mind inward as I was prone to doing anyway. Almost as a whisper, the answer to Uncle Spencer's question wandered into my mind in complete clarity, and the answer shocked me. I stood proud and turned to Uncle Spencer.

"Professor, as impossible as it sounds, my family's lineage can be traced back to the beginning of time." The words sputtered out of my mouth as I slowly recognized what that might actually mean.

"You are correct, Cailyssa!" Uncle Spencer beamed.

Seeing *all* of one's dead ancestors can be a bit overwhelming. *Holy crap!* At that moment there was only one thing I needed. I ran to Uncle Spencer, and he wrapped his big hands and arms around me, surrounding me with the most wonderful, warm hug imaginable. I buried my face in his shoulder and, for a moment, felt like a little girl again. I stepped back from Uncle Spencer and looked boldly into his warm face.

"I know what I have to do, and I'm not afraid to do it!" I said with great confidence.

"I never for a moment doubted that you would, Cailyssa. You have already shown great bravery facing the dark lord and his minions. All the Larkins in this room have been watching you since you were born, and we are all very proud.

Come; let us go. The others are waiting in the field, and there are several things you need to practice before we leave the castle on our journey," Uncle Spencer said.

We walked out of the castle keep and closed the stone doors on my long-dead relatives. I hoped it would be a long time until I joined them, but I wasn't so sure.

CHAPTER 9

THE WOUND

I walked down the stairs to the huge field behind the castle, and I saw Terry flying across the sky. She was swooping down at incredible speed, decapitating dummies that Halodire was running with. Halodire was encouraging her and cheering her on. I couldn't believe the speed and agility Terry showed. She was truly a weapon of mass destruction, and I would hate to see what would happen if anyone really ticked her off. Almost as if she heard me, Terry looked over and swooped down with even greater speed and impaled the dummy that Halodire held. She used her claws to shred the dummy to ribbons. Then she flew over to my side and landed on the grass with the softest touch.

"Hey, Lyssa, whaddya think of that? Am I one dangerous girl or what?" Terry said this as she exposed her razor-sharp claws. "I hope when we go home I can take these wings. They are really beautiful, aren't they? But I don't think they will let me back in school with these claws. You know, the zero-tolerance policy for weapons might consider these bad boys an issue. Luckily, they're retractable; check it out!" Terry said this as her claws disappeared, and her wings crisply folded in and disappeared beneath her short cloak. She jogged off toward Halodire, waving back at me while scooping up the remains of the dummies on the lawn.

I then looked across the field and saw Daemon standing there with his sword in hand. My stomach felt weak as I thought about the upcoming confrontation with him. As I walked up to him, he stared back at me with his most confident look, and I knew it was going to be difficult to talk to him. I didn't want to admit it, but I have to be honest with myself. As I looked at him, the back of my mind screamed, *Oh my God, is he not the most gorgeous male on the entire planet?* He stood there in his tall confident manner, and I could see his piercing gray-green eyes staring at me. He had removed his cloak and was only wearing a tight-fitting sleeveless black shirt. His perfectly sculpted body reminded me of one of the stone statues inside the castle. His handsome face would make any male model envious. Much to my surprise, he actually smiled at me as I approached him. Of course, that didn't help my plan to confront him. His beautiful smile actually made my knees feel weak, and I felt mesmerized by his sheer perfection. *Stop it!* I screamed in my mind. *No boy has ever been able to do this to you, and it ain't gonna start now!*

"So here's the big, cold soldier boy. What were you doing out here? Marching up and down and playing with your sword? Remember, Daemon, I knew you when you really *did* play swords and green army men. You never could hide anything from me then or now," I said with unflappable certainty.

For a moment I thought my bold statement worked, because Daemon's eyes looked to the ground. However, the next moment his smile returned, and he slowly spun his sword in a circle.

"Stand prepared, Cailyssa, I will not provide warning in the future!" Daemon said this as he swung his sword at my head!

Before I could even think about it, I cartwheeled to the left, and his sword missed me by an inch. I returned to my feet and instinctively drew my two swords from the scabbards on my back, prepared for what might happen next.

"What the hell are you doing, Daemon? Trying to cut off my head?" I screamed as I recognized what happened.

"Cailyssa, you're much too fast for me to have cut off your head with such a slow-moving blow. However, I promise that next time I will try much harder to sever your spine promptly." Daemon wheeled about and slashed at me with his six-foot sword.

Before I knew what I was doing, I was in a full-fledged, knock-down-and-drag-out sword fight with my best friend from childhood. I didn't have time to think that we could both be dead. I wielded my two swords with precision and grace that I didn't know I possessed. I mean, I did train with bamboo sticks in kung-fu class, but this was a whole different type of combat. As Daemon whirled and thrust his sword at me, I dodged every blow and began my counterattack. As my blood began to flow, I noticed a strange sensation. Everything turned to slow motion. I could see Daemon's every move, almost before he made it. I knew I had the advantage, and I wanted to prove to him that he could not get the best of me. I shifted my blades to an X position to block his downward slash. Then I spun to my right while kicking him hard in the stomach, hoping that my hidden boot blade wouldn't impale him. It felt like I was kicking a rock when my foot landed against his stomach, so I rolled away from his next blow and prepared to teach him a lesson. Using my newfound slow-motion abilities, I attacked him with a series of blows. Then I jumped away from him, hoping to have proved my fighting abilities. I dropped both my swords and gazed in horror at Daemon.

"Oh my God, Daemon, you're bleeding! I cut your arm. I'm so sorry! I just kind of got caught up in the fight. Let me tie a tourniquet around it before you bleed to death." I was half crying and shaking with fear. I ran up to Daemon and tried to escort him into the castle.

"Please, Cailyssa, it's only a flesh wound. I'll be fine," Daemon said with the utmost calm.

"You need a doctor. You have a huge gash in your arm. I have to get you help before you die or something, you fool!" As I said this, Daemon and I looked at the cut on his arm, and the gash miraculously repaired itself before my eyes. I stood there shaking. *I almost killed my best friend!* And now I watched in disbelief as he quickly healed himself. I ran to him and wrapped my arms around him.

"Thank God you're alive!" I noticed that I was the only one talking and the only one doing any hugging. Daemon was standing there, staring straight ahead, not even trying to return my embrace.

"What is the matter with you? Don't you have the decency to return a hug when your best friend almost kills you? You used to hug me all the time when we were kids, and don't tell me you didn't! I want answers. And I want them now!"

"Cailyssa, please, we must continue our battle training to prepare you for the future." Daemon began to prepare to fight me again.

I was so mad at him at this point that I was almost ready to fight again. Instead, I turned around and ran as fast as I could into the woods at the edge of the castle grounds. I needed a few moments to be alone to sort my feelings out. I came to a ledge that overlooked the lake where my grandfather had appeared to me. I looked down at my reflection and was surprised to see that Daemon was standing behind me.

"So I hope you came to apologize. When a girl lays a hug on her best friend and gets nothing in return, it's like, well, the worst insult you could imagine!" I said as I turned to face Daemon.

"Cailyssa, please understand. I am only trying to protect you," Daemon said as he looked calmly into the lake.

"Listen, buddy. I want the truth. Why were you bleeding from the back the other day? Why do you heal so quickly? Why are you so cold to *me*, your best friend? *Look* at me. What is with you? Don't just stand there staring ahead. Talk to me!" I urged him.

"It's too difficult for me to talk about," Daemon said.

"Well fine, don't talk. Go back to the castle and play soldier boy. I'm staying here," I said firmly. But Daemon just stood there, unmoving.

"Can't you leave me alone?" I hissed at him.

"Actually, I can't. I promised someone I would protect you," he responded smoothly.

"You can't protect me—especially if you can't catch me," I said as I bolted off the ledge.

I ran through the forest as fast as my legs could carry me, never looking back at Daemon, hoping that he didn't decide to follow. I must've run for a while, 'cause the forest changed from a bright green to brown-black gloom. I sat on a rock for a moment to catch my breath, wondering what I should do with my *ex-best* friend. My specular skills were not helping me see this through. I was too upset.

A soft rustling noise in the woods slowly brought me back to reality, and—before I knew it—I heard a swoosh, and an ugly black arrow flew into the tree next to me. I turned to run, but I tripped and fell. Emerging from the woods was an ugly demon like the ones I met when I arrived. He crept toward me slowly on birdlike legs, his green-gray skin covered with what appeared to be dark mold. He was holding a longbow, and he notched an arrow and aimed at me. I froze. He slowly drew the string taut and smiled with his black pointy teeth as the arrow left the bow, aimed at my heart. Out of nowhere Daemon appeared. He stepped in front of me and took the arrow that was meant for me in his shoulder. He then drew a dagger from his right boot and threw it at the demonic creature. The dagger landed square in the center of the creature's head, and he fell to the ground with black blood oozing from his face.

Before I could react, Daemon picked me up and raced back through the woods toward the castle. He didn't stop until we reached the edge of the castle grounds. Daemon gently placed me on a bench next to the castle. To my surprise, he gently kissed the top of my head. Then he knelt down on one knee in front of me, and he gently took my hand in both of his. He slowly kissed the top of my hand and placed it on his cheek.

"Forgive me, Cailyssa. I thought I had lost you. I cannot bear the thought of you dying." A small tear rolled down his cheek. He stood, plucked the arrow from his shoulder, and turned to walk away from me. I noticed all the blood again on his back.

"You're not getting away so easily." I ran after him, grabbing his shoulder and spinning him around. "You're the most confusing man I've ever met. One moment you're cold as stone—pretending that I don't exist—and the next moment you're on one knee, and it looks like you're ready to propose to me. Listen, I don't need a boyfriend, but I *do* need some answers!"

"I will only do so if you require it of me," Daemon said as he turned back into the cold soldier boy. "But please don't require me to explain, I beg of you. It is still too painful for me."

"No deal, big boy. If you're tough enough to pull an arrow out of your chest and heal yourself from a sword fight, I think you are strong enough to talk to your best friend and explain things. So talk. I require it…and no more kissing my hand!" I said with great determination.

To my surprise, Daemon slowly unbuttoned his shirt and took it off. My jaw dropped to the ground, not because I was looking at his perfectly chiseled chest of course, but because I just never knew what to expect from this man. He slowly turned around and showed me two long scars on his back that looked like a letter V. He slowly turned back to face me. "Cailyssa, didn't you ever think that it's a bit odd that we have the same birthday?" Daemon said this as if he expected an answer.

"No, I just figured it was a coincidence, and it was always kind of cool to celebrate my birthday with my best friend. What's the big deal, anyway?" I said as I awaited more information.

"Although it is a vague memory in my mind, my life before I was born into your world was filled with great sadness. I did something horrible, something that is unforgivable," Daemon said.

"What do you mean your life before you were born—like when you were in your mother's belly or something?" I was perplexed.

"I don't have a mother, Cailyssa, only humans do," Daemon said earnestly.

My specular skills started to tingle, and I started to see some images in my mind. They were beautiful but very frightening to me. I blurted, "What do you mean? You're not human? Are you some kind of alien or something?" I tried to say this as I laughed confidently, but I was scared of what I would find out.

I focused on the inside of my mind and tried to organize the various images that floated by. I captured one of Daemon as he was before he was born into my world. My jaw hung open, and I tried to form the words but I had great difficulty doing so.

"You're an, an, an...angel?" I asked in disbelief.

"No, actually, I'm an sentinel angel. There is a considerable difference that you may not be aware of," Daemon said this in a casual manner as if I'd known about it all along. "Cailyssa, at the beginning of time, I was born as a sentinel angel with a duty to serve and protect. There are many types of angels. Many in your world believe there are nine levels in the angelic realm; however, there are *many* more. Some angels are immortal, like me, but they can interact with humans by taking human form. Other angels are spiritual and cannot directly access the human world. The most powerful angels, often referred to as the seraphim by some of your religions, are actually not just spiritual beings. They are also human and have enormous power to change the world for good. I am one of seven of the most powerful sentinel angels. Some would call me an archangel; others would simply refer to me as a guardian angel. So, Cailyssa—as you now know—I am *your* guardian angel, and I will spend eternity protecting you from harm."

Daemon paused and looked down before continuing. "Please forgive me, for this next part of the story is difficult to speak of. But you have required me to reveal it, and I shall. Since I can remember, I have been a sentinel angel for a Larkin. For eternity I served proudly and honorably and never failed in my charge."

Daemon paused and took a deep breath to clear his mind. Then he looked over my head to the sky and continued. "Your grandfather ordered me on a mission, knowing that when I left him, he would die. When the dark lord killed your grandfather, I failed horribly in my duty. I returned to the city of Constantine. There, one of the highest of our kind, Gabriel, cut the wings from my back in front of a legion of angels. I stayed here in Mirror World for years, in mourning, devoured by the blackest sorrow and grief imaginable—wishing every day that I would die. You see, it is my fault that your grandfather died, and that is *not* acceptable for a sentinel angel. When such a thing happens, we become one of the *unforgiven*. To be one of the unforgiven is a shameful existence for any angel. On the day you were born, I was given a second chance to redeem myself. I shall not fail in my charge this time!"

I was stunned and sat there speechless. Daemon bowed before me and then stood tall, spreading his arms wide, and I saw him, for a moment, in his glorious immortal form. It blew me away, and I grabbed the stone bench below me to settle myself. He turned and began to walk away; then he paused and turned to face me. His face showed such incredible anguish and pain that it hurt me to look at him. I felt horrible about forcing this confession and inflicting such pain on Daemon, who had sacrificed so much to protect not just me, but also the Larkin family. He stared at me, and I held his gaze. The power emanating from him did not permit me to look away. His eyes pierced my heart and touched my soul. I stood frozen and stared at his divine beauty and might.

"Cailyssa, I would have you know that—despite my occasional cold, distant nature—since we met on the day of your birth, I have *truly* loved you, *more* than you could possibly ever imagine." Daemon turned and made his way back to the castle, the long scars on his back weeping blood in memory of my grandfather. I sat on the cold stone bench, staring at his back, knowing in my heart that I would never, ever be closer to anyone as long as I lived. Which, considering what I was about to do, might not be that long.

CHAPTER 10

DARK REFLECTIONS

Ttocs flew through the air, supported and swarmed by a cloud of stinging wasps. Since the dragon, Longtooth, had betrayed him and horribly embarrassed him in front of the dwarfs, he had been flying through the air with these nasty stinging insects showing him no mercy. Yet this was only the beginning of the pain he was to endure. The wasps were taking him to the dark lord's castle, where unspeakable pain could be found.

When Ttocs looked down, he saw the barren black ground and knew that he was approaching Castillo Espejos Oscuro—the Castle of Dark Mirrors. The grounds around the castle were swarming with various demons that served as the army for the dark lord. Off to the left, he could see a group of them building something and pointing up at him as he looked down through the wasps. Suddenly, the wasps dissipated, and he fell straight down.

When he finally recovered his senses, he looked up and found the demons—better known as raxs—looking down at him as he lay on his back. Their smell was horrible, and their birdlike legs were stamping up and down with excitement as if he were a new item on the lunch menu. The raxs suddenly became quiet and parted as one of their leaders came to stand over Ttocs. He mumbled something in his grotesque language, and the raxs grabbed Ttocs, picked him up, and placed him on a large cart that they had been building. When he was on the cart, they tied up his arms and legs till he was stretched as far as he could go. Then he noticed that the ropes around his ankles and wrists were attached to wheels at the bottom and top of the cart. The raxs fought each other over the pleasure of slowly turning the wheels. As the wheels began to turn, the ropes around Ttocs arms and legs began to tighten. The pain became unbearable, and suddenly one of the Ttocs's arms was pulled out of its shoulder socket. He screamed in pain, and the raxs laughed at his misery. Then their leader grabbed his face with his long, thin black fingers. He began to lick the blood that covered Ttocs's body where the wasps had stung him. Ttocs screamed in pain as the saliva from the raxs's mouth burned his skin horribly. They wheeled the cart toward the dark lord's castle.

The dark lord's castle was at the top of a small mountain and was surrounded by a black river. The raxs pulled the cart with Ttocs on it up to the edge of the river, being careful not to touch the water. They left him there and walked away, laughing and jeering as they ran on birdlike legs from the river as fast as they could. Ttocs looked down into the river of death and at the hungry souls waiting for him. Suddenly the lines that held him on the cart snapped, and he slid from the cart into the black water. The undead souls swarmed him, and he lost consciousness.

When Ttocs awoke he was on a stone bed. There was food, laced with worms, next to him at a table. He wasn't sure if this was heaven or hell, but he was sure hungry, and he ravenously attacked the food. After he finished, he looked around the room and saw there were no windows or doors. The walls were black and shiny and had an odd curved texture to them. He walked up to the wall and touched it and discovered that the entire structure was made of blackened bones that were somehow made smooth and shiny. The only structure in the room was a large black mirror that held no reflection. As Ttocs stood in front of the blackened mirror, it seemed to come alive, and he began to see himself. The image before him was horrible. He saw himself as a worthless, wretched being who wasn't even able to tame a wretched old dragon or even beat the dwarfs properly. He recalled the dwarfs laughing and mocking him as they pointed at the pee stain in the front of his pants after Longtooth had scared him. This made Ttocs angry, and he wished he could strike back at the dragon and all of the dwarfs. He'd return one day and kill them all for what they did to him.

Unexpectedly, his image in the mirror faded, and the formless face of the dark lord appeared. Ttocs jumped back and held his bowels as best he could. He was sure that if he soiled himself in front of the dark lord, he would be dead.

"Ah, so I see you learned to hold your bladder when you're scared. Since most three-year-olds can do so, you must be at least four," the dark lord said as he laughed at the cowering form of Ttocs. "I pulled you from the river of death just as the souls were about to devour you. Do not make me regret my decision. You are in my castle, but only so long as it pleases me shall I keep you alive."

The face of the dark lord shifted, and his red eyes bore into Ttocs as he spoke. "Now I must ask you a question, and be sure to answer it carefully and correctly. I need to know more about how the dragon betrayed you."

Ttocs blurted, "I was trying to beat the dwarfs to work harder and the dragon refused to eat one of them and then—"

"*Silence*, you blubbering fool," the dark lord hissed. "I care not for your foolish excuses! I need to know one thing. Just before the dragon refused your command, did she look at her reflection in the lake? *Answer* me!"

"I...I...I...don't know, My Lord. I was busy disciplining the dwarfs," Ttocs answered.

"*Think*, you idiot. What did the dragon do right before she disobeyed you?"

"She wasn't paying attention. She was looking away from me, her golden eyes...yes! Yes! She was staring at the dwarf's lake," Ttocs finally managed to say.

"Just as I thought. You answered the question correctly and may live until you are no longer useful to me," the dark lord calmly said.

"Why did the dragon disobey me? I thought she was bound to me. I thought dragons were honorable," Ttocs responded.

"Of course dragons are honorable, you fool, and that's *why* she disobeyed you. I worked very hard so that when Longtooth saw her reflection she was never reminded of her honorable nature. The images I created for her made her feel hopeless and lost." The dark lord seethed as he spoke.

"Then it must have been the old dwarf, Dolhar, who said something to the dragon to change her feeble mind," Ttocs suggested.

"You are by far more stupid than I previously thought. The only way the dragon's will to serve could be changed was if somebody changed her reflection in the water—so that she saw the goodness and honor in herself and decided to do what she thought was the right thing!" the dark lord spit out.

"But, My Lord, that is impossible. No one but *you* can change a reflection in a mirror. Isn't that true?" As Ttocs said this, he realized it was the wrong question to ask. The image of the dark lord became furious, and his wrath was unbearable to look upon. Ttocs cowered in fear.

"A Larkin has recently entered our world again. Her name is Cailyssa, and a company of supporters joins her. I saw her when she first arrived as she sat upon the Larkin throne. I underestimated her abilities, and I will not do so again."

"Let's ready the army and kill her. I need some payback for what the dragon did to me," Ttocs cheered.

"No!" uttered the dark lord. "We shall kill her and all her friends in good time. But first I will show her images from her worst nightmares, and she will beg to be dead upon seeing them. First, you will capture Cailyssa's sister alive; do not kill her. I will make Cailyssa watch in a reflection as I slowly bleed her sister on my black stone altar. Like the last Larkin, she will watch in vain, knowing all that she loves will be lost and that all her efforts were wasted."

"Lord Speculus, I will do what you ask. I live to serve the dark lord," Ttocs said with great pride as a door appeared in the room.

"I do not trust you to do this alone, Ttocs. Leave this room and go to the far end of the castle. There, you will find the two Nephilim; I have preserved their undead bodies. I have waited for a moment just like this to awaken them so that they can unleash their cruelty again. Go now, Ttocs, and do not fail me again."

Ttocs walked through the castle, holding his head high and feeling the power that the dark lord would soon let him unleash. He would find Cailyssa and Terry Larkin, and they would pay and they would suffer and only then would they die.

CHAPTER 11

JOURNEY FROM CASTLE LARKIN

I awoke the next morning and looked out from the balcony of my room. I was still trying to make sense of what happened with Daemon yesterday. I mean, it was kind of cool to have a guardian angel, but at the same time, did that mean I lost my best friend? I wasn't sure; I had a lot of mixed feelings and no time to sort them out. I was pulled from my thoughts by a quick knock on the door. Terry walked in with an impish grin on her face, and I knew she was up to no good.

"So, big sister. I happen to be flying around the castle yesterday, and I caught you," Terry said as she pirouetted on one foot and pointed her finger at me.

"What do you mean, caught me?" I placed my hands on my hips.

"Well…I wasn't spying or anything, but when I looked down I saw Daemon doing the proposal thing on one knee. Are you getting married without telling me?" Terry said, half kidding.

"He was *not* proposing to me!" I screamed back.

"Oh, of course not, he was just kneeling in front of you, kissing your hand, and you were gently caressing his cheek. What was he doing, asking you to go bowling?" Terry said in her most sarcastic voice.

"No! He was simply discussing something with me." I said this way too quickly and then thought how lame it sounded.

"Hey, no problem, if you don't want to tell your favorite and *only* sister about your new boyfriend. But really, Cailyssa, Daemon is perfect. He's drop-dead gorgeous, smart, kind, and I think he'd use that six-foot sword on anyone who tried to hurt you," Terry said with all honesty.

"That's just the problem!" I retorted. "He's not my boyfriend. He never *will* be my boyfriend. He never *can* be my boyfriend."

"Yeah, right. Why not? Looks like a good match to me. You guys have been dating like practically since birth anyway!" Terry said jokingly.

"Shut up!" I howled. "He can't be my boyfriend. He's an angel!" I realized how crazy it probably sounded.

"Sounds to me like you're in love. Every girl who thinks her boyfriend's an angel is definitely in love," Terry said adamantly.

"No, Terry, you don't get it. I mean, I don't *think* he's an angel; I *know* he's an angel. I mean…he's a real angel," I blubbered.

"Listen, girl, the only angel that's been around here is the fat, little cute one called Cupid who shot you in the butt with one big love arrow. You've got one bad case of love-sickness!" Terry said as she walked out of the room.

I was just about to say, "I don't love Daemon," but I caught myself just in time and prevented myself from looking like a total fool. I grabbed my swords, the moonstone, and my leather-bound red book, and I headed downstairs to eat breakfast and clear my mind.

As I passed the dining room, the little elves were mumbling and pointing at me, and I swear they were giggling. If Terry started spreading a rumor about me dating Daemon, I was going to kill her. Right then a voice startled me.

"Good morning, Cailyssa, I hope you slept well, as you know we will be leaving the castle today to begin our journey," Uncle Spencer said as he wrapped his warm hand around my shoulder.

"Thanks, Uncle Spencer, I did sleep well. When you have some time, can I talk to you about Daemon?" I asked.

"Cailyssa, your face tells me that you have discovered who your guardian angel is," Uncle Spencer said.

"You mean you knew all the time and never told me?" I feebly responded.

"As I said before, Cailyssa, you need to work on your specular skills. Everyone expects that you know things and just forgets to tell you," Uncle Spencer said with a light laugh. "Let's go down and eat breakfast. It may be a while till we're able to sit at the table in Castle Larkin and enjoy a meal together. And I promise not to mention a thing about Daemon."

"Did Terry tell you anything?" I quickly responded.

"No, Cailyssa, but the blush in your cheeks at the mention of his name did," he said as he raised his eyebrows. I distinctly heard the elves giggling, and I clenched my fists together and promised myself that I would keep my emotions in control and get on with the business at hand.

As I walked down the enormous spiral staircase to the open dining hall below, I could see that everyone was looking up at me. If my girlfriends at home could only see me now. Here I was, owner of this beautiful castle. I was walking down a marble staircase dressed in black leather pants and riding boots. On top of that, I was wearing a gorgeous off-white embroidered silk shirt with a matching vest, adorned with crimson and royal-blue velvet. Plus, I had two deadly looking swords sheathed in leather scabbards crossing my back. My auburn hair was showing more highlights and curling beautifully as it fell almost a foot below my shoulders. The weather here seemed to be helping my complexion since all my pimples had vanished, and I decided not to even use makeup. I looked across, and I saw the image of myself in a huge mirror adorning the entire wall directly across from the staircase. Was this really me? I guess I thought I might even be looking sort of, well, beautiful today. That's strange; I'm usually not very satisfied with myself.

I stopped in my tracks! Did I just look at a mirror, a gigantic mirror, and not even want to smash it? That never happened at home! I peeked at myself one last time, and the urge to smash the mirror did not return. However, when I looked at myself I was shocked. I did look beautiful. But what really shocked me is that I looked very, very...dangerous. I paused to remember that I did fight with my guardian angel, and I felt ready for whatever dangers I would face in this world. I snapped out of my trance when I saw that Daemon was waiting for me at the bottom of the stairs.

"Good morning, Cailyssa. Stunning outfit, I must say," Daemon said with great enthusiasm as he held out his elbow to escort me to my seat at the head of the table.

"Thanks, Daemon, I like you better acting like a gentleman than weeping blood from your back."

"Cailyssa, I—"

"Daemon," I interrupted. "Let's just forget about yesterday. We need to finish our work here in Mirror World, and we both have to be better about controlling our emotions to get that done. Got it?" I said forcefully.

As I took my seat at the table, I looked around. There was Terry, chatting with Halodire, and Uncle Spencer and Daemon were laughing and eating heartily. The elves were scampering around serving us several courses of the most luscious breakfast I had ever had. My specular skills started to tingle, and I could see what lay ahead for all the folks at this table. I suddenly became sick to my stomach and couldn't eat another thing. I felt for my red leather book and quietly pulled it from my pocket. I opened it up under the table so no one could see and felt comforted by looking at the swirling memories of the many who had come before me. Suddenly, I felt strength surge within me, and I stood up and pushed my chair abruptly away. I walked across the hall to the full-length mirror I had seen as I descended the stairs. My back was to all my friends at the table, but I could tell from the eerie silence in the room that they were all watching me very closely. A flash of light appeared in the mirror that only I saw, and I turned around slowly, put my hands on my hips, and looked at the silent crowd before me.

"Dear friends, you know that I, as a Larkin, am charged with a task that is difficult and very dangerous. As many of you may know, Dark Lord Speculus has used his evil abilities to control all reflections here in Mirror World. When people gaze into a mirror or pool of water, he distorts each image so people see evil and wickedness within themselves. Slowly, he has corrupted many of the inhabitants of Mirror World. His goal is to ruin and then dominate all life here. Next, with this world under his control, he can reach out and use his powers to corrupt the earth. His greatest joy would be to see evil within the hearts of all peoples of the earth. Then he would sit back in his black castle and watch gleefully through his many mirrors as the people of earth slowly began to *destroy* each other!

"The dark lord is also afraid. He knows that people are drawn to also see themselves as good, with kindness and decency in their hearts—not evil. My task here in Mirror World is to remind people of *that*. To do this, I must travel through this world of Speculus Locus, shining as a light, so that each race will step from the dark shadow of evil and embrace fellowship and love."

Terry screamed. "Look out, Cailyssa!"

Without turning to look at the mirror behind me, I knew what Terry was talking about. The hideous face of the dark lord had appeared, his evil red eyes burning with malicious intent as he stared at everyone in the room. The elves scurried under the table, cowering in fear, and Daemon stood up and unleashed his white sword.

Without turning around to face the mirror, I calmly said to Daemon, "Put away your sword. He has no power here. Terry, get Dolhar and the other elves out from under the table. Have no fear."

The dark lord hissed, "You *will* learn to fear me, Cailyssa. When we first met, you sat on the stone throne and gazed into the seven-mirrored pools, and I offered you a gift. *Accept* that gift now, and save the lives of all of those before you. I will not offer you this chance again."

I slowly turned around to face him in the mirror, summoning what courage I could. "Your gift, Speculus, is *nothing* but empty promises and deceit that would lead me to become like you. I will *never* accept such a gift. Now remove your ugly face from my mirror. You have no power here. Be gone!"

At that moment a loud boom, like the sound of a thousand cannons, shook the castle to the core of its foundation. Everyone covered their heads, expecting to be showered with stone. A sharp pain entered my mind, and I almost fell upon the floor. My specular skills were clearly seeing the future. I saw the dark lord torturing my sister and killing my friends.

I did my best to hold back the tears. When I saw Terry's tortured face in my mind, I lost it—but instead of crying I got really pissed off! I jumped to my feet and yelled, "Hear me, Speculus, that is only one possible future you shoved into my mind, and you *know* it. Look at the future I will bring you, filled with goodness and light and the *end* of your rule of this world."

I wasn't sure what I was doing as I held two fingers from each hand to my temples. I felt an incredible power within me; it was warm and glowing, and I felt like it was ready to explode from me. I stared at the mirror in front of me and unleashed my vision of the future to Speculus. The mirror with Speculus's image exploded, glass about to fly everywhere. I held up my hand and stopped the glass in midair. I waved my hand, and the beautiful liquid smoothness of the mirror reappeared. In the mirror I looked at the astonished faces of all of those behind me.

Terry jumped up on top of the table and crowed, "Way to go, big sister, you roasted the dark lord. He is so scared of you that he ran away!"

The elves all cheered and began dancing around the table and singing.

"Hold on, everyone," I exclaimed. "We haven't defeated him yet, and we still have a lot of work to do. I am leaving the castle in one hour. Make sure the elves pack me plenty to eat because they will not be coming. For the rest of you, I love you all too much to risk your lives in what I have to do. Follow Uncle Spencer to the city of Constantine, and gather the angels for battle. I will head to the dark lord's castle and do what I do best. I'm going to break all of his mirrors, and it's really going to piss him off—and I don't want any of you around when that happens. I walked up the stairs to my room and quietly closed the door. I quickly sat on my bed and opened my red book so I could see the loving faces of my mother and father and my dogs. I stared at them for a long time until a knock at my door interrupted my trance.

"May I come in, Cailyssa?" Uncle Spencer's soothing voice said from behind my door.

I ran to the door as fast as I could and flung it open. Uncle Spencer already had his arms wide open. He knew I needed one of his hugs, and I lost myself in his warm embrace. "That was very brave, what you did downstairs, Cailyssa. I don't think the dark lord has ever faced a Larkin quite like you. He fears that you may be far more powerful than he originally perceived," Uncle Spencer said calmly.

"What about my parents, Uncle Spencer? I was just looking at their reflection in the book. They must be so worried about me," I said anxiously.

"Cailyssa, worry not. The perception of time is very different here in this world. I promise you that they are not worried yet."

I hesitated and said, "I'm not sure I like the way you said 'yet.' Do you think I could really do this? Sometimes I'm not so sure. I mean, why did this all have to happen? I wish it could simply go away."

Uncle Spencer put his arm around my shoulder and slowly led me to the balcony, which overlooked the courtyard below. "Unfortunately, Cailyssa, wishing—as you well know—will not change anything. You can stare at a mirror and wish your life away; however, I know that is not to be *your* destiny. Many people gaze into a mirror or their minds, wishing their lives were different. This is the time when people are at their weakest, and that's when the dark lord tries to corrupt them. So you could choose to stay here safely in the castle or, like in my living room, you can make another choice. I know you'll do the right thing, but—whatever you do—I will love you regardless of your decision."

Just then Terry swooped down from above and landed in her perfect, graceful way on the edge of the railing of the balcony.

"You have to stop doing that. You scare the daylights out of me when you do that. Do you always have to make such a grand entrance? By the way, don't even think of coming with me. So go right to your room, and take off that medieval-looking battle suit you're wearing!" I said halfheartedly.

Terry jumped down from the balcony and quickly folded her wings back. "Cailyssa, do you think there's a chance in hell I'm not coming? There is no way I'm gonna let you have all the fun. Besides, we have some friends who can help us out." As Terry said this, she walked backward to the balcony rail and simply fell over.

Even though I knew she had wings, I hated when she did things like this. I stormed over to the edge of the balcony and shouted, "Terry, just because you have wings, it doesn't mean you can do things like that to me. You're definitely not... coming." My jaw dropped to the floor as the words slid from my mouth.

Arrayed in the courtyard in front of me was an impressive display of all my friends. Daemon and Halodire were mounted on beautiful black stallions. They were dressed in shimmering chain mail and looked to have a variety of weapons attached to their horses. Behind them the elves were arrayed in parade formation, all of them dressed in similar attire, and they were holding banners with the traditional Larkin colors of gold and blue. The elves were mounting ponies and had packed huge wagons drawn by workhorses. At the front of the column were two beautiful horses. One was a gray-and-black steed, and it had Uncle Spencer's gear attached to it. Before it, at the head of everyone, was the most beautiful fair-haired horse I had ever seen. His coat was as beautiful as freshly spun gold, and he reared up on powerful hind legs as if he was beckoning me to ride. Terry landed below on the grass and took her place in the grand procession.

Terry looked up and yelled, "Come on, Cailyssa! We were waiting for you. You said to be ready in one hour, and you're already late. Stop doing your hair in the mirror, and get down here!"

I slowly walked down through the castle with Uncle Spencer at my side and opened the two wooden doors at the front of the castle. I proudly walked up to my horse and looked into his big brown eyes. It seemed I had known him somehow. Did I? I jumped into the saddle of my horse and prepared myself to travel. As I spun my horse around, I noticed that Daemon was waving a banner. The elves began to blow their great horns, and the piercing cacophony of sounds rocketed in my years. As the great horns erupted, Daemon drew his white, blazing sword and pointed it toward the sky. All the company followed his actions.

Daemon's powerful voice boomed, "Today we ride with Cailyssa Larkin. All cheer the day, for a Larkin has returned to Mirror World!"

With that, three great cheers rose from the crowd, and they all resheathed their weapons with military precision. As I slowly rode through the outside gate of the castle, I paused to look back at the beautiful structure, hoping I would return. I noticed that the whole company was following me, looking for direction.

"Uncle Spencer, Uncle Spencer, quick," I said anxiously. "Which way do we go?"

Uncle Spencer rocked his head back and let out a hearty laugh. "Cailyssa, with your powers to see the future, do you really need to ask me such questions?"

I felt a little foolish, so I touched the moonstone in my pocket and knew which way to turn. I slowly steered my horse to the road on the right. I felt great! I'll tell you right now. When you're in a tight spot and you have a lot of difficult things to do, there's nothing like having your friends and family with you. I felt comforted by all those behind me, but I also felt a tremendous responsibility to get them safely through this journey, knowing that there was little chance we all would survive.

CHAPTER 12

ROAD TO RUIN

After we left the castle and traveled through the countryside, I could feel the courage that had welled up inside of me being replaced by self-doubt and fear. I shook as a chill crept down my back. Was Speculus watching me? *Stop it!* I yelled inside my mind. *Stay strong*. My mind could be my greatest friend, my strongest weapon, or my road to ruin. My dad always said, "You control your mind and tell it what to think and do; it doesn't control you." Thinking of this made me feel stronger and in control, so I threw any bad thoughts I had out of my head, and I looked at the beautiful road ahead. The road looked ordinary enough and appeared like any mountainside road. It reminded me of my family vacations in the White Mountains of New Hampshire. The thought of being on vacation with my family made me miss them dearly. As I thought of them, my stomach gurgled like a sick, empty pit. I longed for the comfort of my own bed with my dogs on it with me. Up until now, none of this really felt real; it was almost as if I were living a dream. Now the frightening reality of my situation was staring me in the face. My prescience was allowing me to see all sorts of possible visions of the future—some of them good—but many of the visions of the future were too scary for me to dwell on for long.

As we rounded a pass in the mountains, the small elves blew their horns, and we set up camp for the night. We'd been riding all day except for a light lunch, and everyone looked tired and hungry. I didn't want to talk to anyone right now, so I tied up my horse and walked to a nearby rock ledge on the side of the mountain. Of course, Daemon eyeballed me as I passed by him, but the look I gave him said to give me some space. I mean, it's kind of aggravating having a guardian angel looking at you all the time. It was making me feel very self-conscious and uncomfortable. So I walked away and sat on a rock and gazed at the majestic mountains before me. I tried to relax and clear my mind, but when I looked at the beautiful mountains before me, I couldn't appreciate any of it. I wished I could simply crawl underneath this big rock. Why couldn't everybody just leave me alone?

"Cailyssa, dinner will be served soon. Is there anything you need until then?" Uncle Spencer said as he slowly approached the rock, being sure to give me my space.

"No, I'm fine—really I am," I said way too quickly, and I knew for sure that Uncle Spencer knew I was lying right through my teeth. I stood up on the rock and didn't look back at him. I could feel his presence moving closer behind me. I stepped down and walked up to him. Surprisingly, he didn't raise his arms to hug me; he knew that was not what I needed right then. I turned by his side, and we both peered out at the mountains in front of us. Being next to him felt like an anchor grounding me to the earth.

"Hey, Uncle Spencer, ever since I can remember, I've always wondered how you always seem to know the right thing to do or say when you're with me. It's amazing; it's like you can read my mind or something," I said with great curiosity.

Uncle Spencer turned his head and looked at me with his piercing blue eyes. He paused for a moment and then spoke slowly. "Dear Cailyssa, it seems you have finally discovered my special ability. Of course, it's not as obvious as Terry's wings and claws or your specular skills. But, for some reason, I feel my special talents are meant to complement yours and Terry's."

"You're making me feel like a student in your class again because I'm not sure exactly what your special skills are. Should they be that obvious to me?"

Uncle Spencer paused and said timidly, "A minute ago, did you feel as if I was reading your mind?"

"Well, sort of, but it was more like you just really understood me. I felt almost like you gave me something emotional *right* when I really needed it. You've always been like that; you always know what I need. Maybe it was a hug or a kind word or simply just some space and distance. So...did I get the answer right to the quiz?" I asked, curious to know Uncle Spencer's gift.

Uncle Spencer looked out at the mountains and continued speaking slowly. "You're only partly right. When we get to the city of Constantine, the angels will make it even more clear to you. I am known there—ever since I was very young—as a telepathist, which also means mind reader. But you must understand, to an angel a mind reader is very different from what humans might think. We would think that a mind reader could read our thoughts. However, as you get to know the angels, you'll find that they don't have the same thoughts we do. See, unlike our human minds, the angels' minds are all connected by a stronger cosmic force into a huge collective consciousness that has the knowledge and wisdom of the universe. There is literally nothing an angel doesn't know. Unlike humans, they have never had to struggle to master knowledge or their rational mind; they are literally perfect in that regard. However, they have never mastered their emotional minds. In other words, they struggle even more than humans to control and master their emotions—as I'm sure you have noticed in Daemon."

"Oh my God, now I understand him better. He *is* sort of an emotional wreck. He goes through such emotional ups and downs that I can hardly follow him. He seems to feel some seriously deep emotions—almost as if they're controlling him," I said quickly.

"Yes, Cailyssa, angels have great deep wells of powerful emotions within them, and they are *always* working on ways to better control their emotional responses. The reason they are so fascinated with *me* is that I am very good at understanding and reading emotional responses. To the angels, this is a fascinating gift to have, since I am so able to read others' emotions and control my own at the same time. We humans often call it emotional intelligence. It involves keeping your emotions in place and controlling yourself so that they don't get the best of you. To an angel this is a remarkable ability." Uncle Spencer paused and seemed to consider something for a moment. "Let's start walking back to camp. Dinner should be ready soon."

"Hold on, Uncle Spencer, you can't stop there. I could *tell* that you were just about to tell me something important, and you're not getting away from me till you do. Remember, I'm using my specular skills now to see what might happen next," I said as I grabbed and hugged his arm.

Uncle Spencer, who was never at a loss for words, stammered, "I...I...I just don't know how to say this without hurting you, but I think you need to know the truth."

"What is it? I can handle it," I said assuredly.

"It's about Daemon, Cailyssa. There's something you need to know, but you would be better off hearing it from him."

"No way! You can't leave me like this. I have to know *more*," I demanded.

Uncle Spencer let out a great sigh and looked up at me with a great warm smile. "You must understand that angels are different; after all, they are not human. For example, if Daemon were to say something such as...'I love you,' his emotions would be so strong that they could overwhelm him and cause him to lose control. Since angels take great pride in rational thought and self-control, emotions can be a very difficult thing for them to master. Just for a minute, see life as Daemon does. Imagine having the knowledge and wisdom of the universe, a connection with God, sheer bodily perfection, and unimaginable physical prowess. Now imagine that this supreme being can be crippled and become helpless if he lets a simple emotion, such as love, control him. He constantly battles to keep control of his emotional self—and angels don't often do so, as you'll discover when we enter the city of Constantine. There are thousands of angels there who are still working on self-control. Their hope is that they may regain a place in heaven after they do."

"Well, I'll tell you, Uncle Spencer, you sure do know how to make a girl feel confident. Here I am with Daemon, a guardian angel who looks like the most handsome, perfect, and intimidating male in the universe. But you mean to tell me he has the emotional IQ of an adolescent boy," I said confidently as I flipped my hair back. "See, that didn't hurt me at all!"

Uncle Spencer paused and looked carefully into my eyes, and I knew there was something he had yet to tell me.

"Cailyssa, if Daemon said he loved you, it would not have the same meaning it would have if a human said those words to you. He loved your grandfather, too, in much the same way as he may love you. I just wanted you to know this so that you wouldn't be…disappointed if he felt no romantic love for you."

Without thinking I blurted, "But, Uncle Spencer, with my ability to see the future, I have seen a vision of Daemon, and we're…together and there are children and…uh…that has to be *one* possible future, doesn't it?"

Uncle Spencer became visibly anxious, something that was rare for him. He began to walk quickly back to camp as he spoke. "Please don't tell me that, Cailyssa! There has been great tragedy when humans and angels have mated. Your father and I will *never* permit you to be with Daemon. I've said too much already."

I grabbed Uncle Spencer's arm in an attempt to slow him down and talk to him. To my surprise, he forcibly pulled his arm away from me and hurried back to camp. I stood there alone. It felt as if someone had just punched me in the stomach. My knees got weak, and I almost threw up, so I placed my arm on a tree for support. I guess I just always held out hope that Daemon might love me on a romantic level. As I watched Uncle Spencer's shape walking quickly away from me, I blubbered out weak, emotional words that only I could hear. "It's OK, Uncle Spencer. I did need to know that. I have business here in Mirror World. I'm not here to find a boyfriend." I tried to talk myself into this, but it wasn't working, and I knew I wouldn't be able to eat dinner with this sick feeling lingering in my stomach. Damn, love stinks!

I wanted to make sure that I did not make eye contact at dinner with Daemon—or anyone else for that matter. But as I approached the outskirts of camp, I could hear music, and I saw the shapes of what appeared to be Terry dancing with some of the elves.

"Hey, Cailyssa, check *this* out. I'm teaching Grundi and the elves to rap," Terry said. The elves had pulled their pants down to expose the tops of their underwear. Grundi was trying to do a beatbox, and the other elves were trying to learn a rap song that Terry was singing with them. I totally freaked! This crazy scene looked like some sort of sick comedy-horror movie.

I stormed up to them and screamed in my most pissed-off voice, "How can you all be so freaking…happy! Get serious. We're in a war here, not a rap contest." I walked quickly away and immediately felt guilty. All the small elves stopped instantly and looked down at the ground like children who had been scolded.

I ate dinner that night alone with my horse, and I climbed into my sleeping bag early. I was trying to process all the mixed emotions I was feeling, and my prescience skills were starting to feel like a terrible burden. I could see the near future really well. But when I looked out to the distant future, I could see many possibilities, and I wasn't sure what would happen. The choices I made tomorrow or the next day would determine the future we would live in. I rolled over on my side, sighed, and looked at the moon and at the swirling mist floating off in the distance. At the edge of the mountain cliff, there was a figure: an imposing, dark silhouetted form that appeared to be on guard duty. I knew from the physique and the outline of the sword that it was Daemon. Darn it, couldn't the man at least go to sleep for a little while? Then I remembered that angels don't need sleep. I turned over on my other side to avoid looking at Daemon, knowing my dreams would be haunted by surreal visions of overly emotional angels and a bunch of gangster elves doing a really bad rap song.

When I awoke the next morning, I actually felt refreshed. Whatever dreams I had were gone from my mind, so I gathered my stuff and headed to eat breakfast. As I walked through the woods, I heard some gentle sobbing coming from behind a tree, and I went over to investigate. I saw Grundi, the head kitchen elf, sitting there with his hands on the sides of his head. He was wiping the tears from his eyes, and his wife, Nori, was comforting him by rubbing his back.

I bent down on one knee in front of Grundi. "Hey, there's no reason to cry. There's nothing so bad that we can't help you with it."

When he looked up into my face, he began to sob even more hysterically, saying, "I am so sorry, Lady Cailyssa. I didn't mean to offend you yesterday. It was just that Lady Terry was making the music so much fun. I'm so sorry…I'll jump off that cliff if you want me to!"

As Grundi sobbed even more, his wife, Nori, continued to rub his back saying, "He's been out here all night, Lady Cailyssa. Please don't let him jump off the cliff."

I stood up slowly and grabbed Grundi's hands in mine. "Now, see here, Grundi, there will be no jumping off cliffs today. Besides, what would I eat if my favorite kitchen elf was gone?"

Grundi stood up and proudly clutched my hand saying. "Fav—favorite? I'm really your favorite? Lady Cailyssa, that is the most wonderful thing I think I have ever heard!"

Grundi's mood had changed dramatically, and before I knew it, he launched himself at me and gave me the best elf hug that you could imagine. He scampered off, taking his wife along by the hand, singing a song about making me the best breakfast I've ever had.

I called out after him. "Hey, Grundi, by the way, I want to hear some of your music later tonight."

He giggled with glee and ran faster to the camp to make me an absolutely wonderful breakfast.

CHAPTER 13

LEGENDS FOR FRIENDS

After breakfast we headed out. I sat on my horse in front of all my friends and felt a heavy weight on my shoulders. It was difficult to breathe. I was in charge; *I was responsible*. My specular skills were tingling, telling me there was danger and death ahead. As we traveled down from the mountain, the road became more barren. I missed the lush green forest that surrounded Castle Larkin. As I looked out, the land looked dark and forbidding. The road became nothing but an old path, and the landscape was dusted with a few rocks and scrub brush. The trees looked like hunched-over, old witches, fingers grasping for a prize they would never have.

I sensed Daemon riding up beside me. "Cailyssa, we are no longer within the safety of the forest. We need to send a scout ahead. The raxs—which you have encountered—inhabit this land, and they would like nothing more than to bring back one of us as a prize to the dark lord."

I turned my head and stared angrily at Daemon. "I'm not sending Terry ahead, if that's what you're suggesting!"

I knew it would be smart to have Terry fly on ahead and scout the land, but I also knew that the dark lord, Speculus, had sent out a scouting party to capture Terry. I could not let the dark lord capture and torture Terry! That would only further his plan to distract me and perhaps cause me to make irrational decisions. No, I could not let the evil dark lord capture Terry.

Daemon then carefully approached my side again. "Cailyssa, I would send Halodire to ride on with Terry flying ahead. He is descended from a race of large warrior elves, and the raxs would be terrified of his appearance. Remember that he is a bound servant of the Larkin family and would willingly give his life to protect Terry. Your sister will be safe as long as she stays in the air. She's fast enough to avoid any arrow that comes her way."

"But, Daemon, you know as well as I do that the dark lord corrupted a dragon, Longtooth, and it is commanded by Ttocs. If Terry were ever to meet that dragon in the air…"

"I won't lie to you, Cailyssa: she would die, and perhaps we would too if we were caught out in the open. A dragon is a horrible and powerful creature beyond the ability of any of us to defeat."

"Couldn't you defeat a dragon, Daemon? I thought you were an immortal angel."

"Cailyssa, my spirit is immortal, but the human body I reside in is not. I daresay there are few warriors in this world who could slay me in battle. But a dragon is a magical creature, also immortal. Its breath of fire is capable of horrible destruction. None could withstand a dragon if she was intent on destroying us."

I turned back toward Terry. "Terry, fly on ahead. *Carefully* scout the area, and let me know what's in front of us. If you see a huge red dragon, fly back here *fast*. Do not go near the dragon in any way, shape, or form. Halodire! Get up here and ride out with Terry. If anything dangerous comes near her, I expect you to kill it and get her back safely. Is that understood?"

"Yes, Lady Cailyssa, I promise to protect Terry," Halodire said, and he rode proudly ahead.

I saw Terry shoot up into the air, unfurling the razor-sharp claws hidden within her hands. "Don't worry, Cailyssa. I'll be fine, and if I see anything ahead, I'll come back and tell you. Then you *have* to promise to let me fly back and fight. I've been sharpening my claws for two days, and I really need to use them on some foul, smelly raxs."

When Terry flew on ahead, I had an ugly, sick feeling in my stomach. I was so worried about her. Sometimes little sisters can be a real pain. But when it comes to the point where you realize you could lose them forever, you suddenly realize how much you love 'em and how much they mean to you. I grabbed my moonstone to help me, and I prayed that my specular senses would only see good things happening to Terry and Halodire.

As Terry circled Halodire, she said, "Hey, Halodire, can I just call you Hal for short?"

"If it pleases you, Lady Terry, you may call me Hal. I have actually had many names in the past. You may have heard of me."

Terry flew down a little closer. "What do you mean heard of you? People don't often change names; that sounds a little weird."

Halodire rocked his head back and laughed with his most perfect smile as his long blond hair fell down his back.

"Terry, when you have been alive as long as I have, you *need* to change your name."

"OK, Halodire, so tell me one of your names. Are you, like, famous in elf land?"

"Do you know the tale of Narcissus?" Halodire said somberly.

"Yeah, sure, we studied him in my Greek mythology class. Are you telling me you were alive back then and you knew him?" Terry babbled out excitingly.

Halodire looked up and suddenly seemed very sad. "Yes, Terry, I was alive back then, but I didn't know Narcissus—I *was* Narcissus."

Terry paused to consider this. "What do you mean you were Nar—"

"Look out!" Halodire screamed.

Terry felt the buzz of a large black arrow whiz by her right ear. She looked down and saw a group of about a dozen raxs hiding on the road ahead. She flew higher, making sure she was out of the archers' range. As Terry looked down, she could see Halodire charging ahead on his horse.

"No, Halodire, there are a dozen raxs ahead. Stop! They'll kill you!"

Halodire paid no attention to Terry's screams. He charged ahead and pulled out his own bow. He notched three arrows at the same time and let them loose. They flew straight and true and buried themselves in the heads of three of the raxs. Another volley from Halodire's lethal bow, and three more of the raxs were dead. Next Halodire leaped from his horse and charged the remaining six raxs with a spear. Halodire impaled two raxs at one time. He pulled out his spear and used it to pole vault over the last four. He turned to fight three more, and Terry saw one raxs sneak out from behind a rock with an arrow destined for Halodire's back.

"Halodire, look out behind you!" Terry screamed.

Realizing it would be too late for Halodire, Terry tucked her wings in and dove from the sky. The fastest eagle would have been envious. She'd been practicing this technique in the yard with Halodire, and she was amazed how her razor-sharp talons sliced through the shoulders of the raxs so quickly that the creature was still thinking of firing his bow as he looked down at the ground to see his two severed arms still holding it. Halodire then dispatched the remaining raxs. He grabbed Terry, flung her onto his horse in front of him to protect her, and rode hard to warn Cailyssa. They arrived in a few minutes, and Terry jumped off Halodire's horse.

Cailyssa had seen the skirmish in her mind before it happened, and she cried out, "Terry, Halodire, you're covered in blood! What the hell? I told you not to fight anyone."

"Too late for that, big sister. We just met a scouting party of raxs, and those twelve are dead. But I could hear the cries of many more behind them. You better get ready for butt-kicking time."

Cailyssa held her moonstone tightly and went inside her mind in order to see the future. She almost fell off her horse, and Daemon grabbed her shoulders to support her.

Uncle Spencer came up on her other side and said, "Quickly, Cailyssa, what did you see? How many raxs are we facing, and in what direction are they coming from?"

Cailyssa came out of her inner specular mind. "My God, there must be thousands of them ahead of us, and behind them are two giant creatures. I think they're called Nephilim. They're looking to drive us to the road on the right so they can corner us with our backs to the cliffs. There's a fork in the road ahead of us, and they are racing to get there to cut us off."

Cailyssa unfurled her swords, and everyone behind her did the same as they raced off. As the company charged forward, they hit the front ranks of the army like an angry hurricane. Cailyssa went into battle mode, and everything moved very slowly. It seemed like an unfair video game as Cailyssa slew many of the raxs before they could see her move. Daemon had unfurled his huge sword and jumped in front of Cailyssa. He swung his sword, and it gleamed with a white light. The raxs were terrified as he killed dozens at a time. The elves were fighting bravely with their small swords and shields. They were scampering beneath the legs of the raxs so quickly that they were difficult to locate before they delivered their killing blows.

One raxs sneaked out from behind a tree, notched an arrow, and aimed right for Cailyssa's back. There was no way Cailyssa would see this arrow coming. Grundi saw the ugly female raxs aiming the arrow. Thinking quickly, he ran forward and jumped on the raxs's back. He drew his small sword and stabbed her neck. The raxs soldier stumbled awkwardly, still trying to shoot Cailyssa. Grundi held on, twisting the blade in her neck. The raxs archer let the arrow fly. It missed Cailyssa and hit another raxs in the back. Grundi jumped from the back of the dying raxs and scurried away. The dying raxs threw her knife at Grundi as he ran.

Uncle Spencer's voice boomed. "Cailyssa, there's far too many of them. We must make it to the road on the left. We will have our backs to the cliffs if we take the right road."

Even in the midst of battle, Cailyssa dipped into her specular senses. As she killed two more raxs, she jumped on her horse and grabbed Daemon's shoulders.

"Daemon, blow the horn and lead the company to the road on the right. There are too many raxs to fight here."

Uncle Spencer grabbed Cailyssa's arm and spun her around. "Are you *mad*? Cailyssa, if we take the road on the right, it will take us to the edge of the cliffs, and we will have nowhere to go. The raxs will have us right where they want us."

Cailyssa stood tall and confidently said, "Uncle Spencer, *I am in charge here*. Trust me now to do the right thing."

As Daemon led the company to the road on the right, the raxs cheered. They knew that if they could pin their foes with their backs to the cliff, they would be trapped.

As they rode their horses hard to the cliffs, Terry yelled down at Cailyssa, "Not for nothing, big sister, but you're leading the whole gang straight to the edge of a cliff, and there's nothing below but sharp rocks."

"Don't worry, Terry. I have a plan. You'll see."

As they approached the cliff, the horses reared back in fear as they sensed the impending fall. Cailyssa, Daemon, Uncle Spencer, Halodire, and Terry all went to the front to protect the elves. Everyone's back was facing the cliff. It seemed like a difficult situation was about to get a lot worse. The raxs approached. Seeing that their prey was cornered, they slowly crept up. As they did, they slashed at their tongues and began licking the blood from their knives. This blood fever drove the raxs wild! They would charge at any moment and capture Cailyssa and Terry Larkin; then they would feast upon the flesh and bones of the others. It was to be a glorious day; the raxs commanders looked forward to being rewarded by Lord Speculus.

Daemon calmly stepped in front of Cailyssa. "Cailyssa, I can kill hundreds of these foul creatures, but the only way you can survive is if you stand behind me and we flee."

"Daemon, do you actually think I'd run away and leave everyone like this? For an angel who holds all of the knowledge of the universe, you sure don't understand how I think and act."

Daemon yelled back, "You must do what I say. It is your only chance for survival."

Uncle Spencer heard the conversation. "He's right, Cailyssa. Go with Daemon and save yourself. It's most important for you to survive."

Cailyssa stood with her hands on her hips and spun around, screaming, "You know what? I am really sick of you guys telling *me* what to do. Who's in charge here, anyway?"

Before Uncle Spencer or Daemon could mouth an objection, Cailyssa's voice rose over the crowd. "Listen, everyone! Listen! When I say so, I want you all to lie down on the ground and cover your heads. No questions. Just to do it!"

Daemon looked angrier than I'd ever seen him. "You mean for us to lie down like sheep in a slaughterhouse? Have you lost your mind? I will not—"

Before Daemon could finish his sentence, Cailyssa spoke with such regal authority that all who heard it immediately complied. "Lie down and cover your heads *now*!"

As they did so, the wind began to blow with great gusts that threatened to push them off the cliff. As if things couldn't get worse, hideous screaming and flapping noises came from behind them below the cliff. The sounds were so piercing and intense that all who heard quivered in fear. The voice of death itself could not be any worse. From below the cliff, a gigantic dragon appeared. She had been hovering and hiding below. But now she rose up for all to see. Everyone froze, staring at the ominous form of Longtooth. Without warning, all of the air disappeared, and a huge fireball erupted from her mouth. It swept above Cailyssa and her friends, who had taken cover on the ground. As the raxs and their commanders looked ahead, they dropped their knives and began to run as they realized the fireball was headed toward them. The first ball of fire hit the raxs with such force it incinerated hundreds of them so that nothing was left but ash. The remaining raxs fled in terror.

As Cailyssa and all her friends peeked between their fingers and looked up to the sky, they saw that great red dragon blocked the sun. Atop the dragon sat an old dwarf, his long beard flowing in the wind. They watched as the dragon flew over their heads after the raxs. The dragon chased the raxs, spewing flames on them. When the dragon landed, she tore apart the raxs with her massive claws and teeth, making sure not to devour any of the foul creatures. At last only two Nephilim commanders and a few raxs were left of the thousands who had come.

Dolhar, sitting upon Longtooth, looked down upon the two giants as if they were small children. "Go back to the dark lord. Tell him what you have seen here, and tell him that I, Dolhar, and the dragon Longtooth now serve Cailyssa Larkin—not *him*!"

As the two Nephilim giants ran away, Dolhar and the red dragon turned around and slowly approached Cailyssa. They all picked themselves up from the ground and brushed off the soot. The dragon stood in front of Cailyssa; her great golden eyes mesmerized everyone. She was as terrifying and as beautiful a dragon as anyone could possibly imagine. She was also as big as a house.

"Longtooth," Dolhar said proudly, "if you would do me the pleasure, I should like to get on the ground and meet Cailyssa Larkin. We must mind our manners when we address royalty."

At this, Longtooth turned her head so that Dolhar could climb down from the saddle. As she gracefully put her head down in front of Cailyssa, Dolhar jumped down. He approached Cailyssa and shifted his battle-ax to his back, kneeling as if he were bowing to the queen.

Dolhar stood up proudly and bellowed, "My lady, I present to you Longtooth, the great red dragon. I am Dolhar from the dwarf lands of Meridian. We could tell that a new Larkin had returned to Mirror World because the wind has been filled with the essence of hope. We are now here at your service."

"Welcome Dolhar and Longtooth. I am honored to meet you. It seems you have arrived precisely when we needed you. And my friends and I thank you for saving us from the horrible army of raxs."

As Cailyssa said this, she looked back at Daemon and Uncle Spencer with eyebrows raised. They both looked to the ground, embarrassed. They felt foolish for not trusting Cailyssa. She had known all along that the dragon would be coming, and she had set a perfect trap.

Out of nowhere, Terry ran up and unfurled her wings. "Hi, everyone, my name is Terry Larkin. I just wanted to introduce myself. I don't mean to be rude, but I'm just so excited that I now have someone else to actually fly with."

Longtooth looked down at Terry, and her huge golden eyes shone like pools of love. Her heart beat strongly for this young Larkin, and she was quite taken by her. She snorted to be sure that no small fireball was left inside her and then she said in her silky, deep voice, "It is an honor to meet another winged creature. I look forward to chasing the mist of a cloud with you."

Right then Halodire burst forth and shouted, "All cheer Dolhar and the dragon, Longtooth!"

At this the elves cheered and jumped about. Some of them were slapping high fives just like Terry had taught them.

Cailyssa turned and spoke for all to hear. "Despite this joyous victory, we can't stay here—back to the road quickly. There is a small spot of green forest just ahead that will make a good camp spot for the night. They moved quickly and set up camp for the evening. The elves were cooking up a feast to be remembered, and Cailyssa went about the camp checking everyone. Halodire followed with Terry, and they provided medical treatment to those who were injured in battle.

Cailyssa froze. She could see the future, and she could see the icy-cold grip of death about to take one of her friends. She ran as fast as she could to the other side of camp, and there she saw Nori kneeling next to her husband, Grundi.

When Nori saw Cailyssa, she slowly pulled back the bloody blanket. A knife from a raxs had found Grundi's back. Nori cried, "Please, Cailyssa, save my dear husband, please, please…"

Cailyssa knelt down next to Grundi and took his hand.

He smiled faintly and tried his best to pretend he wasn't hurt. He spoke weakly. "Did you enjoy the breakfast I prepared for you the other day, Cailyssa?"

"Yes I did, Grundi. It was the finest I've ever had. Perhaps when you are better, you can make me another. Or maybe I should make you breakfast, since I do owe you big-time for saving my life," Cailyssa said as she held back the tears that began to well in her eyes.

Grundi coughed and struggled to speak. "As much as I wish to cook, I think not. See, I'll be leaving soon to join the halls of my fathers. Please take care of Nori for me. I love her dearly."

As Grundi died a noble death, Nori threw herself on top of her husband and wailed in agony. Cailyssa, Halodire, and Terry stood there, tears rolling down their cheeks. Cailyssa wrapped her arms around herself, trying to keep off the cold. A few moments ago, her specular skills of prescience had showed her this death before it happened. Now she had to see it again—this time for real—and face the pain again. Terry ran over and embraced Cailyssa. They walked back to camp; not a word was said between them. Cailyssa tried to shut down her specular skills, but she knew this was not the last death she would see twice.

CHAPTER 14

PERCEPTIONS OF BEAUTY

The next morning came with dark clouds and rain. Everyone gathered for Grundi's funeral service. He was buried in a grave with a beautiful white headstone that Dolhar had carved with the help of the elves. The gray sky and swirling mists of rain did nothing to wash away the tears and grief of all who were there. Cailyssa did her best to hide her emotions and led them in a final prayer before they departed. They packed up camp and journeyed that day without much talk, each person dealing with grief in his or her own manner.

That night they made camp, and while no one said so, the food did not taste the same without the artful hand of Grundi to help prepare things. Cailyssa sat around the campfire after dinner with Uncle Spencer, Daemon, Terry, Halodire, and Dolhar. Longtooth lay not far away, always staying close to Dolhar and Terry.

Terry broke the silence. "Hey, Halodire, remember yesterday before the raxs attacked us? You were trying to tell me some crazy, made-up story that had to do with you living in ancient Greece. You can't be that old. I mean, you look like you could be in college. Do you elves just make up crazy stories or what?" Terry said as she flipped back her hair and raised her eyebrows.

Before anyone could say a word, Daemon burst out laughing in a scornful way. "I'm sorry to laugh, Halodire, but I can't believe you actually told Terry your past. You realize, of course, that you have piqued both Larkins' curiosity, and now you must tell your tale truthfully to satisfy their interest."

Halodire was looking down at the ground not saying a word, as if no one were speaking to him.

"Now, now…let's not press Halodire to do anything he doesn't want to," Uncle Spencer said to reassure Halodire that his silence would be accepted.

Daemon immediately spoke up, showing his contempt for Halodire. "I'm sure Halodire *wants* to tell his story, and I'm sure Terry and Cailyssa *want* to hear it. Come now, Halodire, tell us the story of the most beautiful man in the world," Daemon cocked his head and laughed mockingly, taunting Halodire to respond.

"Shut up, Daemon," Cailyssa said angrily. "Can't you see that he's truly upset? I thought an angel would have more class than to act like a school-yard bully. Halodire, we don't need to hear your story. Don't listen to Daemon."

Daemon stood up. "He'll tell his story, all right. He has to. It's part of who he is. I've heard the story before, and I have no interest in hearing it again. It makes me sick to even think about it." Daemon stood and began to walk away. Then he paused and looked angrily at Halodire, whose head was still down. "Remember, pretty boy, what I said when you met Terry and Cailyssa at the lake? If I ever hear of you using your charms on them again, I will not hesitate to inflict a great deal of agony upon you."

Without warning, Halodire stood up and charged at Daemon. His seven-foot frame was charging toward Daemon with enough force to crush any man. But, amazingly, Daemon stood calmly waiting for Halodire to arrive. At the last moment, Daemon sidestepped Halodire's charge, grabbed the top of the shirt as he went by, and tripped him so that he fell face first into the dirt. It looked as though Daemon was toying with a little boy.

"What is it with guys, anyway?" Terry said. "Do they think it looks cool to get into arguments and fights? Grow up, Daemon." Daemon disappeared into the woods.

Halodire suddenly stood up. "Don't blame Daemon. He's right. He should be mad at me for what I did at the lake when we first met. It was just that I…I…I have watched you both for so long that when I finally met you, my halo charm just came out of nowhere."

Now Cailyssa stood up. "Whoa, Halodire! What do you mean you had been watching us? You're creeping Terry and me out. We don't much like the idea of a guy spying on us.

Explain yourself, and don't forget to include what a halo charm is."

Terry stood up quickly next to Cailyssa. "You tell him, Lyssa! I want some explaining here, too, and don't go telling me any of those crazy stories about you living in ancient Greece."

"Let us all sit down and talk about this in a reasonable manner," Uncle Spencer said softly.

At that, they all sat down, and Halodire wiped the dirt from his face as he looked into the campfire avoiding eye contact as he spoke. "I will tell you nothing but the truth, Lady Terry and Lady Cailyssa Larkin, but please don't think less of me. I have changed. I am not who I used to be, and I have proudly served at Castle Larkin for hundreds of years."

Terry piped up. "You can't be that old."

"Please, let me tell my tale. Then, if you would like to dismiss me from your service, I will gladly leave." Halodire took a deep breath and sighed. "First, let me tell you that I am a high elf, nearly immortal, and I have been alive for over three thousand years. What I told you yesterday, Terry, was the truth—or at least part of it. Although my true name is Halodire, I was, unfortunately, known as Narcissus when I lived in ancient Greece. Perhaps you know the tale.

"As you may remember, many people of Greece thought that Narcissus was the most handsome man ever created. Word had traveled of my beauty, and people came from all over the world to ask for my hand in marriage. I literally had hundreds of suitors, both male and female, who asked me to marry them. But I turned them all down; I was far too exquisite for any of them. They were all beneath me. And I used my beauty to take advantage of many people. One day an angel appeared to me. I was terrified. His name was Arnon, a friend to Daemon, and he was sent to punish me. I had never seen an angel, and the power and glory that emanated from Arnon was nothing I had ever seen or felt before; I was truly humbled.

When Arnon spoke, I fell to the earth and trembled. "Halodire, we have long watched your arrogant ways. Walk to the edge of the watery pool and face your punishment.'

"I walked to the edge of the pool and knelt down to look at my reflection. It was then that I realized what my punishment was. It was horrible…dreadful…not something I easily share with you. I looked at my reflection but was unable to look away—no matter how hard I tried. I couldn't blink my eyes, and I couldn't move. All I could do was stare at the likeness of myself.

"Arnon appeared next to me and spoke loudly.

"'Your punishment fits you rightly and is just, Halodire. Since you love yourself more than all others, you will spend eternity looking at your reflection, as if you had fallen in love with yourself.'"

Halodire rubbed his temples with his hands as he spoke. "I spent years staring at nothing but my reflection in pure agony, unable to move or pull away. Then Arnon appeared and offered to release me if I would consider serving the

Larkin family in Mirror World. I quickly agreed and have been honored and privileged since that time to serve the Larkin family."

Cailyssa interrupted, "You still haven't explained about watching us."

Halodire looked at Cailyssa and Terry. "When I was in Castle Larkin, I was able to look through the castle mirror and watch you two as you grew up. I saw your grandfather and those who came before him. I watched you through the mirror as a loving servant would, hoping that one day I would meet you and be able to serve you in person. Perhaps you can see now why I was so excited when I met you; that's when I made the mistake of using the halo charm. It happened completely without my awareness. I—"

Terry jumped up. "Even if we believe your story, I don't like the idea of being manipulated by some charm. What is a halo charm?"

Halodire looked sad again. "To some it would be a blessing, but to me it's a curse I have been born with. You see, when you possess remarkable physical beauty, it acts like a halo or as a charm. All people with great physical beauty have some sort of halo charm. I have an extremely strong one. There are—"

"Just give us the skinny, Halodire, no more long-winded stories," Cailyssa interrupted.

"OK, when people see someone with great physical beauty, it charms them. Their impression of the person is distorted.

The more beautiful a person is, the more people think they are intelligent, honest, compassionate, trustworthy, and—"

"That's stupid," Terry interjected. "Just because someone's beautiful doesn't mean they're a better person. It doesn't mean they're smarter, and it certainly doesn't mean that they're more compassionate or trustworthy. Someone could be beautiful but not have any redeeming character traits. Believe me, some of the least desirable boys at my school are handsome-looking guys."

Halodire nodded in agreement. "Exactly. You're absolutely right, Terry Larkin, and you're proving my point. Physical beauty should have nothing to do with what kind of person you are on the inside. Unfortunately, people believe that attractive people are good and kind and trustworthy. Believe me. My halo charm was very powerful. I used to manipulate people and get all sorts of things. When people fell under my charm, they were so enamored with my beauty that they would do anything for me—whether it be right or wrong. This is why I was punished. But I have learned from my mistakes. I may embody physical perfection, but I am no better than anyone else—and perhaps less so. In fact, for thousands of years I wasn't half as good as many of the people who asked me to marry. Now I'm alone and always will be. However, I take great pride in my service to the Larkin family. I have never been happier. I stand ready to serve you—if you'll have me. However, I understand if you see me as a contemptible scoundrel. I will take my leave and never come back."

Before Terry or Cailyssa could say a word, Halodire actually put his head down and wept. Cailyssa could feel the depth of his pain, and she knew through her specular skills that all he had said was true. Halodire had been a tortured soul for many years, and she pitied him. But he had chosen the right path and redeemed himself by working for the Larkin family.

Cailyssa stood up. "Stand up, Halodire. You have paid the price for your errant ways. Stop your blubbering. I do not intend to release you from your commitment to serve the Larkin family. Actually, I think I have a plan to use your exceptional abilities to defeat the dark lord. Are you with me?"

"Of course, Lady Cailyssa!" Halodire shouted. He jumped up and squared his broad shoulders. He looked most impressive. The fire lit his perfectly chiseled face. His long blond hair shone like gold as it cascaded down his shoulders, and his piercing blue eyes looked bright and clear, but nothing was more beautiful than the pride that swelled within him.

CHAPTER 15

A FALLEN ANGEL

The two giant Nephilim warriors returned to the dark lord's castle, after facing the wrath of the dragon, Longtooth. Although their lives had been spared, they had a message to deliver that their master would not want to hear. They stopped at the river of death and waited for the dark lord's permission to cross. Through the swirling mists, a raft approached guided by a black wraith. His long cloak clung tightly to the bony skeleton that composed him. The Nephilim warriors boarded, being sure not to touch the water. As they crossed, they felt the icy chill below them. The dead souls within the river looked like shriveled ghosts floating in the dark waters. They called out to the two warriors, as they called out to all who crossed the river. The whispers of the dead permeated their senses, urging them on to touch the water and join them below.

They crossed the river, while the Castle of Dark Mirrors awaited them. As they approached the castle, Ttocs was standing at the top of the drawbridge with his hands on his hips. "How dare you fools return before the army! I will crush you under my boot, you stupid giants!"

"There is no army. We are all that's left," the Nephilim warrior said.

"What? How can that be? I sent you with the force of thousands. You should have been able to squash Cailyssa and her putrid friends. You were to deliver Terry Larkin *to me*!" Ttocs screamed as he spoke, spittle flying from his mouth.

"My Lord, Ttocs," the Nephilim intoned. "There was nothing we could do. A giant red dragon appeared just as we were about to seize the Larkin girl. The dragon was terrible and enormous. It was by far the most hideous beast I've ever seen. It spewed flames and burned the raxs to ash. The few raxs soldiers that avoided the flames were torn to shreds by her teeth and claws. We were lucky to escape with our lives."

Ttocs slowly walked up to the giants and unfurled his mace, saying, "Kneel down, you loathsome fools." He swung the mace mightily, and the three metal balls with spikes impaled one of the giants in the side of the face. As the other giant attempted to flee, Ttocs swung again, slicing his leg. Ttocs then stormed inside the castle, leaving the giant Nephilim warriors to mend their wounds.

Ttocs walked through the castle entrance and followed the long hallway that led to the throne room. The hallway was lined on both sides with great mirrors. They were all framed with intricate detail, and the dark reflection that Ttocs saw of himself filled him with foreboding. It was almost as if the mirrors were whispering dark thoughts to him. The mirrors were telling him how useless and cowardly he was, how ugly he was, and that only through hate and anger could he achieve greatness. As he imagined killing and hurting other people, he savored the feeling of the floor beneath his feet. It was made from skulls and bones—victims of the dark lord's conquests. As Ttocs approached the dark lord's throne, he felt a cold chill go through his body. He was hoping he would not be added to the skull collection beneath his feet.

The dark lord stood upon the arms of his throne with his back to Ttocs. He was gazing into the largest black mirror Ttocs had ever seen. Usually, the dark lord appeared as an image or reflection in the mirror, or sometimes as a swarm of insects in the shape of the skull. Today, however, the dark lord appeared in bodily form. He turned his head toward Ttocs and jumped from the throne, landing gracefully at the edge of the top stair. He was even more horrible to behold in this fashion. His eyes were blazing with fury, and his hands were on his hips. Ttocs was astounded when the dark lord slowly walked down the stairs in front of his throne and unfurled the largest set of black-and-silver wings he had ever seen. Ttocs was mesmerized as he gazed at the sheer flawlessness and radiance of the wings.

"Behold me. Am I not magnificent to look upon?" the dark lord said as he looked down at Ttocs.

Ttocs was so stunned by the dark lord's question that he couldn't answer. He simply gazed at the dark lord's sculpted muscular form and the incredible span of his wings. Suddenly, the dark lord flew into the air, and a piercing scream that came from the depths of hell shook the castle. Ttocs fell on the floor trembling, truly believing that his life would soon be over. As the screaming stopped, Ttocs looked up and saw Lord Speculus slowly descend upon his throne and gracefully fold his wings behind his back.

"You do not need to tell me your pitiful news, Ttocs. I have seen what the dragon has done to the raxs army in my mirrors. There is nothing that escapes my gaze."

"Yes, My Lord!" Ttocs stammered as he quickly regained his feet and tried to appear respectable in front of his master.

The dark lord tapped his fingers on the throne as he spoke slowly. "This Cailyssa Larkin has made me look a fool. I will crush her—and you will be my hand of death. Behold the mirror to your right."

Suddenly, the mirror next to Ttocs came alive with a vision of a silver-and-black dragon. The dragon was chained in a cave and was forced to look at a huge reflecting pool.

The dark lord waved his hand toward the mirror as he spoke. "As you can see, I have been corrupting this beast as he gapes into the reflecting pool. He is no longer a noble dragon. I have nursed him with lies and deceit, and he has *devoured them gladly*. On him you will ride, and the two of you will rain destruction down upon Mirror World. The beings of this land will again know the power and tyranny of the dark lord. Take this new beast and fly to the woods of ambrosia. There you will find Cailyssa and Terry Larkin, trying again to ruin my good work. This time you will seize Terry Larkin, and I will bleed her on my black stone altar as her sister watches in vain. Do not fail me this time. Be gone."

CHAPTER 16

INNER CONFLICT

I woke the next morning before the sun rose and crept out of my sleeping bag. There was still a chill in the air, but I wanted to go to the open meadow nearby to watch the sunrise and prepare myself for the day. I took a blanket and my hairbrush and headed off to the meadow. As I peered across the greenish-gold blades of grass, the sun touched their tips as it rose in the distance. The water droplets at the edges of the grass glistened, and a cool breeze swayed the grass in a beautiful rhythm that seemed to be waving to me. I began to brush my hair, and suddenly Daemon was behind me. He took the blanket I had brought, unfolded it, and placed it around my shoulders. I flipped my hair outside of the blanket and took a step backward toward him. His arms folded around me in a warm embrace, and I let my head fall back, luxuriating in the arms of my guardian angel—who, at the moment, happened to feel awfully warm and cuddly on this cold, lonely morning. I closed my eyes and listened to his warm breath at the edge of my ear. My God, this might be just the most perfect feeling in the whole world. Daemon slowly took the brush from my hand and began to work it through my hair. I could've melted on the spot. I knew I shouldn't turn around because, if I did, I'd look upon that handsome face and be unable to prevent myself from kissing him like a love-sick fool.

Suddenly, I remembered what happened last evening. I spun around, grabbed the brush from Daemon's hand, and in a blur I bopped him squarely on the forehead.

"You bullying jerk, I can't believe what you did to Halodire last night. You reminded me of a low-life high-school bully. You should be ashamed."

"Cailyssa, I'm sorry but I—"

"Don't even talk to me, Daemon, until you apologize to Halodire. How could a guardian angel possibly be a bully? Ugh! You drive me crazy."

I stormed off through the forest back to camp. But to be honest, I think the hairbrush smack had a lot to do with other things I was feeling rather than just being mad about Halodire. It was scary how much I loved being in Daemon's embrace. Part of me wished that I could suspend that moment in time and have Daemon brush my hair forever as I watched the sunrise. Every time I tried to deny my feelings about him, they seem to catch up to me and overwhelm me. Could I ever stop loving him? I wasn't so sure. Having the ability to see the future sometimes really sucks. One possible future had Daemon and me in an impossibly beautiful and perfect marriage, with wonderful children. In that future he was my perfect soul mate, my perfect partner, and my best friend. Unfortunately, I wasn't sure that was the future for me; there were many other possibilities too. Some of them included Terry and me dying long before either one of us got married.

"Good morning, Cailyssa!" Uncle Spencer's booming voice brought me out of my inner thoughts.

"Morn…ing, Uncle Spencer," I lamely responded.

"Why are we so glum this morning? The sun is shining on our faces, and I just saw Longtooth and Terry returning from a morning flight. I think Terry is receiving some excellent training."

"Hey, Uncle Spencer, can you ride next to me today? I think I need to just talk some things out."

"But of course, Cailyssa, I would be most happy to."

We packed up and headed down the road, following my lead. I rode a few paces ahead and gave Daemon a look that told him not to follow. Uncle Spencer sensed what I was doing and quickly trotted his horse up to join mine.

"Thanks for coming up, Uncle Spencer. I feel like my mind is a jumble of thoughts and emotions. I feel like the bedroom of my mind is filled with piles of dirty clothes, and I really need to clean up my room. You get what I mean?"

"Yes, Cailyssa, I do. Oftentimes life can become very complicated, and we do need to clean our room, as you say, and make sure that we have our priorities in order. This is hard for most of us to do, however. And, Cailyssa, for you it is a much more intense burden. I can't imagine how it must be for you every day, sensing possible visions of the future—and trying to get on with everyday life. It seems extraordinarily difficult for anyone to deal with."

"Man, Uncle Spencer, do I hear you! I just wish some days I could go back to being a simple junior in high school with no specular skills."

Uncle Spencer sighed, and we went on for a few minutes in silence.

"Cailyssa, have you ever heard of the time-traveler's paradox?"

"Yeah, sure, didn't we talk about that in your psychology class?"

"We did, Cailyssa, so why do you think I'm asking you about it right now?" Uncle Spencer said as if he were asking me to respond to a question in class.

"OK, Professor Larkin, I know when you're asking me a question to make me think. Let's see. In the time-traveler's paradox, we speculate that if we went into the past through time travel and changed something, then it could affect the future. Like if I went back in time and did something so that my mother and father were never married, then the question would be, would I actually exist? Am I right?"

"Cailyssa, you are mostly right. But you must understand that you are caught in a similar paradox every moment. Although you may not travel back to the past, you know that every decision you make today can change the future. But you're different from most people. Remember, you actually see the future unfold when your specular skills produce those prescient visions. This is a most difficult position to be in, and it must be extremely stressful for you."

"Yes, Uncle Spencer, it is. I feel I have that thing that you called in class *cognitive dissonance*. It's like I have two thoughts that are in conflict with each other, and I don't know what to do about it."

"Can you give me an example, Cailyssa?"

"OK, but you're going to hate it. Just suppose for a moment that Daemon and I fell in love…"

Uncle Spencer groaned loudly and adjusted himself in the saddle. "Cailyssa, Daemon is your guardian angel. You cannot marry your guardian angel; he is there to protect you."

"Then how come I keep seeing visions of him and me together in the future? It has to be possible if I can see it very clearly."

Uncle Spencer suddenly became very quiet and looked quite nervous, something that was very unusual for him.

"I know that look, Uncle Spencer. Out with it. I know there's something you're thinking about that you're not telling me."

"It's not that simple, Cailyssa. There are things you don't understand. There are things about the angels you don't understand."

"Uncle Spencer, in case you haven't noticed, I'm a big girl now. You must've noticed that I'm actually *here*, trying to *save* the world." I said this in my most sarcastic voice and felt sorry that I'd spoken so hastily. "I'm sorry for that remark,

Uncle Spencer, but I really need to know. What are you not telling me?"

"Cailyssa, the vision you have seen of you and Daemon is simply not possible. Daemon is your guardian angel, and you cannot marry your guardian angel. Daemon would never consent to it."

"So, Uncle Spencer, what you're telling me is that Daemon could not possibly marry me while he's my guardian angel. Correct?"

"Well, you see, a guardian angel is—"

"Uncle Spencer, you surprise me. For a very intelligent man, there is something quite simple *you* have overlooked." I said this in a most satisfied tone, and Uncle Spencer looked worried.

Using his own sarcastic voice, Uncle Spencer retorted, "Well then, Cailyssa, I suppose you will tell me *what* I have overlooked?"

"It's very simple, Uncle Spencer. What if Daemon were not my guardian angel?"

"But he *is*, Cailyssa, and that settles that!" Uncle Spencer said firmly.

"No it doesn't. I'll have him replaced! Then he'll be free to choose me if he desires," I stated flatly.

Uncle Spencer's face was aghast with horror. He almost fell off his horse. He was muttering nonsense to himself. He looked like a crazy man.

"Cailyssa, I am not your father—but *I am* your uncle—and you will stop with this foolish nonsense *immediately*. You cannot simply have Daemon replaced. It doesn't work that way."

"Why not? I'm sure there are other angels around."

Uncle Spencer looked directly into my eyes. "If you asked for another guardian angel, it would look as though Daemon was unable to do his job. The shame and humiliation he would feel would be horrible."

"Don't worry, Uncle Spencer, I have a plan. Remember, I have a secret weapon: I can see the future."

Before Uncle Spencer could say another word, I wheeled my horse around. Uncle Spencer was still muttering to himself, clearly frustrated and upset with our conversation.

I yelled back as I rode away, "Don't worry, Uncle Spencer. I'll work the whole thing out. Thanks for the help."

I rode up next to Daemon and pressed my horse closely next to his. Uncle Spencer rode by, giving me dirty looks as he passed.

Daemon looked over at me. "I hope you are not considering batting me with your hairbrush again. That act did not make you appear dignified."

"Sorry, Daemon, a girl has the right to act on strong emotions once in a while."

"I see," said Daemon. "I have noticed that human females can be extremely unpredictable and fickle."

"Hey, don't go there unless you want me to pull out my hairbrush and begin a smackdown right here in front of everyone," I said as I laughed. I also made sure that I tossed my hair back and gave Daemon my best impish grin.

It worked. Daemon rocked his head back and laughed lightly. He then looked over at me and smiled. I melted. He held my gaze, smiling—and making me feel like I was the most beautiful thing he had ever seen. "Cailyssa?"

"Yes, Daemon?"

"Before you struck me, I wanted to let you know how wonderful it felt to be with you at sunrise. As the sunlight touched the highlights of your hair, I must say…you radiated great beauty."

"Thanks, Daemon, you sure know how to make a girl feel good. Next time, I promise I won't hit you, and you can hug me a little longer. OK?"

We both looked at each other and laughed heartily. I reached out with my left hand and pushed Daemon's shoulder as if to knock him off his horse. He pushed me back in a loving and playful manner, and we continued to laugh, smile, and tease.

"Hey, Daemon, one question."

"Yes, Cailyssa?"

"How would you like to wake up every morning looking at the sun with me?"

Daemon's eyes narrowed, and he looked at me closely. "I'm not sure if I…understand the *nature* of your question."

I sat up erect in my saddle. "Sorry, Daemon, I guess I'm getting ahead of myself here. You see, first of all, I have to find you a new job."

Daemon looked puzzled then laughed. "Do you mean for me to bag groceries at the market?"

"Oh no, I have a much better job than that for you. If you're good, I'll tell you about it sometime."

Before Daemon could answer, I reined my horse to the right and galloped back to meet Halodire and Terry. When I got to the back of the line, Daemon turned his head to look back at me.

Terry whispered in my ear. "What did you just tell Daemon? He keeps looking back at you. Have you two been having a lovers' quarrel again?"

As I stared straight ahead, I answered Terry, "No...nothing like that."

"Come on, Cailyssa, tell your favorite sister the word. What's going on?"

"Oh, nothing much, I just have a surprise for Daemon."

"Really? What is it?" Halodire and Terry said at the same time.

"Oh, nothing really, it's just that his boss is going to fire him."

Halodire and Terry looked at each other, obviously perplexed. I rode off ahead, preferring to be alone with my thoughts. I had such a marvelous plan in place. It seemed almost too good to be true. But I knew I had to be very careful and not screw it up. If I did, a lot of people would get very hurt.

CHAPTER 17

SPIRALS IN THE SKY

"I don't think I can do that," Terry yelled across the sky to Longtooth. "Man, you make it look so easy when you fold your wing and spiral around like that."

"Please, little girl, I am not a man. I am a dragon!" Longtooth said as she snorted out a fireball to emphasize her point.

"It's just a figure of speech, Longtooth. We use that term back home where I come from. And where *I* come from, *I* wouldn't be known as a *little girl*."

"My apologies if I have offended you, young one. It's just that when you get to be as old and big as I am, everyone looks so young and small. In any event, enough with the bantering, we are entering the edge of the mountains where I was hoping to train you. Follow me and stay close!" Longtooth said as she tucked in both her wings and dove down.

Longtooth slowly unfurled just the tip of her right wing, which made her spiral toward the earth with amazing speed. Terry tried to follow but had difficulty catching up. It looked as though Longtooth would crash into the trees. Then she opened her wings and flew sideways between them. Her tremendous speed and energy shot her right back up to the clouds. Terry tried to follow Longtooth's example but clipped several tree branches with her wing tips and lost her momentum to follow the dragon to the sky. Longtooth hovered above, waiting for Terry to reach her.

"Longtooth, that is absolutely amazing. I thought I was fast. How do you do that?" Terry was breathing heavily, trying to recover.

"Young Terry, you must become one with the wind. The wind not only flows through the feathers in your wings but through your body and soul. To become one with the wind is to sense the fabric of life within it and use it to your advantage. Stand prepared! I am about to begin chasing you, and if I catch you, *you* will feel the pinch of my long teeth upon your backside. *Fly now*, young one!"

Terry stood amazed, unsure what to do, until a fireball emerged from Longtooth's left nostril aimed right toward her. Terry ducked the fireball and tried to use the spiral technique Longtooth had taught her to get away from the dragon. When she looked behind her, she saw Longtooth's mouth wide open, snapping at her. Terry surveyed a pass in the mountains and headed for it. There was a small crack between the two peaks, and she used her small size to pass through—knowing that Longtooth could not follow. Then she dove toward the trees with furious recklessness, hoping to prove to Longtooth that she could fly. Terry zigzagged rapidly between the tree trunks. She was sure Longtooth could not follow her between the narrow gaps. The trees ended, and right in front of her was an open meadow of tall grass. Straight ahead, in the middle of that meadow, Longtooth hovered. Her humongous mouth was wide open, and Terry was flying straight toward it. She was going straight in! At the last second, Longtooth lifted her head and Terry crashed with tremendous force into a small spot on the dragon's chest. Terry fell straight down, and Longtooth caught her and gently placed her upon the golden grass.

"Man, wh…wh…what just happened?" Terry said as she sat up, rubbing her eyes in disbelief. "All I remember is that I was flying straight toward your mouth. I thought I was going to be in your belly. Then you stood up, and I was going to crash into your scales…and then I crashed into something incredibly soft. It felt like I hit a marshmallow, and then I remember you putting me on the grass."

"Ah, yes, young one. You have just finished your first lesson in battlefield flying for dragons and other winged creatures," Longtooth said as she lay down upon the grass. Her large golden eyes focused on Terry.

"But I don't understand. At that speed, if I hit your scales, I should be dead, right?" Terry said in disbelief.

"When I stood up, I made sure that you did not strike my scales. You landed right here: it is called my *tendresse*," Longtooth said as she showed Terry her chest.

Magically, one of Longtooth's hardened scales began to glow. There were no words in any language that could describe the color and radiance. The light and beauty that emanated from Longtooth's tendresse bathed Terry in a cocoon of warm love that felt like sheer bliss. Terry felt like she was in heaven. She stood there, mesmerized, unable to move. After a few minutes, Longtooth reached out and gently helped Terry to lie down in the grass. Terry found herself staring up at the clouds, unable to move and unable to understand what had just happened to her. After a few minutes, she stood up.

"Whoo! That was—I can't even describe it—the most amazing thing that I think has ever happened to me. By the way, what *did* happen to me?"

"I showed you my heart," Longtooth said as she put her head next to Terry.

Terry stood up. "But what did I feel? I mean, it felt like, uh, like pure love."

"It was, young one. Legend has it that dragons were placed upon the earth to give men wisdom and to help them touch the power of love in one's heart. It was said that a dragon could remove its heart and show it freely to men so that the love of God would be within them," Longtooth said with unblinking eyes.

"I don't know what to say. Thanks, I guess. But why did you show it to *me?*"

"That would take far too long a time to explain. But if I may have your permission, I will perform a symbiosis with you, and you will quickly understand everything."

"What's a sym—what did you call it—symbas or something?"

"A symbiosis is when a dragon permits another creature to join its consciousness. It is a very rare thing for a dragon to offer. You will feel no pain or displeasure, and you will understand my memories and feelings that I share with you as if you had actually experienced them. It will help you understand angels and defeat Speculus."

"OK, but this doesn't mean you're my mom or anything, does it?" Terry half joked.

Longtooth's head shook back and forth quickly as she spoke. "Oh no, it is nothing like parentage. It is *infinitely* more intimate."

"What? More intimate than…? It's not like I'm scared. It's just that—" Before Terry could stop herself, she stepped forward and placed her hand on Longtooth's nose and looked deeply into her huge golden eyes.

Terry felt like she was falling in an endless void. There were sounds, voices, music, and images. She found herself floating softly down to the grass of Castle Larkin. She was standing there, Longtooth was by her side, and in front of her—impossibly—was her grandfather. She ran to hug him and felt his warm embrace. She looked up at Longtooth and suddenly understood everything!

"Oh my God, how long were we in this symbiotic thing?" Terry stammered as she came back to the reality of the moment.

"We were only there for a few minutes, Terry. And I only chose to show you a small portion of my memories and experiences. You now have some of my same experiences within you, complete with the intense emotions I felt. It is as if you lived them as I did. As you can see, I was very close to your grandfather. He and I were great friends. Your grandfather symbiotically bonded with my master and me. Since he could see the future, like Cailyssa, he told me I would be meeting you one day. And as you now know, when someone bonds with a dragon, they both share their love and all their emotions in a profoundly intimate manner. Now you can understand why I love you as genuinely as your grandfather did."

"You know what's funny?" Terry said as she flipped back her hair. "I kind of knew that the whole time. Remember when we first met: the day you saved us from the raxs? When you looked at me, I felt as if I had always known you—as if we were *connected* in some way."

"That was a very special day for me, too," Longtooth said as a great tear rolled from her eye.

"Don't be sad about toasting all those raxs. You had to do that to save us."

"I see you felt my pain. The destruction of any creatures saddens me. But more, despite your grandfather's specular skills, I was not sure the day would come that I would meet you. I did not show you all of my memories when we bonded. I am ashamed of some of the things I have done. When we bonded and I saw your purity and goodness, it reminded me of my dishonorable behavior."

"Listen up, Longtooth, nobody's perfect, and I have seen the beauty, grace, and honor within you. You're amazing! I feel like you're my second mother."

"Since I share all of your grandfather's memories, I feel that way myself. I only hope that I am worthy of the honor," Longtooth said as she looked sternly at Terry. "The dark lord and Ttocs know of our bonding. There is nothing that escapes the gaze of the dark lord. He will be furious about what I have done with you, and he will, unfortunately, be even more determined to kill us both."

"Good! Let him try, but he has to catch us both first. Doesn't he?" Terry said with a broad smirk on her face. She reached out and smacked Longtooth on the nose and flew off quickly into the sky. "You're not gonna catch me this time, old one. When we bonded you also shared with me all of your secret battlefield flying techniques." Terry flew quickly away from Longtooth.

"The unbridled enthusiasm of a young one is good to see," Longtooth roared toward the sky. "Yet there are many things you have yet to learn, and I am about to teach you one of them when I catch you!" Longtooth took off into the sky.

The great red dragon and the young girl from Boston, now one, chased each other through the mists of the clouds. Just as they had promised when they first met.

CHAPTER 18

MY FAULT

"Cailyssa, wake up quickly! Uncle Spencer is dead, and we need to get to the funeral. You're gonna be late." My dad was standing over my bed, shaking my shoulder.

Then I woke up, still in Mirror World, and the vision of Dad faded. Quickly turning to prescience, I scanned the future to see if the dream of Uncle Spencer's death would come true. When I looked into the future, I kind of felt like my body was floating in a ribbon of time, and various pictures and symbols were riding along with me on this wavelike ribbon. Some of the pictures were very clear, and others were very blurry. Sometimes when I touched a picture, it opened like a video on my smartphone. Other times, I grasped a picture, and it simply faded away in my hand. Now I was desperately searching for any images of Uncle Spencer; the few I found did not predict his death. Thank God, time to get up and go to work.

When I opened my eyes, I was a bit startled. I was lying on my side, and my horse's nose was about two inches away from mine. He was lying down too—something that was a bit unusual for most horses. I looked into his chocolate-brown eyes, and it was like I could read his thoughts. He had noticed I was struggling in my sleep, and he sought to comfort me by lying down beside me—just as he would have done back home. *What?* I jumped to my feet. I didn't have a horse at home. What did this mean? I needed to ride with Uncle Spencer today and talk things out. I saw Uncle Spencer in the distance and ran up to him.

"Good morning, Cailyssa, I hope you are well rested for our trip."

I didn't say a word in response, and Uncle Spencer knew exactly what I needed.

"Cailyssa, I was hoping we might ride together today. It appears that you have a lot on your mind."

Uncle Spencer didn't have to use his skills of telepathy. It was pretty obvious from the blank stare in my eyes that I was lost in some pretty disturbing inner thoughts.

"That would be awesome, Uncle Spencer, and I promise not to talk about Daemon. I can't let boyfriend issues get in the way of some important work I have to do today," I said in my most determined voice.

I walked by Daemon. Of course he wasn't sleeping, he never did, and I told him to rally the troops for our journey to Ambrosia. I walked right past him, giving him a sideways glance, and I could feel his eyes follow me as I passed. I wanted to turn around and look at him, but I knew that if I did, that damn gorgeous face of his would distract me from what I needed to do. Our troop set out for Ambrosia, with Terry and Halodire acting as scouts for the road ahead. I moved my horse alongside Uncle Spencer.

"Cailyssa, how are you managing the experience of your specular skills? Are the visions overwhelming for you?"

"To be honest, I'm actually getting quite good at traveling the ribbon of time and picking out events in the stream of my mind. But something is freaking me out. I saw some images today. They were really clear, but I just can't believe what I saw."

"Um…I may have some experience that could help you," Uncle Spencer said as he stroked his goatee slowly. "Did any of the persons seem familiar to you in some way?"

"Exactly!" I sat up straight on my horse, intent on hearing what Uncle Spencer had to say.

"It's not unusual in Mirror World to experience others here—even those we knew back on earth."

"You know what brought this on? I woke up this morning, and my horse was looking in my eyes. It was so familiar that it absolutely freaked me out. I just reached out and hugged this beautiful golden horse I'm on right now."

At that moment my horse turned his head and looked up at me as if he knew I was talking about him.

"See what I *mean*, Uncle Spencer!" I screamed. "Cali is looking at me as if he knows I am talking about him."

"Excuse me for pointing out the obvious, Cailyssa, but what did you just call your horse? Up to this point, I have not heard you use his name." Uncle Spencer said this as if it were an examination question. He paused for a moment and looked over at me. "I have only heard you use that name in reference to your most beloved golden retriever at home."

Then the revelation hit me. "Oh my God, Cali, is that really you?" I said as my fingers immersed themselves in the beautiful golden mane in front of me.

"That feels really good. I wish you'd pet me more, but I know you're really busy."

Zap! My horse—I mean my dog from home, I mean… I don't know what—just connected with my mind as if he spoke to me.

"Cali, can you hear me?" I whispered in my mind.

"Of course I can. I could always hear your thoughts at home too, but you just never answered me back until now."

Then I freaked! "You stupid dog! You could get hurt here. There are lots of evil creatures that would be too quick to kill a dog—I mean horse. Argh!" I screamed in my mind.

At that moment Terry flew overhead. "Stop screaming at the dog, Cailyssa. You're making him feel bad."

"Am I the dumbest person in the world, Uncle Spencer?" I said sheepishly as I patted Cali to make up for yelling at him. "How did I not know my dog followed me here?"

Uncle Spencer's head rocked back, and he laughed. "You're by far one of the most intelligent people I have ever met. But you should realize that you are overwhelmed at times managing your specular skills. By the way, both of your dogs followed you here. Have you not noticed the markings of my black-and-white 'Bernese mountain dog' horse?"

I floated inside my mind and dipped my hand in the specular ribbon of time. Whoa. I finally understood what I was experiencing, and it helped me get through what I needed to do today.

"Hey, Uncle Spencer, how did everyone get to be here? Terry, Daemon, and you followed me here through the mirror, right? I don't think my dogs did."

"We did follow you through, but others that you may meet here did not—such as your dogs. It is a mystery, but quantum physics has shown us that an electron can be in two places at once. Why can't people? Besides, you needed us here, Cailyssa, so we came," Uncle Spencer stated compassionately.

"Oh great, major guilt trip here! I'm responsible for bringing you, and maybe others, here. So I'm responsible for making sure the dark lord and his nasty raxs don't pick the meat from your bones. Great! I really wanted to be burdened by more responsibility. Can't a girl catch a break once in a while?"

Uncle Spencer sighed. "We all came freely. Nobody was forced to come here by you. We love you dearly, and we would not consider abandoning you to the dark forces of this world. I need to tell you something important, Cailyssa." Uncle Spencer looked directly into my eyes. "Your grandfather and my dad, Artemus, sought to protect his friends and family at his own peril. This was his greatest weakness, and the dark lord used it against him and killed him. You cannot make the same mistake. Remember what we saw in the mirror back home. I will gladly die to stop the ruin of this world and ours back home, and so will everybody here with you." Then Uncle Spencer stared straight ahead and sat very erect in his saddle.

I looked across at Uncle Spencer; he did not look back. Daemon turned around to look at me, and I saw his beautiful face. I glanced up at Terry flying overhead. I hated having the responsibility for their lives. The only thing I could do was fight damn hard to make sure the dark lord would never have time to make trouble for my friends or anyone else ever again.

I connected my mind to Cali. "Thanks for coming, Cali. You're the best dog in the whole world. I can't wait to get home and have you snuggle up in bed with me."

"Lyssa, if you don't mind me asking, can you find me some of those bacon dog treats? Hay is for horses, and I hate eating it. Please, please, please!" Cali wagged his horse's tail and did the best imitation of a horse trying to look like a dog that I could ever imagine. I laughed at his playfulness and sense of humor.

"I don't think they have bacon dog treats here, but I saw the elves had some real good-looking meat bones from dinner last night. I'll be sure to get you two! Let's ride a little faster. I want to get to Ambrosia by lunchtime. It should be interesting reuniting with some old friends, I think.

CHAPTER 19

HELPLESS FRIENDS

We entered the woods of Ambrosia, and the landscape changed dramatically. If you've ever read a book about fairy creatures and envisioned the colorful floral world where they would live—you'd know what this place looked like. The ferns that encompassed the walls around me were so vibrant and bright that it looked like someone had sprayed fluorescent paints. Golden hues were imbued with pastel shades of blue and green that seemed to wave a welcoming hand to us as we slowly rode by. The path in front of us appeared to be a shimmering compilation of smooth water rocks. The smell of the ocean enveloped me, and I breathed deeply—savoring the sweet saltiness I loved more than anything.

My specular sense flashed, and I got a nervous empty feeling in the pit of my stomach, knowing who I was about to meet. That's when whispering started, "Oooooooh, noweee, weeedooo, pleeeeease goesssss awayyzzz." The voices were so soft it may have been the ocean breeze playing tricks on me.

The stone path led us by saltwater pools and eventually to the white sand beach known as Anac Atnup, which had many small, beautiful islands close to shore. It was simply paradise. All around us now was sea grass; the waves could be seen and heard as they tickled the sand ahead.

"Whoa, Cailyssa, this place rocks! I want to paint my room these colors when we get home," Terry said as I dismounted from my horse and stood next to her.

Uncle Spencer and Daemon joined us. We were all dazzled by the spectacle of nirvana before us. Daemon's voice pierced our ears. "Beware of the creatures who live here. To underestimate their powers could prove fatal. Watch out especially for Halodire. These women can charm men and easily bring them to their death."

"Daemon, they're my friends—not creatures," I sternly said. "These amazing women are Amazons!"

All of a sudden the water stirred, and dozens of beautiful women emerged from the waves. They fled silently into the tall grass, seeming to be hiding from us.

Using a language I knew they would understand, I called, "Nosidam, Acissej, Ebeohp, please come out. It's been too long. I really miss you! It's Cailyssa."

"Cailyssa, do you really think you know some of these people?" Terry said in her most curious voice.

Rustling could be heard among the ferns, but none of the dwellers would show themselves. Terry turned to Daemon. "Daemon, you seem to know what's going on. What is an amazon and why did you call them nymphs?"

"Etymologically, the word *nymph* is related to the Greek word for bride. They are exceptionally beautiful and enchanting and have often been lovers of gods and heroes. But some of them can be exceptionally dangerous. These women are goddesses of the sea and are descended from the great race of warrior women known as the Amazons," Daemon said in his most serious tone.

"So we have a bunch of tough supermodels who came out of the water and just ran into the woods. Sounds like they have a self-esteem issue, if you don't mind me saying," Terry said as she turned to Cailyssa.

"It's much worse than a self-esteem issue, Terry. Be quiet, and I'm sure they'll come out," I said softly.

"Nosidam, Acissej, Ebeohp, please come out. It's me, Assyliac," I said, using my Mirror World name.

"Cailyssa, what did you just call yourself?" Terry said.

"Spell it backward, Terry. You're in Mirror World, after all."

"Spell it backward," Terry said mockingly.

Terry thought for a moment. Assyliac backward? C-A-I-L-Y-S-S-A. "Cailyssa, it's backward but not a palindrome. Leonardo da Vinci often used it in his writings. Thought you would trick me didn't you? Holy crap!" Terry screamed.

At that moment three Amazons appeared from the thick foliage with ferns covering most of their bodies. They walked with such awesome grace and beauty that it would have made any runway model jealous.

"Cailyssa, look who they are. How can that be?" Terry pulled excitedly on Cailyssa's arm.

My best friends Madison, Jessica, and Phoebe appeared in the form of goddesses in front of us. While they were all very cute back on earth, they were absolutely gorgeous here. Halodire, and even Uncle Spencer, were enthralled by their overwhelming beauty and stood there with mouths agape. Daemon had no expression on his face.

I stepped up to them excitedly. "Girls, group hug here. I missed you all so much. But can we say our names normally for the benefits of the others here? Your Mirror World names are much too difficult to pronounce."

But my three friends just stood there, looking terribly embarrassed.

Jessica, the boldest of my friends, looked up. "Assyliac—I mean, Cailyssa—we missed you too, but we are too embarrassed to have you see us like this. Please leave." The tears began to roll down Jessica's cheeks.

Phoebe broke loose and ran toward me for a monstrous hug. Madison and Jessica followed, and we four girls shared a tight embrace. It was then that Phoebe's emotions caught hold of her, and she fell on her knees crying hysterically.

"I'm so sorry, Cailyssa, that you have to see me like this. It's so disgusting; I want to kill myself," Madison said through tear-filled eyes.

Terry jumped in. "Hey, girls, you look *great!* Madison, don't be embarrassed about being half-naked and covered with leaves. The boys always thought you were hot back at home, but now you look like a freaking supermodel. My God, you three are absolutely gorgeous. Can I have some of the water you've been drinking?"

At this comment, the three Amazons' bawling intensified.

"Terry, please don't say anything else," I interjected.

"But I was only trying to hel—"

"Sh! Terry, look at the water in the pools."

As they all turned to gaze at the water, Madison, Jessica, and Phoebe's reflections appeared. It was cruel! They were grotesque. Boils and scabs covered their backsides, and when they turned around to face the water, their faces could have appeared in any horror movie starring the undead.

"What the hell is going on?" Terry said.

I walked up to the edge of the water. "That is what they see; that is what they think of themselves. That is just *plain wrong*!" I said in my angriest voice.

Daemon stepped up to the edge of the water. "It is obviously the work of the dark lord, Speculus. He will rue the day he meets my sword!"

Phoebe ran up to the edge of the water. "See what we are? Run away from us, before it happens to you. When we came here, we heard voices calling us to drink from the waters. We thought it would make us beautiful and give us everlasting life. Look what it has done to us!"

Jessica joined her. "Hideous beasts are what we are. What sort of cruel joke is this? How could anybody be so mean?"

"Step *back*, everyone," I shouted, using my commanding voice and presence. When I got in this state, everybody listened and obeyed—partly in fear, but more due to the awe-inspiring power that emanated from me. Even Daemon took two steps back.

"Speculus!" I shouted across the pools of water as I held my hands at my sides, palms facing out toward the water. "Your cruel distortions end *now*! I will end them now, and when we meet I will end you! Hear me and feel fear, because you *really* pissed me off this time. Nobody messes with my friends!"

The air became cold, and the water slowly rose up in front of everyone. The perfect and terrible image of the dark lord appeared. He was in full bodily form, and his great wings were spread out before him. His handsome chiseled face was marked by a cruel grin as he crossed his arms and looked down. "Cailyssa Larkin, do you suppose I am some schoolboy that you can rid the world of by slapping a sneaker across my face at the mall? I have been to heaven and hell and have faced enemies far more formidable than an imbecilic teenage girl. Ask Daemon. He has done battle with me, and he knows I can crush you where you stand."

Daemon jumped out, drawing his blazing white sword. "I will meet you in battle in heaven or hell, and this time I will prevail!" he shouted at the dark lord.

"Relax, Daemon, I've got this," I said very calmly for someone who was facing such an evil foe.

Lord Speculus's voice boomed. "You see how I have reduced your friends to the sniveling, miserable wenches that they are? I will twist the reflection of all people in this world and in your own—until you all wallow in misery. You will then worship me and beg for redemption and my mercy."

I cocked my head. "Worship you? Worship *you*? I am going to kick your ass!" I mocked and taunted him.

"Maybe you should try your roundhouse kick to my head." Speculus laughed in jest.

"Oh no, I wouldn't do that to an *angel*. I have something much more appropriate in mind."

Speculus's evil laugh boomed across the water, sending spray everywhere. I held my ground with my palms facing the water. I dipped inside my mind and grabbed hold of the ribbon of time. My hands seemed to glow, and I began to very serenely adopt one of my favorite kung-fu postures: bagua, the crouching tiger. As I did so, my hands began to slowly trace a bright-blue ribbon of light between them.

Speculus stopped laughing. A hint of fear slid across his face. Speculus grabbed his black snake belt, and it turned into a long black knife—the head of the skull on its hilt. "Perhaps I should kill you and your sister now. Your trivial banter annoys me, and I have always enjoyed killing Larkins. I clearly remember when I dispatched your grandfather."

I paid no attention. I simply continued what I was doing, and the blue ribbon I was mending between my hands grew larger and into the shape of a tiger.

"You will not undo my spells, Cailyssa. If I was there in person, I would sever your head from your body."

"Not when I remain alive, old foe," Daemon said as he stood next to me.

In the next moment, everyone was looking at me—unsure what exactly happened. As the blue tiger dipped into the water, she seemed to look different: more graceful, more beautiful, and certainly more powerful than ever. Next, as the tiger entered the water, I did something that nobody expected. I knelt down and clasped my hands together—seeming to be in prayer. The bright-blue tiger was shimmering and tearing up the water in front of me.

Speculus screamed, "He cannot help you here! Those are the rules. Fend for yourself, you weakling!"

I continued kneeling and then slowly stood up. I adopted the crouching tiger position and began to kick and punch. The tiger fought the water in rhythm to my movements. The luminescent tiger grew terribly large. She tore at the water with tremendous force and shredded Speculus's reflection, dismantling his image into a million droplets of water. A tremendous explosion rocked the earth. Everyone was blown backward. Even Daemon was on the ground, covering his ears, and attempting to recover from the earsplitting boom.

Terry got up and dusted herself off. "Way to go, Cailyssa. That's kicking ass…I mean butt! The dark lord's not gonna mess with you now—but don't use the 'A word.' Mom and Dad always hated it if we swore; I…"

Before Terry could finish her sentence, I dropped to the ground. Everyone rushed to my aid, and Daemon was there first, placing his coat under my head. I awoke in a moment to the beaming faces of my loved ones around me. Daemon helped me to my feet and stood next to me to ensure I was steady.

"Uncle Spencer? Is he gone?" I asked.

"He is gone for now, but you must be careful when you use the ribbon to help you. It is simply unheard of for a Larkin of your age and experience to be able to conjure up such power. You could have died. Thank God that you're still here."

"Thanks, Uncle Spencer, I'll be more careful next time. Madison, Jessica, Phoebe, come here! I have something to show you," I said as my three closest friends timidly approached from the confines of the woods.

Phoebe spoke first. "Thanks, Cailyssa, I know we're too ugly to look at, so if you want to leave, no problem. Maybe we can—"

"Phoebe, stop babbling, and come up to the edge of the water—Madison and Jessica, you too. Come forward, please."

The three friends approached the edge of the lake and gazed down at their reflections—steadying themselves to see their hideous forms. Their eyes grew large, and some of the leaves fell from their bodies. Speculus had corrupted them by bending their reflection in the daytime to reflect unreal beauty, but at night he would turn them to ugly hags. All this was done to control their minds. But now they were no longer perfect supermodels or hags, but they were back to normal—still beautiful, stunning, and radiant—just as they were meant to be.

They all ran toward me, hugging me and weeping. "Thanks so much for changing us!" they all blurted out excitedly.

"Stop!" I screamed a bit too loudly. "You're missing the point here. I didn't change you."

Jessica said, "What do you mean you didn't change us? Now we look like our old selves! Too bad we're not supermodel gorgeous during the day...but—"

"Stop it!" I yelled, again too loudly. "You were *always* beautiful. That's the point! All the dark lord did was change the reflection. But *you* gave him the power to do it! He baited you and promised you unreal beauty. And you took it. You accepted his distorted gift. He used it and further corrupted you until you became the beast you saw. All the time, you were still you; *none of you ever changed a bit*! The only thing that *changed* was your perception of yourself."

Phoebe whimpered, "But Cailyssa, we're not supermodel gorgeous anymore. We're just—"

"Stop right there, Phoebe. I'll finish the sentence for you. You should say we're...*beautiful* just the way we are. That's how God made you, and that *is* truly beautiful. Nobody looks like a supermodel in real life. It's all airbrushed fantasy. Speculus knows that, and he preyed on your insecurity and desires. Be confidant and love yourself, and he will have no power over you."

Madison stepped up. "Cailyssa, you're a girl; you know that sometimes you just don't feel good about yourself. What are we supposed to do?"

"Madison, listen. You're only as beautiful as you think you are. When you finally come to realize and accept what you look like—you will then be truly happy."

"That's easier said than done, Cailyssa," Jessica retorted.

"Maybe you need someone to tell you about the perils of obsessing with perfectionistic beauty," I chimed back.

"We all know Daemon over there. You probably told him to tell us we're beautiful to prop up our worthless self-esteem," Madison said with her arms crossed.

"Actually, I had someone else in mind. Halodire, would you mind stepping out here for a moment? I wanted you to meet the three friends I have been talking to you about."

Halodire stepped forth, and the three girls melted with sheer adoration, as did all who met Halodire for the first time. Because he was so tall, he knelt before them on one knee and kissed each of their hands. "Dear ladies, you are all far more beautiful than Cailyssa had described. You each possess remarkable natural beauty, and I am fortunate to be in your presence."

"Hey, big guy, take the girls over to the grassy glen there and tell them your story. I'm sure they'll understand the curse of beauty in a whole new way."

I walked away with everyone else to make camp near Halodire and the three girls and noticed that hundreds of the Amazons had slowly approached and were peeking out of the tall grass.

I walked to the beach to be alone for a moment, and suddenly Daemon was in front of me. He stepped up, and in a rare moment of spontaneous affection, he grabbed me and hugged me firmly as if he was cradling the most precious thing in the world. Then he looked into my eyes, and I was mesmerized. For a fleeting second, Daemon's lips brushed mine.

I pulled my head back a bit. "Whoa, easy does it there, angel boy. I'm not used to you like this—not to say I don't like it," I said with my best coy smile.

"I was very proud of what you did today. I have seen many people deal with Speculus, but I have never seen anyone face him like you. Your skills in battle are formidable. I actually think I saw fear flash across his face," Daemon said.

"Thanks, Daemon, but after kissing me I was sort of hoping you were going to say something else. Really? Battle skills?"

Daemon stood tall and shouted, "I did not try to kiss you. I was only complimenting you as you deserved. And rightly so." Daemon appeared cold and took a step back.

"Ugh, you're impossible. How can an angel with infinite wisdom be a dumb knucklehead when it comes to simple human emotions? You don't try to kiss a girl and then compliment her about *fighting*!"

Demon stammered, "I...I...I only sought to..."

"I only sought to, I only sought to," I said, mocking him. I turned around and stormed off. "Good night, Daemon, and grow up. You have the emotional intelligence of a twelve-year-old!"

Daemon ran after me and spun me around, looking intently in my eyes. "I'm sorry. As your protector and guardian angel, certain feelings are...*unavailable* to me."

I responded, "Such as love? How could any being exist without love?"

"Cailyssa, if you hoped for me to say romantic things, I cannot. I'm sorry. My duties prevent me—"

"Then why the hell did you come up and try to lay a romantic kiss on me? Huh? And don't tell me you didn't feel it too. You love me, and deep inside you damn well know it. You're just too stupid to realize it."

Before Daemon could respond, I stormed off and curled up in my sleeping bag. The day's events overwhelmed me, and I looked forward to some rest. Thank God Cali came by and rested his head next to mine.

"Hi, Cali—you cute horse-dog—let's get to sleep. I've seen a vision. Ttocs will be here in the morning, and Phoebe is going to absolutely flip out when she sees him."

CHAPTER 20

STILL BEST FRIENDS

I woke up slowly the next morning, lying on my side, rubbing my eyes, and expecting to see the cute face of Cali before me. Instead, about ten feet away from me, I saw a pair of black boots.

"You freakishly weird man!" I yelled. "What are you doing there staring at me?"

"I hope I didn't wake you, Cailyssa. I was waiting here quietly while you were sleeping."

"You mean you were watching me sleep? You don't watch a girl sleep. What's the matter with you?"

In his softest voice, Daemon responded, "I'm sorry. I love watching you sleep, and I'm supposed to watch over you as your guardian angel."

I stood up and tried to compose myself. "Listen, Daemon, I don't want to start the morning off with a fight. But it's just not cool to stand and watch a girl sleep, and it kind of freaks me out. Do you know what I mean?"

"I am familiar with the term *freaks me out*, but I fail to see how a guardian angel watching over you should freak you out. It should give you a sense of safety and comfort to know that you're safe. Since I don't sleep, I often watch you sleep."

I looked up at Daemon and saw the true complexity of an angel. He was one of the most powerful beings in the universe, but he had the innocence, charm, and naïveté of a young boy when it came to emotions and girls.

At first I was mad. But when I walked up to him and looked at him, I began feeling sorry for him. I could see he was struggling to tell me something, and of course I knew what it was. "Daemon, take a walk with me while I stretch my legs."

As we walked, Daemon looked distressed. I desperately wanted to reach out and hold his hand, but I dared not.

"Cailyssa, I was waiting for you to wake because I wanted to apologize for my shameful behavior yesterday. I did not mean for our encounter to be romantic in any way."

"So you are admitting that you tried to kiss me?" I quickly responded.

"I am not!" Daemon retorted.

"So how do you explain that your lips just happened to brush against mine? Do you have an explanation for that—Mr. I-know-everything-in-the-universe-angel-boy?"

"Perhaps it was a mistake and I was standing too closely to you and had a momentary lapse in judgment," Daemon responded lamely.

"Daemon, listen. It's OK if you have feelings for me. It's only natural for us to be attracted to each other, OK?"

"Perhaps if I were not an angel that could be so, but—"

I blurted out, "So you're admitting that if you were not my guardian angel, we would have a relationship. *Right*?"

For once Daemon just stood there. I don't think he really knew what to say. I could see he was in great pain, and I walked up to him and held both his hands, looking up into his eyes.

"Daemon, can I ask you a question? And you have to be totally honest, promise?"

"You know I dread such questions, but if you must do so, go ahead."

I clasped Daemon's hands more securely and shook them in a loving way. I said softly, "Daemon, tell me honestly. You've been alive for thousands of years. Haven't you had a girlfriend or a partner of some sort?"

"No, Cailyssa, I have never been involved in a romantic relationship."

"That sounds like it must be a terribly lonely existence. I couldn't imagine that." I noticed Daemon's eyes looked away from me. I hugged him lightly and placed my hand and left ear on his chest so that I could hear his heartbeat. He wrapped his arms around me, and I could feel my best friend's anguish. He loved me and he knew it, but he was equally sure that we would never be together.

"Daemon, you know I have the ability to see the future. My power to do this has grown stronger every day. I know

I have seen a future where we could be together; you must know that this is true, too."

Daemon stood there proudly, unable to utter a sound. I looked up at his beautiful face, and a drop of moisture fell upon my cheek. My world exploded around me; I felt like I was falling into a vast abyss. I felt connected to Daemon in a way that I didn't think was possible. I held on to him tightly so that I didn't fall down. I suddenly understood from his perspective the great love he had for me. But sadly, he also believed that he was destined to be alone for eternity.

"Oh my God, Daemon, what just happened? I feel weak and fuzzy all over."

"Cailyssa, you have experienced the tear of an angel. I am embarrassed for my weakness. I lost control, and this has connected us in a way that is most intimate. When an angel sheds a tear and it touches someone, he shares part of his soul. That person then understands the angel in a very deep and special way. I believe you now know *exactly* how I feel." Daemon stepped back and gazed above my head.

"Daemon, that was very special to me. Don't let it worry you; I'll take care of everything."

"*That's* what I'm worried about," Daemon said as he looked down at me, raising his eyebrows and giving me a questioning look.

"No worries, angel boy! We have a lot of work to do here in Mirror World, and we can't let our relationship get in the way of our duties," I said this with great confidence, but I knew in the back of my mind that I loved this man and would always be with him. And of course I had a great plan to make this happen, but I wasn't ready to tell him about it yet.

"I don't believe I enjoy being called angel boy. Perhaps that is vernacular I am not familiar with." Daemon said sternly.

I cocked my head and did that cute smile that I knew Daemon always loved. "Hey, Daemon, you have something on your chin," I said as I pointed my finger at his chin. He looked down, and I flicked my hand up quickly and caught the tip of his nose.

Daemon smiled. "Cailyssa, you used to do that to me back when we were young children. You could always make me laugh!"

"So that means we're still best friends, right?" I quickly retorted.

"Of course we are, Cailyssa!" Daemon said with a bright smile.

"Remember what else I used to do to you when we were little?"

Before Daemon could form a reply, I lurched forward and grabbed the beautiful medallion Daemon kept on the top right of his tunic.

"Here now, Cailyssa, give that back to me!"

"If you want it back, you gotta catch me. You couldn't catch me then, and you still can't catch me now!" I shouted as I scampered away, using my specular skills to get ahead of Daemon. We ended up in the middle of the grassy clearing with all of the elves and Amazons watching this spectacle. They were all laughing as Daemon tried in vain to catch up to me. I finally stopped and held up the medallion. As Daemon reached out to get it, I tweaked him one more time and threw it straight up in the air. He finally caught it in his left hand and looked at me, smiling.

"Still best friends?" I raised my right hand for him to give me a high five.

"Of course, but I hate this human ritual of a high five," Daemon said, shaking his head.

Daemon slapped me a weak high five with a beautiful smile on his face. All of the elves and Amazons cheered. I'm not sure exactly what they were cheering about, but it sounded great to me. I walked away from Daemon and dipped into my specular skills, seeing my future self in a stunning white dress on my wedding day. I was running from the church with Daemon, and the crowd was cheering, just like a moment ago. I lost myself in this beautiful daydream.

Later I went to hang out with my friends. I needed some girl time. Madison, Jessica, and Phoebe were hanging out near the sea grass. They were all speaking with hushed voices to the Amazons and seemed to be pointing in the air. They all looked nervous.

"Hey, girls, what's going on? We all got some secrets to share or what?"

Suddenly, the Amazons disappeared back into the thick grass.

"Hey, Phoebe, what is it with these women? Every time I come near, they seem to run away."

"They're just scared, Cailyssa. They keep talking about this guy called Ttocs and how he's gonna be really mad since you changed the reflection in the water. Who is this Ttocs guy, anyway? Do you know him?"

"Phoebe, I don't know how to tell you this. But you know him better than any of us."

"Cailyssa, I don't even know how I got here. I don't know anyone here, and there is nowhere to get a pedicure. I can't even find a nail file!"

"Phoebe, some things about you just don't change, but that's what I love about you. Hey, P-girl, listen up. Remember how I always knew what was about to happen?" Madison and Jessica wandered over to listen in on the conversation. "To make a long story short, I *can* kinda see the future. I was brought here to Mirror World to defeat that guy you saw emerge from the lake. He is one bad dude. He's trying to bend everybody's reflection so he can ruin this world and our world back home. His name is Lord Speculus."

At the sound of his name, the Amazons began to panic and cry out as they tried to hide farther in the flora.

Using my commanding tone, I told Madison, Jessica, and Phoebe to ask the Amazons to come out and talk to me. We walked over to the edge of the thick grass, and reluctantly they began to emerge. There were many more than I had imagined. They were so good at hiding; I didn't realize that there must have been hundreds of them. But I couldn't understand why they were so scared. They seemed safe here in their idyllic little floral haven. They were also some of the most amazing-looking females I had ever seen. Not only were they beautiful, they were all extremely athletic and strong. When they emerged from the forest wearing only their green shorts and tops, it appeared to be a photo shoot for a fitness magazine. They were also tall, averaging over six feet. They walked with the grace and presence of panthers on the hunt for dinner.

"Phoebe, these gals are amazing. I can't believe they're so scared. They look like they could kick butt on any guy at our school," I whispered in her ear. "Since I'm a little slow on my nymph speech, could you ask them why they're all so petrified?"

My three girls walked up to the Amazons. They seemed to be accepted by them, since they had lived with them. Several of the Amazons who appeared to be leaders walked out and spoke, pointing to the sky, obviously with great agitation and worry. Phoebe walked back, ahead of the other two.

Phoebe whispered, "Here's the scoop, Cailyssa. Many years ago, the Amazons lived in freedom. Many of them were actually married to some big-shot guys: kings, great leaders, and long-lost heroes. They said they were highly valued as brides because they are descendants of the Amazons. I guess the Amazons were very proud, warrior-like women who also possessed amazing beauty to attract men. I mean, take a look at them. They all look beautiful and dangerous; guys would love that. When I look at them, I feel…inadequate."

I jumped in quickly. "Phoebe, don't go down that road. Finish the story."

Phoebe sighed but seemed to stand up a little prouder. "I guess they didn't live up to their Amazon heritage, and they let their powerful husbands abuse them and then send them here. Then the dark-lord dude offered them the chance to join his army. When they refused, he imprisoned them here so they could never leave."

"I don't see any walls or fences, Phoebe. How could they be imprisoned here?"

"Did you see that stream when you came in here? It circles this entire paradise to the ocean on both sides. If any of the Amazons try to cross that stream, they think they will die. One of their great leaders, Sariel, tried to cross that stream hundreds of years ago. They say when she touched the water. It sucked the life-force out of her, and she fell to the earth like a dried-up corpse. Her bones crumbled into ash as she hit the ground. Now they say some guy on a dragon flies by once each year and points out the lethal stream. They said he reminds them of their abusive husbands. He comes on a powerful dragon and insults and belittles them in any way he can. He's wicked mean!"

"Phoebe, tell them I'll help them. We all crossed the stream when we entered here, and nothing happened to us. It's a trick of the dark lord. Remind them of what I did when the dark lord appeared in the water. Ask them to join us in the fight against him," I said with great urgency.

Phoebe, Madison, and Jessica understood what I said and went up to the Amazons. The discussion seemed to become heated. I didn't know Phoebe could be so intense. It looked like she was really trying to push my point. Her hands were flipping up and down, and she seemed very frustrated. Jessica and Madison started yelling, and the Amazon leaders started yelling back at them. Then the Amazons turned their backs to us and walked away into the woods.

"Cailyssa," Phoebe yelled, "I can't believe it. They refused to help us in any way. They said we should leave and go fight the dark lord ourselves. They will not help. I can't believe such powerful women can be such wimps. It's like they've just *learned to be helpless!* I'll never let a man tell me what to do again or make me feel helpless."

"I'm glad you said that, Phoebe. Remember, you promised me at the mall that you would never date Scott again or let him abuse you. Remember that today!"

"What are you talking about, Cailyssa, why do you bring up Scott now?"

"Just remember what I said, Phoebe. I'll always be there to help you."

I took Phoebe's hand, and Jessica and Madison followed. We joined up with my gang, and it seemed like my girls knew everyone except the elves. I noticed that they gave Halodire some distance. I guessed that it was because he had told them his sad story about Narcissus. I hoped that they understood the lesson. I knew from my specular skills that it was extremely important for my three girls to feel confident and happy with themselves. They would soon be tested, and if they failed they might die.

I was brought out of my inner thoughts by the sound of Terry singing with the elves. She'd already taught them rap, and now she was teaching them some famous Beatles songs. The sight of all the elves and Terry singing "Twist and Shout" brought a smile to my face. Even Uncle Spencer's foot was tapping. Madison thought this was hilarious, and she joined in. That's what I always loved about my sister: she could always make the best of any situation. I bought her a T-shirt once that described her perfectly. On the back it said, "Instant party—just add water." She just had the ability to pump fun into any situation. That's why I sometimes called her "fun pumper." Today, however, my specular skills were telling me to worry more about what might happen to my little fun pumper. Ttocs and a dragon were on their way here, and I knew they would like nothing better than to take her back to the dark lord.

"Terry, come here for a sec. I want to talk to you."

"Hey, big sister, did you like the song? Look at Madison; she's adding a new level to my elfish band."

"I loved it, Terry. You're the best! But listen, I have something serious to talk to you about. Ttocs is on his way here today, and you have to promise me something."

"Sure, Cailyssa, anything. Whose butt do you want me to kick, anyway? My claws are really sharp, and I haven't had a chance to use them lately!"

"Terry you're *grounded*!" I shouted louder than I wanted to.

"You can't ground *me*, Cailyssa. You're not my parent! Besides, how you gonna keep me in my room for the weekend? We're in Mirror World, remember?" Terry said sharply.

"Terry, I'm sorry I screamed at you," I said. "But my visions of the future tell me you're in danger today. And by "grounded" I mean stay on the ground—no flying. I don't think you'll be doing much fighting today. I have a plan for dealing with Ttocs. But you have to promise me something. Cross your heart and hope to die. No flying under any circumstances. *No flying*. Got it?"

"Come on, Cailyssa." Terry was disappointed. "Is it just for today?"

"Just until I get rid of Ttocs—then you and Longtooth can go flying tomorrow anywhere you want. Sound good?"

"OK, Cailyssa. But if I'm on the ground and Ttocs or any of those raxs give me a hard time, I'm gonna slice them up like a hot knife through butter," Terry said as she unfurled her razor-sharp talons.

I grabbed Terry and gave her a big hug. I was always amazed how Terry could go from one extreme to the other. One second she was singing gleefully with a bunch of elves, and the next second she became a deadly weapon ready to slice and dice.

Terry retracted her talons and gave me a hug while she whispered in my ear, "Don't worry about me, Cailyssa. I'll be fine."

"Sure, Terry, sure. I know you'll be OK," I said to myself as Terry walked away to rejoin the singing elves. My head dipped into the ribbon of time to see the several futures awaiting me today. My stomach felt sick because in one of those futures, Terry was dead.

CHAPTER 21

FREEDOM AND FEAR

The afternoon of that same day brought a damp chill to the air. I wasn't sure if the dark lord was manipulating the weather or if I was just feeling the cold more because of the visions I had about Terry. My visions of the future were becoming *much* clearer to me now, but I was never sure which one was about to happen. When my visions of the future unfolded, some of them were good, and some were very, very bad.

Right now, as I dipped into my mind, I could see the two Nephilim warriors running through the forest toward us. They would be here soon. Nephilim are not big beastly guys, like the football players in my high school. They are giants! One Nephilim warrior could destroy an entire city back home. They looked like hairy men in medieval battle armor. They were massively muscled with extremely broad shoulders and large heavy bones. Each stood at least fifteen feet tall and must've weighed more than an elephant. The

Nephilim were mean, built for battle, and nearly indestructible. During battle they relished pulling the heads, arms, and legs off men and placing them in a pile. Later the arms and legs were roasted and devoured like chicken wings at a restaurant. The skulls of the men, women, and children they killed were boiled until only the bones remained. They were placed in bags according to size—the children being the smallest, of course. And they were used for decoration and a weird game that looked like a cross between baseball and bowling called *calva*, which is the Latin word for skull.

Why couldn't I have simple, beautiful visions about hanging with my best friends or going to the prom with a handsome young man? *No!* My head had to show me pictures of these stupid beasts tramping through the forests intent on messing with our skulls. *Damn*, some days I hated the responsibility of being Cailyssa.

Like a movie screen in my mind, I could see the Nephilim running through the forest, smashing trees in their paths. A shadow above them flew toward us—Ttocs on his new black-and-silver dragon leading a horde of raxs. I shut down this vision in my head and decided to rally my friends, knowing that some kind of ugly encounter was going to happen today.

Pulling my shoulders back and trying my best to look like a leader, I barked orders to all, preparing them for the arrival of our visitors. At the edge of the small stream that circled this beautiful land, we formed up in our skirmish line, ready to fight. I was at the front with Daemon, joined by Uncle Spencer and Halodire. Off to our right were Terry and Longtooth—who was watching Terry like a protective mother and scratching her claws in the dirt. I had taken a moment earlier in the morning and told Longtooth to watch out for my sister and stay on the ground with her. Behind us stood all the elves. They were dressed in their armor and were clanking their small swords against their shields. The Amazons were nowhere to be found. They were probably hiding in the forest.

A sharp cry was heard in the air, and the black-and-silver dragon that Ttocs was riding raced across the sky in front of us. The dragon unfurled its claws and spit a fireball onto the field across from the small stream in front of us. That scared Phoebe, Madison, and Jessica, and they ran up to stand behind me. As they did, the Nephilim warriors came crashing through the trees. They stopped about a hundred yards away in a grassy clearing across the small stream in front of us. They roared in anger and lit the field on fire. They pulled rocks from bags on their back to throw at us—except when I looked closely, those were not rocks—they were skulls. Phoebe was really going to flip out now.

"Holy crap!" shouted Phoebe. "Who lit the field on fire? And what are those horrible-looking things across from us near the forest?"

I put my arm around Phoebe's shoulder. "Pheebs, I'll explain this all later. For now, trust me. Stay strong, and do what you know is right. No matter what happens today, be brave, and *do what you know is right*! You have an important part in helping us win today."

"*What?* Me, help win a fight? I can't fight. You know *that*, Cailyssa. I'm so scared my knees are knocking, and I gotta pee really bad."

I grabbed both of Phoebe's hands and looked into her eyes. "You have a lot of friends here to help you. Let our strength help you."

I'm not sure what happened right then. It felt like tingling between our hands, and our hands seemed to be glowing. Phoebe's knees stopped shaking, and she stood up, proud and tall.

"Whoa, Cailyssa, thanks for whatever you just did. I feel something, but I'm not sure what. I think I feel *brave*. I'm usually so scared, especially around boys, but—"

Before Phoebe could mouth another word, Ttocs landed in the middle of the field, his black-and-silver dragon spewing fireballs from his nose. The dragon was by no means as big as Longtooth, but its eyes were lifeless, and it looked evil. An eerie silence enveloped the crowd. The wind stopped, and the cold, damp air crept in around us as if the fingers of death were attempting to drag us into their clutches.

Ttocs came forward on his dragon, adjusting his body armor and clanking his sharp boots against the armored scales of his dragon.

"Good afternoon, everyone. Isn't it such a beautiful day? Cannot you feel the cold chill of death upon you? The dark lord and I have brought this weather to remind you that your miserable lives are at our whim. And we may snuff out your pitiful lives at any moment we choose," Ttocs said boldly before breaking into a fit of laughter.

It was a good thing that Madison and Jessica and I stepped in front of Phoebe, because she almost fainted when she got a look at Ttocs's face.

Phoebe turned to me in shock. "Why did you bring my cruel boyfriend, Scott, here? What is going on? Am I in hell?"

"Phoebe, believe me, I did not bring Scott here, but I know who did. You had a glimpse of that evil angel yesterday in the water. By the way, as you might've guessed, you're looking at Ttocs. That's what your boyfriend Scott calls himself here. It's not hell; it's Mirror World."

Ttocs slowly made his way up to us, and his dragon stepped over the stream in front of us, making sure not to touch the water. All of this commotion had brought the Amazons out of the woods, and they were peeping out, watching in horror. Daemon's sword was blazing, and Terry was raking her claws on rocks. Both of them looked like they wanted to kill Ttocs on the spot.

"Hold your place everyone!" I bellowed. "Nobody move until I say so."

"I'm sure that doesn't pertain to me, Cailyssa," Ttocs said as he approached us, unfurling his mace and exposing the chains and skulls at the tip. He swung it around with his right hand. "I have come here to see my girl, Phoebe. Surely none of you would stop Phoebe from running up to me and worshiping this most *desirable male*."

"Leave me alone!" shouted Phoebe as she marched forward toward Ttocs. "I don't want any part of you! After the way you twisted my arm and humiliated me at the mall, do you think any girl in her right mind would still talk to you?"

"Dear Phoebe, my love," Ttocs said with great anger and disdain. "Surely you know how much you love and adore me *and* that your rightful place is here with me—*at my feet!*"

At that moment, Ttocs moved quickly and grabbed Phoebe's wrist. I told everybody to stand still. This was something Phoebe had to do alone. Phoebe tried as hard as she could to pull away, but she could not get out of his vicious grasp. His armored glove was biting into her wrist, and blood was dripping down her arm.

Ttocs flashed his evil smile at all of us. "I think Phoebe and I will take a little walk across the stream. Then you will see how this fat, useless pig wilts into a charred corpse. Let this be a lesson to all of you who dare to defy the dark lord!"

The Amazons could be heard crying in the forest as they saw Ttocs drag Phoebe into the stream where their great leader, Sariel, had died many years ago. The water was now up to Phoebe's knees, and Ttocs pulled harder, dragging her through up to her waist. But nothing happened! Ttocs dragged her across the stream to the other side. Phoebe arrived on dry land unscathed by the water. The Amazons gasped.

It was taking incredible willpower on my part not to interfere, but I knew Phoebe had to do this on her own.

Daemon, Terry, Longtooth, and the others also looked on anxiously, but they followed my lead and did not interfere.

Phoebe suddenly drew on an inner strength she didn't know she had and broke free of Ttocs's grasp. "Leave me alone!" she screamed at Ttocs. "No girl in her right mind would want an abusive loser like you for a boyfriend. Go crawl back into your cave and pet your filthy dragon. *You're the pig, not me!*" Phoebe spit in his face.

The Amazons walked out of the forest, amazed by what they'd just seen her do. Phoebe was not helpless; she was *strong!* And she crossed the stream of water—the same stream that had killed Sariel and the same stream they had feared to touch or cross for a thousand years! The Amazons were enraged, knowing that they had been confined here by the trickery of the dark lord. Then the Amazons did something that they had not done in many years. They grabbed their weapons and prepared to go to battle.

The phrase "nor hell a fury like a woman scorned" sprang to mind. The emboldened Amazons quickly dispatched the raxs army and had the fearsome Nephilim in full retreat.

Ttocs wasn't sure why the water didn't eat Phoebe alive like he thought it would. And now he was looking at a whole bunch of people who weren't scared of the water any longer and would quickly cross the water to skin his hide. Before anyone could catch him, Ttocs jumped on his dragon. The dragon reached out with its long claw and grabbed Phoebe as she walked back across the stream to join us. Everyone stood astounded and watched Phoebe being helplessly carried off into the sky with Ttocs and his dragon.

"No!" I screamed at Terry. But it was too late. My sister launched herself into the sky after the dragon, doing exactly what I feared she would do.

Terry raced toward Ttocs and the black-and-silver dragon, intent on rescuing Phoebe. Longtooth saw her shoot to the sky and quickly followed. "This is my fight, little one. Let me dispatch this miserable little dragon, and I promise I will save Phoebe. Go back on the ground as your sister instructed."

"Don't worry, Longtooth. You taught me well. I want Ttocs to feel the pain of my claws when I rake them across his back," Terry replied.

"Do not disobey me!" Longtooth spit fire at Terry, trying to stop her relentless pursuit of Ttocs.

Terry simply spiraled away and avoided the fireball. She knew Longtooth wouldn't really hit her. She pumped her wings harder and chased after the black-and-silver dragon. She flew straight up to the sun and came diving down at Ttocs with the sun to her back, which blinded them to her approach. She unfurled her claws. Her right hand sliced through Ttocs's armor and his back, and her left hand raked across the back end of the dragon. Both of them screamed as Terry's claws sliced through them and drew blood. The dragon and Ttocs were so shocked by this attack that the dragon dropped Phoebe. Longtooth saw her fall and knew that Phoebe would be dead if Longtooth did nothing. She flew across the sky and grabbed Phoebe, praying that Terry would be OK. Enraged, Ttocs and the black dragon spiraled back to pursue Terry.

Ttocs screamed at his dragon, "After her! I want you to send a fireball to roast that little Larkin alive."

Terry's battle-flying skills were indeed impressive. The black dragon and Ttocs could not keep up with her acrobatic flying. She dove backward, flying directly under the dragon, and raked his underbelly—the softest part of a dragon's armor. The dragon roared in pain, and Terry turned around to look at the damage she had caused. When she turned, Ttocs aimed his crossbow and shot a lethal dart at her. She easily avoided the dart by spiraling to the left. The dragon, recovering from his wounds, spit a fireball a second later. Terry swung to the right as quickly as she could to avoid the fireball. She thought she'd made it until she looked at the tip of her left wing, which was now on fire. The small difference in weight ruined the balance of her wings, and she spiraled to the earth out of control. She folded up her wings to put the fire out, but it was too late.

CHAPTER 22

A LESSON FROM DEATH

A moment after Terry's demise, Daemon saw Cailyssa suddenly fall to the ground. He checked her quickly for wounds, thinking that one of the shards from the skulls might have injured her. But he found no wounds. Cailyssa's eyes were closed, but when Daemon moved closer, he could see that her eyeballs were moving rapidly from left to right beneath her eyelids. She was alive and apparently uninjured. But Daemon could sense that her life-force was weak; she was near death! What had happened?

Daemon stroked her head lovingly. "Cailyssa, please answer me. Are you injured? Did you hit your head?"

No response. Daemon prayed and held her close for what seemed like an eternity. Cailyssa slowly opened her eyes and grabbed Daemon tightly. He did not let go. Cailyssa buried her head in his shoulder, and she cried and shook uncontrollably, obviously tortured by some internal agony. By now Uncle Spencer, Halodire, and all the elves were surrounding

Cailyssa. They all watched and felt her pain. These were the type of tears that came from the soul and could not easily be stopped or soothed.

Suddenly Cailyssa stood up, supported by Daemon. With great distress Cailyssa screamed through her tears, "Has anyone seen Terry?"

They all looked to each other in silence, shaking their heads, offering no answer. There was a commotion from the back of the crowd. The elves parted, and three people walked through: Madison, Jessica, and Phoebe, with Longtooth in the back.

Cailyssa cried out, "Longtooth, where's T—Terry?"

Longtooth walked forward slowly and lay down; her huge golden eyes were rimmed with sadness when she looked up from Cailyssa's feet.

"I fear I failed in my duties, Lady Cailyssa. Terry attacked Ttocs and the dragon, and she was winning. Then the dragon dropped Phoebe, and I had no choice but to catch her as she fell. I placed her upon the ground, and by the time I was back into the air, Terry was nowhere to be found. I circled overhead and searched, but there is no sign of her." As Longtooth said this, a great tear rolled from her eye. It turned to a crystal as it sank in the sand.

Cailyssa could barely form a word. She croaked out, "*Everyone*, go find her, please! Find her, please, for me?"

Everyone ran off to look, and Cailyssa buried her head in Daemon's shoulder. She was inconsolable, and not even the warmth and love of an angel could help her now. Darkness fell, and no one had found Terry. That night Cailyssa wasn't sure if she slept. It was like a living nightmare. She was trapped in her grief; her visions of the future were now gone. She had seen Terry die, but she had never believed that future would come true. Now it had! What was she to do? She closed her eyes, and the next moment she was back at home. It was so real.

It was the week before Christmas. She was still a little girl, and she and Terry were so excited. Their family always had such wonderful Christmases together. Terry, in her one-piece jammies, came into Cailyssa's room with her *Winnie the Pooh* book tucked under her arm.

"Sa-Sa?" Terry used the name she called Cailyssa when she was too young to say the full name. "Can you weed me da *Pooh* book in your bed?"

"Sure, Terry, climb up the steps!"

Terry's little body tried to scramble up the three steps to Cailyssa's high bed, but she slipped, falling back toward the hard floor. She'd be hurt! Cailyssa reached out and grabbed her arms, pulling her to safety. Terry snuggled up next to Cailyssa, not realizing the disaster she had narrowly missed, and her big sister read the book. Cailyssa sighed with relief. She was so big and strong; she could protect Terry from anything. Right?

"Again, again, again," Terry chirped, hoping to have Cailyssa read the story one more time.

"Not now, Terry, it's getting late, and Christmas is coming soon. We better get to bed."

"Otay," Terry said sadly. "Can we play Piglet and Pooh before we go to sleep, p-please?"

"Sure, Terry, I'll be Pooh, and you'll be Piglet—just like we always do…"

Terry climbed down and stood up straight—bright-eyed just like Piglet—and proudly said, "We'll be fwends forever, right, Pooh?"

Cailyssa walked toward the adorable little girl before her and held her hands. With deep love she replied with the line Terry loved so much. "Longer than that, Piglet, longer than that."

Cailyssa woke up and screamed at the top of her lungs. "No!"

She was back in Mirror World—no comforts of home, no *Winnie the Pooh*, no Terry. How could that be? How could she live? Her vision of Terry dying replayed in her mind and consumed her with grief. She saw Terry falling from the sky, her wings on fire, and then drowning under the waves of the ocean—cold and still.

With help from Daemon, Cailyssa slowly made her way back to the beach. Everyone was there, not saying a word. They had all searched through the night for Terry, with no success. They walked away, and only Daemon and Uncle Spencer stayed with Cailyssa.

When Cailyssa saw Uncle Spencer, she said, "Help me, please."

"If there was anything I could possibly do, Cailyssa, I would. You know I would die for Terry." Uncle Spencer moaned, unable to hold back his own tears.

"How can I explain this to my parents? I have to go home. I don't even know where her body is to have a funeral."

"We must stay and continue on, Cailyssa." Uncle Spencer tried to sound enthusiastic, but he knew it was a weak attempt.

"No way, Uncle Spencer. I'm all done with this Mirror World crap. Tell me how I can get home. I'm outta here—for good!" Cailyssa barked.

Cailyssa stormed away. She just wanted to be alone with her agony. She felt so overwhelmed emotionally. It felt as if somebody had reached down inside her and ripped something out, something that could never be replaced. Cailyssa sat down, hidden in the tall grass, with her back to a big rock. She pulled up her knees and put her head down. She tried to enter the ribbon of time and find Terry's body, but her skills were gone. She couldn't see the future anymore. Maybe she'd lost her powers. Who cared at this point anyway? Without Terry she couldn't go on. She staggered slowly back to camp and could see fires in the distance. The elves were making too much noise! Were they singing? How was that possible? Terry was dead, and the elves were having a party. As Cailyssa approached, she was sure she heard singing now. Enraged, Cailyssa ran up to the singing elves. She saw Daemon and Uncle Spencer run up, too.

"How can you possibly be singing at a time like this?" Cailyssa bellowed before anyone could say a word.

The elves turned to face her in silence; they always listened to Lady Cailyssa's orders.

"I can't believe you fools would sing at a time like this!" Cailyssa said as she noticed that a few drops of water had landed on her cheek. "This is a time of mourning, not singing." Cailyssa again noticed water lightly splashing on her cheek, and she wiped it off. "I am very disappointed in all of you and—" Before Cailyssa could finish her sentence, a whole bunch of water sprayed on her cheek. And the elves were giggling.

"How could you possibly be laughing at a time like this? What is this craziness?"

Before Cailyssa could utter another word, two small white wings—one burnt—shook behind her and absolutely soaked her with water. The elves roared with laughter.

Cailyssa was enraged and spun around screaming. "Who the hell is splashing…water?" Cailyssa's voice trailed off.

Behind her was Terry—soaking wet from head to toe! She stood there in her typical confident stance, hands on her hips and a mischievous expression on her face. Her wings were fluttering droplets of water, and her hands were shaped like two squirt guns—since she had pretended to squirt Cailyssa from behind, to the elves' great delight.

Cailyssa's emotional chemistry went berserk. An overwhelming flow of conflicted feelings engulfed her. Terry was alive! She felt pure joy and love for her sister, but that didn't last long because another emotion came far too quickly: anger. Cailyssa walked up to Terry and almost slapped her across the face but decided to punch her shoulder. Hard.

"Ow! Hey, that really hurt, Cailyssa. I'm back from the dead, and you're not even glad to see me?" Terry said rubbing her shoulder.

Cailyssa, red in the face, yelled much louder than she wanted to. "I told you *not* to fly! I told you! I told you! I knew what could happen." Cailyssa's emotions shifted, and the tears could not be held back. The two sisters reached out to each other and embraced.

Terry was the one crying now. "I know you told me not to fly, Cailyssa. I just couldn't help myself when I saw them snatch Phoebe."

"I thought you were dead. My visions told me you were. I can't understand why you're alive."

Terry spoke aloud for all to hear. "You see, I put a real hurtin' on Ttocs and the dragon. They were bleeding so much that they dropped Phoebe from the sky. Longtooth snagged her, and I went back to finish off the dragon. I tore his belly open, but he managed to burn the tip of my wing. When I fell from the sky, I angled my wings to land on the beach, but I didn't make it and fell in the ocean. The water put out the fire, and my wings helped me swim. I almost drowned, but I saw a light, and it felt like it pulled me to shore. I must've passed out when I crawled to the beach. Anyway, I can't fly until my wing heals, but man, can I swim fast!"

The crowd cheered upon hearing Terry's story. The elves worked very hard to have a wonderful banquet that night in honor of Terry's return. Their new friends, the Amazons, joined them, and they all became fast friends. After a day that felt like an emotional roller coaster, Terry and Cailyssa decided to go to bed early. As they left the party, their hands just fell together. The loving bond between two sisters was still there.

"Terry, you don't know what it was like for me when I thought you were dead. I mean, it was really bad. I don't think I can handle this again. You gotta be more careful," Cailyssa said as she crawled into her sleeping bag.

Terry slid into her sleeping bag next to Cailyssa. "Don't worry, Cailyssa. We're gonna be friends forever, right?" Terry reached out and held Cailyssa's hand. "This is like when we were little, Cailyssa—holding hands, reading *Winnie the Pooh* books." Terry giggled.

"Longer than that," Cailyssa said, finally feeling overwhelming joy that her sister was still alive.

Cailyssa sat up in her sleeping bag. "Terry! What made you think of *Winnie the Pooh* right now? I mean, after all these years, why right now?" Cailyssa whispered.

"Oh nothing, it was just a dream I must've had when I passed out after almost drowning. It felt so real. I'll tell you about it sometime. Good night."

Cailyssa looked to the stars, relishing the warmth of her sister's hand. She could feel the ribbon of time and knew that she could use her visions again. That could help her explain a lot. What she couldn't explain was how it was possible that she and Terry had shared the same dream. But then something struck her. Maybe it wasn't just a dream; it had felt far too real for both of them.

CHAPTER 23

ABODE OF THE DEAD

Atop of the Castle of Dark Mirrors, Lord Speculus was perched like a giant bird of prey on the highest point in the castle. In his crouched form, his enormous wings could be seen from the ground, and blazing flames now ringed his black eyes as he peered downward. The raxs, who looked up quickly, were horrified at the image above them. They quickly carried on with their work, hoping that the dark lord would not single them out for punishment.

Down below, Ttocs and his dragon headed into the castle, and the servants tended their wounds from Terry Larkin's attack. The Nephilim had just arrived, each holding their severed arms—which they had tied with vines as tourniquets to stop the bleeding. The Amazons had taken a hand from each. They staggered toward the castle, looking for a place to recover from the Amazon's blades.

The miserable Larkin sisters had again foiled the dark lord's plans—but how? Speculus had been sure that his plan would work. By now, fat Phoebe should be dead, the Amazons should again be living in fear, and Terry Larkin should be his prisoner. Who could have spoiled his plans? Certainly the Larkins were not this powerful!

Fury boiled within the dark lord's mind, and he stood up on the peak of his castle. He let out a savage cry, and the raxs below wailed in terror. He swooped down from his perch. As he approached the ground, he tucked in his wings and flew only a few feet above the earth. As he approached a group of raxs, he spiraled so fast that he was only a blur; the tips of his razor-sharp wings cut through the raxs, leaving only a pile of bloody meat. As he flew into the castle, the other raxs approached the hideous mound of their former comrades and began to squabble over the tasty, large chunks—leaving only the putrid entrails for the weaker raxs.

Lord Speculus was not feeling any better after venting his frustration on the raxs. He stormed into his castle, looking to further punish anyone he came across. Suddenly, a siren sounded in his mind. It was a sound he had not heard in many years. He stopped abruptly, his body frozen in fear. He dared not even move or breathe. How could this be? A faint whisper crept into his mind. He was right to be afraid. His master was calling him.

The dark lord walked with purpose to the sleeping chambers on the second floor of the castle, knowing what he would find inside. Ttocs was standing in front of the mirror, joyfully picking his nose. He had shed his battle armor and was now wearing only his underwear and his favorite AC/DC shirt, featuring their album *Highway to Hell*. The dark lord kicked open the door, and Ttocs spun around quickly—afraid—and wiped his finger across the front of the shirt.

"Picking one's snout has always been one of the most disgusting human habits I have observed," the dark lord said with great disdain. "At least you have a proper shirt on today. Follow me and say nothing, or I'll kill you where you stand."

The dark lord stormed out of the room and marched down the hall. Ttocs scrambled to put on his pants and shoes. He stumbled after the dark lord while attempting to snap his pants. The dark lord marched out the front door of the castle, and Ttocs did his best to keep pace with his master's stride.

"Master, where are we going? I wanted to expl—"

"Silence, you blabbering fool, and follow me!"

The dark lord grabbed Ttocs and pushed him forward. He stumbled and fell as the dark lord kicked and pushed him toward the end of the castle courtyard. Ttocs could see that they were heading straight for the river of death, and fear gripped him. He was sure that he was about to be thrown in the river because he had failed to capture Terry Larkin.

"Lord Speculus, please, please, don't kill me. I beg you." Groveling, he wrapped his arms around the leg of the dark lord and kissed the tops of his boots.

"You are indeed a pitiful creature. I should've selected another human to help me. Today you will not die, but when you discover where we are going, you'll wish you had." The dark lord shook his leg to free himself from the sniveling Ttocs.

Through the swirling mists, a raft slowly approached, guided by a black wraith. His long cloak clung tightly to his bony skeleton. The dark lord and Ttocs boarded the raft. Ttocs made sure to stay in the middle and not touch the waters below, fearing that the tormented souls drifting beneath would pull him to his doom. The wraith stopped rowing when they reached the middle of the river. A hideous laugh erupted from the wraith, and he turned around to look at Ttocs, pointing his bony finger at him while his laugh echoed louder across the water. The raft began to sink slowly, and Ttocs curled up like a baby and cried.

When Ttocs awoke, he opened his eyes and found that he was on dry land. He quickly checked all his body parts to see if any were missing and to make sure he had not shriveled up like the dead souls in the river. He found his feet and managed to stand up. The dark lord was nowhere to be found. He looked around, and fear crept through him. He was cold, colder than he had ever felt before, and he wrapped his arms around himself to stop the shivering. Where was he, and where was his master? He looked down at the cracked dirt below his feet and saw that smoke and steam were rising through each fissure. It appeared as though he was inside some type of volcano, and the hot lava was below. How could he feel so cold in a place so impossibly hot? He cried out for his master, but he heard nothing. Not knowing where to go, he crept forward, hoping to find someone who could help him.

Ttocs moved in a dreamlike trance, not knowing if he was going straight or in circles. He had felt fear before, but he had never felt anything like this. There were no words to describe this emptiness, this dread. This feeling was worse than death. He had to escape. He heard a noise and quickly turned around. Six red dots could be seen shaking back and forth and up and down. Maybe they were laser pointers wielded by people who knew the way out of here! As he walked toward the lights, a low growl erupted, and a hideous beast appeared from the blackness in front of him. It looked like a gigantic dog. Its black fur was matted, and Ttocs now realized that the six red dots were really blazing red eyes from each of the dog's three heads. Ttocs reeled in fear and ran backward, keeping his eyes on the accursed dog, hoping it would find another, more interesting meal. Ttocs backed into something hard. He turned around quickly and found that he was in front of the biggest stone door he had ever seen. Above the door he could see the words *Lasciate ogne speranza, voi ch'intrate*. His brain actually remembered reading about this in high school, and he understood. "Abandon all hope, ye who enter here." And he knew where he was, but he dared not go inside.

As he looked up, the stone gates transformed. There were faces of people, animals, and grotesque beings. They swam together in the stone, wallowing in agony and sorrow. The gates began to open. Ttocs turned to flee, but Cerberus—the three-headed hound—was behind him, snapping his jaws at Ttocs. Not knowing what to do, Ttocs ran through the gates, screaming in a high-pitched wail. He saw Speculus flying on ahead, and he ran headfirst into a huge rock.

He must have passed out because when he awoke he was on a hillside, and he could see a small house at the top of a hill in front of him. Where was he now? He looked around and saw that everything was gray—absolutely gray. There was no color anywhere on anything. He slowly walked up to the house before him. The front of the house was drab and gray, and there was a small door, blackened windows, and seemingly no one at home. Ttocs stood at the door, and the chill in his bones deepened. He felt as if all his feelings were being sucked. The door slowly opened, and he was forced to walk inside.

"Sit down. I will read your fortune," an old, scratchy voice crackled out to him.

Ttocs looked across the room. Although the house was small, it now felt as long as a bowling alley. At the end of the room sat an old woman gazing into a crystal ball.

"Don't just stand there. Come to me; come to me. Your fortune will be revealed to you," the old woman said in a singsong voice.

Ttocs wanted to run for his life but couldn't help himself. He slowly walked up to where the woman was seated. He could see her face. It was just as old and gray as this house and all of the surroundings. Her hair was gray, and her dress was gray.

"The future will be told to you; it will." She laughed lightly. "Place a nickel in the box for payment, and I—Zelda, the great fortune-teller—will tell you what I see in my crystal ball." She laughed again, but in a sinister manner, as she dramatically announced her name.

Ttocs didn't have any money, so he dipped his hand in his pocket and pretended to drop a nickel into the box. He stepped up to her table. He had a plan.

"OK, old hag, tell me my future, and tell me exactly how I get out of here," Ttocs bellowed.

For a moment the old lady did nothing. Then she burst into laughter. It was so unexpected that Ttocs jumped back.

"How do you get out of here? How do you get out of here? Young boy, you've always been here and always will be!" The lady laughed and choked upon her words.

"Just tell me how to get the hell out of here, and cut the crap. I don't want to smack an old lady on the side of the head," Ttocs screamed as he clenched his fists.

At that moment the old lady jumped up. Ttocs noticed that something was wrong with her. Her head was on backward, and her eyes were solid black—not a hint of white or any other color. She looked directly at Ttocs as she spoke, and Ttocs again felt weakness in his bladder as fear crept through him.

The old hag bellowed as if speaking to a crowd. "I was once the greatest fortune-teller in the *world*. People came from afar for Zelda to read their fortunes. But I never read a fortune." She paused and tilted her head, cracking her neck as she spoke in a loud whisper. "But I did tell them what they wanted to hear. They worshiped me and paid me handsomely. I cheated them, stole their money, and some I killed!" She laughed hysterically as she shuffled out from behind the desk toward Ttocs, who was frozen in place.

"Wonder why my head is backward and my haunches point toward you as I walk? Do you wonder why someone would be so cruel to Zelda? See the irony of my punishment! In life, I pretended to look forward, and now I shall always look back, spending eternity in this pitiful house alone. But enough of my story, it is time to reveal your story, for I *truly know* what is in your future." She began to laugh again, and this time her voice was a lot lower and a lot scarier.

"Give me your hand, and I will read your palm!" She intoned in a demonic voice that echoed throughout the house.

Ttocs stood unable to move, and her twisted body hobbled to him. She grabbed his hand and slowly began circling his palm with her right index finger.

Ttocs felt like he was in a vise; he couldn't move his hand. He couldn't move his body. She raised her head from his palm and grabbed his throat. Her large black eyes bore into him, and—to his amazement—she began to open her mouth. The inside was blacker than her eyes and grew enormous as she pulled him close and swallowed him whole.

When Ttocs awoke, he was on the floor of the dark lord's castle, covered with smelly saliva. He looked up at the throne, where Speculus was sitting and gazing down on him. "You are fortunate the old crone decided to spit you back here. For a minute I thought she liked you so much that she would keep you." The dark lord laughed.

Before Ttocs could utter a word, the dark lord stood and spoke harshly to him. "Do not ask me what just happened. Even one as stupid as you should know where we were. You were there before, as a small boy!" Speculus walked down the stairs. His back was now to Ttocs. "When you were young, I nursed you through the mirrors in your home, and I corrupted your soul. You looked into the mirror one day and begged me to make you powerful; in return for that, you promised me your soul. Yours is one of the many souls I have presented to my master."

"Your master? Do you mean the dev—?" Before Ttocs could get the words out of his mouth, the dark lord backhanded him, sending him flying across the room.

"That is one name by which he is known. There are others: Satanael, Prince of Darkness, Azazel, the Antichrist, the serpent. They are all incorrect. Most of the beings that deserved those names were simply demons, or perhaps lower-level angels that were given those names for the evil deeds they undertook. My master—the only true god—is omnipotent and beautiful, and he will one day rule everything! Did you know he was God's favorite angel? His angelic name is Lucifer, and he is truly the most perfect angel—even compared to me." Speculus sat back on his throne, looking up at a great mirror in the ceiling. "Your human history and religions distort my master's true purpose. He wanted to help humans to show them a different path, but God is cruel and does not take well to disagreement. He punished Lucifer by creating hell and sending him there. But I, and a third of *all* the angels in heaven, knew *God was wrong*! So we followed my master, because *he* will one day be the righteous one, and God will rue that day!"

Speculus's voice softened, and a smile slunk across his face. "While you were with Zelda, my master Lucifer gave me great knowledge. You see, I could not fathom how Cailyssa Larkin could foil my well-designed plans. Now I know that Lucifer was trying to test Cailyssa. He let Phoebe go free so that Terry would follow her. Terry should have died, but her sister saved her. My master and I were unsure of Cailyssa's powers. She seems to be able to use the ribbon of time for much more than seeing the future. She was somehow able to remove herself from her human body and travel the ribbon of time to save her sister. Now we know what we are dealing with! There hasn't been a Larkin who has ever been able to accomplish what she has at her young age. All Larkins who have left their bodies and traveled the ribbon of time to help someone have died in the attempt. Artemus died that way to help Daemon save his sons. We are dealing with an enemy who is far more powerful than I initially imagined. I have consulted with my master, and I have a plan. When we are successful, he has promised us both the most wonderful of rewards. He will allow us to leave this Mirror World and travel to earth. There, we will be treated like royalty, and we will be able to reshape that world in our own image. And do you know what that image is? Do you remember being in hell and feeling coldness, fear, and emptiness?"

Speculus flew up and hovered in the air, arms widespread. "You see, hell is the only place where there is a total absence of God. Isn't it a delightful feeling? Can you imagine how beautiful the earth will be when all the humans feel that, too?" As Speculus ended his speech, he flew out of the castle laughing with glee, hoping to visit the earth soon.

CHAPTER 24

CRAZY ANGEL

I woke up the next morning early and rolled over to see Terry's beautiful face just peeping out of her sleeping bag. I turned over to lie on my back, rethinking the events of the last few days, knowing how lucky I was to have my little sister alive. But I couldn't help thinking that maybe I'd made a mistake. I knew now that something miraculous had happened. I had sensed that Terry was dying and somehow—I'm not really sure how—I saved her. But I saved her when I was asleep, or at least passed out. I was all too sure that the dream about Winnie the Pooh was really about me pulling Terry from the water, not helping her to get back on the bed. I'm not sure *how* I did it. I knew it had something to do with my prescience skills and entering the ribbon of time, but I thought that all I could do was see the future. Don't get me wrong. That's a wonderful ability sometimes, but it seemed like I could do some other things—some other things that might just get me killed. The worst part was, every time I replayed this whole thing in my mind, I had this creepy feeling that somebody had set me up. Somebody was watching me do this and was very interested in my newfound abilities. It was probably the dark lord, but I wasn't sure why he would do that. I thought he wanted to kill Terry.

I didn't have time to deal with all this now. I had promised Longtooth and Dolhar that we would return to the dwarf mines on our way to the city of angels to try to get them to join us in our fight against the dark lord. We certainly could use all the help we could get. And I had a special plan to get the dwarfs to *see* things differently.

A few flicks of water almost hit my face, and a familiar giggle told me that Terry was awake behind me and was messing with me.

"Cailyssa, I hate when you do that. Can't you let a girl have a little fun sometimes? Just because you can see the future doesn't mean you have to duck out of the way right before the water hits you." Terry flicked the tip of her wings, and this time I accepted drops of water gracefully.

"Hey, big sister," Terry said somewhat sheepishly. "I'm not usually as good as you in talking out my emotions, but I have really thought about what happened the other day, and I wanted to say, uh…thanks. I was just thinking that I'm pretty lucky to have a big sister like you who's got some pretty amazing abilities. Of course, you'll never have my wings, razor-sharp talons, or my special style. But you're pretty cool in your own way," Terry said as she jogged off, shouting a quick "love you" in my direction.

I busied myself getting ready for the day, making sure to show appreciation to the elves for making us breakfast, and I told everybody that we were off to the dwarf mines. Dolhar was very happy. I knew how hard it was for him to leave his family the day Longtooth flew them away. In addition, he had some unfinished business there, and I was happy to help out. If it wasn't for Dolhar and Longtooth that day at the edge of the cliff, the raxs would've had us for lunch. They were some good friends to have in battle.

I was about to jump on top of my horse when Terry arrived behind me. "Cailyssa, I was just thinking. I'm always flying around, and I really should learn to ride a horse. Do you mind if I try yours today? He kinda reminds me of our dog back at home—I don't know why—but I just want to give him a big hug. Look at those chocolate-brown eyes!"

"No problem, Terry, take the horse. Maybe I'll go ask the elves for a lift," I said as I walked away.

Halodire had heard the conversation and cantered his horse over to us. He whispered, "Lady Cailyssa, I would be honored to offer you my horse. I'll walk beside Terry and teach her how to ride."

"Thanks, Halodire, but I can't let you walk all those miles. I'll just jump on in back of you, if you don't mind." I grabbed his shoulder and swung myself up behind him.

Halodire looked a bit nervous and began to stutter. "I'm not sure if this is a good idea. It's not that I—"

"Just start riding, big guy, and chill out. I'm not gonna bite you or anything."

"It's not you I am worried about, Cailyssa," Halodire replied anxiously.

I slapped the horse's butt, and Halodire and I shot forward. The weirdest thing was that when we passed Daemon, he looked at me on the horse and had the strangest expression on his face. I'm not sure what it was. His face was all scrunched up like he had a fly on his nose. Maybe it was nothing. Sometimes it's sure hard to figure out what an angel is experiencing. Just then I heard a loud yell, and Daemon's horse galloped away in front of us. I presumed he was going out as a scout or to check the road ahead. But why wouldn't he ask me? It was very unusual for him to leave without saying something. I shut down my specular skills because I wanted to stop worrying about analyzing every bit of the future. I'd figure out what Daemon was up to later.

"Hey, Halodire, thanks for the ride. There was no way I was gonna let you walk all day, and Terry will be fine on the horse." I looked over at Terry, who was bouncing up and down, trying to get the rhythm of riding. Halodire saw this too, and we both laughed as Terry cantered by, mumbling something about how bumpy horses were.

I had my arms wrapped around Halodire, sort of hugging his back as we rode. I looked up at his flawless blond hair. He was truly gorgeous, and I thought for a moment about my friend Madison and how jealous she must be. Just as I thought this, I turned around and saw Phoebe, Madison, and Jessica peeping out of the carriage driven by the elves. They were giggling and pointing at me. I then realized what this must look like.

"Listen, girls, I'm just getting a ride from Halodire. Terry took my horse for the day, and I needed a lift."

Madison looked incensed. "If you need a lift, Cailyssa, you can take my place in the wagon, and I'll be glad to ride with Halodire. But I'm sure you're not gonna give up your place. Tough choice isn't it? Ride in the wagon, or ride on the back of a horse with one of the hottest guys I've ever seen."

"That has nothing to do with it. I just needed a ride and…" I stopped talking as I looked at my girls and their faces. Nothing I could say would sway their opinion.

Maybe they were right. I did jump on without even asking Halodire. It's not like I am attracted to Halodire. Right? No way! I just needed a ride. Then I caught myself as I looked up at Halodire's perfectly chiseled cheek and jaw and had to admit to myself that he was beyond supermodel hotness. After all, he was once—and still is—Narcissus, the most desirable male in the world. Just as I was thinking this, Halodire turned his head and flashed that pearly white smile of his. My heart skipped a few beats, and I found it difficult to breathe. After all, I'm just a seventeen-year-old girl.

Halodire broke my trance as his smile quickly disappeared and his face grew sullen. "Cailyssa, please excuse my jovial mood. I shouldn't be smiling."

"I have to admit, Hal, I'm a bit confused. A person has the right to smile if he wants to."

"I stopped smiling when I saw Madison's face. It was obvious that she felt envious of you. I could see the disappointment in her eyes. She wanted to ride on the horse with me. You see, Cailyssa, I have seen that face a thousand times or more. Remember, I am the scoundrel who rejected suitors time and time again. I saw the look of rejection upon their faces and laughed at them in a scornful manner. It was a horrible and cruel thing I did. As you know, I was punished for a very long time."

"Listen, Hal, you offered me your services, and I accepted. But I gotta tell you, you've got to get over this guilt thing. It will eat you up. You made some mistakes; you paid the price. You asked God for forgiveness, and it was granted. Now it's time to move on. If I ever hear you start speaking again of all the mistakes you made, I will release you from my service. You are now ordered to start enjoying life!" I said with my most charismatic voice.

"I will do my best, Cailyssa. But it's difficult for me. I am sometimes not sure what to do." He looked down like a young boy.

"Hal, it's really easy. Just be yourself, be genuine, and be honest with people. That's all you can do. Just be yourself, and quit beating yourself up."

He raised his head and boldly said, "I will do my best, Lady Cailyssa."

I grunted back, somewhat annoyed. "Last thing—no more calling me Lady Cailyssa. Most people call me Cailyssa, or Lyssa for short."

Halodire let out a genuine laugh at this. It was good to see him in a better mood. I don't think I ever met a person, except Daemon, who harbored more guilt over what he had done. Speaking of guilt, I was starting to feel some of my own. I didn't want my girlfriends to think of me as some flirt.

How could they? Back at home I was one of the few girls who wasn't boy crazy. I rarely dated, and I always avoided the conversations when my friends were rating guys on the hotness scale. I was proud of myself for this. I despised seeing girls throwing themselves at the feet of boys or gaining their attention by flirting or dressing like tramps. It drove me crazy to imagine my friends might think that I was doing that now. I made a point in my mind to talk with them later.

We stopped for lunch and enjoyed each other's company and some good food. It was a beautiful spring day, the sun was shining, and the smell and feel of the beautiful forest felt refreshing. I saw Daemon sitting alone a few feet outside of the circle. I know he doesn't usually eat much; he's always drinking that angel-nectar stuff. But today he looked in an especially sullen mood. He was making no eye contact with anyone. Was it possible that he was actually pouting? He briefly made eye contact with me and looked away quickly as he kicked a small stone toward the forest. I guess angels can be moody just like anyone else.

Halodire came over and sat next to me. "Lady Cai—I mean Cailyssa—thank you for riding with me today. I have taken your advice, and I feel much happier. I am now focused on being genuine."

"Hal, that's great, but don't try too hard. If you try too hard to be yourself, you're not yourself. It has to come naturally, and hey, why are you so nervous?" I said as I shook my head.

"Of course, Cailyssa, you're absolutely right. It's just that I caught a glimpse of Daemon, and he is making me nervous. I don't think he appreciates me talking to you."

"Halodire, he's probably just being protective. You know how guardian angels can be."

"I'm not sure if it's just that—" Halodire stopped in midsentence.

"Come on; out with it. What do you mean?"

Halodire looked uncomfortable and whispered into my ear. "I believe that Daemon is jealous of my time with you, and I am worried that he may lose control and harm me."

I whispered back in Halodire's ear but in a commanding tone, "Listen, Hal, I talked to Daemon before about his bullying, and there is no way he is going to do something like that to you again."

"Thanks, Cailyssa, but I'm not so sure. I have seen Daemon when he loses his temper. It is a scary sight. I'm not sure if you realize how precarious his emotional state is. He is *not* always fully in control. He can be very dangerous."

"Oh come on, Hal. Daemon might get a bit grumpy at times, but he's not gonna hurt anybody," I said assuredly.

"Maybe not you, but the way he just glanced at me was definitely one of those if-looks-could-kill moments. Nonetheless, I am very glad to be here talking with you. You don't treat me like a servant, which I am. You treat me with respect and friendship, and I truly appreciate that. In some ways you and I are kindred souls, both suffering and lonely."

I replied angrily, "Whoa, don't throw me in the suffering and lonely camp with you!"

"Dear Cailyssa, I meant no offense. But it must be so hard for you. I see how you look at Daemon, and I know you have feelings for him. So it must be difficult to know that the thing you most greatly desire will never be within your grasp. I don't want you to be alone like me. You deserve to be loved, and you must find someone other than Daemon to share your life with."

I snapped. "I am really sick and tired of you, Uncle Spencer, and everybody else telling me what I can do." I stood up, saying far too loudly, "I am the *only* one who can see the future around here. Don't you think *I* might have a clue about my own future?"

"My apologies again, Cailyssa, just be careful. Daemon can be very dangerous. He would never wound you, but nothing could hurt you more than breaking your heart."

I was getting a little tired of this emotionally thick conversation, and I was feeling a little bratty anyway, so I jumped up and pointed with my finger toward the forest. "Halodire, quick! Look, a raxs!"

Halodire jumped up and spun around, and I yanked the back of his shirt open and poured the cold water in my canteen down his back. You should've heard him yell in surprise. I laughed and jogged off to the horses. Halodire quickly followed, unscrewing his canteen, hoping to get some payback. When he caught up to me, he grabbed the back of my shirt and started sprinkling the water on my head. Since he is seven feet tall, I had no chance of jumping up and grabbing the canteen, so I grabbed him under the armpits and tickled as hard as I could. He howled even louder than when the water got him. Who knew that a giant-size elf was extremely ticklish?

Just then Daemon stomped on up to us. "What devilry is going on here? If you are hurting Cailyssa, Halodire, I will—"

"Chill out, Daemon." I quickly cut him off. "We're just having a little *fun* here. It looks like you could use a little fun too, judging by the pouty little face you have screwed on."

Daemon's face turned bright red, and he just stood there not knowing what to say.

"Come on, Halodire. I'm riding on your horse again this afternoon." I said feeling a bit of guilt.

Halodire ran away from Daemon and jumped up on his horse, and I jumped on the back. As I rode away, I looked back at Daemon, who was just standing there and not uttering a word. His face was as red as a tomato. It looked like he just might explode.

As we rode on, Uncle Spencer came to my side. His horse trotted beside me, and I knew he wanted to say something. "What's up, Uncle Spencer? Looks like you have something on your mind," I said in a bratty little tone.

"Cailyssa, perhaps this bantering with Halodire is fun and distracting. But if the purpose behind this is to anger

Daemon, I would be very disappointed in you. It's not proper to torment a tutelary angel whose sole purpose in life is to protect you."

All of a sudden the icy-cold grip of guilt crawled up my back. What was I doing? Was I really doing this to make Daemon jealous? That was definitely not me, and it's definitely not the girl I want to be. Just then Daemon's horse rode by at a furious gallop, and he charged into the woods. He disappeared quickly. Halodire freaked. He jumped off the horse and ran as fast as he could to the wagon the elves were pulling. He jumped inside the wagon and hid under the canvas. I could hear the giggling from Madison, who was certainly happy to have this beautiful man within her grasp.

I took control of the horse and rode up to the wagon. "Halodire, what is going on? Get out here and tell me why you ran off like that."

Halodire replied from under a blanket, where I could tell he was shaking with fear. "Lady Cailyssa, I am hiding in the wagon. Please don't tell Daemon where I am. I saw the look in his eyes as he charged past us. He is in the zone of fury and cannot control himself. If he gets anywhere near me, I'm sure he will kill me. I warned you about how dangerous he could be!"

"Aw, come on, Hal. Just because Daemon might be a little jealous doesn't mean he's gonna lose his mind and kill anybody."

"Lady Cailyssa, I wouldn't be so sure of that. I'm not sure if you've ever seen him when he—"

Before Halodire could finish his sentence, the elves screamed, and an enormous tree flew over our heads. Everyone stopped for a moment. There was complete silence. Then a furious chopping sound came from the forest, and tree after tree flew through the air. It sounded like a million crazy lumberjacks were chopping trees and catapulting them into the air. I engaged my specular skills, and I could see what was going to happen. I was shocked. I rode as fast as I could. Trees were flying in every direction. A wide swath of the thick forest was reduced to nothing but tree stumps. In the middle stood Daemon, his white sword severing a tree in one slice. Before the tree could fall, he grabbed it with one hand and launched it through the air as if it were a javelin. I rode up to Daemon. He didn't see me coming, and one of the trees flew close to my head.

I screamed. "Daemon, you almost killed me with that tree. Stop! What the hell are you doing? Have you lost your mind?"

Daemon turned around holding his white sword. He was wearing only his black leather pants, and he was...glowing! His face looked scary. This was the zone of fury that Halodire had warned me about. I knew he wouldn't hurt me, but he projected such rage and power that I was really frightened. Sometimes I forgot that he was one of the most powerful angels. Then it *hit* me! I thought of what I had done with

Halodire. Could I have caused this? I jumped off my horse. My hands came to my face. I was ashamed. When I peeked out between my fingers, Daemon was standing in front of me. He had resheathed his sword. He was still angry but not glowing.

"Cailyssa," Daemon said sternly as he looked over the top of my head, not connecting with my eyes. "I should not have lost control. My emotions got the best of me, and I apologize. But I do not appreciate being toyed with. Your overly flirtatious game with Halodire was obvious to all. It is certainly beneath you to stoop to such a level!"

Now *I* was a bit angry. "Daemon, don't you think you're taking this jealousy thing a little bit too far? Chopping and throwing trees at people is not a normal way to handle jealousy."

"Jealousy?" Daemon screamed at me. "Is *that* what you think this was about?" Daemon then paused, crossed his arms scornfully, and said, "Don't kid yourself, Cailyssa. I am not some boy infatuated with you! In my lifetimes, I've had thousands of beautiful females beg me to wed them. I was angry because I was disgusted with your behavior. You were acting like a traipse!"

"What? What did you just call me?" I shot back angrily.

Daemon stood there, looking very cocky. "I said you were acting like a traipse! A tramp! It is one thing to behave in a playful and alluring manner. But you were acting in a disgustingly flirtatious manner with Halodire, purposely flaunting yourself and throwing it in my face. It is far beneath you to behave in such a manner. And I'm very disappointed."

My hands balled up into fists, and I used my semi controlled screaming voice. "I can't believe you. You can't even admit it, can you? *You* were jealous, and now you're blaming it all on me. I was having a little fun with Halodire, and you can't handle it." I got louder and angrier. "Who are *you* to say that you're disappointed in *my* behavior? I don't care if you're an angel with a thousand ex-girlfriends. You're obviously a *boy* incapable of emotional control. You feel a bit jealous, you lose control, and you start chopping down trees in the forest. Suppose I was attacked while you were out chopping? Huh? I'm the one who's *disappointed*! You're supposed to be a guardian angel, not a jealous lumberjack who can't control himself!"

The look on Daemon's face was hard to bear or to understand. I never saw an angel really swell with emotion. His face contorted in rage, confusion, sadness, and finally, deep despair. He walked away from me slowly, not saying a word, back to his horse. The V-shaped wound on his back started dripping blood as he strode away.

Then my face contorted into despair and guilt. My stomach felt weak, and I almost threw up. What did I do? How could I keep hurting the man I loved more than anything? He would give his life for me without a second thought! Was I really that selfish? If I couldn't have him, would I stoop to torturing him by flirting in his face? My father always said, "Do things you're proud of Cailyssa. You'll always feel good about yourself if you do." Right then, I didn't feel proud. I felt shame. I was there to do a job, save the world and everything, and I was acting like a childish girl who only cared if she had a date on Friday night. This had to stop. I *needed* to talk to Daemon!

CHAPTER 25

TRUST IN KINDNESS

That night I tried to fall asleep curled up in my sleeping bag. From a distance I could see the outline of Daemon on a hill near me. I felt like I didn't deserve him. Every night he watched over me as I slept—forever keeping me safe—even after the way I treated him. The guilt crept up inside me, and the sniffling and tears almost broke out of me. I slept fitfully that night. The next morning I awoke with a cloud of guilt hovering over my head. As I reflected upon the events of the previous day, I honestly didn't even want to leave the security of my sleeping bag. Couldn't I just bury my head in the pillow and avoid Daemon today? As soon as the thoughts from what happened the previous day hit me, I felt like a dark, gloomy cloud was over me.

"Come on, Cailyssa, you can't stay scrunched up in that bag all day," Terry said as she knelt down behind me and rubbed my shoulder. "Try to put yesterday out of your mind. Those things just happen. We're all a little bit stressed out.

I mean, we could get killed at any moment and become a chicken wing for those Nephilim. It's no wonder that we have a little emotional upheaval."

I sat up fast in my sleeping bag, mumbling, "Did you hear what Daemon and I were saying?"

"Uh, well, maybe just a tiny bit. I was worried when you ran off alone to the forest, so I kinda flew overhead just to make sure you were OK. I didn't mean to eavesdrop. I'm the only one who heard you, but everybody else knew there was a lot of yelling going on."

"Terry, I'm not mad. Thanks for looking out for me. I'm so embarrassed. I'm supposed to be the proud leader here, and I looked like a flirtatious tramp," I said sadly.

"Whoa, Cailyssa, stop right there! You were not a flirtatious tramp! Pouring a little water and tickling the big guy were teasing—all in good fun! It's not like you were trying to get him to kiss you. Maybe it wasn't the best idea to do it in front of Daemon, but hey—I gotta tell you—Daemon lost it! No one should get that jealous and mad over a little, stupid water fun. That's a bit much, don't you think? You're being way too hard on yourself." Terry put her hands on her hips. "Here's my take on the whole situation. *Clearly*, you and Daemon are absolutely in love with each other—and, in my opinion, a perfect match. Everybody knows it; everybody sees it. So stop denying it and treating each other badly. You two just need to chillax and get over the hump. Go *make out* or something 'cause…Well, we can't stand it anymore!"

"I wish it were that easy, Terry, but he's a guardian angel and all. It's not like he's just some boy at our school," I said sadly.

Terry wasn't buying what I was selling! She raised her eyebrows in disbelief, took a deep sigh, and grunted loudly before she continued. "There you go again, Cailyssa, making a big deal out of a simple thing. Here's the dealio; now listen up! When two beings are in love, I don't think it matters much if they are angels, humans, or llamas. When people love each other, they take *care* of each other! You know what Mom and Dad always said: *care shows love, and love multiplies the joys and divides the sorrows!* So cut the crap, and start taking care of Daemon; you know he's always gonna take care of you! Let's go. Time to eat. I can't wait to visit the dwarf lands today!"

I jumped up, grabbed my little sister, and gave her a great big hug. "You know, you're a lot like Uncle Spencer. You know the right thing to say. And you're certainly not afraid to say it, but that's what I love about you."

"No problem, Lyssa," Terry said as she jokingly punched me in the arm.

I went down to breakfast, and I saw everybody eating and talking in the distance. I felt disappointed in myself, and I was embarrassed to have everyone see me. But I stood up tall and proud and vowed to myself to make this a different day. As I quickly stepped around a tree, I bumped right into Daemon. I think I startled him a bit, and he turned around.

We looked at each other with our eyes wide open and the drumbeat of our hearts thumping loudly. But neither one of us could say a word. I wanted to apologize, but every time I tried, my mouth just hung open. Daemon seemed to be doing the same thing. He was breathing quickly, but he couldn't form a word.

I swallowed my nervousness, and finally my voice softly croaked out. "G-Good morning, Daemon."

"Uh…good morning, Cailyssa," Daemon said as he bowed slightly toward me as a small warm smile began to form on his face.

"Daemon, I acted pretty badly, and I wanted to say I'm—"

"No, Cailyssa, it is I who must apologize," Daemon blurted out. "I failed in my responsibilities, and I am very sorry." He held out his hands, palms open, toward me. I gently placed my hands on top of his and immediately felt the warmth of his touch. His hands closed around mine, and he slowly pulled them toward his heart as he kissed them gently. He looked into my eyes, and I felt as though my heart would explode out of my chest! We stood there, our lips inches apart. I was melting inside.

I blinked, embarrassed, and said, "I'm so sorry, Daemon. It's my fault the whole thing happened, not yours. I would never want to do anything to hurt you."

"No, Cailyssa, it is my fault. An angel needs to be better than—"

"Let's not argue any more about whose fault it is," I said as I clasped his hands a bit tighter, knowing that I sounded like an emotional wreck. "I just want my best friend and my guardian angel back."

Before I could blubber another word or do anything, Daemon enveloped me in the warmest hug imaginable. I buried my head in the side of his neck and held on, hoping this dream would never end. We squeezed each other tightly and rocked in a loving embrace for a long time. I did not look up at his face, knowing that I would kiss this most beautiful man right on the spot. I felt him sigh, and the wonderful aroma from where my nose was buried into his chest and neck made me weak in the knees.

I finally whispered in his ear, "Daemon, is this the most perfect feeling in the whole world?"

For a moment I did not hear any response. He wouldn't leave me hanging, would he? Then, slowly, his hands slid up my back, and he pulled me closer to him. I could feel the side of his face brush against mine, his lips sliding slowly from my ear across my cheek.

Daemon's deep, husky voice whispered. "Um…yes, Lyssa, it certainly is."

He turned and kissed me gently on the cheek. I totally melted. My whole body was filled with a feeling so strong that I almost fell backward. I think Daemon noticed and grabbed my hand. He led me slowly down the forest path to breakfast. All I could think of was how I wished this was the aisle of the church, and we were heading to the wedding reception.

Breakfast was wonderful as usual, but what felt better was that I thought—or I hoped—that Daemon and I had a better understanding of each other. I used my specular skills and looked at what appeared to be in our future for today. This was going to be an interesting day! I hoped it would end as well as it was starting.

I told Uncle Spencer to take all of the elves to the outskirts of Constantine, the city of angels, and we would meet them there in a couple of days. Daemon and I would be riding to the dwarf lands today. Dolhar, Longtooth, and Terry would fly and meet us there. I had a special mission for us. Camp broke, and I noticed that Terry was galloping away with my horse with Longtooth flying overhead. What the heck? When I turned around, Daemon had already prepared his horse for me and was waiting to help me up.

"If you think I'm gonna ride your horse and make you walk, you're one *crazy* angel." I smirked at Daemon and pushed his right shoulder playfully.

"Is your horse strong enough to carry us both, or are you just too scared to ride with me next to you?" I winked at Daemon, trying to actually use what little beauty I had to pull off the wink.

The strangest thing happened. Daemon's head rocked back as he smiled broadly. He seemed about as excited as I think I had ever seen him. He jumped up from behind the horse from where he was standing. And let me tell you, if you've never seen an angel jump up on a horse, it is done with such grace and beauty that you'd think it was like sliding a feather on top of the saddle. He then reached out his hand to me with a dazzling smile. I just stood there for a moment, looking at this sight in front of me. Here was prince charming, offering me a ride on his horse to live happily ever after. Nope! Got that one wrong! This was even better! This was the most perfect male angel in the universe, and he wanted me! I didn't think a girl got luckier than this.

Knowing that I had him in my power, I tried to use that coy smile again, and I stood there for a moment just to cause a little drama, hoping he might think I might not take his hand.

I slowly reached out my hand and said, "Thank you, Daemon, I would love to!"

He swung me into the saddle in front of him. I assumed I'd be riding in the back. He grabbed the reins of the horse, and his strong arms enveloped me as we rode off to the dwarf lands. My only hope at this point was that it would take us about five hundred years to get there.

I knew we had arrived in the dwarf lands, since the mountains loomed ahead. These mountains were more spectacular than anything I had ever seen. They began with a beautiful blue-and-green cascade of hills that turned into mighty snowcapped peaks. The highest mountain peaks had no snow at all, and it looked like they had been clipped by a mighty storm and had lost the tip of their white hats. We would be traveling through these mountains on a narrow pass to see the dwarfs who lived here. As our horse slowly cantered through the rocky path, I looked up and saw large breaches in the mountains to each side. It looked as though a mighty hand had come down from the sky and clawed deep rows out of solid rock. I knew from my visions that this had once been the beautiful mining community of the dwarfs. Thousands of them had once lived here happily—until Speculus twisted their reflections in all of the lakes that adorned these mighty mountains. When a dwarf looked into a lake, he hated himself. The dwarfs fell into great despair. Then Speculus and Ttocs, with an army of raxs, came and took all the women and children. The remnants of this once-great community now lived in just one mountain, digging coal for the dark lord's furnaces. I felt a knot in the pit of my stomach when I looked ahead to meeting my old friend Yllib and all the dwarfs. Suddenly a loud scream brought me back to reality.

"Whee-hoo!" It was Terry doing her best to imitate a jet doing a flyby over my head.

She zoomed overhead, and I could not believe how fast she was soaring; did that girl have wings, or what? Just then I discovered why she was flying so fast. Traveling close behind her—snapping her jaws in a playful manner at the tips of Terry's feet—was Longtooth, with Dolhar on her back. Dolhar's bushy beard was flying in the wind, and he looked as happy as a young boy on a roller coaster. I came to appreciate the size and strength of Longtooth when she passed overhead. She blotted out the entire sky, and I felt like a jet airplane was about to snip the top of my head. As they flew away, they both began to gain altitude, and they spiraled into the sky with great acrobatic skills. It looked very cool. I was also very happy to have my own lethal, private air force, in case Ttocs came by with his evil dragon. Daemon and I stopped up ahead, and I didn't want to get off the horse and leave my cozy spot between his arms. Daemon jumped down and gracefully placed his cloak over the puddle there.

"Daemon, did you just toss your cloak over a puddle so I wouldn't step in it?" I said with great surprise.

"Of course I did, Cailyssa. It's what any decent gentleman would do," Daemon said as he stood proudly.

I wasn't quite sure what to say or do until a scene from an old movie flashed in my mind. "OK, Daemon, I did see that in an old movie. I guess it's kind of nice to know that there are a few gentlemen left in this world," I said as I jumped off the horse.

Of course I had to step on the cloak just to make it look useful, but the tough girl part of me wanted to jump over the puddle. Daemon held my hand, and I walked across the small puddle. He quickly gathered his cloak and shook it once. Of course, since it was angel cloth, it never even got wet. There were certain advantages to having heavenly clothing.

"Hey, Daemon and Lyssa!" Terry said as she made one of her typical graceful landings in front of us.

Good thing I have visions of the future because I braced myself for the small earthquake that was about to happen. Even Daemon braced himself against the rocks when the earth shook. It wasn't technically an earthquake; it was a seventy-five-foot red dragon landing behind us.

"Lady Cailyssa," Dolhar shouted as he slid gracefully down Longtooth's neck. "It is with great pleasure that I am here to accompany you on your journey through the mountain. I am proud to be your guide and protector!" Dolhar bowed before me.

"Master dwarf, it is my pleasure to have such a brave and handsome dwarf as my guide," I said.

Dolhar was blushing a bit. He stammered and cleared his throat. "Milady." He pointed his hand toward the entrance to an enormous cave.

A small fireball erupted over the top of the cave entrance, and we all turned around, knowing that Longtooth wanted to gain our attention. Her eyes bore down on us as she walked forward, and we all felt like small children being lectured by a gigantic dragon teacher.

"I will find no pleasure here! Of course my girth will not permit me to enter the mountain caves with you, but I don't like to leave you unprotected—especially my flying partner, Terry," Longtooth said. She stood up on her back legs and crossed her arms in front of her.

Terry jumped forward and flew up into her arms to give her a big hug. "Don't worry, Auntie L, we'll be fine. And I promise to fly with you when we get to the other side of the mountain at daybreak tomorrow," Terry said as she slowly fluttered her wings and landed back on the ground.

We entered the cave, leaving Longtooth behind. Dolhar led the way.

"Terry, did I hear you just call Longtooth *Auntie L*?" I said with great curiosity.

"Yeah, why? That's my nickname for her. She kind of adopted me, and since we're family, she told me I could call her that."

Dolhar said, "That is quite an honor, Terry. Any other being would be roasted alive had they attempted to address Longtooth in that manner. I noticed when we were flying today you seemed to be communicating without saying a word. I suspect that she has shown you her heart, which is an experience few people have ever had."

Terry beamed with pride, and I made a note to myself to ask her later what this was all about. Right now I had to focus my attention on looking ahead to the future. My visions told me that not everything in this cave was friendly, and I wanted to make sure we got through in one piece.

Dolhar was surely in his element here. He told a long-winded story about how the dwarfs had hewn this tunnel out of solid rock. It made me really appreciate how tough these little guys were. Dwarfs were short; five feet was considered tall among them. But they were extremely sturdy and very heavy. For some reason they were blessed with an extremely long life and incredible density. Even the smallest of them weighed over five hundred pounds. Their legs and arms were massive, and they could wield a twenty-pound ax so swiftly that it could cut through solid rock. They were also amazing metallurgists, and they used the titanium they dug from these hills to build their axes. Some of the axes were even tipped with diamonds. Dolhar told us that no rock could withstand a blow from a dwarf's diamond-bladed ax. As Dolhar said this, I remembered my job was to convince the dwarfs who lived here to join me in our battle against Lord Speculus. It would be a great advantage to have the dwarfs on our side in the battle against him.

As we continued to walk through the cave, the opening became quite narrow, and we faced a labyrinth of tunnels with no light. Dolhar grabbed a flint, and with one strike he lit a torch that had been left there from years past. He found a few more, lit them, and passed them around. When all our torches were lit, we realized what the crunching had been beneath our feet: bones!

"Dolhar!" screamed Terry. "I've been walking on top of bones all this time? I thought they were just leaves or something. Is there anything in these tunnels that we should be worried about?"

"Bones, bones, bones, left from small vermin a thousand years ago. Have no worry. Dolhar is here to protect you!" he said proudly.

"But Dolhar," I protested. "My visions have told me that there are creatures still alive in these tunnels and that we could run into a few. Don't you think—"

Dolhar interrupted, "Lady Cailyssa, the snargulls will give us no problem. There's probably very few left of them anyway. Besides, they haven't eaten a dwarf in many years. They don't like the taste of male flesh."

Terry stopped for a moment. "Master dwarf, in case you haven't noticed, Cailyssa and I are *fe*male! Are you telling me they only eat females?"

Dolhar looked a bit confused and stuttered. "Ah…forgive me, forgive me, of course, of course. It is true that the snargulls only eat females. You see, about five hundred years ago when the dwarfs dwelt in these caves, Speculus took all of the females, so I had almost forgotten about the female gender. And now you have me worried. The snargulls gave up eating dwarfs since they detest the smell of a male. Uh…but they can become extremely interested if they catch the smell of you lovely ladies," Dolhar said as he readied his ax and walked ahead of us to ensure our safety.

"Hey, everyone," Terry blurted. "Look at this over here. It's the cutest little thing in the whole world. What an adorable face on this critter. It looks like the most lovable teddy bear in the whole world. Look how tiny he is. Don't you want to just reach out and scratch his ears?" Terry stuck out her hand.

"No!" Dolhar roared from the other side of the tunnel.

Before anyone could move, the tiny teddy bear's head was eclipsed by a set of serpentine jaws, with four huge fangs and rows of teeth that curled into its mouth. The creature unhinged its jaw and launched itself at Terry. For a moment, Terry was no longer visible as the creature's enormous mouth enveloped her. Suddenly the creature's head flopped down, severed from its neck by Dolhar's well-thrown ax. The disgusting head of the creature was still hanging on by thin skin, and Terry's eyes could be seen peeping out of what used to be the creature's head.

"Ew!" Terry screamed as she lifted the disgusting head of the creature over her head. She then unfurled her talons and shredded it to pieces. "That thing had the most disgusting breath, and now I have its drool all over my shirt. If I see another one of those teddy bears, it's gonna get torn apart!" Terry cleaned off her claws.

Dolhar ran up to Terry. "I'm so sorry, Ms. Larkin. That snargull must've gotten past me. He was only a baby, and sometime they're difficult to see in this light. If I may—"

"What?" Terry snapped before Dolhar could finish. "What do you mean that was only a baby? That thing was gigantic! Do you mean to tell me there may be bigger ones?"

Dolhar looked stunned. "I hope not, but if so they will meet my ax before one of them touches you. The snargulls are despicable creatures. That cute little head you saw was its tongue, used to lure prey. Creatures find it irresistible, either due to its cuteness or its tastiness. Once a snargull lures its prey close, the true head of the beast becomes visible, and it pounces on its meal. They have a snakelike body and stubby legs like a lizard. They cannot run very fast, but they are extremely agile and stealthy. A snargull can change its body color to match the background of any rock in here. That's why you couldn't see it."

I pushed Dolhar to escort us quickly through the labyrinth of tunnels and to the other side. I didn't want to risk losing one of us to a creature that was almost completely invisible. I turned on my specular skills to see the short distance in front of us; none of these creatures waited in our path. I explained to Dolhar that I could see the tunnel ahead, and I urged him on. We began jogging, and slowly the tunnel opened up into a large cave. At the end of the cave there was light ahead, and we could see our way without the torches.

"*Run!*" I shouted as loud as I could.

We all took off—and not a second too soon. One of the enormous boulders in the cave was not a boulder at all but an enormous snargull that was waiting for us. Its jaws opened up, and it snapped at us with incredible speed as we ran by. I thought I was about to become its lunch until Daemon ran in front of me. I was sure the snargull had him, but with lightning-quick reflexes he evaded the jaws of the creature and jumped on its head. His sword was already out, and he struck down with two hands, piercing the immense single eye of the creature. It howled in pain, and Daemon skipped off its head and ran after us until we were all safely out of the cave.

"No need to run anymore," Dolhar shouted, out of breath. "Snargulls cannot come into the daylight. We are safe."

We all stood there with our hands on our hips, trying to catch our breath. When we began to recover, I looked out. A dark lake was in the distance, and the caves the dwarfs lived in could be seen all around. Here was the lake where Lord Speculus bent their reflections. These once-noble dwarfs were tricked into hating themselves and all those around them. Speculus knew that if he could stop the dwarfs from forming friendships with each other, he could dominate them, and they would serve him.

Longtooth came flying overhead, carrying Daemon's horse in her massive claws. The horse was not too thrilled about flying in the claws of a dragon. Longtooth placed the horse carefully on the road below us and quickly flew back, landing on the ledge in front of us.

"If I may offer you a quick ride down, I shall be most honored," said Longtooth. We all jumped on her back.

She flew us down, and Daemon and I ran to the horse, which still seemed quite upset after the long flight. I gathered the group and told them what I planned to do. Dolhar, Terry, and I would go on ahead and sneak aboard the dwarf train. The rest would stay here and wait for our signal. Daemon was very unhappy about the prospect of leaving me unguarded, so he demanded that Longtooth fly him over the train so he could keep an eye on things. I consented. Dolhar took us down a back road and through a small underpass.

"The train should be returning from the mines very shortly. We will have to jump from here onto the train's caboose, and then we will make our way to the front of the train. Yllib will be at the front of the train, anxious to be the first one off and the first one in the dining hall," Dolhar said excitedly.

Before the train came, I sat quietly and entered the ribbon of time. Visions of the past, present, and future danced about my inner mind as I tried to sort them out. I was trying to focus my will upon the dwarfs' lake so that I could prevent Lord Speculus from using it against them. I usually hadn't had a problem doing this in the past, but some unknown force seemed to be blocking me. I challenged it! It felt cold, and it felt evil. I wrapped my arms around myself and began shivering. This wasn't just Lord Speculus. I knew what it felt like to touch his mind. This was his master, and he did not seem too happy that I was playing with the dwarfs' reflection. I reached into my pocket and grabbed my red family book and moonstone. I hugged them both, rocking myself back and forth to stay warm and to shake off this evil chill. I felt the ribbon of time shift within me, and I tried my hardest to use my power on the lake. I was hoping to show the dwarfs the nobility and pride they once had, but I was unable to control the lake's reflection. But suddenly the evil, cold feeling disappeared, and I felt a warm presence within me. *What?* I wondered. The image in the lake flattened. Lord Speculus and his master would not be able to change the reflection in the lake either. It was a tie! The next time the dwarfs looked into the lake, they would see whatever they chose to—without my influence or the influence of the dark forces allied against me. I wasn't sure what had happened, but it seemed fair enough to me.

"Jump!" Dolhar yelled as we launched ourselves on top of the train.

Terry had no problem since she could use her wings to guide her, and Dolhar had jumped on a few trains in his lifetime. But I didn't hit the top of the train quite right. I was still weak from my encounter with evil, and I fell—sliding off the roof of the train toward the rocky cliffs below. Terry grabbed my leg with her right hand, and she impaled the top of the train with the claws of her left hand. She stopped me just as my head slid over the edge of the train.

"Thanks, Tink!" I yelled as I got myself up, brushed myself off, and tried to look dignified.

We climbed down the back stairs of the train and opened the door. Dolhar entered first. It was quite a sight! The dwarfs were stunned when they saw Dolhar. They had not seen him since Longtooth had embarrassed Ttocs and flown away. They stood up and cheered and swarmed him. Then they noticed Terry and me. They were speechless—their jaws hanging open.

Dolhar stood up proudly and said, "Dear friends, let me present to you Lady Cailyssa Larkin and her sister, Lady Terry Larkin."

The dwarfs were shocked to hear our names. They also had not seen a female creature in many years. They gasped, trembled, and quickly bowed in reverence, treating us like royalty—for what reason, I'm not sure. We made our way through the train, and in each car the same thing happened. We continued to the front car, and I could see the back of Yllib, who was sitting alone up front. We quietly moved up to the front of the train, motioning to the dwarfs to be silent. We sat down a few rows behind Yllib and waited. The train approached the dining hall and stopped.

Yllib stood up and turned around. "All right, you bunch of mangy, worthless pieces of trash, no one gets to the dining hall before me, and make sure you save me some of your f... foo...foo..." Yllib stood there sputtering and couldn't finish the word.

He stared at us. His mouth was wide open, his eyes were as big as the moon, and—for one of the few times in his life—he had actually lost his appetite. Dolhar walked up to him and wrapped his arms around him, giving him a big hug.

"My friend Yllib, how I have missed you. I have brought two friends with me, and they are here to help," Dolhar said as Yllib's eyes still looked back on us in shock.

Yllib tried to speak. "It can't be; it can't be. I thought it was..."

Terry walked up to him, and I was right behind her with my hand on her shoulder.

Yllib seemed scared. He pushed Dolhar away and stumbled backward until his back was flat against the boxcar. "You came here to tease me, just like you always used to. Now you're gonna make fun of the jelly on my shirt again, and the whole train will laugh at me. You want to humiliate me again. This isn't the school bus; this is my train!" Tears started to form in his eyes.

"Billy, wait! Terry and I are not here to do that. I promise. Please listen to me."

"No! You've come all this way to make fun of the fat kid on the bus again. Go ahead if that's what makes you happy. Go ahead!"

"Billy, we're not here to do that. Terry and I want to tell you something. Please listen," I said as sincerely as I could.

"What? Is this a trick or something?"

"No tricks, Billy. Terry and I just wanted to tell you that we are sorry—very, very sorry—for the times we said or did anything that insulted you. It was wrong. Can you forgive us?"

Terry gently wiped some of the food off the front of his shirt. "I'm sorry I said that about the jelly doughnut on the bus, Billy. You didn't deserve that teasing."

Billy looked stunned, but part of him looked really happy. Terry grabbed his arm and led him off the train. I ran around to the other side of him and locked my arm under his and escorted him into the dining hall. The dwarfs cheered, and Dolhar led the rest in, too. The dwarfs were stunned when they entered. At the front stood Daemon. He had lit all the fireplaces across the wide wall, and in each fireplace was a huge slab of roasting meat on a spit, courtesy of Longtooth's quick hunting. Dolhar told his friends where a secret stash of ale was, and they began eating and drinking heartily. The only thing a dwarf liked better than roasted meat was ale. These dwarfs had spent hundreds of years eating gruel without even a drop of precious ale. I don't think I had ever seen a more outrageous or joyous feast.

After the dwarfs had eaten their fill, they began drinking even more ale—and let me tell you, a dwarf can drink a lot of ale! They began dancing on the tables, which of course spilled the ale, so they decided to use the tables as a slide.

You haven't seen anything until you've seen a fat dwarf get thrown across a table full of ale, knocking down the three dwarfs on the other side like bowling pins. These dwarfs knew how to party!

Terry and I got to talk to Billy. We explained to him about Mirror World and how Yllib was some type of mirror image of himself back at home. He seemed to appreciate and understand it, but we weren't really sure how the whole thing worked anyway. We talked about some of our earliest memories in grammar school together. We used to play together at the local playground, and Billy was really good at football. We talked like the childhood friends we once were.

Billy put his massive arms around Terry and me in a brotherly sort of way. "Ya know, Cailyssa and Terry, I wasn't too kind to you on the bus either. I guess I just forgot how to treat some of my friends. I thought that being loud and obnoxious would get me attention and friends."

"I know, Billy. Whenever we feel worthless and not deserving of a friend, we can be cruel to each other, and then we lose friends. A little kindness can go a long way toward changing that, don't you think?"

"Absolutely!" Billy shouted with great enthusiasm. "I can't believe I spent all this time here without letting any of these dwarfs become my friends. I was really acting like a jerk!"

While Billy was talking, Dolhar came around from behind and gave him a great big bear hug. We all laughed. I asked Billy to come outside with me for a moment, and I told him all about Lord Speculus and his plan to dominate the dwarfs by ensuring that they never made friends. I told him how that each morning when the dwarfs woke, Speculus bent their reflections in the lake so that they would see badness within themselves. I also told him about Ttocs and how he was part of the evil plan to corrupt Billy and the dwarfs. Billy became furious on hearing Ttocs's name. He slammed his fist down on a massive rock beside me, and it shattered into pieces. "Tell me where Scott is, Cailyssa, and I'll do the same to his head!"

A big smile spread across my face, and I put my arm out, resting it on Billy's wide shoulder. I looked into his eyes and said, "You know what, Billy? I came all the way here because I was really *hoping* to hear you say that!"

CHAPTER 26

CONSTANTINE

We gathered our things and said good-bye to the dwarfs the following day. Yllib was beaming with pride, and the dwarfs seemed happy to have friends again. They all promised to help us in any way possible in our battle against Lord Speculus. Yllib had spread the word throughout the dwarfs about how the dark lord and Ttocs had corrupted their images in the water. The dwarfs were angry, and many of them were sharpening their axes in the background as we left. Lord Speculus and his minions would soon feel the dwarfs' wrath for taking their children and women and corrupting their reflections. I was sure happy they were on my side, knowing what was to come.

We arrived at the outskirts of the city of Constantine and met up with all of our other friends. Uncle Spencer, Halodire, and the elves were so happy to see us. I briefly told the story about the dwarfs and how they would help us in our battle. Then we marched down the road toward the city of angels. As we approached, the tip of the great city could be seen. There were great cruciform structures and spires on top of tall steeples that radiated incredible brightness and color—even from far away. As we moved closer, we could see the many buildings that looked like a city of small castles. Each building was unique in shape and size, but none had doors. Rows of windows and balconies adorned the top of each building. As we approached, a sound drifted to us from the city. It sounded like the whispers of some enticing music, and we became entranced. Our eyes gazed at the sheer perfection and beauty of the city, and each of us saw blazing colors of blue, crimson, and gold that swirled in a mesmerizing wave of beauty that stunned us all. We all stood with mouths open in total shock. Anything we held in our hands, we dropped. Anything we pondered was lost. Our only thought was to walk into the city and let it envelop us and take us in.

"Stop!" Daemon said. "Proceed no farther. The city is not ready to receive you, and it could be very dangerous to take another step. Please, everyone, try to sit down and gather yourselves. It can be an overwhelming experience to visit the city. The angels need to be warned of your visit. To see even one angel in its purest and most glorious form can be absolutely intoxicating. Humans of earth have been known to faint, and others have died upon seeing even one angel. You must be prepared to experience them. Uncle Spencer is well-known among them, so he and I will journey forth and let them know of your coming. Please do not leave until we return."

As Daemon spoke, we found ourselves seated on the ground, but our mouths were still agape. It almost felt as if some cosmic force had wrapped itself around us and smothered us in a straitjacket. Our emotions were split. We felt overwhelming fear and overwhelming desire and love at the same time. We all continued to stare straight ahead at the city, not saying a word. About an hour later, Daemon and Uncle Spencer came riding back to us. They helped us to our feet, and we approached the city. As if on cue, the sunlight faded and nighttime rapidly unfolded, even though it was the middle of the day. I knew from my specular skills that the angels had changed the light cycle in order to help us enter the city. The road beneath us changed from a rough pathway to a smooth semiporous surface. It felt as if we were walking on soft ice, and our feet seemed to glide without any effort. The road was amber in color, and small waves of magenta and green were flowing by—almost assisting us in our sliding steps. It was good we had help walking. We could now see the tremendous white wall that surrounded the city and the small mountain the city was built on. At the top of the mountain sat an enormous churchlike castle with the biggest spire and the most striking array of colors. The wall in front of us seemed to flow much like our pathway, and we found ourselves at two tremendous gates. They looked like they were carved of the most beautiful white marble I had ever seen. There were faces and images of angels that shifted within the gates. And I had the strangest feeling as I looked at the images. As strange as it sounds, I had the feeling that the images were trying to tell me a story.

Uncle Spencer intoned, "Behold the gates of Constantine! In front of us is the history of the angels of this great city. We could stay here for hundreds of years and never truly understand these remarkable stories. Open your hearts; open your minds. I have asked Gabriel, the highest angel of the city, to permit us to enter."

Slowly the gates began to open inwardly, and we slowly continued along the angel-powered walkway. We could see the buildings and the tremendous lights, but there was not an angel in sight.

Terry piped up, "Uncle Spencer, I came all this way to see an angel. Where are they?"

"Dear Terry," Uncle Spencer said loud enough for all of us to hear. "Gabriel has told the angels to expect us. You will not be able to see an angel until you're ready."

"Come on, Uncle Spencer. I'm definitely ready to see an angel. I really want to go fly around here and check the place out," Terry said with great enthusiasm.

"Terry, please stay on the ground. I appreciate that you're eager to see an angel, but obviously you're not ready. You see, if you were ready to see an angel, you would have. There are many walking by us right now, and you can't see them." Uncle Spencer waved his hand to show us where these invisible angels were walking.

"Cailyssa, can you see anything?" Terry asked me.

"I'm not sure, Terry. I feel their presence, and I see that the light is different around me, but I can't really see an angel. My specular skills are tingling out of control. It's almost as if I can feel them all trying to touch my mind at the same time." Then I fainted.

"Daemon, grab Cailyssa. I think we may have entered the city too quickly," Uncle Spencer said quickly. "All of you, quickly follow me without question or delay. Daemon, get us to safety. We must make it to the tavern of Evad the barley man. It's the only place in the city where Cailyssa will be safe from the angels."

I awoke the next morning in a strange place. It was like a big dormitory with beds lined up in long rows. It looked like others may have been sleeping next to me, since the beds looked messy and unmade—but I was totally unsure of things at this point. Had this all been a dream? I vaguely remembered entering the city of angels, and then I had felt their overwhelming presence trying to connect with my mind. I remembered feeling that my head might explode, and I didn't remember a thing after that. I heard snoring in the distance and saw several bodies sleeping at the far end of this big room. The door at the hallway began to open, and I looked around under my bed in an effort to retrieve my swords. Behind the door, light crept into the room, and I saw the familiar outlines of Uncle Spencer and Daemon.

I blurted, "Thank God you're both here. Where are we? What is this place? Is everybody OK?" My hands were shaking, and my head was still throbbing.

Daemon ran up behind me, fluffed my pillow, and helped me to lean back. Uncle Spencer sat on the side of the bed and used his big warm hands to stop mine from trembling.

"Cailyssa, we're both very sorry. We should have foreseen this. But we had no idea that your specular skills were this highly developed. No Larkin at your age has ever been able to enter the ribbon of time at such a deep level. When you tried to do so yesterday, the angels in the city could sense it, and all of their minds tried to contact you at the same time. The mind of a single angel is an amazingly intense experience for anyone to contact—never mind a city of angels. I'm just glad we got you here in time; the minds of the angels cannot enter this place. When you have built up enough strength to deal with the angels and feel ready, we can reenter the city."

"So is everyone OK? And what am I doing in this old attic with a bunch of beds?"

Daemon suddenly laughed. "This is the top floor of Evad's tavern. People find refuge here when they need a break from the intensity of angel city. Some people also use this room to sleep if they have had too much to drink in the tavern below. As you can see across the room, several of the elves are still sleeping off the effects of Evad's malts. If you feel up to it, Cailyssa, Uncle Spencer and I would like to take you downstairs to have something to eat. But I have to warn you: this can be a crazy place. Many of the people who live in angel city, including some angels, come to this tavern to eat, drink, and be merry, but sometimes it can be a little unnerving."

"Daemon, after all of the crazy things I've seen since I've been here, what could possibly shock me now?" I said in my most confident voice.

The stairs led to the street below. We turned the corner, and I found myself standing in front of what appeared to be an old tavern. It certainly looked different from all the majestic buildings of angel city. It looked like an old pub, and it was the only structure with a doorway. I guess if you have wings, doors are useless. Over the doorway was a round sign that read Evad's Tavern, All Are Welcome Here, est. 2850 BC. In the middle of the round sign was a beautiful Scottish family crest adorned with a golden lion and a blue cross. It looked magnificently medieval, except for the fact that above the lion's head there appeared to a hockey stick and a golf club crisscrossed. What kind of a bizarre place was this? I would soon find out. I found myself walking through a doorway that had big red roman columns to either side of it. They looked strangely out of place in the old-pub atmosphere. As I walked in, I realized just how large the place was. In the middle, there was a gigantic bar shaped like two big angel wings, and it was surrounded by barstools. On each side there seemed to be endless rows of wooden tables and chairs. The place was crazy with noise; music, laughter, and loud voices rattled my brain. Then suddenly, like some old western movie, dead silence—and everybody turned and stared at me as I entered.

Oh great, I thought, *I was really hoping to remain low key so I could focus on the work I have to do here.* As if a light switch had been turned back on, all the noise erupted again, and the patrons seemed to be back at whatever they were doing. As I looked around, I was amazed at the various types of people, angels...and other beings? Whoa! There were angels of all different shapes, sizes, skin colors, and wings. There were people here, too, who appeared to be human or part human, along with all different types of creatures. It actually looked like I was on some movie set for the filming of *Hercules* or some crazy movie with demons and demigods. Terry was at the bar waving enthusiastically for me to come over and join her. I ran up to her and almost tripped over the faun who was carrying four enormous, foaming mugs.

"Terry, you're not old enough to be in a bar! What are you doing sitting up there?" I knew how stupid it sounded right when it came out of my mouth.

"Aw, Cailyssa, chillax and belly up to the bar, sister. This place rocks." Terry hoisted a big mug and began to drink.

"Terry, if you're drinking beer, I'm gonna kill you!"

"Relax, big sister. It's angel nectar, and it's perfectly acceptable for someone of my age to have." She winked and took a big sip.

I turned to Daemon. "Daemon, is she really supposed to be drinking that stuff? Can she get drunk or anything?"

"It is certainly not like alcohol in its effect on humans, but it can produce a state of euphoria that is quite pleasant. I don't think it will be harmful for her."

I wanted to run out the front door and go back to bed. This place was just too much for me. I saw that the elves and Halodire were having a grand time, and it looked like they were drinking the real alcohol—not the angel-nectar stuff. I reluctantly took a seat next to Terry and Uncle Spencer, and

Daemon sat next us. I tried to look small, hoping that no one would notice me. I looked down at the bar and noticed that two big, meaty hands were in front of me; it was obviously the bartender, looking to take my order. I looked up at Evad the barley man! I knew it was his place from the sign outside. He wasn't what I expected. He was definitely human looking, with a handsome, rugged face and a big, happy smile. He also had a twinkle in his eyes, and I sensed incredible intelligence. I reached out to touch his mind, and I could tell that he knew all about me. For some reason he had the same effect on me that Uncle Spencer did. I just felt warmth and safety being here in front of him.

In a thick Scottish accent Evad asked, "Will ye be havin' a malt wit your beer, or should I git a little warm milk for yah?"

As he said this, the whole bar suddenly grew silent, and everyone turned to look at me. They were all waiting for my response. If I said the wrong thing, I'd look foolish.

So I cheated a bit and dipped into my specular skills. I stood up from my barstool, adjusted my clothes, and stood tall and proud. "I'll have your best single malt whiskey and the largest tankard of Scottish ale you can find in this rat's nest of a bar!"

There was silence in the bar. Evad's face looked deadly serious. Had I said the wrong thing? All of a sudden Evad slammed his hands down on the bar, and a broad grin appeared across his face. The bar erupted in applause and laughter.

Evad bellowed, "Free drinks on the house! All cheer the return of a Larkin to the Tavern of the Barley Man! Here be Lady Cailyssa and Terry Larkin, and anyone who touches 'em will answer to me!"

The crowd roared again, and I again tried to make myself look very small. I felt every eye in the bar was on me. When Evad returned, he had a wonderful plate of food prepared for Terry and me and two angel nectars for us to drink.

Evad then bent over so only Terry and I could hear him. But when he spoke this time, there was no Scottish accent. "I only did that for the crowd, young ladies, but I meant the last part of what I said. If you need anything here in angel city, you let me know. Your grandfather, Artemus, told me you would be coming here one day, and I have always looked forward to the day I would meet another Larkin!"

Terry and I dug into our food, and it tasted absolutely wonderful. It had been a long time since we'd had spaghetti and meatballs, and I was wondering if Evad somehow knew it was our favorite dish. As we finished eating, I observed the variety of characters in the tavern. There were two large elves and some smaller angels playing darts in the far right corner. I couldn't see what the dartboard looked like, but I knew it was alive, since it yelped every time a dart was thrown at it. Across from the dartboard, several dwarfs and humans were playing some game with a dagger on top of the table. It appeared that they were jamming the sharp blade into the table between their fingers to test each other's bravery. Suddenly, two angels on the other side of the bar started arguing. Their wings flared out, and they became very red-faced. They started pushing and shoving.

Evad's voice boomed out. "Take it outside, my feathered friends. You know the rules in here. Break them, and there will be no angel nectar for you for a hundred years!"

The angels took the threat seriously and pushed each other out the front of the building, still arguing. I saw my first angel fight. My blood ran cold, and I was glad when Daemon came up behind me and wrapped his arms around me. These angels were not the cute ones I thought of in the Bible stories. These were vicious warriors, and they were hell-bent on killing each other. Their wings flared out, and they used the edges as razor-sharp swords. Their hands and feet were also lethal weapons, and they moved with such speed and violence that it was truly horrifying. When one angel took a kick to the stomach, he flew across the street and right through several sets of buildings. It appeared that the other angel, a female, had just won the fight.

Daemon whispered in my ear. "I know how scary this appears, Cailyssa. Remember, the angels in the city do not have control over their emotions. You must be very careful when dealing with them."

Terry elbowed my arm. "Whoa, Cailyssa! Did you see that angel brawl? I didn't notice it at first, but she was a female angel. I guess they've worked out some of the sexist attitudes here. Maybe it's a place that truly respect females as equals. What do you think?" Terry said as we sat back on our stools at the bar.

As soon as Terry said this, I felt a hand fondle my butt and pinch it from behind me. What the heck? Could that be Daemon? I spun around, and there seemed to be no one there—until I looked down. I couldn't believe it. Before me was a short angel—kind of like a cherub (the cute, chubby ones that shoot the love arrows in the paintings), except this one had a beard and a hairy chest. He was extremely dirty and appeared to be drunk.

He looked up at me and smiled with filthy teeth. "Hey, sweet cheeks, wanna party with me?" He then raised up a huge mug of ale and drank it so fast that it poured down the sides of his mouth and stomach. He let out an enormous burp in my face. He rubbed the beer over his belly as he tried to do a sick, little sexy dance. He laughed hysterically, turned around, and rejoined his cherubic partner at the table. They began drinking more, laughing as they pointed their tiny fat fingers at us. Daemon's back was to us, and he was talking with Uncle Spencer. It was a good thing he had not noticed this, since I think he would have beaten up those two little cherubs.

Evad came up and gave us enormous bowls of ice cream—our favorite dessert. "Have those two cherubs been giving you any problem? They can get quite nasty when drunk. They haven't shot a love arrow in a long time, and now all they do is come in here and cause trouble. Watch out for them!"

"Terry, you're not gonna believe this, but do you see those two little baby-looking angels with beards?"

Terry looked over my shoulder. "That's disgusting. It looks like somebody took those cute, chubby angels and ruined them. Look at them; they're absolutely drunk. They're spitting and drooling while they're talking to each other." We turned around to finish our ice cream.

"Watch out for them, Terry, one of them sneaked up behind me and grabbed my butt—"

"What the heck?" Terry screamed out as she spun around on her barstool, hoping to punch whoever just grabbed her. "Touch my butt again, and you're dead!" Terry said as she punched over the little angels' heads.

We stood up. The filthy, drunken angels had sneaked over behind our stools and grabbed both our butts this time—with two hands. We instinctively turned around and swung our fists, connecting with the air. We looked down, and both of the scumbag cherubs were laughing and dancing. I'm not sure if someone with a body like a baby can dance in a sexy way, but they were sure trying.

"C'mon, you hotties, dance with us," the drunken little angels said as they motioned for us to come with them.

I think they were just about to reach up and try to grab at us again when a large shape vaulted over the bar with an incredibly athletic move. In front of us stood Evad. He was one big dude. He was angry, and he had a hockey stick in his hand. When the cherubs saw him, they stopped dancing and dropped their beers. The bar became silent. Evad swung the hockey stick with incredible force and caught the hairy little angel on the curve of the stick. The cherubic little hockey puck sailed toward the front door, bouncing hard against the big red column and screaming with pain as he rolled down the street. The other little angel turned to flee, but Evad was too fast for him. He swung the hockey stick again, and the cherub flew through the air like a puck and slammed off the red column on the other side of the door. Evad then used his hockey stick in a pole-vaulting maneuver, and with athletic precision he launched his imposing form back over the bar.

Evad turned to look at us. "If you see those two hairy beasties return, you let *me* know, and I'll slap shot them to the other side of the city. Finish up your ice cream. It's starting to melt."

Uncle Spencer and Daemon wandered over. "Are you two enjoying the food here? Be careful, there's a lot of crazy people in this place!"

Terry and I just looked at each other and laughed. We finished our ice cream. Then we walked up the back stairs to crash on the beds in the attic. I think the ice cream and nectar made us a little sassy, and we giggled our way to sleep, talking about drunken little angels and how they reminded us of a bunch of stupid guys in our school. We laughed even harder when we tried to be quiet. Maybe we could bring Evad back to Boston with us. He'd make a great principal in our school. He could walk around with his hockey stick and get rid of the male trash.

CHAPTER 27

THE CITY OF ANGELS

I floated in a dream at the edge of consciousness, knowing I was about to wake. I wanted to stay in the dream. I was young again. My parents, grandparents, and much of my family were surrounding me at a picnic at the beach. I felt their love, and I relished the notion of being a carefree little girl.

My eyes peeled open, and I realized I was in a bunk staring at an old wooden ceiling. This sure wasn't my bedroom at home! If I had any doubt, all I had to do was look across the room and watch a whole rack of little dwarfs snoring away. I crept out from under the covers and quietly made my way to the balcony, closing the small doors behind me. Here was Constantine, the angel city! And it would be the biggest test yet of my abilities. I put my hands together as if I were praying and then slowly stretched my arms, taking a deep breath as if I were doing my favorite yoga position.

I carefully immersed myself in the ribbon of time, and my specular skills tingled.

I knew clearly what had happened with Terry. It wasn't a coincidence that we had the same Winnie the Pooh dream. I had seen the future, and Terry was going to die! Without knowing it, I had somehow left my body and became the white light that she saw in the ocean. I wasn't sure exactly how I saved her, but one thing that I was sure of was that if I did it again, I could die. But there was one other option, and I knew I had to make it work or die trying—because it was the only way I could save my friends and defeat Speculus. Uncle Spencer was about to open the door and join me. Sometimes seeing the future was pretty cool.

"Good morning, Uncle Spencer," I said before I turned around to see who it was.

"I see that your specular skills are working quite well this morning. You knew I would be coming to greet you." Uncle Spencer chuckled. "You obviously have turned to a new level of your revelatory awareness. And the angels' minds are not overwhelming to you?"

"Not at all, Uncle Spencer. I'm really glad you came out here. I have something very important that I need to discuss with you." I looked directly at Uncle Spencer's eyes. "I…I just wanted you to be here with me. I have to try something. Tell my mom and dad that I love them, and tell Terry too—"

Uncle Spencer interrupted me hastily. "Cailyssa, if you have any intention of going off by yourself and trying to defeat the dark lord, let me tell you right now—"

"No, Uncle Spencer. It's nothing like that. It's just that I've recently discovered what I need to do to defeat him. You don't know what it's like to see the future and watch your sister or your friends die. I *have* to be able to do something about this. I *have* to!" I cried as I vanished before Uncle Spencer's eyes.

"Good Lord!" Uncle Spencer stammered, pushing open the doors of the balcony.

I instantly appeared at the other side of the dormitory; I was already there when Uncle Spencer opened the door. Then, somehow, I popped myself right back onto the balcony. Uncle Spencer's face was gray, and his hands were trembling. I got there just in time to steady him before he fell.

"Cailyssa, what in God's name did you just do? You're dabbling in areas that no Larkin should. Don't think your specular skills can—"

"Uncle Spencer, I can do it. I can fold time. I knew I could; I saw it in the visions of the future. Now that I know I can do it, we can use it to our advantage. You made me think of it. Remember in your class, talking about the wormholes and stuff? You had us write the letters A and B on the corners of a piece of paper, and we all used our pencils to try to draw the quickest route between the two points. We all drew a straight line between the two letters. You surprised us all and folded the paper, touching the letters."

"I remember, Cailyssa," Uncle Spencer said as he gathered himself and his wits. "The point of the exercise was to expand my students' minds so they could think of the possibility of two places that were very distant actually being very close. We also discussed the possibilities of being in two places at the same time. Wait—you're trying to distract me with academics! You should not be using your specular skills to travel the time continuum. There are unheard of dangers. What would happen if…"

I silenced Uncle Spencer as I wrapped my arms around him and gave him a big hug. "I know, Uncle. It's dangerous. But trust me. You brought me here to do a job, and I'm gonna do it the right way."

"I hate to be reminded that I had a hand in bringing you here, Cailyssa. If I don't bring you back in one piece, your mother and father will be very disappointed in me and…" Uncle Spencer's wise eyes began to well up.

"I love you, too, Uncle Spencer. I promise I'll be careful. Let's go visit the angels. I'm dying to get a tour of the city."

Uncle Spencer and I met Daemon and Terry, and we walked down the back stairs to the alleyway outside of Evad's tavern. Daemon held my hand, and I knew he was worried about me. He warned me that a city filled with angels is not safe because not all angels are good. The other buildings of the city had no doors. There were no entrances at ground level. Why would an angel need a door? They have wings. Each building had a large balcony without rails. Angels were flying throughout the city and landing gracefully on the balconies. I could see them! There were also angels walking the streets. Although none talked to us, they did make brief eye contact, usually bowing their head slightly to the left or right. Some were grim and straight-faced. Others had a hint of a small smile, I thought. And others simply paid us no attention.

We continued to walk until we came to the center of the city, where there was an enormous fountain surrounded by a large pool. The fountain was adorned with intricate artwork that had images of angels woven into various landscapes. The fountain itself must have been hundreds of feet tall, yet the water fell so softly; it was magical. The most amazing thing was the way the stone angels slowly swayed and changed color. Daemon explained that the fountain was made out of a special type of marble infused with heavenly substances he couldn't explain. We strolled through the astonishing city, amazed at its ethereal nature. To say this was a mesmerizing, dreamlike sequence would not do it justice. We were heading uphill now to the largest and most glorious building in Constantine: the home of Gabriel, one of the greatest archangels known to God or man. I was frightened at the prospect of meeting this angel, but I knew I had to if I wanted to complete what I came here to do.

"Hey, Cailyssa, this is awesome. Why didn't I think of this before?" Terry said as I saw her softly land in a fountain off to our right. "These fountains have the most amazing misty water. It's just fabulous for cleaning off my wings." She flipped the water off her wings and flew over to land next to me. "Hey, Lyss, did you see all the angels cleaning their wings in the fountains?"

"Sure, Terry, it makes sense that angels would need to clean off their wings."

"Yeah…but there's something going on here. Remember that big fountain in the middle of the city? That had the best water and a deep pool but not *one* angel in it! Now we've passed a dozen other fountains. They're all small and crappy—compared to that big one—and they are filled with angels. Not only that, the strangest thing is that there are always two fountains right next to each other. Look over there—two fountains and two different groups of angels in each fountain. But here's the weird thing, look at how those two groups of angels are treating each other! One group is acting as if it owned the place, and those angels are being so rude to the other angels—even the little ones! That group over there just looks sad and beaten down. I saw one of the little angels wander over to the other pool to pick something up. When the little angel picked it up, that big angel slapped him to the ground with its wing. It's also really clear that those angels are not allowed to go in the other pool. It feels like a bunch of bullies to me," Terry said sadly as she shook her head.

Daemon cleared his throat and interrupted. "This is horribly embarrassing, but as you know, many of the angels here are still working on controlling their emotions so they can regain their place in heaven. There's a problem here that's been going on for a long time. I hate to admit it because it is humiliating to think that angels could do such things."

Uncle Spencer said, "Human history is replete with examples of one group oppressing another group. Genocide, ethnic cleansing, and domination of groups are very sad pieces of our history."

"I see," Terry chirped. "Some of these angels are racist or something. I see there are many angels with different skin color and different ethnicities; that's what it must be all about."

"Skin color and ethnic features are not of any concern to angels. We are all seen as equals—except for one small thing," Daemon said as he looked down, embarrassed to continue.

Uncle Spencer jumped in to rescue him. "Angels are not racist, Terry. In fact, ethnicity is truly not an issue. But perhaps what is most troubling is that there is one small feature that the angels look at. They use that one feature as the basis for oppressing and dominating others. I know this is hard to believe, but if you look at the tips of all the angels' wings, you will see that the outermost edge is outlined either in gold or silver. The angels with the silver-tipped wings are the dominant angels, and the gold-tipped angels must be subservient. The angels with the gold-tipped wings are seen as inferior. They are not allowed the same privileges, such as using the same fountain."

"That's crazy!" said Terry. "All of their wings are so beautiful. How could a stupid thing like the color of the tip of a wing have anything to do with how good a person—or an angel—is?"

"It's very sad but true," Daemon said. "For thousands of years, the silver-winged angels have dominated the city, and to make it more confusing, for many years before that, the gold-winged angels dominated."

Cailyssa stopped. She glanced at the reflection in the fountain to her left. Her specular feelings zapped her hard. "This is sounding all too familiar. I know one bad angel with black-and-silver wings who absolutely loves the idea of what's happening here: breeding discontent and hate and infecting the minds of others so they become cruel tormentors. This dark lord is really starting to tick me off, and I can't wait to smack his head off the big black mirror behind his throne. Let's go see Gabriel. We have work to do!" I barked as I marched up the street, trying not to look at any more angels.

CHAPTER 28

THE HOUSE OF GABRIEL

I was feeling pretty good about myself. I was in Constantine, the city of angels, about to meet Gabriel. I was going to secure the help of the angels and vanquish Lord Speculus to a rotten place in hell. After that I'd probably go back home, see my parents, get my haircut, and then wait for Daemon to take me out on a *real* date. Suddenly I stopped and almost fell. My specular skills flashed, and I freaked.

"I *can't* read the future; no one can. What was I thinking? Oh no, bad things…gotta find help…" I spoke so loudly that everybody turned around and looked at me.

Daemon came up and touched my arm gently, looking at me as if I had just lost my marbles. "It's all right, Cailyssa. Your specular skills are causing you to contact the minds of many angels. Put up walls against them if they overwhelm you. They can be rude and invade people's minds. Don't let them bully you!"

"It's OK, Daemon," I said as I collected my emotions and myself. "They helped me to realize something. No one can really see the future; the future is constantly changing. There is no one set path; there are many possible futures. It just makes me feel so much pressure, since everything I choose to do sets in motion a different future. Although I can't read the future as I used to think, I'm beginning to understand my specular skills in a different way." As I said this, I popped and disappeared—landing right behind Daemon and tapping his shoulder. His reaction was hilarious; he jumped into battle mode, drew his sword, and screamed my name. All the while I was behind him with my hands folded, and I was laughing. When I tapped him on the shoulder, he turned around and almost took my head off with his sword. But of course I saw the sword coming in slow motion, and I casually ducked under the blow.

"Cailyssa!" Daemon screamed. "What devilry is this that you should disappear before my eyes?"

Now it was my turn to calm Daemon down. I'd been mean to him, so I wrapped my arms around him, whispering, "I know it really scares you when you think you've lost me, but you're never gonna lose me. I promise." And with that, I gave him a classy little kiss on the cheek.

Daemon resheathed his sword and exhaled a calming breath. I told everyone how I'd found a way to use my specular skills to make baby wormholes and travel time. Daemon looked at me with awe, but I think Uncle Spencer almost toppled over. Terry giggled the whole time and said it was just way cool. I knew they were all worried about me, but before we could get into a long-winded conversation explaining this phenomenon, Terry helped me out by screaming and pointing in the air. "Look! There's an angel up there with only one wing, and it's falling out of the sky."

Everyone turned to look, but there was nothing there! Terry winked at me. "I knew you needed a little distraction, Lyssa." She shouted, "Let's get on with exploring the city. I can't wait to fly around with these angels."

We laughed and walked away. Daemon and Uncle Spencer looked at each other, shook their heads, and just followed, mumbling about my difficult nature.

Terry was flying around as we walked up a slow incline toward the biggest building here. The architecture was ethereal and graceful. We were still walking on multicolored bricks that felt like gliding over warm ice. We took a turn and crossed a parapet walkway over a stream of the most beautiful blue water I had ever seen. We continued up the hill and saw many of the angels soaring off those balconies and landing on the walkways. It was getting crowded. Many of the angels were now staring at us, and the childlike angels pointed to us and giggled.

My nerves were starting to jangle as I sensed that we were approaching Gabriel's house. The enormous tower was decorated with an amazing spire with a flaming white cross on the top. As we came closer, I noticed that this was the only structure in the city with a door. Across the top of the door were crenellations adorned with images of angels. I was no longer under my own power but was compelled by forces beyond me to enter.

We walked into the most spectacular chapel I have ever seen. The beautiful sculptures and images that surrounded the cruciform-shaped room were from every religion I had ever read about. More than that, the images were moving and slowly transforming themselves as they cascaded around and up and down the walls.

"Awesome!" Terry whispered in her loudest voice. "I feel like I just made it to heaven. Look at that wall with the moving pictures of heaven on it. It's like all the religions of earth are flowing together. I'm not sure I even know what I'm seeing…"

"No one can describe this place," Uncle Spencer chimed in. "I believe I was here as a small boy. Legend has it that everyone sees something different here. You will never forget this day. Relish it while you can." Uncle Spencer slowly raised his hands palms up and spread them slowly as he looked around the room. "This room is also in many places at the same time. It is here in Mirror World, on earth in places of worship, and in heaven. This is the closest a mortal can get to truly experiencing what heaven might be like. Steady yourself! Gabriel, head of all angels, approaches!"

We stood in the middle of the glorious chapel, and a form appeared from mist in front of us. She was wearing a simple, white, flowing garment and walked toward us quite gracefully. As she approached we could see more clearly. Her hair was beautifully wrapped with a fancy bun on top, her skin was flawless and brown, and her eyes were deep but sparkled with a brilliance that was captivating.

"Stand around me!" she said in her intoxicating voice. "I will take you up to the most comfortable of rooms in the house of Gabriel." As she said this, we floated up, up, up to the top of the tower. At the top we slowly glided in and landed in a beautiful room filled with the most comfortable crimson and blue couches and pillows imaginable. Warm multicolored drapes hung from the walls. Paintings on the walls featured famous human singers. *What?* I wondered.

Terry whispered, "I don't like it. Gabriel has an African American maid who looks like a soul singer. What gives? That's wrong, and I'm gonna let him know it, too."

The angel who guided us here began to laugh in a hearty manner. "That's what I have always liked about you, Terry. You're an honest one, sugar. I used to travel to earth and listen to you and Cailyssa sing at church. I could hear ya loud whisper then, and I can hear ya loud whisper now. But that's what I always loved most about you, Terry. You are never afraid to point out what's wrong—and stand up for what's right."

Our guide added, "Now, believe me, Gabriel has visited your world many times and has seen firsthand the pains of oppression and slavery. None of *that* will be stood for in *this* house! I wish I could say the same for the angels in this city. Now y'all come up and stand in front of me. I have a question for you. When you meet Gabriel, what will you see?" She winked at Daemon and Uncle Spencer as she said this.

Terry and I just stood there sheepishly. We put our hands in our pockets, shrugged a bit, and tried to find the right thing to say. My skills tingled a bit, so I knew she was an angel.

Terry finally broke the silence. "An angel?" She had an embarrassed look on her face.

"And what do angels look like? Do they have wings? Do they always look human? Do they sing like me?" And in that instant, the figure before us broke into the most soulful rendition of a gospel song.

I was transfixed. The sheer beauty of the voice before us was like nothing we had ever experienced. We cried, we trembled, and our hearts pounded with joy. But more importantly, we discovered through this song that she was talking to us. The archangel Gabriel stood there before us, her glorious angelic form encircled by a halo around her entire body. We became overwhelmed and dizzy, and it's a good thing the couch was behind us. The sight of Gabriel was too much for us. We fell, landing in the soft pillows.

We looked up with awe, and I stood and tried to compose myself. I turned and saw Uncle Spencer and Daemon snickering in the background. "You knew this was Gabriel the whole time, and you didn't tell me?" I said in my loudest whisper.

"Don't blame them." Gabriel placed her hand on my shoulder, and I felt her incredible presence. It was as if a jolt of electric love and comfort flew through me—impossible to describe.

"I know I shouldn't, but I like to have some fun sometimes," Gabriel said as she stepped back and smiled in a warm, radiant way. "I just *love* to see the expression on people's faces when I first meet them. I was chuckling a bit when ya both fell back on the couch. I remember when I announced the birth of Christ to three shepherds. One of them ran away screaming, and the other two fell down like you did. One of the lambs keeled over and died on the spot. I felt bad for the little thing, so I brought it back to life. Ya can't go around killing little lambs, can ya? I'd be in big trouble with the boss—Lamb of God and all that stuff."

Gabriel's mood then turned serious, and she folded her arms before her and turned her head sideways. "So tell me, Cailyssa, what brings you to my house?"

I stood up tall, trying to stop my fidgeting. I was addressing one of the most powerful angels of the universe. I felt so *small*.

"I've...uh...come here to ask for your help, and the help of the angels, to defeat Lord Speculus and to stop his evil plans. He has corrupted the waters here in the city and has turned the angels against one another. They should be angry. I want them to join me and my friends to overthrow him." I felt I sounded silly, trying to act proud and confident.

"Hmm..." Gabriel said in a smooth low baritone that literally shook us to the bone. "Speculus, eh? That's not his real name. I knew him before he was thrown out of heaven. I'll tell ya, I'd like to march over there right now and slap him upside the head for all the wrongs he's done. But I can't. There are rules! Rules you don't understand."

"Do you mean you can't help me?" I squeaked, feeling more nervous than I thought was possible.

Gabriel walked over to me, took my hand, and folded it in both of hers. I can't tell you what the experience was like. It calmed down my whole body instantly. I felt this incredible warmth and love. "Now, now, young one, I didn't say that. I can't force the angels to help you; it's up to them. But I can help you get in touch with them. Every day at midday, all the angels gather on their balconies and sing. Angels *love* to sing! At that moment all of their minds are connected. You can use my balcony and your specular skills to ask them for aid. That's the best I can do, honey." Gabriel softly took my hand and walked me over to the couch. I sat down. All the others sat too.

"Cailyssa, Terry, search your memories. Do you remember me?" Gabriel said softly.

Terry sat straight up in her seat and raised her hand like an eager second grader. Gabriel softly laughed.

"I remember—my grandfather and…you. You were at our church with him, back home. You were saying something about me singing in the children's choir!" Terry blurted excitedly.

"I visited you many, *many* times—not always meeting you—but I have long waited to see you here," Gabriel said with a sincere smile. She then sat down and held our attention as she gazed in our eyes. "What you're doing here is good work. It's hard work. It's God's work to me, but...it might not end exactly as you have planned. Keep the faith and find strength from others," Gabriel looked directly at me, adopting a serious tone. "Cailyssa, now fess up! I asked you why you came here, and you only told me one reason. Might there be *another* reason for your visit?"

Oh my God! A great lump made its way into my throat, and I started to croak out a very lame reply. "Uh, yeah, um—"

Gabriel saved me by interrupting. "Honey, we don't have to talk about it here. But don't forget; we got business together."

The others all looked around with quizzical faces. I averted my eyes from Daemon, hoping he wouldn't look at me and ask any questions. I was getting really nervous and began rubbing my hands together while hunching over.

Again, Terry had my back and saved me. "Uh, Ms. Gabriel? I mean...Ms. Angel Gabriel? I think Lyssa and I need to use the ladies' room and freshen up a bit."

Gabriel raised her eyebrows. "Of course, of course, my apologies for not offering sooner. Go through the door over there, and you'll find what you need."

Thank God Terry saved me; I was starting to lose it. She escorted me down to the door that Gabriel had pointed to. As I approached the door, I heard a voice. Gabriel was whispering in my mind. "Cailyssa, I know the other reason why you've come. I'll be waiting."

I ran into the restroom with Terry and closed the door quickly behind us. I fell against the door with my back, my hands flat on it to support me. I was breathing quickly. I was in panic mode!

"Hey, big sister, what's going on?" Terry sat with her arms outstretched.

I whispered at Terry, "*Nothing*, Terry, I just need to talk to Gabriel about the most important decision I'll ever make in my life!"

"Ah…" Terry said sarcastically. "I know it's about Daemon because you got that love-sick look again."

I shouted.

"It's *not* just about Daemon!" I was shaking as I said this, regretting my loud voice. *Did he hear?*

Terry came over and gave me a hug and propped me up. She didn't understand. I had to make a choice! I could see some possible futures. Some of us would live; some of us would die. I just wanted to make sure I was the only one doing the dying.

"Hey, Cailyssa, I'm always there for you if you need me." Terry gave me a parting hug and then took a step back.

"I know, Terry, I know. I'll tell you everything after I talk to Gabriel. Let's go back in there. I'll fix my problem with Gabriel. Then I'll talk to the angels and convince them to help me. At the end of the day, everything will be good, right?" My voice sounded like I was trying to convince myself.

CHAPTER 29

ANGELS AND DEMONS

When I returned from the ladies' room, Gabriel was gone, and the others were sitting quietly off to the side of the room. Terry joined them, and I heard another whisper in my mind. Gabriel was calling me, so I walked behind the couches, parted the thick drapes, and entered another room. Gabriel was there with her back to me, looking out the window.

"Do all angels have wings?" I asked.

Without saying a word, Gabriel walked across the room. I knew I had to follow. We walked around the corner, and before us stood a glass case. In the case was the most amazing set of angel wings I had ever seen. The tops were imbued with a golden brown that morphed into blues and greens. The tips were bright white. And then I looked closely; the tips were sharpened like razors.

"Are these yours?" I said to Gabriel.

She gave me an intense look. "Sharpen your mind, Cailyssa! You know whose wings they are! Don't play coy with *me*! I know of your incredible abilities. Use 'em. Yet I also know that your emotional mind is still one of a young lady who has a lot to learn. You *know* they're Daemon's wings!"

"I do." I looked down as I said this, knowing that I had to be totally up front and honest with Gabriel. "I'm sorry; I'm just really nervous."

Gabriel frowned and continued. "What you don't know is the story behind them. I'm sure you've heard from him that he stood here on the balcony of my house, and I cut his wings off in front of all the angels. He turned his bloody back in shame. What you don't know is that I didn't want to; it was *Daemon's* choice! He didn't deserve any punishment, but he is one stubborn angel. He thought it was the penance he earned for letting your grandfather die. But as you know, your grandfather forced Daemon to protect your father and Uncle Spencer. He died so they would live, and Daemon saved them both from death. Had he not done so, you would not be here before me. I'm telling you this because you need to know that Daemon is among my most favored angels—but he can be very emotionally impulsive. We could've done without the wing cutting and the drama, my Lord. He left the city, blood dripping from his back, and he disappeared to mope around for eternity. I thought he was like a little boy pouting, and I told him just *that*! The only way we could convince him to get out of his sulking mood was to promise him an opportunity to redeem himself. That's when he reentered earth—born the same day you were—growing into the knowledge that he would be your guardian angel. If he fails in protecting *you*, I'm not sure what he's capable of."

Gabriel placed her arm around my shoulder, shoring me up. "So tell me what's on your mind, sugar, and be straight with me. There's nothing I haven't heard before. Believe you me!"

I pulled down my vest and straightened out my shirt, hoping to gather courage as I mumbled. "This is hard for me. I really don't want to seem selfish."

"There's not a selfish bone in your body, Cailyssa. Please continue," Gabriel intoned.

"Well, you see…it's like…I…well," I looked up at Gabriel as I said this, and I gathered the courage just to tell it like it was. "I love Daemon!" I confessed.

"Lordy, girl! Everyone knows that, including Daemon. Tell me something I don't know. You make it quick now. We don't want to be late to hear the angels singing."

I went on. "My prescience has told me that one possible future has Daemon and me together forever, deeply in love. I honestly don't think I could live without him. I know I'll never love anybody like I do him. I know I'm young, and I may seem foolish, but I truly believe this."

"This doesn't seem so foolish to me, especially since Daemon loves you, too!" Gabriel stated flatly.

"He does? You mean romantically? You're sure he really does?" I cried out.

"Cailyssa, please, you both know that you love each other. What are you going to do about it?" Gabriel looked at me expecting an answer.

"Well, I was hoping to get married and everything, but I guess we can't do that since he's my guardian angel. *Right?*"

"Who told you that?" Gabriel raised one of her eyebrows.

"There are many rules governing the angels, and some of them are not *so* clear." Gabriel started to pace back and forth. "Rules or not, he will not give up being your guardian angel to marry you, even though he loves you, because doing so would place you at risk and would violate his duty to you."

"I'll renounce *him*!" I cried a bit too loudly. "I'll fire him as my guardian angel, and I don't even care if you get me another one. I mean, he can't think for a minute that I'm going to let him follow me around for the rest of my life protecting me. I'd be tortured! I'd have to look at him every day, knowing how much I love him but knowing that I could never have him. No way in *hell* am I doing that."

"Please don't use the word *hell* in anger. It bothers me," Gabriel said as she turned around to face me. Gabriel looked up and sighed, and then she softly said, "Love is the most powerful force in the universe. You need to find yourself! Remember, love is not only who you can see yourself *with*, but it's also…who you can't see yourself *without*. So what did you want to ask me?"

"Can I renounce Daemon, and what will happen if I do?" There it was. I'd finally said it.

"So you've heard of renunciation. It has rarely ever been done, so I can't tell you what will happen. You'll have to ask yourself. What I can tell you is, *yes*, you can renounce Daemon. You simply have to ask me. Then I will sing to all the angels and let them know. Know this, Cailyssa!" Gabriel said in her powerful angelic voice. "It will humiliate and shame Daemon to no end. It'll be big-time gossip among the angels. He'll think he's failed again as a guardian angel. It could be worse than the first time when he asked me to cut off his wings."

Gulp. A lump formed in my throat, and a queasy feeling crept into my stomach. I thought I was going to barf right there on Gabriel's beautiful rug. I croaked out, "Do you mean he'd be so mad at me that he'd never talk to me again?"

"It could be worse than that, Cailyssa, he could—"

"Kill himself?" I burst out.

"Angels can't really kill themselves—at least not in the human sense—but he could choose to disappear. If he so chose, none of us could *ever* find him."

Gabriel grabbed my shoulders for support. The faucet behind my eyes could not be held back any longer. I tried rubbing away the tears as I said, "So what am I supposed to do? If I don't renounce Daemon, we'll never be together. If I do renounce Daemon, he could disappear forever! Either way, I have already *lost* him!"

"Dear Cailyssa, you are very dear to me, but I can't make this decision for you," Gabriel said kindly. "Trust me, when the time comes, you *must* find a way to work this problem out *with* Daemon. Don't do everything alone. Ask for help! Most importantly, remember to find your real self, and you will find the answers you seek."

I'm not sure I understood everything she told me, but I straightened up proudly and stamped my foot on the floor. I was embarrassed about the way I carried myself. I must have appeared like a weak little girl, not some force here to set things right. "Gabriel, I'm so embarrassed. I must look like a love-sick fool—only thinking of myself when I should be thinking about what I need to do to defeat the dark lord."

"Not at all, Cailyssa," Gabriel said in her most comforting tone. She stiffened. "I wouldn't add this weight to your shoulders unless I knew you could take it." Gabriel looked deeply into my eyes, and I felt she was touching my soul. "As you know, the decision you make regarding Daemon will not just affect the two of you; it could hurt others. It could affect your ability to *defeat* the dark lord. He will use everything in his power against you. It was terrible what he did to your grandfather. By the way, Cailyssa, I'm always around to listen, to help. And if I may offer one small piece of advice—pray. Lord *knows* it helps!" Gabriel began walking out of the room. "Let's go, honey. Time to hear the angels sing!"

I walked out of the room with my chin held high and a bounce to my step. I laughed lightly as I glanced back at Gabriel. I didn't want to give anybody in the room, especially Daemon, a clue about our conversation. I clapped my hands together and announced, "Hey, everybody, it's almost time for the angels to begin singing. I can't wait!"

Daemon walked toward me with a stern look on his face. I faced him with my brightest smile. He looked at me silently for one moment and then said, "Cailyssa, may I have a word with you?"

Oh shoot. He knows, he knows, he knows. I said to myself. *No, he doesn't, Cailyssa. He knows absolutely nothing.* My mind battled with itself as Daemon lightly took my arm and escorted me to the far side of the room.

"Cailyssa, I'm very upset, and I need to speak with you alone. I have to ask you something about your conversation with Gabriel. Please answer honestly," Daemon said with a very worried expression. He was using his angel power on me, and I knew I could not lie.

"Did you and Gabriel discuss anything about—"

"Your wings!" I interrupted Daemon and spoke a bit too loudly. "Yes, I have to be honest; Gabriel did show me your wings. They were the most beautiful things I've ever seen."

Daemon looked at me and then over at the room I had been in with Gabriel. Did he believe me?

"Well, Cailyssa, that means she told you her side of the story about when my wings were removed from my back." Daemon stood very tall and looked over my head. "I wanted to let you know that I will *never* fail you as I did your grandfather. It has been hard for me to be in the city. I'm so ashamed of what I did that I cannot bear for another angel to look upon me. It is very important for me, as one of the highest guardian angels, to be respected by my brethren. When the angels sing, I will stand next to you, proudly knowing that I am fulfilling my duty as your guardian!"

Great, just great! Daemon didn't know that it he was making it awfully hard for me to consider renouncing him. How could I hurt him like that?

Daemon began to walk away, but I grabbed his arm and spun him around quickly. "Daemon, from what Gabriel told me, it wasn't your fault one bit about what happened to my grandfather. If it wasn't for you—"

"Silence!" Daemon actually screamed at me. "We will never talk about this matter again." He walked away.

I was furious and humiliated. If I had the time, we would be having another one of our full-fledged arguments. So I chose to take a different tack. "Daemon, Daemon," I said just enough over a whisper so that he would come back and talk to me.

Before I said a word, Daemon blurted, "I'm sorry, Cailyssa. I should never have said that to you. That was disrespectful. Please accept my heartfelt apology. Mastering one's emotions is difficult for me. In a few minutes, I'll be standing on the balcony with the angels singing. As you know, the last time I stood there was the last time I had my wings. There is nothing more precious to an angel than his wings, except his honor. It will be hard for me to stand there, knowing I have not fully regained my honor among the angels."

I looked at his handsome face. Angels can really project emotions, and the sadness and pain I saw in Daemon's face was overwhelming. How could he still blame himself? Man, this angel needed a therapist! That was a dumb thought. He'd tell a therapist he was a guardian angel, and they'd have him in a mental hospital. I brought myself back to reality and noticed Daemon was still standing in front of me. It was as if he wanted my permission to leave.

"Hey, Daemon." I reached out and grabbed his hand. "Do you think it would be OK if we held hands out on the balcony when the angels are singing?"

"Of course it would be, Cailyssa. I would greatly enjoy that," Daemon said as his huge hand enveloped mine.

We all went to stand on the balcony, waiting for the angels to begin singing in a few minutes. Angels don't talk much unless they have to; they prefer singing. I closely clutched Daemon's hand. We needed each other's support here for different reasons. I dipped into my specular abilities to ready myself for this experience.

Gabriel walked out and stood in front of us. "I have to warn you about what you'll hear. This isn't like a concert back at home. Although angels' singing is the most beautiful sound imaginable, its purpose is not just entertainment. It's how angels choose to communicate. In a minute you'll see all of the angels flying toward their balconies. There will be a dust falling off the edges of their wings. It is one of the most valued commodities in the universe, and it has hypnotic effects on humans. Be prepared."

I gripped Daemon's hand even tighter. Terry was bouncing up and down on the tips of her toes, and Uncle Spencer looked out in awe. The rolling thunder began as the angels flew in and landed on their balconies. The dust was lingering in the air. It was reflecting the light, and colors were dancing in all directions. Then it began. The thunderous sound of angels flying was replaced by total silence as angels stood on their balconies. Angels of all shapes and sizes—big and small, young and old—slowly opened their wings, and we saw them in pure angelic splendor. The singing began, but it sounded like orchestral music. It was soft and melodious; it drifted into our minds and through our senses. We had the feeling that we were floating. How long this went on, I wasn't sure, but I do remember being stunned as Gabriel broke forth in song. She was singing to all of the angels. There were no words, but I understood her meaning. She was saying that three Larkins were here on the balcony with her, and she asked the angels to give us their blessing and to also listen to what I had to say. Out of nowhere a voice rose next me. It was Daemon singing! His voice was so strong and beautiful. He was telling all the angels about me. I blushed. He told them I was beautiful, intelligent, charming, and witty, and he also told them how much he loved me, as my guardian angel. His voice then changed. He told them how important it was to help me to defeat the dark lord.

It was my turn next. I couldn't sing, so I entered the ribbon of time using my specular skills and connected with the minds of the angels. Things go so fast when your minds are connected, and words are not needed. I told them the whole story from the time I left Uncle Spencer's house till now. They knew about my work here in Mirror World and how I had assembled an army no longer under Lord Speculus's control. I then showed them how Speculus was corrupting them by bending their images so that the gold-tipped and silver-tipped angels would always be at odds. It served his purposes to keep the angels separated so they would not unite against him. I did a great job! And at the end, I asked for them to help me—to join the battle. I was so proud of myself.

The singing changed. The voices were getting louder and a lot more intense. All of us felt like we had heavy weights on our chests and couldn't breathe. The singing became more passionate, as if one group of angels was trying to oust the other. They were arguing; they were angry…They were gonna help me! Everything became a blur. I fainted. And when I woke up, I was on Gabriel's couch, and the singing had stopped.

"Oh my God, I must've fainted," I said as I jumped off the couch. "Thank you so much, Gabriel. Thank you, Daemon. I knew the angels would help me." I looked around at their solemn faces. "What is it? What's up? You look like you're all going to a funeral. Let's have a party before we gather our forces and go smash that bad angel's mirrors."

Nobody moved, and I kept talking. "Hey, so what did the angels say after I fainted?"

Daemon looked down at the floor. "They said *no!*"

"What do you mean *no*?" Then it struck me, and I moaned. "No? You mean they said they wouldn't help me? They can't do that. Gabriel, Daemon, you have to go tell them that they *have* to help me. That's why I came all the way here. You know we can't defeat the dark lord without their help. Please, please, please!"

I continued my blubbering, begging each person. But no one could help. Terry just sat there and did something she rarely ever does—cry. I was lost. What could I possibly do now? We gathered our things, and Gabriel led us down the tower. There were no more words to be said. I was moving in slow motion. I have never felt such an overwhelming wave of disappointment and depression. Everything I had worked to accomplish was ruined. Without the help of the angels, we could not defeat the dark lord. We all made our way out of the front door. Everyone was glum, avoiding all eye contact.

Terry stopped and said to me, "Cailyssa, I've got an idea. Meet me at the big fountain—the one that none of the angels use." And with that, Terry rocketed off into the air.

"Wait," I called after her. "There's nothing you can do. There's nothing anyone can do." My voice trailed off to a whisper.

It's a good thing that angel streets are smooth, because my feet could barely leave the ground. I was hunched over, shuffling, staring at the top of my shoes. What should I do now? Tell everybody it was a lost cause? Go home? Let Speculus ruin this world even more? What would he do to the dwarfs and Amazons after I'd left? Then I had no doubt that the vision I'd had in Uncle Spencer's mirror would eventually come true when I got back home. I couldn't see any way out of the situation.

"Cailyssa," Daemon said softly to me. "I'm sorry the angels decided not to help you. I did the best I could to convince them, and so did you. But they have been divided for so long, and there is much frustration and pain."

"They're stupid!" I yelled in frustration. "They're stupid angels. Can't they see that they are all angels, alike except for the color on the tips of their wings? How could one group think it's superior? It's crazy. How could angels do such a thing? Can't God just tell them what to do?"

"It doesn't work that way," Daemon said sadly. "All angels, as humans, have free will. They can choose what to do."

I just shook my head. I was so angry! We walked on in silence for a while. Then in the distance, we heard singing. But it sounded like human singing. Maybe I was just hearing things, but I thought I heard an old Beatles song. There it was again. *There's nothing you can't do that can't be done.* As we rounded the corner, we saw Terry in the ornate fountain that none of the angels used. She had all of the smaller angels—the ones who looked like children—in the fountain, and she was teaching them to sing. She was prancing around, getting them to sing, hold hands, and even splashing a little water. Just like with the elves, when my sister started a party and got people singing, everybody wanted to be around her. Terry, the ultimate fun pumper, was trying to cheer me up. All of the small angels had now joined voices with Terry, and a resounding chorus of "All You Need Is Love" reverberated through angel city.

"This is bad, very bad," Daemon said.

"What could be bad about a little fun, Daemon? I don't care what these angels think anymore; let them sing."

"It's not the singing I am worried about, Cailyssa. Look in the fountain! The reason the angels never use that fountain is that you can't see the tips of the wings. This could get dangerous. Stay close to me."

"Who cares—" I couldn't finish my sentence because I was knocked over by an angel flying right above my head.

Things became crazy. Angels were coming from all over. The big ones were pulling the little ones out of the fountain. I'm not sure what they were saying, but there was a lot of fighting and a lot of arguing. I yelled at Terry to get out of there, and I ran across to her. Daemon ran after us both. Then it occurred to me what had happened when I saw the smaller angels being carted away by the bigger ones. When the angels couldn't see the tips of their wings, they put aside their differences. They sang together, and they played together. And something happened that had not happened in millennia in Constantine: the gold-tipped angels and the silver-tipped angels actually held hands. But now they were all gone, pulled away after a brief moment of being united. How could angels be so mean?

Everything was really quiet. All of the angels were gone. Daemon, Terry, and I were soaking wet in the middle of the fountain. Uncle Spencer was soaked too as he waded in to try to help.

"I love what you were trying to do, little sister. You always try to cheer me up when I'm down," I said as I walked over to grab her hand.

"Look out!" Daemon screamed. He pulled out his sword.

I looked up. The sky was blotted out by enormous sets of wings. There was a group of angels descending on us fast, and they weren't there to pull the kids out of the fountain. These angels were dressed for battle and had all sorts of weapons. I pulled the swords out of my back scabbards and prepared myself to kick some angel butt. I'd had enough of angels today!

"Cailyssa, duck," Terry screamed as she flew straight toward me.

I did as she asked, and she impaled her claws in the chest of a large angel who had just landed behind me. Terry then placed her feet on the angel's chest and kicked off as she pulled out her claws. Unfortunately, angels heal very quickly, and this one was already reaching for his sword. Six angels were battling Daemon at the same time. He was like a whirlwind. His sword was spinning faster than I had ever seen it, and he sliced through the neck of one of the angels. His head dropped into the fountain like a big rock, and his body followed. Uncle Spencer and I were doing our best to deal with two mean-looking angels who had just landed in front of us. I was using all of my specular skills and the best of my fighting abilities, but all I could do was hold these angels off. I slashed at them, chopping some of them pretty good. But as soon as I did, they healed right up and came after me.

"Daemon," I yelled. "Have you seen Terry? I can't see her in the air."

Terry was over our heads, and she was dealing with four angels. She looked like a tiny wasp as she battled relentlessly. Her incredible speed and acrobatic ability made it very difficult for the angels to keep up with her. Every time an angel came near her, he paid the price as her long claws drew blood. The battle raged on. It seemed to be a draw. A squad of angels against the three of us, and we were holding our own. Something had to give.

"No!" Daemon roared as he sliced the head off another angel.

Daemon dropped his sword and began hurling his throwing knives at the angels who had now taken off into the air. I was just about to crow with delight, thinking we had beaten them, when I saw what they were doing.

"Save her, Daemon!" I shrieked. Four of the angels were carrying Terry away, each holding an arm and leg.

Daemon stopped throwing his knives. The angels were already high up in the sky.

"Do something!" I tried to yell as I fell to my knees in the fountain, pointing to the sky above.

"If I had my wings, perhaps I could have…helped. I'm so sorry, Cailyssa."

I ran over to him, sobbing. I pounded his chest with my fists, and I wept more. I tried to hit him anywhere I could. He just held on to me and let me whale away. I went crazy.

"You have to save her Daemon; you have to…" I cried. With my sword, I pierced one of the heads that had been severed from an angel. I threw the head against a nearby building. Then I began kicking and spitting on its body—feverish with rage—not caring that the blood had drenched me.

I don't know how I made it back to Evad's tavern. Daemon and Uncle Spencer later told me that there was nothing they could do to calm me down. I entered the tavern covered in blood. Evad was aghast. Everyone cleared out quickly. The elves and Halodire stared at me. I sensed that Uncle Spencer and Daemon were behind me.

I turned and said in my most menacing voice, "Don't even think about telling me to calm down!" I pointed my sword in a complete circle at everybody. "That goes for all of you, too." I turned to the elves. "Grab your stuff, we are *outta* this place! And if I see an angel on the way out, I'll have its head!"

Still covered in blood, I traveled the ribbon of time and appeared instantly in Gabriel's tower, carrying a sword that I had taken from one of the headless angels. I held it up and, with two hands, firmly impaled it into the floor.

"Thanks for your help!" I said to Gabriel.

She said nothing. A tear started to form in her eye, but I disappeared before she had a chance to say a thing.

No one prevented us from leaving the city, and we didn't see another angel. We marched on with my whole company until I couldn't see the rotten outline of Constantine anymore. I hated that city. I hated the angels. The dark angels that took Terry had been working for Lord Speculus. Terry was already a prisoner in his castle. This was one vision of the future that I never thought would come true. I didn't have time to feel sad. I had to hold onto my anger and save her. I saw a small pool of water—and in it I saw the face of Lord Speculus.

"Dear Cailyssa," he hissed. "I thought you'd like to see your sister's sleeping accommodations." His evil laughter trailed away.

I couldn't look away. An image of Terry appeared in the water. She was in one of the highest towers of the castle. The room had one small window, and in the middle was a black stone altar. One of the giant Nephilim was holding Terry down. Ttocs was standing over her. He turned toward me and smiled. Then he picked up a heavy hammer and a sharp metal spike. Turning back toward Terry, he held down her wing and searched for the most sensitive joint. He put the spike there, turned to give me another rotten smile, and proceeded to pound away, piercing Terry's wing and pinning her to the altar. Terry screamed in pain. Ttocs finished the other wing, relishing each hammer blow. Terry looked like a crucified bird. She was sobbing and shrieking in agony—arching her back off the table, only to find more pain in each movement. The image of the dark lord returned. He was on his throne, tapping his fingers, looking at me, and shaking his head.

"You really shouldn't have let your sister be captured," he said in a smooth, sarcastic voice. "I thought you were *the* Cailyssa Larkin: powerful, specular abilities, time traveler. Yet you can't seem to keep your baby sister safe." Contempt oozed through his voice. "But please don't fret, my dear. I'll be sure to have Ttocs take good care of her. He always fancied her; perhaps he should—"

"Screw you!" I stamped on the puddle in front of me. "If he touches her again, I'll kill him myself!"

"You are welcome to try. Meanwhile I'll check what other diabolical tortures are available to Ttocs. One of the advantages of having been to hell and back is that you know *all* of the best tortures." Speculus sneered at me and laughed.

"After I'm done with Ttocs, you're *next*!" The swords flew off my back, and I drove them through his image in the puddle.

CHAPTER 30

THE CASTLE OF DARK MIRRORS

When Longtooth heard the news that Terry was captured, she bellowed and spit a fireball so far into the sky that the end could not be seen. She was almost uncontrollable, and I knew she wanted to fly to the dark lord's castle for an immediate rescue. But I needed her to wait. Dolhar calmed her down, and I promised her that she would be able to unleash her fury very soon. I called a meeting of all of the leaders to organize the plans for battle. Yllib, Sariel, Daemon, Uncle Spencer, and Halodire sat around a small campfire at dusk. Longtooth joined the meeting. Her golden eyes were dark and ringed with fire.

I started the meeting by pointing to Longtooth's eyes. "The fire you see in the eyes of the dragon should be within all of you. The dark lord's days of corrupting people's souls will soon be *over*!" My commanding tone surprised even me.

I grabbed a spear that I had taken from one of the angels we had battled, and I snapped it over my knee with a strength

I didn't think I had. Good thing it broke. I used the tip of the spear to draw a circle around a large rock. I continued making marks in the sand until I had finished my map. Seeing the future is great when preparing for battle!

I pointed with the spear as I spoke. "The stone in the middle is the dark lord's castle. That's where Terry is, and that's where all of the black mirrors are that Speculus has been using to corrupt people's souls. We will rescue Terry, and I will destroy the dark lord's black mirrors and then banish him to hell."

I used the tip of the spear to explain the battle plan. The dark lord had lined up a huge army of raxs. Since there were so many of the foul creatures, he had them lined up in rows, which were driven by their leaders from behind. Their lines stretched for over a mile and ended at the edges of the forest on each side. The dwarfs would form in dozens of phalanx formations across from the lines of raxs. These wedge formations of powerful dwarfs, armed with hammers and axes, would seem nearly indestructible to the raxs army. The Amazons—with their incredible speed—would act as cavalry, working behind and in between the dwarfs as these two forces mowed down the raxs army from the front. My company of elves—along with Daemon, Uncle Spencer, and Halodire—would adopt flanking positions and hide in the woods on the right side of the raxs army. Longtooth and Dolhar, an army of two, would lie hidden in the woods to the left side. The dwarfs and Amazons would engage the raxs from the front. On my command, we would surprise the raxs and attack from each side—pinching them to destruction. The raxs would not be able to flee, since the river would be behind them, and we would crush them all from the other three sides. Lord Speculus was foolish to have left most of his army near the river. I had been deeply riding my specular skills and could see how this battle would go. At the end of the day, we would be victorious!

"That's the plan. Have everyone ready to go before sunrise tomorrow." *Time for a motivational speech?* I wondered to myself. I paused, thought of Terry, and got really angry. "Don't expect any help from the angels. If we encounter any dark angels working for Speculus, this is what will happen to them!" As I said this, I reached into a bag behind me and grabbed the long black hair of a dark angel's head. Daemon had severed it from one the angels in the fountain when they took Terry. I turned around slowly to show it to everyone. I then spun it several times and whipped it high into the air. Longtooth was only too happy to incinerate it to ashes. So much for speeches before a great battle. I was more of a person of action anyway. As the ashes from the head fell down, I turned my back on everyone and walked into the woods, alone.

Of course I'm never truly alone. Angel boy had followed me out to the woods, and I could tell without turning that he was behind me.

"Cailyssa, if I may—"

"Say what you want, Daemon, but don't try to talk me out of what we're doing."

"Actually, Cailyssa, I was going to say that I was most impressed with the way you handled yourself. You projected power, confidence, and a regal presence that inspired us all."

"Thanks, Daemon, I have to stay focused if I want to save Terry. I'm worried sick about her, but I know if I open the door on those emotions, I will lose control. I'll be on my knees crying and puking, and I don't have time for it."

Daemon came up and put his large hands on my shoulders. His steady gaze was on me, and for a minute I became lost in his eyes. A few emotions leaked out, and I grabbed him in the tightest embrace I could. He responded and wrapped his arms around me as we rocked back and forth for a long time.

Daemon whispered in my ear, "Just promise me one thing, Cailyssa. Don't try to go anywhere during this battle without me. We can defeat Lord Speculus and save Terry, but we have to do it together."

"I can't promise anything," I said as I stepped back pushing him away harshly.

Daemon looked shocked. "I will not permit any harm to come to you. Do not make my job more difficult by trying to do something on your own!"

"I'll do whatever I have to do in order to save Terry."

"So will I," Daemon said, shaking his head, looking truly worried. "But *please*, Cailyssa, don't consider asking me to do anything that would require me to leave your side. I will *never* abide by such a request."

"Right now, Daemon, I'm not making any promises to anyone except myself. I will do whatever I have to do to save Terry and to rid this place of the dark lord."

"Cailyssa, I have been in many battles before. Heed my advice. You're strong, capable, and highly skilled. But you can't do this alone; you *need* help." Daemon grabbed my shoulders, and I pushed his hands away. He whispered, "There comes a time when leaders must make some very difficult decisions."

"I *know*!" I yelled too loudly. "Sometimes it comes to a point where you have to decide *who* lives and *who* dies. Don't you think I *know* that? That's what I came here to *do*! I'm a Larkin!" I turned my back on Daemon and fled into the woods to pray.

Everybody woke up in the dark. I heard the sharpening of weapons and quiet voices readying themselves for what would prove to be a bloody day. I vanished and reappeared to speak and show encouragement before each group of warriors. I hoped that showing them that I possessed such an ability would inspire confidence. I stood proudly before them, showing no hint of fear but knowing that not all would return.

It began in the dark. We slowly crept up on the sleeping raxs army, everyone in place. Speculus must have somehow seen what we were doing, and we heard screams from the raxs as they rallied their troops. Some of the Amazons had brought longbows, and they began raining arrows upon the raxs as they tried to ready themselves. I told the dwarfs to move forward before the raxs were prepared. The battle began.

Each wedge of dwarfs pierced the first lines of the raxs army like giant arrows, cutting an enormous path. The raxs were furiously battling the dwarfs. Dwarfs are extremely hardy and can withstand an amazing amount of wounds. But there were just too many raxs. Some of the dwarfs began to fall, but others replaced them to keep the wedge in place. It looked like we were winning until the earth cracked. From the crevice a huge hoard of the evil creatures climbed out and charged. Speculus had prepared a surprise for me; I had not seen this coming. But he didn't know that I had a few surprises of my own. There were now just too many raxs, and the dwarfs were fighting just to not be driven back. The Amazons were in a blood lust, each killing a dozen or more of the raxs with their spinning lanza blades. Wave upon wave of the raxs moved in, and the battle began to turn for the worse. Our forces were starting to be decimated, and we were being pushed back.

My flank force was hidden in the forest. I drew my swords, and everyone followed my lead. We began to attack the raxs army from the side. We stopped at the edge of the forest, and I disappeared for a few seconds and appeared in front of Longtooth and Dolhar—who were hiding on the other side of the forest. I wanted to coordinate the timing of our attack so that we both hit the raxs simultaneously. We did!

The raxs army appeared shocked. They didn't expect forces to attack them from the sides. My plan was looking successful. I knew that Speculus was using his mirrors to find how forces were aligned. I could feel his presence in the ribbon of time. Every time he probed, I pushed back. I wasn't able to hide everything from him, but he didn't know about our pincer maneuver until the last moment. The raxs were being squeezed from three sides. Longtooth and Dolhar were incredibly effective. They incinerated thousands of evil creatures, and Longtooth fought as she never had before, knowing that Terry was being tortured in the castle.

We were driving the creatures back. Some of them were beginning to fall into the river of death. The souls within claimed them, and fear was creeping through the back of the raxs army. Now all we had to do was unleash part of my secret plan. Since Longtooth had almost completely slaughtered her side of the raxs army, she flew back into the woods. She grabbed two tremendous wooden bridges that the dwarfs had secretly constructed. She flew over the river of death and dropped the bridges on each side. Done! We could cross those bridges, and our army would charge across to the doors of the dark castle. The dwarfs and Amazons began crossing, but when they touched the other side, an evil shriek came from the castle. Two black cloaks fell to the ground, and behind them were the two Nephilim, cranking catapults with immense flaming boulders. The rocks crashed into the bridge. I screamed, but it was too late. The bridges exploded in a fiery crash, and the dwarfs and Amazons who were left fell in the water. They swam, trying to reach shore and climb out. Their comrades on the shore were holding out their hands and throwing lines, but the dead souls in the water below slowly dragged the swimmers under. I had just sent hundreds of people to their deaths. I watched as each one was dragged below. The screams for help were horrible. I was sick. The survivors who were still floating looked at one another in horror, awaiting their doom. How was it possible that I didn't see this? Perhaps Speculus had hidden something from me, too. At this point there was nothing we could do. I used my time-travel skills to vanish and reappear, calling our forces to retreat. We had almost completely destroyed the dark lord's forces—over ten thousand raxs! But what good was it? There was no way that we could cross the river of death now.

That night, we set up guards and licked our wounds. Daemon and I went around to give support and encouragement. Many had fought bravely that day, and many had died. Unfortunately, there wasn't time for mourning the dead. Terry was still stuck in the castle, and Ttocs was still hurting her. He planned to break her will, and if he did Speculus had promised him a reward: Terry would be his bride. I couldn't ever let that happen. I went into the woods to be alone, so no one could hear as I poured some water into a small bowl.

"Your army is gone, Speculus. You're next," I said to the water bowl in front of me. I wanted to be first in our next contact.

"I was waiting for you to call," Speculus said as he sat upon his black throne. "You must be very impressed with yourself today. Look how many of your friends have died. I especially enjoyed watching the elves and Amazons slowly fall to the souls from the river. Did you see their faces right before they were dragged under: each painted in a portrait of pure terror—knowing what would come?" He snickered.

"You lost an army today! Don't lecture me about loss!"

Speculus laughed in that spiteful way that I hated more than anything. "Loss? Loss? Do you think I consider losing raxs a loss? I kill the foul creatures myself when I'm bored! I have an endless supply. They respawn from the bloody depths behind my castle. I have an endless supply of raxs soldiers for my armies." Speculus paused and stood up in front of his throne. "You, however, Cailyssa, do not have an endless supply of friends—nor an endless supply of…sisters. Behold the wonderful new toy I have given Ttocs."

As he said this, the image of Terry appeared in front of me. She was semiconscious and obviously still in a lot of pain. Ttocs came into the picture, always being sure to look at me in the cruelest fashion he could conjure. From a table next to Terry, he raised several small chains. At the end of each was a very large fishing hook; on the other end of the chains were black steel balls. He turned toward Terry and slowly slid the hooks into her, piercing her flesh between each rib.

"No! I'll kill you, Ttocs!" I screamed.

Ttocs turned around toward me and held the small steel balls at the other end of the chain between his fingers. He smiled and let them drop. Terry screamed.

Daemon was close behind me. He must've seen my knees buckle. I did not want to show any fear to Speculus, despite the horrors he was inflicting on my sister. I touched the water and bent the image away from Terry and back to the dark lord's throne room. Daemon stood close behind me.

"Must we fight over changing the TV channel, Cailyssa? I want to switch us back to the horror movie that your *sister* is starring in. I'm recording it on my DVR, and I'll probably watch it many times." The dark lord sat back on his throne and crossed his legs. "I see my good friend Daemon is there—"

Daemon roared, "I should've killed you when we last met!"

"Daemon, in case you don't recall, you failed when you tried. Just like you failed the last time you were playing guardian angel. When will Cailyssa realize that you will again fail in your duties and let her die, too? It's only a matter of time till Larkin history repeats itself."

"Not this time, Speculus," I said in a calm, even voice.

I knew Speculus was about to speak, so I kicked over the bowl of water. I dipped into my specular skills and let out a burst of energy that prevented him from using the image of any of the water in the area. I needed time to think.

Daemon and I returned to camp. I could tell Daemon was so angry that he was ready to spit some nails. First, he loved Terry, and second, Speculus just tossed him the worst insult imaginable. When we returned to camp, I told everybody to try to get some sleep. I tried to sleep too. I slid into my sleeping bag, feeling safe since Daemon was close by watching. Some type of fitful sleep approached, and I immersed myself in it, knowing I could touch on my specular skills in a dreamlike domain to plan what I needed to do the following day. Visions of the future floated before me like wisps of smoke—some clear and others fading rapidly. The faces of my parents, my past relatives, and even Gabriel spun around in my mind, whispering advice and giving loving support. I awoke the next morning but kept my eyes shut. The sequence of dreams last night laid out all the cards on the table for me. Now it was time for me to make the hard choices. What was it that Gabriel had said? *Love is not only who you can see yourself with, but it's also…who you can't see yourself without.* Great advice. Who should I let die first? Maybe me? Maybe that's how I could save Terry.

I gathered all the leaders from the battle and sat them down again. There was no way to cross the river of death, and I didn't want any more of them to die trying.

"We killed many raxs and destroyed an army, yet our plan to cross the river of death failed, and we will not try to do it again. I don't want to lose any more lives that way. What I do want you all to do is to pretend as though we are preparing to attack. Move up toward the river, make a lot of noise, shoot a bunch of arrows, and pretend that you're gonna attack. But don't. You're the diversion. Hopefully your antics will distract Speculus and his minions long enough so that a small force of us can secretly cross the river to save Terry and finish what we *came here to do*!" I walked away with Uncle Spencer, Daemon, Halodire, Longtooth, and Dolhar.

"Here's the plan. Halodire is going to use some of his famous charms, and we are going to cross the river of death."

"That's impossible," Daemon interjected. "His charms have no sway over the dead."

"That's true," I retorted. "But I spoke with Halodire, and he said his charms work perfectly well on a wraith. Halodire will summon the wraith with his boat, and we will use that to get to the other side. Longtooth and Dolhar will wait in the woods. I will keep in touch with them, and at the perfect moment, they will fly in and help. The first thing we will do is to find Terry and rescue her—after we kill Ttocs. Longtooth will fly in and take all of you to safety. Daemon and I will go alone to face Speculus."

We waited until night, and my remaining army began to cause a distraction. I had to focus on using my specular abilities to hide us from the gaze of the dark lord. Daemon, Uncle Spencer, Halodire, and I crept forth to the river of death. As we approached, Halodire made a soft cooing sound, and the wraith and his boat appeared, creeping toward us. We stayed hidden in the shadows, our black cloaks covering us. As the wraith approached, Halodire called out to him, speaking to him in some elfin language I'd never heard. When the wraith's boat came to shore, Halodire did his magic. His halo charm went into full effect, and he spoke to the wraith in some manner that captured this entity and enthralled it. Daemon crept up slowly and grabbed the wraith. His superhuman strength and speed were incredible. He grabbed the creature and twisted its head off. He threw the carcass and the head into the river, and we all sneaked on the boat.

Halodire, wearing the wraith's cape, used his expertise as an oarsman to guide us across. We huddled low until we reached the other side. Now was the tricky part. I concealed us from Speculus's gaze and contacted Longtooth, and she flew overhead spitting balls of fire at the raxs in front of us. At the same time, my army on the other side shot arrows in the air. The coordinated effort scattered the raxs, and we sneaked around a small gully and made our way to the castle. As we approached, we silently killed any raxs that took notice of us. When we reached the castle wall, Uncle Spencer took a rope with a grappling hook and threw it into a window. We grabbed the rope and climbed up.

We landed in an empty stone guardhouse and crossed the parapet walkway. A guard appeared, and Halodire shot two arrows through his head before he had a chance to make a peep. We continued onward and made it to the back of the castle and to the tower where they were keeping Terry. Daemon muscled the door open, and we crept up the spiral stone staircase to the room at the top. We burst through, weapons ready. The room was empty. Except for a mirror on the wall.

"Cailyssa, you should've knocked, and I would have been happy to greet you at the door. I am not without manners," the dark lord's face said in the mirror. "Your specular skills are weak. I foresaw that you would be coming to this room, so I moved Terry to a new location—equally painful. You could wander in my castle forever and I would anticipate your every move and you would never find her. I do, however, offer you one other option. Join me, Cailyssa!" The dark lord gushed as his whole form became visible. "Join me. I will release your sister, and no harm will come to your friends."

I grabbed one of Daemon's throwing knives off his belt and hurled it through the mirror. We heard the noise of a bunch of raxs—the welcoming committee. Everyone else bolted out of the room to make sure they had space to fight. However, I stayed behind in the room; I needed to do something important. I closed my eyes and reached as deeply into my specular skills as I could. I could see that the raxs in front of us were simply a ploy. Speculus was trying to use them to herd us in a different direction; he wanted us at a certain point in the castle where he would have us surrounded. I had to be careful. Speculus was in his throne room looking at all his mirrors and using his skills to see the future, but he was also trying to bend the visions I saw in my mind. This would be a *specular* chess match: the dark lord versus me, fighting mind to mind. But I was ready to make the next move.

I ran out of the room and found my friends battling the raxs. The raxs's leader was driving them forward, trying to push us down the walkway to the left. I grabbed my swords and charged straight through the middle of the raxs—each of my hands swinging wildly and hacking everything in my path. The raxs looked stunned. I was now on the other side. I was out of Daemon's protection zone, and he launched a vicious attack with his white sword, cleaving through several raxs at a time. I watched as Daemon demolished the entire company of raxs just to get next to me. There were piles of disemboweled raxs everywhere. When Daemon got into the zone of fury—when he was trying to protect me—I didn't think there was any force in the universe that could stop him.

"Cailyssa!" Daemon bellowed, not even out of breath after his exertion. "I told you to never leave my side. You must stay with me and let me protect you. I will *not* tolerate—"

"Sorry, Daemon," I quietly interrupted. "We don't have much time. Follow me."

Daemon stayed right next to me, and I looked back and saw Uncle Spencer and Halodire walking through the piles of raxs meat, shaking their heads at what Daemon and I had just accomplished. I held up my hand to stop everyone, and I made my next chess move! I sneaked into the back door of Lord Speculus's mind and mirrors. I used an image from the raxs that I captured in my mind. I showed him that the raxs were winning, driving us to where he desired. The ruse wouldn't last long, so we ran ahead, but—hopefully—by the time Speculus found out what I had done, we'd have Terry.

CHAPTER 31

GAMBIT

We ducked into a small door and ran down an undersized corridor that was used for carrying supplies through the castle. I stopped us at a drainage gate that was above our heads. Daemon reached up and pushed it open and helped us all climb through. We were in the middle of a large stone courtyard, and behind us was the edge of the castle wall—and beyond that was a deadly drop to the rocks below. To the front of us was a large stone building. It looked like an old church with no cross. It had a stone staircase leading up to an enormous set of wooden doors. I ran up the stairs and pounded on the doors.

"Terry, are you in there?" I screamed.

"Lyssaaa!" Terry answered weakly.

Then I heard a wail, and I knew Ttocs had embedded another one of those torture hooks to punish Terry for her outcry. Daemon and Halodire broke down the door. Daemon's sword cut through it like butter, and Halodire burst through the timbers. We entered a large room, and way in the back was Terry, impaled on the altar. We ran across the room as

Daemon shouted warnings I didn't listen to. When we approached the altar, Ttocs stood behind it, swinging the torture chain, and the two Nephilim stood at his sides. Terry turned her head and looked at me. She looked horrible. There was blood dripping down her wings, her eyes were bloodshot and tearing, and trickles of blood fell from the hooks that Ttocs had used on her. She was moving her mouth trying to form a word, but all I could hear was a croaking sound.

Ttocs spoke. "Hellooo, Cailyssa, nice to see you, baby sweets. I was just chatting with your lovely sister. She's a cutie."

I took a step forward—Daemon right behind me—with both my swords and my soul lusting for blood. "I've been waiting for this moment, Ttocs. You'll pay for what you did to Terry, but I plan to kill you very slowly."

Ttocs laughed. "This won't be like at the mall, *Cailyssa*. You're not gonna smack your sneaker across *my* face again. In fact you're going to do nothin'—except when I tell you!" He pointed at me.

Before I could make a move, I heard a dozen doors surrounding the room open. Out of doors came dark angels, just like the ones we had encountered at the fountain in Constantine. They surrounded us and cut off our path to Terry. But nothing would stop me now! I went into my crazy battle mode, using my abilities to see time in slow motion. I spun my blades with furious abandon and whaled on the angels. I disappeared and reappeared, taking an angel with me each time. Daemon was with me. His sword was swinging, and the white light was never brighter. I saw the faces of the dark angels, ashen with fear at the sight of my guardian angel. He slew them handily. Halodire and Uncle Spencer did the best they could, but against the fury of a group of angels, they just did their best to try to stay alive.

Daemon and I were finding some success. We had killed or maimed half the angels—at least enough to take them out of the battle. Ttocs became nervous and ran. The Nephilim stormed forth, and Halodire was on them, shooting them with multiple arrows and fighting with a long spear. I ran to Terry, but before I could cross the length of the room, the floor gave out, and a deep crevice appeared in front of us. Daemon was yelling at us to go back. We heard a great rumbling sound, and more angels appeared from the crack, all ready for battle. "Follow me," I yelled, and I ran back out the wooden door into the large courtyard. The angels all came out the door. They were grinning, as they could now use their wings to attack us from the air.

They marched forward. There wasn't much room left in the courtyard. Our backs were to the edge of the castle wall and the deadly drop below. Time for another surprise. We had lured the angels right where I had hoped to.

"Take this, Speculus!" I screamed.

Just then, a dozen angels shot into the air, and a huge fireball engulfed them and charred them to cinders. The ashes fell upon the other angels as Longtooth and Dolhar landed behind us. More angels came forth, and Longtooth's rage was incredible. She spewed forth flame and tore through angels with her claws and teeth. When she left for battle in the air, her anger was even more terrifying. There were now hundreds of angels encircling her, but none of their weapons could pierce her scales. It's rare to see fear on the face of an angel—but when I looked up, I could see that now. The angels were falling from the sky; Longtooth was swatting them like flies. She then landed in front of us. Dolhar and his ax took care of the few angels that were left. Longtooth and Dolhar, with us behind, stormed up the stairs to save Terry. Longtooth was too big for the door, so she tore apart the stones with Dolhar by her side. The room was empty of enemies except for the giant Nephilim warriors who remained behind the stone altar that held Terry.

Longtooth looked down at Terry, her golden eyes tearing. She connected with Terry's mind. "I have felt every hook and spike, as our hearts are connected. I'm sorry it took so long to save you. But Cailyssa has a plan to save us all."

The Nephilim warriors stood still as stone behind the altar. Longtooth reared up on her hind legs. Fury boiled from her eyes. She opened her mouth and was about to engulf the Nephilim, but they raised weapons that were hidden behind their backs: enormous crossbows with magically tipped arrows, designed by Speculus himself for one purpose—to kill a dragon! Before Longtooth could bring her head down, the Nephilim shot the arrows straight into Longtooth's heart. Terry's back arched off the table as if she had been shot, too. For one long moment, Longtooth just stood there. Then she collapsed—her great body crashing down and her head right next to the altar.

Her golden eyes met Terry's for the last time as she whispered, "I wish we could fly together one more time, Terry. You know how special you have been to me. Take care of what I gave you."

And with those last words, Longtooth died. Before anyone else could move, Dolhar charged the Nephilim, hacking insanely with his ax. One grabbed him from behind, and the other took out a sword and pierced Dolhar's chest. He died quickly. They tossed his body like a piece of trash, and he landed on top of Longtooth. Now, both dead, their bodies slowly faded away.

"Oh my *God*!" I wailed at the ceiling.

I didn't expect this! In my visions Longtooth had saved Terry, and we had all flown out of here on her back. This turn of events knocked me down. I stood there stunned—as we all did—until I saw Terry crying, reaching out her hand.

"Longtooth, no, no...Longtooth, please," she whimpered.

I refocused on my sister and yelled, "Daemon, Halodire, jump over the crack in the floor, and grab Terry so we can get out of here."

Before anyone could move, the crack in the floor widened. It spread across the entire room, and the walls fell down. The crack became a crevice and spread out along the whole length of the castle. A wall of flame billowed from what had now become a monstrous crevice. It was so powerful that it blew us all backward with incredible heat and wind. Then it stopped, and after a long silence, a massive black wall erupted from where the flames had come from and shot into the sky. But it was not a wall at all. There were bodies and wings filled with weapons. It was a host of dark angels, and they flew into the sky and swarmed around us in a gigantic circle. From the middle of that dark circle, a form emerged and flew toward us. As it landed in front of us, concealed by black-and-silver wings, hundreds of angels landed at our sides. Others continued to fly above.

"Peekaboo!" The dark lord snickered as he unfolded his wings and gazed at us. "Another Larkin plan foiled. And now I have *both* Larkins in my grasp," he said as he slowly walked toward us with arms akimbo. "Did you really think your pitiful specular abilities could match mine? I've been a step ahead of you every inch of the way. I saw in your mind what you were doing. A specular chess match—is that how you saw it? Well, if so the appropriate term at this point would be…*checkmate*!" Speculus's voice carried such power that it made us all take a step back—all except Daemon.

Speculus stood with his hands on his hips, his eyes laced with small flames. I could see him now as the horrible angel he was. He was pure evil. The tremendous malicious powers within him pushed against me, and I suffocated for a moment.

"Did you really think you had any chance of winning? Each of your gambits has failed. You were even foolish enough to assume that the raxs were my army, but they are nothing but pawns. Here is my true army," Speculus said as he held up his hands and pointed at the angels flying above. "A legion of angels from hell, a force that has never been defeated!" Speculus looked up and smiled, basking in his victorious moment. "Chain them and take them to the dungeon. Cailyssa will then choose to join me, or they all die," Speculus said to the angels surrounding us.

I looked at Daemon and he at me. This was not the time to fight. We were all manacled and pushed out of the room. Daemon was raw fury, and he stared into the eyes of Speculus the entire time as we were dragged away, never turning his head from him.

"This isn't over, Azazel!" Daemon shouted, using Speculus's true name.

The four of us marched slowly down into the bowels of the castle under the watchful eyes of the dark angels. None of them said a word. They were horrible for me to look at. Although they had the beauty that all angels possess, they did not have the grace of God. Every time one of them got near me, I felt a dark presence, and a cold feeling swept through me that felt as though it was emptying the goodness from my soul.

"They will not harm you," Daemon said to comfort me. "What you're feeling is the darkness of their souls; there is nothing good within them. These are some of the angels that left heaven for hell."

We were thrown in a small dungeon, and the door was locked behind us. There were several angels outside guarding us. We sat down—sort of falling down—with our backs against the icy, wet walls. Our hands were still in shackles. I noticed that Daemon still stood. He screamed and broke his shackles off. He stared straight ahead, not saying a word. Uncle Spencer was softly praying and so was Halodire. I put my head between my knees and looked down at the metal cuffs holding my ankles. I tried to cry but couldn't. The pain was too much to bear. Thoughts of Terry and all those who had died overwhelmed me. I couldn't breathe. Every breath strained. I was trying to draw in air, but it was getting harder with every breath. Daemon came over to me and picked me up—with one hand under my knees and one hand behind my shoulders. He slid down the wall, and I sat there on his lap like a child. A tear fell from his eye and touched my cheek, and some of his angel magic rushed through me—just enough to hold my breath steady.

I couldn't see any future. All I could see was the past. I saw visions of the people I had gathered—those who had died—in the hope of defeating Speculus: Dolhar, Longtooth, the Amazons, and the dwarfs. And finally I saw a vision of Terry, still impaled upon that altar, with Ttocs at her side. Would all of us be dead soon? A feeling crept into me that I had never truly experienced—a sick, black, empty feeling of complete dread. Now I knew. I truly knew what it felt like when all hope was lost.

CHAPTER 32

AMAZING GRACE

I'm not sure if it was morning or night, but I awoke to the sound of Daemon whispering in my ear. "Cailyssa, I've given you enough strength with my tears for you to overcome the evil curses of this cell. You need to use your time-travel abilities and leave this place. It's the only hope you have. Save yourself, and perhaps one day…we will meet again. I'll always *love* you."

I was stunned. I hadn't really thought about leaving. Of course I wouldn't leave my friends to die. But perhaps there was some way I could use my abilities to jump to another place in this castle and defeat the dark lord. I didn't want to give up.

Daemon sensed my thoughts and quickly said, "Cailyssa, do not try to venture out in this castle alone. There is no hope that you can defeat Speculus by yourself—or save Terry. The dark lord will see all of your moves."

I wasn't sure what to do at this point. Daemon was right. What chance *did* I have against a legion of angels? But I couldn't simply leave my friends to die. I was boxed in. I tried to take a calming breath and think. As I did this, I remembered being in Gabriel's tower and her parting words to me: *Pray. Lord knows it helps.* So that's what I did. I didn't always find it helpful reciting the prayers I had learned, so I just kind of talked things out in my mind, hoping that someone was listening. My specular abilities started to get back online, but the convoluted visions before me overwhelmed me. Guilt overwhelmed me. *How many did you let die, Cailyssa? You have failed!* I thought.

There must be something I could do—something to ruin Speculus and his plans. But what? My mind started arguing with me. *Maybe you didn't fail, yet, Cailyssa,* a voice inside my mind intoned.

I screamed back at the voice. *How can you have any hope at a time like this? Maybe this praying stuff isn't all it's made out to be. Sometimes it's OK to give up and die. Isn't it? I tried my best; I did what I could.*

Then I got angry and shouted, "Why did I have to come here anyway? If I had to do this all over again, I'd stay safe and sound at home with Terry."

Everyone turned to look at me screaming at the wall. They were all in deep despair, and they didn't blame me a bit. I was still sitting next to Daemon, staring down at my feet, when I noticed something small floating down to land at the tip of my shoe. It was the tiniest white feather. Where had it come from? Maybe one of the dark angels had dropped it? That couldn't be; it was smaller than my thumb. I picked it up, held it between my fingers, and looked at it closely. My specular skills boiled with power; I could time travel again despites the curses Speculus put here! Then it hit me, and I disappeared. Daemon, Halodire, and Uncle Spencer were relieved that at least I had saved myself.

I reappeared in Gabriel's tower, free of the handcuffs. Gabriel was waiting there for me.

I started speaking frantically. "Gabriel, please, I didn't know what to do. But then I saw this tiny white feather. It reminded me of you when you showed me Daemon's wings."

I walked quickly toward her, and she held out her hands palms up—just as she had when we first met. I placed my hands upon hers and let her good graces flow through me and calm me. I looked up into her eyes. My eyes were like giant saucers, and my face was drooping as I stammered, "Gabriel, there's got to be something you can do to help us."

I started telling her the whole story, but after a few words, I realized she knew the whole thing.

"I wish I could send forth my own legion of angels and rid this world and the universe of Azazel!" Gabriel shouted. But she looked down and said, "But I can't. Things don't work that way. There are rules."

"Screw the rules!" I yelled back as I took my hands away. "Somebody has to help! How can you just stand by and let evil take its course? I thought angels were good. Can't you just contact God and get me some help?"

For a moment Gabriel looked at me, and a small smile on her face told me she was going to help me. My heart leaped for joy. I could save Terry and all my friends!

"Cailyssa, I can't help you directly. But let me give you a little advice. When you leave the city—walk by the fountain that Terry was singing in and say a prayer."

"Is that it? That's it?" I squeaked. "I need an army of angels who want to kick butt. I can't waste my time praying at a stupid fountain when my friends are dying. What kind of advice is that, anyway?"

I stormed out of Gabriel's room, using my feet rather than my specular abilities. I walked out the front door of her house and slammed it shut. What the hell? I knew I was not supposed to use that word in anger, but I didn't give a crap. I was sick of these angels. The only ones that seemed to do anything were the bad ones.

I walked listlessly through the city of angels. It looked like many of them were avoiding me—for good reason. I looked like a bloody mess. My hair was matted down and caked with blood, there were cuts all over me, and I walked as though I was ready to kill. I walked right by the stupid fountain. If I'd had a penny, I would have thrown it in, but I wasn't gonna waste my time praying in front of it. Then I stopped, as if I had hit a wall.

I walked up to the edge of the fountain and looked at the reflection of the water in front of me. There I was in the reflection, but it was a hideous form looking back at me—just like at home, when I woke up in the morning and smacked the mirror with my brush. It's no wonder I hated mirrors. I looked like hell, literally. Then I had an idea. Placing my finger into the fountain, I summoned my specular abilities to show the stupid angels of this city what their inaction had caused. I began using my skills to change the images in the water. My mind was exploding—bursting forth an HD video from my brain. It showed the whole battle, from our early victories to our horrible defeat. And just like a good horror movie, it ended with a picture of Terry tortured on Speculus's stone altar.

I opened my eyes and saw that many small angels surrounded the fountain—all the small angels who had held hands and sang with Terry. They stared at Terry's image, their eyes moist and their lips trembling. They stepped into the forbidden fountain pool, the gold tips and silver tips of their wings held above the water. They all held hands as they looked down at the image of Terry floating before them. They began to weep small tears with no sound. As they did so, they wrapped their wings around themselves to use the tips of their feathers to wipe the tears that slid down their cheeks. Some tears were missed and finally dripped into the fountain. Everything suddenly stopped. Nothing could be heard except the fountain and the tears of angel dust hitting the water. Softly, they began to sing with the grace of God powering their tiny voices. The sound was like nothing I will ever hear again in my life. It was the sweetest sound in the universe. The small angels had put aside all of their differences. The colors on the tips of their wings meant nothing anymore. Suddenly, the tips of their wings began to glow—all turning white—and a heavenly light burst forth and engulfed their wings. All of the vibrant colors exploded before me! Their wings looked even more magnificent—if that was possible. They had *passed* the test; the doors to heaven were open for them. But they continued to sing on, their voices staying true, as their unity and oneness brought incredible power to their song. The voices rang through the city of Constantine with such incredible force and loveliness that every angel hearing the sound was overwhelmed and stood frozen. Every angel in the city—more than I could've possibly imagined—flew to the fountain.

The small angels continued their melody, but now their voices changed. They had shown all the angels the power in putting differences aside, and they had shown the path to heaven. Their voices were strong and pure. They were asking everyone to help—to help Terry! My heart filled with hope, and the singing stopped. I blinked. The angels looked at each other, almost as if they didn't know what to do. I touched the water and showed them a vision of Speculus and the black castle. At that moment, they realized the true extent of the dark lord's manipulations and how they had been corrupted for so long. The singing began again, but the song was not sweet; it was angry, very angry. And something happened at that moment that had not happened in the history of Constantine. All of the angels joined together, grabbed their weapons, and flew off into the air.

I cried into the air with fury, and my voice echoed off the walls of Constantine. "This is *my* chance to move a chess piece, Speculus. I'm gonna make you pay—*pay for everything*!"

CHAPTER 33

PAYBACK

I jumped into the ribbon of time and landed back in the dungeon. Before anyone could say a word, I whispered that the angels from Constantine were coming to help. A look of shock and hope was on their faces. I told them I would be staying in touch with the angels, and we would be coordinating our attack.

"How is this *possible*, Cailyssa?" Uncle Spencer's whole body shook with excitement. "How did you change their minds?"

"I didn't, Uncle Spencer. Terry did." They looked dumbfounded. How could Terry have helped if she was pinned to the altar? "I don't have time to explain. We have to get Terry *now*! When the angels from Constantine attack, all hell will break loose. Ttocs will kill her, rather than let her be rescued."

As I said this, a great screeching voice echoed throughout the castle. Speculus was gathering his forces in preparation for the attack. The angels guarding us in the hallway ran away. I reappeared outside of our dungeon door, grabbed the keys off the wall in the hallway, and opened the door. Everyone removed their manacles, and we charged down the hallway with our weapons. We sprinted up the stairs of the dungeon to the castle above.

Uncle Spencer turned to us at the top of the stairs. "Cailyssa, if I may be so bold to suggest it, let Halodire and me go to rescue Terry. We can dispatch Ttocs, and the dark lord will not anticipate us coming. He will see you in his mirror if you try. As you said, he'll kill Terry rather than let her be rescued."

"I like it," I replied in my commanding tone. "Go save Terry! Daemon, you're with me. We have an appointment with Speculus!"

Uncle Spencer was right. Speculus could anticipate my every move—but I could also anticipate his. I knew that he was shocked that the angels of Constantine had united. He definitely hadn't seen that one coming. With their help, I could see that the legion of angels that Speculus had gathered could be defeated. Now all I had to do was destroy Speculus's ability by smashing all his mirrors and making sure we all got out of there alive.

Daemon and I crept along some of the lesser-known hallways of the castle, trying to make it to the dark lord's throne room without being detected. There were mirrors everywhere in this castle, and I had to make sure that when I used one to see what was going on, I was able to block Speculus so he couldn't find us. As I used one of the mirrors, I could see that the angels of Constantine were just now approaching the castle. Great cheers erupted from my army below! I could see the elves, dwarfs, and Amazons shouting as the gigantic angel flock flew overhead to attack the castle. The dark angels, directed by Speculus, saw them coming and met them in the sky. This would be a battle for the ages.

As the angels clashed overhead, Uncle Spencer and Halodire moved through the castle to the room that still held Terry. Halodire and Uncle Spencer had been talking the whole way, strategizing about the best way to save Terry. One of the reasons I let Halodire go was that I knew his special charms would be of great use today. Halodire crept through the broken bits of stones and yelled out to Ttocs, who was still guarding Terry, as Uncle Spencer hid in the shadows.

"Lord Ttocs, it is I, Halodire. I escaped the dungeons, and the great Lord Speculus has shown me, through my reflection, how I can be great and strong again."

Ttocs was stunned. He did not know if the dark lord was specifically recruiting Halodire. He was suspicious, but it made sense. The dark lord was always able to turn people into traitors.

Halodire walked up to Ttocs. "Lord Ttocs, I have come to serve. The dark lord suggested that I come here and help guard the Larkin girl."

Halodire said this as he started to ramp up his halo charm.

Ttocs drew his mace. "I don't trust you, elf. Kneel before me."

Halodire did so. He slowly went down on one knee and then looked up into Ttocs's eyes. He turned his halo charm on fully. Ttocs's face was ashen, and his mouth was wide open as he lowered his mace. He walked down the stairs with his back to Terry, who was still impaled on the altar behind him.

Halodire stayed on one knee. "I only come to serve the great Ttocs." At that moment Halodire smiled, and his halo charm enthralled Ttocs.

Ttocs didn't know what to think. He was entranced by the vision of this handsome elf standing in front of him. It was obvious that he was trustworthy—look at his eyes and that smile. The thought of being attracted to another man crept through Ttocs. His eyes widened, and his head was spinning with embarrassing thoughts. But he could not look away from this man's face.

Ttocs fumbled for words. "Off your knee, Halodire. Take my hand. We will guard the Larkin girl together."

Halodire stood up. The whole time he had been entrancing Ttocs, Uncle Spencer had sneaked behind the altar and was slowly undoing the torture hooks. He was getting ready to take the spikes out of Terry's wings and carry her off the altar.

Everything was going just as I planned. Terry would soon be safe, and now Daemon and I would have the enjoyment of crushing the dark lord. We made our way through the castle without encountering an angel or a raxs; they must have been all busy trying to fend off the angels from Constantine. We walked up to the door of Speculus's throne room. Daemon unleashed his sword, fury blazing in his eyes. Before Daemon could kick the door down, it opened. There was Lord Speculus, calmly sitting upon his throne, tapping his fingers as he usually did. Beside him to the right and left were the Nephilim warriors with their arms crossed and their heads almost touching the ceiling. I could see that Lord Speculus had replaced their missing hands with sharp blades.

Before I could say a word, Daemon charged right for Speculus—his white sword blazing above his head. Daemon was out of control; he was in the zone of intense fury, where he was unstoppable. He approached Speculus upon his throne with unimaginable speed and slashed his sword downward. In that instant Speculus was gone. We looked up, and he was floating above his throne slowly flapping his wings.

"Did you think you were the only person able to bend time and use specular skills in this fashion?" the dark lord said with arrogance and anger. "Did you really think your pitiful angel boyfriend could defeat me?"

The two Nephilim warriors hurled themselves toward me. They had grabbed shields with their good arms, and the cutting blades replacing their missing hands ripped through the air. As if things couldn't get worse, a group of raxs—Speculus's special bodyguards—came charging from behind me through the door that we had entered. Speculus's laughter could be heard above the clanging of metal. I disappeared and popped up on top of his throne. For a minute Speculus was above me, and I jumped as my swords ripped through the air toward his legs. In a split second, his legs moved out of the way, and his wings carried him higher. Even using my specular skills I could not slow down time enough to get an advantage over him. This was definitely going to be a difficult battle.

Daemon and I were still in the room, back-to-back and surrounded by the Nephilim and raxs. The dark lord hovered overhead, enjoying the spectacle.

"Welcome to my throne room, Cailyssa. I'm going to show you first how we kill guardian angels. Then you and I will have a little chat about joining me!"

Daemon jumped so high into the air that I didn't think it was possible. He actually caught hold of the dark lord's ankle and dragged him down to the ground, slamming him so hard that it cracked the floor in all directions. Not letting go of his ankle, he spun him around in a circle; the razor tips of his wings sliced through the contingent of raxs right where their backward-jointed knees met. They all fell and began trying to move around on the stumps of their severed legs. Speculus then managed to kick Daemon in the face with his other leg. Daemon flew across the room, his back crashing into a mirror and breaking the stone wall behind it. He slid down the stone wall but quickly regained his feet. Speculus was already up and spinning his way toward Daemon, his lethal wings forming blades of death.

Speculus flew off the ground to attack. Daemon slid underneath him and pointed his sword toward the ceiling. A white beam of light shot out of the top of the sword, and it went through the ceiling of the throne room, through the rest of the floors above us, and up into the sky. Speculus couldn't stop, and he hit the beam of sword light. The room exploded, and massive rock was strewn everywhere. When the dust cleared, Daemon and the dark lord were fighting hand to hand. I was doing my best—keeping one eye on them and fending off attacks from the two Nephilim, who were doing *their* best to chase me around the rubble with their blades spinning. I couldn't believe that with all the destruction that had occurred in this room, none of the mirrors were broken except for the one that Daemon had been thrown into. One of the mirrors flashed, and I saw what was happening with Terry.

Just when Uncle Spenser was about to take Terry off the altar, Ttocs's dragon appeared behind Halodire. The dark lord had not been fooled by Halodire's charms, and he had sent the dragon to kill him. The dragon charged Halodire, spewing flames, and Ttocs turned and ran back to the altar—only to see Uncle Spencer trying to secure Terry's release.

Ttocs pulled out his mace and walked angrily toward Uncle Spencer. "My least favorite teacher in school is now trying to mess with my new little girlfriend," Ttocs screamed as he charged Uncle Spencer. His fury was inflamed knowing that Halodire had just duped him. Uncle Spencer grabbed his sword and was able to fend off Ttocs's vicious blows. Trying to draw Uncle Spencer in, Ttocs grabbed one of the hooks and planted it in Terry's stomach. She screamed in pain.

"Don't be touching my torture toys, old man!" Ttocs said as he readied another hook for Terry.

Terry looked over at Uncle Spencer, her face contorted in agony. "Uncle…Spencer," she cried as she held out her hand toward him.

Uncle Spencer's fury boiled, and he charged Ttocs, swinging his sword in a wild manner. Ttocs danced around the altar, swinging his mace at Uncle Spencer with one hand and impaling Terry with a hook with the other. One of the hooks caught Terry right in the neck. She shrieked. Uncle Spencer could not bear to watch the torture, and he removed one of the hooks that was hurting Terry. Ttocs had waited for this, and his mace found Uncle Spencer's hand, shattering all the bones as he dropped the hook that was in Terry's neck.

"Uncle Spencer, *no!*" Terry cried with whatever voice she could manage.

It was too late. Uncle Spencer had fallen for the ploy, and he worked feverishly to remove the hooks from Terry. But in the process he left himself vulnerable to attack. Ttocs's mace caught Uncle Spencer on the side of the head, and the spiked balls embedded deeply in his skull. His body slowly slid off the altar as Ttocs continued to beat him. Uncle Spencer's eyes never left Terry's, and hers didn't leave his. He slid to the ground, and his eyes drifted closed as his fingers released all the hooks he had removed from Terry.

Halodire was in a vicious battle with the dragon. Consumed with a lust for battle, Ttocs clambered onto the dragon's back. Halodire was hurling every weapon he could find at the dragon and Ttocs. He fought bravely, as very few could do when facing the onslaught of a dragon. Halodire picked up a shield just in time; another powerful stream of fire blew him out the door and onto the courtyard below. The dragon flew a short way and landed on top of Halodire.

"I've been waiting for a dragon to eat someone's head. Looks like it might as well be an elf's rather than a dwarf's," Ttocs said as the dragon stepped on one of Halodire's hands, crushing it to the floor. Halodire howled in pain. The dragon's gaping maw moved toward Halodire's head. During the fight, Halodire had grabbed a spear, broken it in half, and stuck it in his quiver of arrows. He waited till the dragon was close, and then he grabbed the spear. With all of his strength, he rammed it upward into the dragon's mouth, and the spear went straight through, its tip coming out between the dragon's nostrils above. The dragon howled in pain and sent an enormous stream of fire at Halodire, who was just able to bring his shield up in time. The next stream of fire blew him farther back and off the edge of the castle wall, his massive elf body tumbling end over end toward the rocky ground below.

CHAPTER 34

RENUNCIATION

A vision flashed in my mind, and I ran out of Speculus's throne room. Daemon, my guardian angel, reluctantly gave up his battle with the dark lord and followed me. I ran to the closest empty room with a mirror, and no one chased us for the moment. I saw the entire failed rescue attempt and Uncle Spencer. Daemon didn't know. Now I could see what was about to happen next. The angels of Constantine were starting to win the battle, and the dark lord had instructed Ttocs to kill Terry if the angels tried to rescue her. Ttocs had jumped off the back of his dragon and was returning to the black altar in order to carry out the dark lord's wishes.

I closed the door, and Daemon looked around.

"Cailyssa, that was the first skirmish. We did well. We shall return and defeat him!"

"No, Daemon," I said as I stood tall in front of him. "Halodire and Uncle Spencer lost, and Ttocs is going to kill Terry!"

"Then we shall save her," Daemon said as he started toward the door.

"No…we won't," I said in my most commanding tone, as I grabbed Daemon's arm.

Daemon was stunned by my words. His eyebrows furled together, and he looked at me with the most intensely worried face imaginable. I steadied myself, knowing I was about to do one of the most difficult things of my life. I let out a quick breath and then took control.

"*We* won't be saving Terry, Daemon. *We* won't, but *you* will!" I firmly said to him.

"Cailyssa, my love for Terry goes beyond the land, and I would certainly do anything to save her or to help you. But my duty as your guardian angel does not permit me to leave your side. I need to protect you. We can do this *together*!"

I held my breath and steeled myself for what was to come next. I pushed Daemon slightly in the chest, and in a steady voice—making sure I sounded like I really meant it—I said, "You are no longer my guardian angel!"

"What foolishness is thi—"

I interrupted Daemon and said forcefully, "I renounce you! I renounce you as my guardian angel! When we were in the city of Constantine, that's what Gabriel and I discussed."

Daemon looks stunned. "You wouldn't…You didn't…It's not possible—"

I interrupted again. "It is possible, Daemon, and you know it. Renunciation is complete and unchangeable."

Daemon's face flooded with emotions. Denial, shock, and then incredible anger overcame him. "*How dare you!*" His fury took the air out of the room.

Before I could say a word or react, Daemon slumped over and held his hands to his face. As he slowly removed his hands, the pain and agony I saw in his face was beyond belief. He looked almost unsteady on his feet—something that's not really possible for an angel. "But, Cailyssa, I thought you loved me. How could you possibly do this? Have I not done a good job protecting you? You know I love you and would gladly give my life for you, yet you discard me like a piece of trash." His voice was gaining in anger. "Do I mean *nothing* to you?"

I held my ground and drew upon all the strength I had left. I gave Daemon the coldest stare I could and turned my back on him. I couldn't let him see my face, or he would know how I really felt. "In case you didn't hear me, I'll make it *more* clear," I said smoothly, trying to keep my voice steady as my emotions threatened to overwhelm me. I dared not turn to face him. "I renounce you as my guardian angel!" I gulped hard. The next words left my lips as if a stranger controlled my body and forced me to utter cruelty. I used my meanest and most scornful voice. "Why would I want *you* as a guardian angel, anyway? You couldn't save my grandfather. What makes you think you can save *me*?"

Daemon's angelic roar pierced my ears and soul. It was the saddest sound I would ever hear in my life.

I didn't turn around, but I said in my most commanding tone, "So, as I see it, you have two choices. You can run off and pout like you did before, or you can *save my sister!*" I bellowed at the wall in front of me. "That way at least you will save *some* of your honor." My voice softened. "It's your choice. But know this: you are *not* coming along with *me*!" As I finished my rehearsed speech, I immediately disappeared.

I materialized in a storage room at the far end of the castle, breathing heavily and trying to hold back the tears because I knew that if I opened the faucet, the waterworks would come out in great heaving sobs that would never stop. The actions I had taken would determine the future. *I had just done it. The choice had been made.* I had just destroyed my best friend and the man I loved more than anything in this world. At least he and Terry would be alive; they would see that I sacrificed myself for them.

Taking a deep breath, I sat down for a minute and tried to figure out how to deal with Speculus. My mind was an emotional wreck. Then it hit me. That was the *last* time I would ever see Daemon, and that was the *last* memory we would ever have of each other.

From the beginning I had made a promise to myself after seeing all the possible visions of the future. If anyone had to die, I wanted it to be only *me*! I screamed the last word up at the ceiling. I had already let so many people die already. I couldn't let Terry and Daemon die, too! I stood up strong and proud. I needed to go face Speculus alone. My swords flew into my hands. My mind was beyond furious, and my body was crouched and ready for battle. All of the fury within me would be released upon Speculus for everything bad that had happened. He would pay the final price. I entered the ribbon of time, knowing I would land directly in Speculus's throne room.

CHAPTER 35

A PROPOSAL

My swords raised above my head, I hit the floor running directly toward Speculus, who was standing in front of his throne.

I had the edge on him with my specular abilities. I materialized a few seconds before he thought I would, and I saw the look of surprise on his face. I charged toward him drawing upon all my skills—using them to anticipate his every move—in the hope of hacking him to pieces.

My body whirled with a sense of fury, and my swords slashed with more speed and precision than I ever thought was possible. Speculus put up one wing to protect himself, but I saw it coming, and I lashed out low with my other sword—under his other wing—and I cut into his left thigh right to the bone. He screamed in pain and kicked me away as he flew into the air. The throne room had an incredibly high ceiling, and he was hovering far above me. I had avoided most of his kick, and I was happy to see the blood on the floor in front of his throne.

A voice boomed out from above. "Cailyssa Larkin, is this the way you greet your new betrothed? I have known many girls who enjoy a good fight before their wedding day." He laughed with his ominous tone and landed in front of me, perched on top of his throne like a great bird.

What was he talking about? Wedding day? Was he taunting me about Daemon? All I could remember from his words was something about a good fight. And that's what he was in for now. I ran toward his throne, knowing that he would attempt to fly over my head. In the middle of my run, I stopped, grabbed one of Daemon's throwing knives I had in my boot, and threw it straight up to the ceiling. The knife looked as though it was heading toward empty space until Speculus flew into it, my knife impaling itself deeply in his stomach. I heard another grunt, and more blood fell from above me. If he could bleed, he could die! I spun around. Speculus was now on the ground in front of me. He stood up and spread his wings out. He was frightening and terrible to look upon. He folded half of each wing in front of him, and I could see the razor-like edges on each side. He approached me slowly. We were two warriors, ready for battle.

My body was still a furious killing machine, and I wanted to keep the momentum on my side, so I charged toward him again—slashing and stabbing with my two swords as fast as I could. This time he was ready for me, and his wings were blocking every blow. The huge bones on the outside of each wing must have been made out of titanium because every time

I hit one, I felt the vibration right through me, and no damage was done. I could sense his every move, and up till this point, I was staying a split second in front of him. The only problem was that he could see the future, too. He began anticipating my moves and was now flashing his wings in a complex battle sequence that was like a blur of razors slashing at me. I was lucky enough to hold my own during his vicious attack. He sensed he had the edge on me. He kept moving forward, slashing, kicking, spinning, and laughing with his hideous voice. I had to move backward to avoid being killed. I was using every defensive skill I'd learned, but I knew I was starting to lose.

I vanished before him and reappeared on the other side of the room. For a moment, I thought this newfound ability would be an advantage. Then I noticed Speculus had disappeared. I ducked just in time. Speculus had materialized right behind me, anticipating where I would be, and he slashed his wing right over my head—cutting off some of my hair! The battle changed from a physical battle to a battle where time was folding—each of us vanishing and rematerializing—each of us trying to gain an advantage. There was none to be had. I used every ounce of my ability to slow down time, anticipate his next move, and then reappear in time to kill him. The only problem was, he was doing the same thing, and he had the same abilities I did—and more.

"I'm done playing with you, little girl," Speculus hissed as he landed on his throne. He looked down for a moment at his feet, and then his head snapped up, and he looked at me with a cruel, evil grin. He clapped his hands, and a loud boom broke through the air and pinned me against the wall. "We will have no more of your childish antics—folding time—trying to avoid me."

I dipped into the ribbon of time and discovered that Speculus had somehow removed my ability to vanish and reappear. I wouldn't be leaving this room unless it was on my feet. My only chance to kill him was to do so now, before I tired. Again I charged toward his throne, and he walked down the stairs and met me in battle. I slashed with my sword. He parried with his wings, and then he beat me back. Slowly, I was backing up...step by step by step. I was almost against the wall. I was losing. There was no way I could physically compete with an angel of his ability. So this was how I was to die. I wouldn't die in vain. I would die fighting!

Speculus paused for a moment. "I tire of sparring with you. Did you really think your pitiful abilities were any match for *mine*?" When Speculus said this he roared and came toward me with his hands raised and his wings pulled back. I arched my swords behind my back as far as I could and slashed down directly over my head. My swords landed in both of his hands, and he caught them. Blood dripped down his forearms. He snapped my blades, grabbed the hilts from my hands, and threw them on the floor. His bloody hands healed immediately. Before I knew it, the back of his right hand hit me squarely across the side of my face. I crumpled to the floor and blacked out for a moment.

When I awoke I was at the bottom of his throne. He was sitting on it, looking down at me. The two Nephilim warriors were at my sides. They roughly picked me up. My legs were barely able to support me. The Nephilim walked away, standing behind Speculus's throne.

"So, my dear..." Speculus said as his fingers tapped upon the giant dragon heads that composed the arms of his throne. "I hope you enjoyed our little contest. As you can see, you are no equal to *me*. Neither your specular nor your physical abilities could ever hope to be as astonishing as mine." Speculus slowly stood up. His wings folded open, followed by his hands, and he presented himself as a terrible angel, projecting his evil presence on me. "Am I not magnificent?" He slowly turned around, making sure to rip off his shirt and expose his perfectly sculpted body.

I always hated guys who were in love with themselves, and this guy took the cake. The fury began to boil in me again, but I wasn't sure what I could do about it at this point.

"Worship me!" Speculus bellowed. The Nephilim warriors pushed my shoulders down and made me kneel before him.

Speculus retracted his wings and held out his hands almost as a peace offering. "Dear Cailyssa, you should have taken the gift I offered you when you first entered this world. Recall, if you will, when you sat upon the Larkin stone throne; I showed you your images in the pools. I again offer you that gift. But now you are forced to accept it—willingly or unwillingly."

I stood up and spit as far as I could. I knew I wouldn't hit him, but it was the only thing I could think of doing to show defiance. "I'll never accept any gift from you! I'll continue to fight you till the day I die."

Speculus laughed. "I must say, your spirit is quite admirable. I've always enjoyed conquering women of your nature. Did you think I was going to kill you? If you did, you're quite wrong. You are going to live a long life by my side."

This I didn't expect. What was he saying? I knew I could face death, but I didn't think I could face life knowing I'd be trapped here.

Speculus pointed down at me. "Cailyssa Larkin, don't you understand—with all your great abilities—that everything that has happened has happened according to my *plan*?" Speculus started pacing. "Do you really know why you hated mirrors so much? I have been looking at you since you were born, nurturing you and shaping you, knowing the whole time that you would be right here at this moment."

My mind was spinning. I had always hated mirrors, and I had an idea that a dark force was behind some of them. But what did he mean by his plan? I tried to sound tough. "You don't control me, Speculus. I know what you are!"

"Do you now, Cailyssa? Do you know how I've been controlling you all along? I led you here by capturing Terry. I knew that you would not let her die, and I also knew that you would do anything to save her." Speculus smiled a bit. "Of course my plan worked perfectly, and it led to this very moment. So the two of us could be…alone," he said in what sounded like a flirtatious, romantic voice.

What the heck? At that moment another smaller throne appeared next to his. It was covered with black roses. I was completely thrown off track. What was going on?"

Speculus began walking down the stairs, each of his feet gracefully landing upon the next step as if he were the lead in the final act of a dark opera. "My dear Cailyssa, I must say that your specular skills are not what I thought they were. You didn't even realize that it was *my* plan for you to renounce Daemon all along. I planted that seed in your mind when you looked at a reflection of me. You see, specular skills are not simply about reflections, they are about controlling other people's minds. Inside each mind is a mirror. And I control the mirror in *your mind*!"

I stumbled backward. It couldn't possibly be true. I renounced Daemon to save Terry—and to save him. It couldn't be possible that Speculus had told me to do it.

"I don't believe your lies!" I retorted. "You spew nothing but lies and deceit. You're a disgrace to the angels!"

Speculus slowly took another step forward saying. "That would depend on which angel you ask, Cailyssa. My master is quite proud of me, and he is the greatest of all the angels." Another slow step. Speculus's eyes bore into me. "Foolish girl, I captured Terry, knowing that you would eventually renounce Daemon, thinking that was your only chance to save her. I planned it. I saw it all coming in my mirrors. What you didn't see is that Daemon will be too late. He will find Terry dead and will go off to an endless void, wishing death for himself." He took his last step toward me, and now he was standing directly in front of me. "Everyone has died according to my plan. Now it is just we two." Speculus had a very intense look in his eyes. I began to walk backward—away from him.

"Stay away from me, Speculus. I know who you are, and I know your real angel name." My voice sounded courageous and sharp. "You were in heaven once, but you came to the earth and forced yourself upon human women. You became a fallen angel, and God threw you out of heaven. I know what your forced matings produced: *them*!" I screamed as I pointed at the two Nephilim. "Those giant abominations are your sons, your spawn!"

"I am most impressed, Cailyssa. I'm glad you know that one of my favorite activities is forcibly mating with a human. Do you *now* understand *why* you're here?" Speculus pointed toward my throne. "You will be my bride. We will wed, and you will spend eternity at my side. You will worship me, you will adore me, and you will eventually love me. And of course, my two Nephilim sons here will greatly enjoy the brother that you will produce from our marriage!" Speculus said as he quickly came up to me and pushed me onto the ground.

Before I knew what was happening, Speculus was on me. He pinned my arms over my head, his powerful hands crushing my wrists. His terrible face was looking right at me. I was reeling with disgust. How could this possibly be happening? I felt his hot gaze on me, and I knew he was slowly moving forward to kiss me. No words could describe the disgust I had for him. My head was moving back and forth as fast as possible trying to avoid his lips touching mine. Everything slowed down. I prayed and I became strong. I knew one thing for certain. There was no way in hell I was going to be the bride of Speculus!

I stopped moving my head. Speculus paused for a moment. He thought he had me. For a moment my lips were still, and he was about to finally kiss me. I clicked my boot on the floor, and the knife popped out of the toe. Using all of my specular skills to gain an advantage in time, I kicked upward as hard as I could. My blow landed precisely where I meant it to land. Angels are tough, but anyone who gets kicked in the groin with a knife and a boot feels it. Speculus groaned in pain, and I took the moment to push his nauseating form off me. My plan at this point was to get him so angry that he would finally kill me. I backed away from him, trying to plan my next move.

"I'll die before I marry you, you loathsome piece of trash!" I shouted at him in my most confident tone.

He slowly stood up. The pained expression on his face vanished and was replaced by anger that was staggering to see. He screamed! And every rock in the castle trembled. A great crack opened before us, and an enormous flame licked up and disappeared. I knew I was looking into the flames of hell.

"I am *done* toying with you, Cailyssa Larkin. I will bend your mind to my will. And you will marry me in hell on this day!" As Speculus said this, every mirror in his throne room began attacking me with evil thoughts. They placed self-doubt in my mind and made me feel that everything I had done was selfish. My mind was spinning; the power coming from him was unimaginable.

Thoughts came to me. Were they his or mine? *The choices I made killed all my friends.* He entered my mind more deeply. *Did I rid myself of everyone to be alone with him? He suggested it but I did it. Was I evil? Marrying Speculus was what I was destined to do?* I struggled against his thoughts, but he pushed back, reminding me that I was already evil—that I had killed and desecrated the bodies of angels. I had turned to the path of darkness. I was ready to be his bride!

I held my hands over my heart and thought of every happy thought I owned. Then I slowly spread my arms palms up. He hadn't seen my last surprise.

"Now you know, Cailyssa, that your destiny was always to be with me," Speculus said as his face softened a bit.

"You're not quite right, Azazel. Your destiny is to be with me!"

Speculus was disarmed when I used the name he had been known by when he lived in heaven. I took control of all the mirrors in his throne room and pushed back all of his evil thoughts. I let the power of my specular skills flow through me, and I pushed forth a series of heavenly images that Gabriel had shared with me when we talked.

"Azazel!" I said loudly to gain his attention. I looked into his eyes as I took control of the mirrors. "I have a gift for you that I was waiting for this very moment to share." As I said this, all of the mirrors projected the images Gabriel had given me—of Azazel before he was a fallen angel. He was in heaven. There was great joy and beauty there, and he was within the grace of God.

"Look at the reflection of who you were! You were not always what stands before me now. You remember the feelings of goodness and God." Standing up tall, I spoke to him in a calm, easy voice. "Azazel, I forgive you for all that you have done. Hold my hand, and join with me now. Put away your past. Fly with me to Constantine, and again enter the realm of the good angels. You will be welcome there; I promise." I knew that as I said this Speculus would dip into his skills and see the future. He knew what I said could be true! For a moment his face softened. He looked at the mirrors, and he looked at me. For a moment the beautiful angel that had once been reappeared! Suddenly he looked confused, and he gazed at me with fearful eyes.

A loud boom shook the castle. An evil force erupted from the crack below us. It grabbed Speculus and the two Nephilim, slowly dragging them down the crack into hell.

A voice burst forth from the depths below speaking in the language of hell. The pure evil and power of it washed over me like a plague of death and horror. "Cai...lyss...aaa, you will *not* succeed in corrupting my lieutenant. I have now turned my attention to you! You have no idea of what I am capable of."

I trembled as the overlord of the underworld, the most powerful angel ever—Lucifer—spoke to me.

Speculus and the two Nephilim were slowly dragged down into the crack. They were screaming as demonic creatures engulfed them, hungry to do their master's bidding. The crack before me became enormous and came toward me. I was frozen in shock. The whole castle began crumbling around me; everything would be sucked into the depth below.

I can't describe the feeling of fear within those few seconds as the icy grip of evil wrapped itself around me and began to drag me down. Perhaps I could find some way to die there. I wasn't sure. I had lost all hope. I fell to the ground, trying to dig into the stone with my nails. I tried to scream for help, but nothing came out of my throat. My feet were now over the edge the crack, and I could feel the intense heat—but worse, an evil presence. I smashed my head on the stone floor as hard as I could, hoping to kill myself. Blood covered my eyes and face.

"You will not have her in this way! *Lucifer*!" A powerful voice bellowed from behind me. Was I dead? Was this a dream? With the warmth and slowness of a sunrise, a cocoon of white light surrounded me. I looked up, and Gabriel was hovering above me. I must be dead. Her wings were slowly flapping, and it was perhaps the most beautiful sight I had ever seen. The light coming down from her was warm and filled with loving calmness. I began to breathe again.

"You know the rules, Lucifer. She has *free will*. She did not choose Speculus! You failed." Gabriel's voice radiated such power that the crack of hell felt small and powerless. "You cannot take her in this manner. She has made her choice. She is with me, in the hand of God. Be gone before I unleash my fury upon you…as I did when I threw you from heaven! Go back to the depths from which you came!"

As if in a dream, the cocoon of white light held me, and Gabriel came down and wrapped her arms around me. She flew away with me, and all I could see through the white light was the dark castle crumbling and being sucked into the void below. What had happened to Terry? Was she really dead? Where was Daemon? I passed out in Gabriel's arms.

CHAPTER 36

CONSTANTINE RENEWED

I woke up in a soft bed. My wounds had been bandaged, but I could still feel the pain throughout my entire body. I sat up straight in bed and almost passed out. I wailed, "Terry! Daemon!"

I fell back to the bed, the pain searing me from head to toe. I dozed or passed out—I wasn't sure which—and when I awoke again all I heard was a clicking sound from behind me. It sounded like somebody was rolling marbles. What the heck?

"It's about time you finally woke up, Cailyssa. I've been waiting here for...ever. I almost splashed you with water, but you look in tough shape. Look, this game is so cool. It has these magical little angel balls to play with," Terry said as she stopped rolling the marbles and finally came to the side of my bed.

We looked at each other for a long time without saying a word, glad to see each other alive. We hugged gently, trying not to hurt each other, since we were both still wounded. We cried only a bit, hugged some more, and it finally turned into a crying, sniffling laugh with a bunch of words that neither of us could understand. We shared a close bond that could *not* be put into words.

"Get some sleep. You look like sh…crap!" Terry playfully said as she gently pushed my shoulders back down to the bed. She had woken earlier and had spent time with the healing angels. I lay back down, trying to make sense of the incredible experiences I'd just had.

I sat straight up again. "So Daemon must've saved you. He's alive! Where is he?"

Terry sat down next to me. "He was incredible, Cailyssa. He saved my life. I'm not sure what happened. Uncle Spencer, Halodire, Daemon—they might be…" Terry stammered as she turned away, lowering her head and covering her face with her hands. Her wings looked so tiny, tucked in and bandaged. Terry was sobbing in great heaves.

The thought of Uncle Spencer and Halodire hit me hard.

Terry wiped the tears from her eyes. God, she was strong. "Daemon came in. His sword was incredible; he slew all of the raxs and angels protecting Ttocs. Ttocs had grabbed my hair and bent over me with a knife. He was just about to kill me, but when he saw Daemon, he dropped the knife and ran like a scared baby in the other direction. That was when the dragon appeared. The fight between Daemon and the dragon was incredible. The dragon had no chance. He only had time to shoot one fireball at Daemon! Daemon attacked him so fast that it was a blur. He cut off the dragon's head and threw it as far as I could see. He then came up to me and gently picked me up. He didn't say a word. He looked horrible. His back was bleeding, and his eyes had deep gullies under them. I think he was crying. I tried to talk to him and ask what happened. He wouldn't look at me or answer. It was strange.

I asked him if you were all right. When I mentioned your name, it looked like I'd stabbed him in the heart. His face contorted in pain, and he covered his heart with both hands. For a minute I thought maybe an arrow had hit him in the back. Then his face changed to this distant, haunted look. I had never seen him like that. I thought you might be dead! I asked again about you, and he just looked at me, straight-faced. Without saying a word, he picked me up and took me outside. He motioned to a bunch of angels from Constantine who were flying above, and they carried me off. When I looked down—I…I…don't want to tell you this, Cailyssa—I saw Daemon jump off the edge of the castle wall. Those sharp rocks were hundreds of feet below. I screamed his name! Then the whole castle was closing in on itself, and it looked like everything was being sucked into this big crack. I'm not sure, but I…" The tears were now running down Terry's cheeks, and her whole body was trembling. "I think Daemon might've been sucked in. I mean, the castle disappeared, and there was nothing left of anything! The crack spread and became a black canyon. All the dark angels and raxs were sucked in, too! Only the angels from Constantine who were in the sky were left. Our other friends had been running away and escaped the carnage. I'm sorry, Cailyssa. I wish I had better news." Terry looked down sadly.

Gabriel appeared in the distance. I didn't have to ask her the same question I had asked Terry. She shook her head, and I knew that she had no idea what had happened to Daemon. I lay back and let the grief consume me. I was as still as night—frozen.

"Leave me alone, please," I whispered.

Gabriel and Terry left. I'm not sure what happened next. It must have been several days. I could barely breathe, and I was in a black void somewhere between sleep and wakefulness. My mind was a live dream full of nightmares, full of screams, and full of friends dying—my best friend dying. For a moment I was back in first grade, and Daemon was holding my hand as we walked to the swings. I was pushing him, and he was swinging higher, smiling and laughing as he said my name. He swung back toward me, and I pulled out a knife! I woke up shaking and sweating, only to find the pain in my body too much to bear, and I passed out again. I had refused help from any of the healing angels. I deserved the pain! When I finally woke, there was no one in my room. I saw that my old clothes had been laid out before me. They looked like they had all been cleaned.

I did not shower, wash my face, or brush my hair. I put on my jeans, shirt, and Converse sneakers. I dressed slowly, each small movement hurting, but it was the emotional pain that hurt worse. I looked out the window over Gabriel's balcony. The city was having an exuberant celebration. The angels were singing, and the golden nectar was flowing. It looked like New Year's Eve. The angel dust was falling like confetti, but I didn't care. I turned my back and walked to the farthest side of the room. I sat down and put my head between my knees. I had held it together all of this time. I was always the brave one, never shedding a tear. I was here to save the world, right? Too bad I blew it! If it wasn't for Terry changing the angels' minds, we'd all be dead. *Nice job, Cailyssa!* I screamed at myself. *You think you're so tough—so smart. You killed Daemon and a bunch of your closest friends, and you didn't save the world. Terry had to do it for you!*

I cried. But I didn't just cry, I wailed in agony for all of the deaths that I had caused, until there were no more tears left. My emotions finally trailed off to a soft whimpering as I replayed my final time with Daemon in my mind. He died thinking I had renounced him. He died believing I didn't love him. What did he ever do to me to deserve that? Protect me? Love me? And then die for me? This would torture me for the rest of my life. How could I possibly have done what I had done? Speculus could have been right. I might have been able to save Terry without renouncing Daemon. He might still be alive.

I stood up straight, staring into space. I just stared straight ahead, seeing nothing except visions of all the horrible things I had done.

The next day I woke up physically healed, but mentally I was a mess. I grabbed the only possessions I had with me: my moonstone and red book. Thoughts I couldn't catch flew through my mind, shouting at me, taunting me. It was almost like part of Speculus was still in there torturing me. *Why'd you let them die? You didn't need to renounce Daemon, did you? Not so tough now, are you?*

"I have some good news for you, Cailyssa," Gabriel said as she walked into the room. My eyes perked up. Could it be Daemon? "Some of the angels found Uncle Spencer. He is in our healing facilities. He was very close to death. Our healers can support his health, but if he leaves us, he may die."

Terry and I went to see Uncle Spencer. Angels surrounded him, and he seemed to be in a coma. We gave him a hug, and I left feeling the weight of another life that I had ruined. We went to the balcony, and we said our good-byes to Gabriel and angel city. I could barely wave. During the last few days, I had been so consumed with grief that I couldn't take part in any of the celebrations. I knew that Terry had been a good ambassador, saying thanks—and of course joining in the party. Terry put on a good front, but underneath I could see a deep sadness in her. Would either one of us ever be the same? Probably not. But the angels loved Terry; after all, she had saved them and Mirror World! She would always be welcomed back here. What did *I* do?

A group of angels approached us. They picked us up and flew us across Mirror World. I passed by Castle Larkin and eventually came to the place where I'd first entered this crazy place. They carefully dropped Terry and me and said goodbye. I looked at Terry, and then I looked at the stone throne before us with "Larkin" engraved on the back. I looked at the luminous pools below me, but they were all blank. No reflection was there. Maybe my specular skills were gone. I really didn't care. Without a word between us, Terry grabbed the throne. As she did, we felt the liquid essence of time surround us, and our next step was back into Uncle Spencer's living room, where we faced the couch we had sat on so long ago.

I looked at the clock and remembered what time can do. It was it was half past ten o'clock; barely five hours had passed since we'd left our parents' home. So much had happened, and so little time had passed on earth. We didn't turn around to look at the big mirror—or any other mirror—as we walked out the front door of the house. We dragged ourselves toward the car. There it was: Daemon's black Mercedes! It felt as though a knife went through my stomach. We drove back to our house; not a word was exchanged between us. It began to rain. We parked the car, took deep breaths, and walked toward the front door. Before we could open it, our father charged out. I thought he was going to question us about where we had been.

"Cailyssa," he said. "You weren't answering your phone. I wanted to get in touch with you as soon as possible. I'm afraid I have bad news. Your uncle Spencer has had a severe stroke; your mom and I are on the way to the hospital now. I'm sad to say that the doctors tell us it doesn't look good."

My mom flew out of the house and quickly gave us a hug as she ran to the car. I wish they could have stayed with me. I tried to wave to them, and I babbled some words that sounded like "I hope he's OK," but I was the only one who could hear them. Terry and I walked inside, absolutely exhausted. Dogs are proof that God loves us, and both of mine came bounding up. But I could barely pet them. I was totally spent. *At least they're still alive*, I thought glumly. I guess things could be worse. I could have returned home to see their unmarked graves in the backyard. My pep talk didn't work; the thought of Daemon crept in. Terry and I barely made it upstairs to our bedrooms, and without even saying good-night, we flopped on our beds fully dressed. Terry fell asleep, and I could hear her breathing softly in the other room. I was so drained and tired, but I couldn't fall asleep. Every time I would doze off, I would find myself in a nightmare filled with vivid recollections of everything that had happened. Then I would wake up and sit up in my bed, shivering and sweating, only to repeat the whole process again. I wished I were dead.

CHAPTER 37

THE REAL ME

It had been three days since Terry and I had returned from Mirror World—the three worst days of my life. I felt like I was sleepwalking, and nothing seemed real except the incredible grief and heaviness that was on me. I couldn't eat or sleep, and I often found myself unable to move. My parents were starting to get worried, and I told them I was just sad about Uncle Spencer. The only thing I liked to do was visit him in the hospital. Sitting beside the bed, staring at his unmoving face, somehow made me feel better. I guess I felt in some way that he knew how to help me, but at this point he couldn't even help himself.

School was an absolute disaster for me. I often found myself late for class or wandering in the hall. School counselors came and took me out of class one day and asked me if everything was OK. I again used the excuse about Uncle Spencer. Sure, I was incredibly sad about him, but I knew it was much more than that. It was Daemon. He had been around me ever since I could remember, and not having him now—when I needed him the most—felt like somebody had ripped me apart and thrown half of me away. Would I ever be a whole person again? Would I ever let myself out of this personal jail? I was an empty person going through the motions of life. Nothing felt real. Nothing felt good. Sometimes I wasn't even sure if I was awake or not, since I never slept much anyway. Friday came, and I looked forward to the weekend, when I would just stay in my room and mentally beat myself up.

It must have been nighttime because, when I opened my eyes, it was dark outside. Something woke me up, and it wasn't a nightmare. It was a sound like a tiny rock hitting the window of my room. I dozed off. *Plink, plink!* I sat straight up. There was definitely something hitting my window. Maybe there was a storm outside? Dragging myself out of bed, still in my clothes—which I usually slept in these days—I shuffled to the window and drew back the drapes. No storm. It was a quiet June night with a full moon. I opened the window and looked out. There was a pile of tiny rocks on my window ledge and on the porch roof, just a couple of feet below my window. Maybe it was some punk kid trying to mess around. Or maybe this was a bad dream. I was just about to close the windows when I heard a creaking noise. Suddenly two boots appeared out of nowhere, and a large dark figure landed on the roof in front of me. If I hadn't been so depressed, I would've jumped backward. Instead, I just stood there with my mouth open.

"Cailyssa!" A stern voice spoke. "I need to ask you a question!"

My mind and body were totally in shock. The unmistakable outline in front of me was Daemon.

"Cailyssa!"—a louder voice this time—"I need to ask you a question. You will answer it! Approach me!" Daemon said as he reached in, grabbed my arms, and somewhat roughly placed me on the roof right in front of him.

"Daemon, you're alive? But I thought…I mean…it's so—"

"Silence!" Daemon bellowed. "Stop your blabbering, and gather your wits so you can respond to my question appropriately."

He was really angry! I could see it in his eyes and in the way he had his arms crossed in front of him. What was he going to ask me? How I wanted to die? I just wanted to say I was sorry before he killed me.

Reality hit me. "Daemon, you're too loud, and you're on the roof of my house! My parent and the neighbors will probably call the police."

Daemon didn't say a word. He slowly placed his hands on his hips. He shook his head and then grabbed my arms and turned me around so that my toes were at the edge of the roof. Was he going to push me off? It sure felt that way. I deserved it. Daemon's hands became firmer, and before I knew it, he shoved me off the roof. I was heading straight for the ground when, suddenly, his strong hands wrapped around me, and I flew straight upward in the sky at an incredible rate. I was breathing quickly, trying to catch my breath. He had wings! My mind was scrambling to make sense of this, and I began babbling about how sorry I was and how glad I was to see him. In typical Daemon fashion, he did not say a word. After about ten minutes of my yammering, he interrupted me.

"Quiet! I did not think it was prudent to continue our discussion on a roof, so I'm taking you somewhere we can talk." Daemon flew onto one of the highest cliffs in town that overlooked Spectacle Lake. It was very secluded. He placed me on the rocks, and I was overlooking the water when he came and stood next to me.

Looking across the water, Daemon spoke without making eye contact. "I'm only here for one night, to ask you a question. I need to hear you say it in your own words. After you answer, you will not hear from me again." Daemon lapsed into silence.

I turned toward him and looked at him, ready to do whatever he asked.

"Answer honestly, and don't babble. *Why* did you renounce me?" His voice was so forceful that the word "why" echoed off the rocks below—and through my mind.

"Daemon, I'm so sorry about what I did. I thought it was the only way I could save Terry. I wish I didn't have to—"

"Do not *lie* to me, Cailyssa Larkin." Daemon turned to face me when he said this, and I thought I would almost fall off the cliff from the power of his voice.

"But I'm not lying," I replied in a lame tone that sounded like I didn't really believe myself. "There was no one left to save Terry. Everyone had died trying. I knew you wouldn't leave my side unless I renounced you. And I knew you'd save Terry; you would not let her die."

Daemon looked down at me as if he were speaking to a child. "With all of your specular skills, Cailyssa Larkin, you're a fool! Did it ever occur to you that we could have saved Terry together? Then we could have faced Speculus together!" Daemon began pacing back and forth. "Think, Cailyssa. By splitting us apart, you foolishly risked Terry's life and your own. You're very lucky that Speculus didn't rape you. If it wasn't for Gabriel, you'd be a bride in hell at this moment." Daemon turned to face me. "I asked you a simple question, and I wanted an honest answer—and you can't give me one. I'll ask you once more, and if you don't answer honestly, I will fly off this ledge, and you will never see me again. Search inside yourself. Why did you renounce me?"

The thoughts inside my mind were jumbled up, and I couldn't sort them out. Speculus told me that it was his idea to renounce Daemon. Did he do it to get me alone? Was I following his wishes? "Daemon, I know that Speculus suggested in a reflection that I renounce you so he could get me alone with him."

"And so he did," Daemon said. "But if you recall, you are a master at resisting his influence. Perhaps you're not being honest with yourself. I know you're not being honest with me. Good-bye!" Daemon began flapping his wings, lifting off the ground.

"Wait!" I screamed as I ran up and grabbed his ankles, trying to pull him back to the earth. "Just give me a little more time. My mind has been a mess. You don't know what it's like to be without you!"

He shook me off, and I fell. He landed above me, looking down. "Oh I do, Cailyssa, I certainly do. How do you think it feels to be renounced by the one person you love more than anyone in the universe? Do you think I do not feel heartbreak or pain? As an angel, I feel these emotions even more intensely than you. At this point, I don't care how you feel. I only care to hear an *answer*!"

Why was this so hard? What didn't I want to admit to myself? Part of the reason I renounced Daemon was because I hoped that he could be with me if he wasn't my guardian angel. I was being selfish. Maybe that was the real reason I renounced him. Maybe I had risked my life and Terry's life foolishly—like a selfish little girl whose only care was to have a boyfriend. Daemon was standing in front of me, so I stood too and tried to appear proud and honest.

"Daemon," I said quickly—and then took two deep breaths before continuing. "Part of the reason I renounced you was because I wanted to be with you. I love you. I renounced you as my guardian angel so you could be with me."

"Honest you are, Cailyssa, but still foolish. What made you ever think that my being a guardian angel prevented us from being together? That's simply not true. I spoke with Gabriel, and I know she spoke with you. Her advice to you was to work it out with me—to talk with me about it! Instead you took matters into your own hands and renounced me. And you risked your life and your sister's life needlessly."

I stumbled backward. "You mean, I mean, uh…we could have been together if you were my guardian angel?"

"*Yes*, Cailyssa! And if you had asked me that, I would have told you," Daemon said as his voice softened a bit.

"Oh my God, I never thought of it, I guess. I just thought you needed to protect me and—"

Daemon interrupted. "Why? Why could I not protect you if we were together? There is no rule that states a guardian angel cannot also fall in love with the one he is protecting. This has happened many times."

My heart leaped for joy. "Daemon, I didn't know. Please forgive me. You know that everything I said—I didn't mean. And you know now that I didn't do it just to save Terry. I did it in the hope of being with you. Is that so bad?"

"Yes it is, Cailyssa. When you renounced me and went to face Speculus alone, you almost died. Can you imagine for a moment what it was like for me when I knew you would face him alone? I have known him forever. I know the atrocities he's committed. Yet you made me walk away from you at the time you needed me most. I was left unable to protect you, knowing that you were in the clutches of a dark angel who raped and killed countless humans! I didn't think I would ever see you again! Do you understand how hard that was for me?"

"I do, Daemon. I do." And I ran over to hug him. Unfortunately, there was no hug coming back my way. Daemon simply stood there like a statue.

"Did I answer your question, Daemon? I was selfish. I renounced you 'cause I love you. Please tell me you'll stay."

My eyes were looking up at him, and I was pleading with all my might.

Daemon slowly shook his head and started pacing. "Cailyssa, you have been aware of a great reluctance in me to be with you. Is that correct?"

"Yes, Daemon, I thought you didn't want to be with me because you had to be my guardian angel, but now—"

"You're wrong!" Daemon quickly shouted. "There is a divine reason why we cannot be together. And even with your wonderful specular skills, you still can't see it."

"What do you mean? We can be together now, can't we?" I weakly croaked out.

Daemon remained serious. "*No!* There is something else that is preventing that from happening."

"What could it be?" I pleaded. "Is there some angel rule or something? Gabriel didn't say anything about it; she told me that you truly love me."

Daemon sighed deeply. "She also told you to find your true self for the answers!" Daemon began pacing again. "I brought you to the lake for a reason: a reflection. Look into it, Cailyssa, and search within yourself as you have never done before. This is our last chance to be together. There is something inside *you* that is preventing us from being together. It's not *me*; it never has been!" Daemon spun me around and forced me to look at the reflection below.

"But Daemon," I said, gesticulating as I tried to tell the story. "I know in my soul that I absolutely love you and will never love anyone more. There's not a bone in my body that doesn't love you."

"That's not the point, Cailyssa. *Look* into the lake," Daemon said as he moved away from me. "You carry that red book with you, and you know the simple poem inside."

It floated in my head.

See me not, yet I see you.
Trust in me to find what's true.
Closer now, it's you I see.
Can you see the real me?

"But you've never been able to figure out what it means, have you?"

"I know what it means, Daemon. It…it—"

"It!" Daemon interrupted. "It's something that you don't want to see in *yourself*! This is the real reason you renounced me! You did not renounce me for love, Cailyssa. Be honest! You have seen it in your visions. You renounced me because part of you knows that I am not worthy to be with you—that we should never be together."

"*What*? But Daemon, you're an angel; you're absolutely perfect. I'm just a human. How could I think you're not worthy to be with me?"

"Cailyssa, do you know how foolish you sound? Do you know any other humans who have your specular skills? Do any of your friends have a castle named after them in Mirror World? Do you not understand the spectacular powers you possess? Did you ever wonder why none of your friends has a guardian angel assigned to her like you do? My God, Cailyssa—and I use that term with all due respect. Ask yourself the last line of the poem and look out at the water, and I pray that you finally get it."

I looked out toward the water, and slowly the last line of the poem floated through my mind. *Can you see the real me?* Suddenly, it was as if Daemon had punched me in the stomach. I lost all control. If he weren't there, I know I would've fallen off the cliff. My mind was floating in the specular ribbon of time as it never had before. Visions were coming to me, and I was trying to sort them out. I looked down at the lake below. It couldn't be. It was the same thing Lord Speculus had showed me when I first came to Mirror World. Speculus said it was a gift, and he'd wanted me to accept it! I slowly replayed the event in my mind. I was looking at seven small pools. Seven images were before me, and I couldn't believe my eyes. As I looked from one image to the other, I became more magnificent. By the time I reached the seventh image, I was the most glorious, beautiful, intelligent, powerful, and graceful person I could ever hope to become. I was pure angelic perfection!

"Oh my God, it can't be!" The images before me were a reflection of what was inside of me, not what I physically looked like! How had I missed that? When I finally came to understand who I really was, two small luminescent wings sprouted from my back. They weren't real feather wings like Daemon's; they just kind of floated there like pale magical lights.

"Yes, Cailyssa, it's true. You're an angel!" Daemon nodded. "You're a seraph, a human angel with extraordinary powers. There are only seven others like you at any one time, all working to shape the course of humanity toward paradise. You inspired us all, and you did save Mirror World and your world—for now." Daemon walked over to me. "So now you understand your family secret, Larkin: a lineage of seraphim, dating back to the dawn of humanity!"

I turned toward Daemon. And then I ran. I hugged him so hard that I thought I would squeeze the stuffing out of him and never let go. And this time…this time, he hugged me back.

"I still love you, Daemon—even if I'm some kind of angel!" I said as I looked up into his eyes. He didn't need to answer. His face was glowing with a radiance that was overwhelming. I don't think I'd ever seen Daemon like this—so happy. We looked into each other's eyes, unable to turn away. He tilted his head slightly, and his lips brushed mine. He kissed me deeply, and I felt like I was floating on a cloud of love. Neither of us could stop. Our love was too strong. We stayed in that embrace for what seemed like a lifetime. The only thing that let us part was knowing we would be together forever. We sat down, overlooking the lake, and I crept in front of Daemon. He wrapped his wings around me and kept me warm as I lay back, tucking my head just under his neck. This was heaven on earth. We stayed there for a long while, not saying a word.

"So Daemon," I finally mumbled in a sleepy voice, "did you really think that I wouldn't love you when I discovered I was a human angel?"

"I was hoping you would still love me. But I was filled with self-doubt."

"Daemon, any girl would be lucky to be with you! You're powerful, intelligent, caring, and absolutely drop-dead gorgeous—"

Daemon interrupted. "Cailyssa, you're just beginning to understand the rules regarding angels. One of the rules is that everyone was forbidden to tell you that you are a human angel; you needed to figure that one out on your *own*." Daemon laughed lightly and tickled me a bit with his wings. "Did you ever wonder in Mirror World why you were treated like royalty, Lady Cailyssa? You had a castle, servants, even a guardian angel."

"I thought they were just being polite. I guess I never really thought about it too much."

"To everyone else it looked like you were lost. And it looked like you were denying your true self." Daemon stood up, but I still stayed under his wings and turned around to face him. "The best way to explain the rules of the angels is to think of this as a fairy tale. You were a powerful, lost princess. Everyone knew you were a princess except for you. Then you fell in love with one of the guards who was assigned to you. The guard loved you too, but he did not think it was proper to court somebody who was royalty and didn't know it, since the guard was from a lower class. Angels are very snobby, and in the angelic realm, I am considered a guardian-angel worker, and you are considered upper class. If I had willingly accepted your love before you knew you were a seraphim, the angels would have seen it as treachery! What if you came into the knowledge of being an angel and decided not to be with me?"

"That's silly!" I said as I laughed.

Suddenly Daemon picked me up, and we were flying through the air. He still spoke softly in my ear. "It is *not*! You know how Speculus and other angels came down to the earth to force themselves upon human women and create the Nephilim, right? Well, the angels have rules regarding relationships with humans. One rule is that you cannot marry somebody unless that person consents. You don't force anyone into a...relationship, especially someone who is unaware of who she is! Before you knew you were an angel, you couldn't give your consent for our relationship. If I had forced you before that, it would have been as if I had stolen your virtue and pushed myself upon you! I would have become a dark angel, just like Speculus, and you would have spawned a Nephilim baby! I would like to see you explain that to your parents and Gabriel!" Daemon said with a bright smile and a laugh.

"I understand, Daemon. But now I have to ask you a question. How did you get your wings back, anyway?" Daemon said nothing. "Daemon! C'mon, tell me. How did you get your wings back?"

Daemon relented grudgingly and sighed. "Gabriel set off to find me after you left Mirror World. She had a message for *me* from the boss."

"What was the message?" I quickly asked.

"She sang to me—in your vernacular—to *grow up!*"

"Whoa, wait a minute. You're telling me that Gabriel brought you a message from the boss—God—and the message was to *grow up?*"

"Well, actually, it was God's son who sent the message through Gabriel—and not in precisely in those words—but I understood they were disappointed in me. Basically, I was told to stop blaming and punishing myself. Gabriel also told me that you never really renounced me. None of the angels ever knew what you told me that day. Gabriel gave me my wings back and told me to stop moping around and to follow my heart. She told me that if I didn't at least try to win you back, I would regret it for the rest of my life. She was right! By the way, the boss had a message for you, too!"

"What? Me? A message from Jes…us?"

"Yes," Daemon said smoothly. "He wanted to let you know that you did a good job! And he's proud!" Daemon's lecturing voice continued. "You did what you were supposed to do in Mirror World. *You* united us. *You* inspired us, and *you* broke the dark lord's mirrors and vanquished a terrible and powerful angel! So stop moping around and beating *yourself* up. You weren't supposed to save the world by yourself, you know."

We landed outside the window of my room. I cracked the window open and slipped into my room. Daemon followed me in. I can't tell you how happy I was. The half of me that had been ripped away had been restored. I felt whole again.

"Cailyssa, please excuse my presence in your bedroom. As a gentleman, I should not be in here. I only want to make sure you're safe, and then I'll leave."

"So, Daemon, are you still my guardian angel?" I lightly kissed his cheek.

"I never stopped being your guardian angel, Cailyssa, and I never stopped loving you—never will!" Daemon said this in such a sincere manner that it brought a small tear to my eye.

"Well then, I guess it's time to say good night...I—"

Crack! The mirror above my bedroom dresser smashed! It was totally in fragments, but the fragments just hung in space. An evil, burning face could be seen within the mirror's shards. I held up my hand, and in a second the mirror became whole again. Daemon crouched, ready to fight. I noticed that I was also in a fighting stance.

"What the hell was that? I thought Speculus had no power over this world."

"Your first question is most appropriate, Cailyssa. Speculus does not, but his master does! You have garnered his attention, and his gaze will be on you. He now knows we are together, and he hates the idea. Lucifer will be watching, waiting for the right moment. The war you became involved in is not over. It has been going on since before man walked the earth."

I remembered the last few minutes before Gabriel had saved me; the memory of Lucifer made me shiver. *Sounds like there's more work to be done*, I thought.

"Cailyssa, for now you're safe with me here. The mirror was only a warning of things to come. Please go to sleep. You know where I'll be—always watching, always there to protect you. Good night, Cailyssa. *I love you!*"

Daemon said it! He really said it! He really loves me! I whispered in my mind. I lay down, and he tucked me in. He gently kissed my forehead and headed out the window. "Love you, too!" I mumbled softly. *Love you, too!* I said to myself. And for the first time in what seemed like years, I actually fell asleep.

Coming in 2016!
Mirror World: A User's Guide for understanding famous psychological studies in the book

Be sure to check out my website www.johncalicchia.com to see a chapter from the next book in the *Mirror World* series and for more information about *Mirror World* and the psychology behind it.

John Calicchia PhD is a professor of psychology who also works with children and young adults as a licensed psychologist. He lives near Boston with his lovely wife and two amazing daughters. You can usually find him in the pool swimming with his two big dogs.

Made in the USA
Middletown, DE
25 February 2016